THE CLAY GIRL

Heather Tucker

a misFit book

For my clay children,
Sarah
Mike
Ben
Mary &
Elisabeth

ART APPLETON'S FAMILY TREE

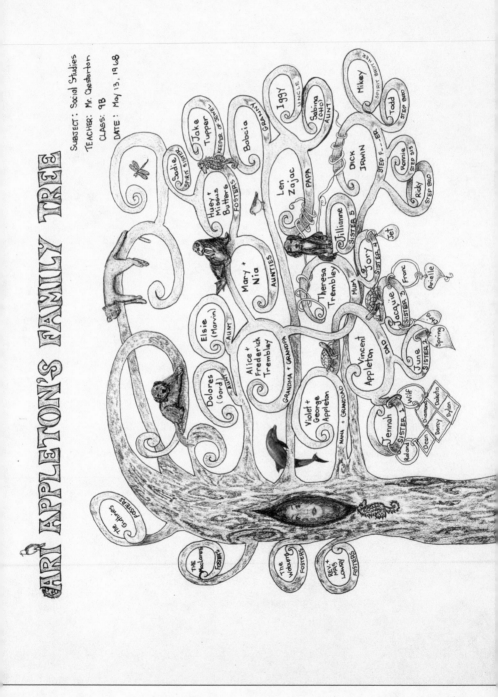

ONE

My sister-house collapsed—again. Our aunties collected us up.

St. Patrick's midnight bells shiver up my neck hairs. I quiet-step over my sleeping sisters, sneaking through Auntie Elsie's front door to the wishing sewer. Carved on the iron grate is 1953, the year I came out of the water and became a girl. I release one smooth stone, a wish. *Pebble small, pebble white, let me stay here all my nights.*

Second stone carries a spell. *Abra-can't-grab-ya, no beans can have ya.*

Third stone, an offering, a prayer. *Oh, suffering children Lord, deliver us from Aunt Moral Corruption.* Sacrifice swallowed. *There, that's done it, Jasper. We'll be okay now.*

Back inside, I crawl into the spy cave, resting my cheek on a rug that smells like an old man's suit.

Tires ringing over the grate snap me up. I peek through the curtains. A car marked POLICE MONTRÉAL creeps like a panther against the curb. *Bleedin' Jesus, they're back.*

Auntie's slippers slap down the hall to the knock. Boots, big as tool boxes, step in, crushing the blue flowers on the runner. "Just checking everything's settled, ma'am."

"Their mother is at St. Mary's and we've made arrangements for the girls."

"You hear of these things, but you never think . . . Hope things improve."

"Well, they can't get worse."

Hear that, Jasper? No worses. We're staying.

In the kitchen Auntie hums "Joyful, Joyful" and motes swirl on the sunstream like they know the words by heart.

Sister number one skedaddles out the front door and into Scotty Davenport's convertible.

I duck when Reverend Lowry swoops in like an angry owl, snatching sisters two and three, walloping them with a prayer before leaving, "And for these lambs, so scarred by man's depravity, give strength and travelling mercies. Amen and amen."

Down the path they go, shoulders freshly loaded with the sins of our father who aren't in heaven.

Aunt Dolores pulls into the empty spot by the curb. Sister four bounces away. "Hey, Auntie Dee, you get the pick of the Appleton tree."

Sister five slips out the back door without making a sound.

Mr. Whiskers chases rainbows sprinkled on the rug from the fancy vase. *Look, Jasper, a sign, like when the Almighty delivered Noah.*

Tell me the boat story, Hari.

Um, one night, a slice of moon fell into the ocean. Kangaroos welcomed us aboard Jasper's Jewel. We sailed to Kentucky where all the reindeer wore blue sweaters and—

"Hariet." Aunt Elsie tilts the green velvet chair. "Come on out, now. Mrs. MacLaren is here. Where's your coat?"

"At the MacLaren's. Under Jinxie's head."

"It's near freezing today." A grey sweater is sacrificed from the back of the closet. "You know, we wish we could keep you, too, but one is all we can manage and Jennah needs to be near her job." Auntie's pretty fingers triple roll the sleeves. "There, how's that?"

The wool is the prickly kind. "Spectacular, Auntie."

At the train station I wait where I've been told to stay put. I can't see the dragon's tail, but a worrisome blackness puffs from nose to middle. *Cripes, Jasper, it's coughing like Grandpa before he went to meet his baker.* Riding a red-nosed dragon train to the ocean twists Jasper with excitement. I shove him down. *You forgetting the horrification waiting at the end? Indescriptable acts upon my person, that's what.*

Mrs. MacLaren comes hurrying down the platform with the ticket and takes me by the hand to feed me to the dragon. "Up you get." The step is half as high as me, which would be no trouble except for the situation under my dress. "Come on, Hariet, you're too heavy for lifting."

I oblige, hoisting up my eight years of flesh and bone.

"Good Lord, child, where are your panties?"

"Jory got the last ones." One thing learned being smallest of six: you get what you get and most times you don't.

She sacrifices fifty cents. "No time now. If you see a five-and-dime could you manage to buy a pair?"

If I can travel my lone self from Montreal to Halifax to Sydney, I can buy underwears. They'll be pink . . . no, green, with little flowers. "Mrs. MacLaren?"

"Yes?"

A salt-moon winks on my scuffy shoe as I tap the metal step like a world famous rocket dancer.

"Spit it out."

"Is Daddy in a whale like Jonah?"

"He's where he can't hurt anyone ever again."

"But what if his going hurts in my belly?"

3

"Just drink some warm milk and you'll be fine."

"Mrs. MacLaren?"

"What is it now?"

"Jinxie likes her white ear scratched best."

"Soon as your mummy is on her feet you'll be back scratching her ear yourself. Off you go now and find a seat."

I can read so I know the brass-buttoned ticket-puncher is William. Jasper quivers in my pocket. *Don't be scared. Mr. Brassbuttons is just a walrus with a fancy biscuit tin on his head.*

"Ticket, miss." I dig inside Grandma's broke-strap carryall, past my swirl-coloured ball, Jasper's matchbox bed, toothbrush, bottle of hero ashes, and mittens that Grandma knit, to reach the ticket. "Quite the journey you're taking. Someone meeting you in Halifax?"

"No. My Auntie Moral Corruption is collecting me in Sydney."

"Who?"

"After my sisters got doled out she was the only one left." I heave the God-have-mercy load off my chest. "Beans. There's big trouble with them."

"There's no trouble in beans, little miss. Settle in. You've a long haul ahead, but there's nothing like October pictures from a train to pass the miles."

Walruses have lovely whiskers and a lot of goodness tucked in their folds. I push back the stress-curls forever jouncing out of my braids. "You got kids?"

"Three little misses and a mister."

Well, there's a universe of a letdown, Jasper. He won't be wanting another miss.

A stop brings travelers hurrying for seats. A green-suited badger. A silky Siamese, her *parfum d'lilac* tail brushing noses down the aisle. A plaid-vested beaver risks sitting with a half-dressed Hariet. Not that the lady has big teeth, she's just the busy kind that thought to pack a good lunch, plus she knows about

4

dams, and that too many paper cones of water has me at bursting. "Come on, little dearie, facilities are this way."

I've never had anything so shocked with tongue pleasers as what Mrs. Beaver stuffed between two pieces of bread. "Thanks, lady, this is spectacular."

"And where are you from?"

"The sister-house is where I live most the time."

"Like a convent?"

"Nothing like. There're no grey nuns with rulers. In my sister-house, June makes the walls. Jory is the roof. Jillianne is the floor. Jennah, she's the windows, fluttery with lacey curtains. And Jacquie is the yellow door. And Jasper and me tuck ourselves safe inside and tell stories."

"Well, yes. I'm sure you do." She licks her hankie and swipes mustard from my cheek. "You're awfully little to be travelling on your own."

"My mummy's sick with a conniption. Auntie Elsie's keeping Jennah. Grandma's puttin' up with June and Jacquie. Auntie Dolores nabbed Jory. Jillianne and my dog are with Mrs. MacLaren. But Jasper's come along with me."

"Jasper your brother?"

"No, ma'am, my seahorse."

"Let me guess, your name is Jane or Jessie?"

"I was a hoped-for Joshua. Everyone said with another girl my daddy had a string of jewels."

"Ah, so it's Jewel."

"No, Hariet. A one *r* Hariet. Mummy messed up the papers on account of I used up her neverlasting nerve."

"Bet your father is Harold then."

"No, Vincent."

"And where is he?"

"Um . . . incarcerated in a Turkey prison."

"Why?"

5

"For . . . poaching tigers."

"Really?"

Don't tell he put a bustard in Jacquie's oven or we won't get another brownie.

"What really happened is . . . this flash tidal wave reared up and he drowned trying to save my dog who fell into the vast Saint Lawrence. Jinxie washed ashore downriver but a giant otter dragged Vincent out to sea."

A consoling brownie lands in my hand. "And where will you be staying?"

"With Auntie Mary Catherine and her lady friend. They eat little girls like bean burritos, but everyone else was already too full up with me. You got kids?"

Mrs. Beaver opens a photographic accordion of kids dancing ballet and blowing at birthday candles. The pictures make a grey-socked, one r'd Hariet wish she hadn't swallowed the second brownie.

"Let's get you comfy for the night." William Walrus makes a bed on two seats with sheets that don't smell a bit of piss or snot and a pillow so feather-puffed a thousand eider-ducks must be naked somewhere. He gives me three digestives and warm milk. On the strawberry side of his chocolaty hand he writes: 1961. "You know what this is, little miss?"

"The year of our Lord?"

"Watch old William's hand." He turns it right around. "See? The whole world can get turned upside down and this year still lands right. There's good ahead. Old William sees it."

"You see a store to buy underwears for fifty cents?"

"There's an hour between trains tomorrow and I know just the place. Hunker down this way so you'll see the sky when you wake."

When riding a dragon, chomp-chomp, chomp-chomp, chomp-chomping away the miles from where you came there's nothing nicer than a walrus singing, "There's a place for you, somewhere a place for you. Peace and quiet and underwears. Take my hand and we'll buy a pair . . ."

Mrs. Kramer of Kramer's General Store is a hen clucking over my circumstances. My new panties are white with a tiny pink flower and a green bow so I get everything I ever wanted.

"Lord a tunder, darlin', Sydney's too cold this time a year for bare legs. On with these woolies." She snaps me into tights like Dr. Herbert takes to a glove.

It'd be nice living with a wing-over-the-shoulder hen. "You got kids, Mrs. Kramer?"

"Comin' out my ears."

"Oh." I hold up the fifty cents. "I can special deliver the rest once I get settled."

She plucks a quarter. "This'll do it, with change for a sweet."

William Walrus tucks a wrapped sandwich into my carryall. "This train will take you right to Sydney."

I hug him big. "Thank you, mister. It's been spectacular knowing you."

"Hang onto that little fellow riding with you."

"Jasper?"

"He'll lead you to your heart's double." He buttons my sweater. "And your true home."

With my bum snugged into blue woolies I'm set for anything, even the devil herself. Binocular-eyed, I search for a wolf or a serpent.

7

"Hello, sweetheart." She sneaks up from behind. "I'm Mary. Just look how you've grown." She's transfigured into a gentle-Jesus-sweet-'n-mild getup, but Hariet Appleton knows about the snake hiding under the *little sweetheart*.

"Under this sweater I'm scrawnier than a starving weasel. Dr. Herbert says there's not much on me worth eating, and for certain I'd give a body heartburn."

"Is your trunk inside?"

"Wasn't much for bringing."

"You're shivering. Come on, there's a blanket in the truck."

No matter how hard I swallow, my bally lunch scrambles up, landing a whisker away from Auntie's red shoe.

"You're safe here, I promise." She offers a tissue. "Come meet your cousins."

"You've got kids?"

Three exuberant mutts leap from the truck. "This is Hoover, Cork, and Wabi-sabi."

"Can I ride in back with them?"

"The road can be a little bump-and-throw, but Wabi loves a lap up front. Let me get a bucket in case your tummy ups it again." She moves butterfly-over-flower quiet. A fat rope of hair hangs to her bum and the escaping curls are more like a party than a stress.

"If you're my mummy's big sister how come you're younger?"

"Your mummy's had a lot of hard things."

Wabi has one ear up and white splotches like paint spilled on her black fur. "Could she ever sleep with me?"

"She'll have your bed warmed before you climb in." I sometimes wondered where Mummy's smile went and here it is on Auntie Mary Catherine's face.

On the long drive, Jasper wraps his tail around an escaping curl and near unscrews my head from its connecter. *Look, over there. Mmm, smell that. Oh, what's that?*

8

"You okay, Hariet?"

"You grow jewels here?"

"You're seeing the sun on the ocean. Just so happens it's in our backyard."

Up ahead, a painted roof on a fat grey barn looks like the tin has been peeled back to let fish swim in the sky. *Oh, don't you wish we could live there?* Like the god-listeners hear us the truck turns into the lane. A stone-faced house with two big window eyes says hello. Jasper's nose squishes against the windsheild. *Look, it has a yellow door.*

"Well, here we are."

"It's . . . it's like the sister-house."

"Where's that?"

"Inside the locked room."

She hushes my hair like she knows everything about outsides and ins.

Jasper, there's a pot boiling somewhere, sure as sure.

TWO

I wait, like Gretel, for the beanwitches to pitch me into the oven. Fourth morning, first light, Auntie's friend, Nia, comes for me. She's a polar bear, all tall and silky white. "Hariet, come meet my friends."

Jasper bows his head. *Our father who harps in heaven . . .*

"Here, put on my sweater."

Forgive us our messes . . .

9

"Be very quiet."

Yea though I walk to the belly of—Bambis?

Outside the back door, Bambis gather. Auntie Mary is the mother deer, offering apples, and quiet-like they take them from her hand. Long grass glitters all fairy feathers and the ocean looks like the dragon dropped his whole treasure load. Hariet Appleton lives with a polar bear and a deer in a house that smells like Christmas at Mrs. MacLaren's. "Do you have kids, Auntie Nia?"

"No, but I always wanted a little girl."

"To eat like a bean burrito?"

"Just to teach her things I know. Have her teach me back."

"Could you teach me to feed the deer?"

An apple slice smiles into my open hand. "Walk slow to them. If they startle and run, just joy in watching. They'll come back."

Auntie Nia spreads out Scrabble squares. "You keep working and by January you'll be ahead of all the grade threes."

"Jacquie's the smartest Appleton. I'm dirt stupid."

"Watch your mouth, you hear. You're clay, not dirt." Auntie Mary pulls cookies from the oven. "One cookie for three words."

I spell: SEAHORSE, JASPER, MARY, NIA, INX.

"You want two cookies, do you?"

"I want another J for Jinx. You have nice names."

"My given name is Eugenia. Always hated it. Mary found me Nia. It means shining purpose."

Oh . . . a silvery dolphin.

"Could you find one for me, Auntie Mary?"

She mixes HARIET tiles. "How about RITA?"

"What does it mean?"

She checks a big book. "Pearl."

"That's nice, I guess."

Jasper pokes, *Oyster insides aren't near as good as shiny dolphins*.

"Well, merciful heavens, look what's been hiding in your name all along." She spells A-R-I. "It means lion. It can also mean eagle." She lifts my chin. "Ari Lioneagle. Suits you."

Pleasant Cove's grade three/four teacher has paint splatters on her white runners and hair bursting wind-happy red.

"Mrs. Brown," says Auntie Mary, "this is my niece, Ari."

"Well, aren't you a bright penny."

"Your turkeys are spectacular."

"Pardon?"

I point to the apple turkeys with marshmallow heads lining the windowsill.

"So happens, I'm one short." She plunks me down with supplies. "Trace your hand on the paper then cut it out."

They walk to the door for some shushed-up hallway talk.

Mrs. Brown comes back, situating her bottom into a chair. "Your auntie will be back at three thirty. How about you and I get to know each other before the others arrive. What were you learning at your old school?"

"Well . . . I didn't have much time for regular school 'cause . . . I was in Siberia hunting pandas."

"And did you catch any?"

"No, ma'am. They're good hiders."

"So what did you do?"

"Well . . . my daddy got sick with frostbite so I captured some wild huskies and made a sled out of a crashed airplane door and mushed him across the tundra to a hospital in Mexico."

Mrs. Brown snatches me from my chair like a lizard takes a fly. "Glory beaver, you're a story weaver."

Her chest clouds under my cheek. *Jasper, look at all her goodness poking out the sides of the chair.*

My stick loops in the water, churning out sister-mail. *Dearest Jennah, June, Jacquie, Jory, and Jillianne: Moral Corruption is turning out to be a stupendous place to wait out the glorious revampment of the Appletons. I've got a job earning a whole dollar a week collecting shore treasures with my best-ever friend Sadie O'Shaughnessy.*

The aunties' old barn is a skyfish gallery, where driftwood becomes mystical beings with sea-glass eyes and red dirt changes into turtles swimming from the sides of shiny pots.

There's more musical wonder here than at the First Pentecostal on Hallelujah-Jesus-is-Risen Sunday. Huey and Jake fiddle and have me clogging out the Lioneagle dance. It all sets a body wondering why the Almighty is so spit-faced mad at the aunties for the less beans horrification.

Sadie settles on the rock beside me. "Sending story waves to your sisters again?"

"Yeah." I open my hand in the little rock pool. "Have a swim, Jasper."

"Jasper's magic, ain't that right, Ari? Can he rides in my pocket for a while?" Sadie knows about pocket friends. She lives two plots over with Huey Butters and his Missus. Huey and the Missus go together like a strong mast and a fat-bottomed boat, a perfect pair for stormy seas. Sadie told me they had a son never returned from war, one lost to the sea, and a wee girl buried in the churchyard. The Butters' house is filled with a half-dozen of other people's kids. Sadie says it's the best place she's ever stayed and, like me, she's stayed around a lot.

Day's end lands me in a forest-scented room where logs sleeping one atop the other make my walls. The ocean hush, hush, hushes up over the cliff, sneaking along the grass, through the window and into my breath. I wonder if the dragon hid me inside his mountain and no one knows where I am. Not that I want to be found, just maybe wanting to know that some persons notice I'm missing.

Auntie Nia asks, "Having trouble sleeping?"

I say yes because that brings honey-vanilla chamomile tea and a story about Ari Lioneagle's adventuring. Then, a whispered prayer, *you're a treasure girl, and nothing that anybody did, nothing that happened was ever your fault.*

"Is there a God of our Mothers?"

Auntie Nia sparkles in the moonspill from the window. "Of course. You've seen her breath on the morning grass." She unburies my face from its stressload of hair. "Sleep now."

"Auntie, walruses know secrets."

"Aye, they do. Listen and they'll whisper you to dreams."

Auntie Nia makes clattery kitchen noise to let me know I'm welcome on the morning hunt. She says I've an eye for the creatures hiding in the driftwood that the sea ladies leave for us overnight. "Does the sun's mother yell at him for spilling all this colour?"

Her pale eyes soak up the rainbows filling the new-day ocean. "It's her who kicks him out of bed saying, 'Make me another pretty picture.'"

"The sun has a nice mother, eh." I push up a smooth curve of wood, taller than me. "Look, a dancing porpoise."

"Is there any better find to start the day? Let's go spill some colour on it."

Back at Skyfish, Auntie Nia sets to coaxing an ocean fairy out of an arch of driftwood with sandpapery hands, two Band-Aids covering yesterday's nicks.

Mummy's hands were like the row of pink pencil crayons at Ted's Hobby Shop, sharp and perfect.

Jasper rides the turn of Auntie Mary's wheel as her mucky hands birth a pot. The clay bits she trims away are mine. Sometimes a fat chunk, like an extra serving of cake, drops my way and Auntie winks. It feels live-earth as I pat it flat. I make stars or moons or suns with tin cutters, fancying them up with pearly shell bits, sea-smoothed glass and glazes. Auntie tucks them in the kiln whenever there's room and you just never know what surprises will come out. Big mitts protect her hands as she lifts out a tray.

"Your pots are spectacular, Auntie."

Nia says, "Because Mary knows the clay has the spirit of a child in it."

"Like a ghost?"

"No, it's mouldable, a ball of possibilities. And clay absorbs water, same as you soaking up everything in your path. And with a little added grit, but not too much, the clay becomes stronger."

"Will you teach me?"

"After this order is shipped, we'll start lessons. You're going to make a great potter."

Yellow balloons float from my belly to my heart. "Really?"

"Look at these." Mary shuffles the bits on a tray. "They're pretty enough to sell. What are you going to do with them?"

"They're for my birthday. I'm just waiting on something from Huey."

I unpocket the agreed-upon dollar for twelve brass rings and fishing line. Huey pushes back my hand. "No need, dolly. I got the materials for free. It just took a little bend and solder."

Mrs. Butters snatches up the dollar, tucking it between her sugar-sack mammers. "Now, girlie, what's you a doin'?"

"Making presents. Auntie Mary read me *The Hobbit*. They give gifts on their birthdays."

Before the clock reaches bedtime, twelve chimes hang from the rafters. They tinkle fairy-like when the oldest foster, Jake, opens the door, all tired and fish-soaked. He looks up. "That's a pretty sound to come home to." He loads a bowl with down-home stew and opens a homework book. Music always taps in his foot and sweetness stirs in his butterscotch eyes. Jasper says I'll marry him when I'm filled out as beautiful as Jennah. He looks up from his book. "Come out on the boat Saturday, if you like. I'll show you a family of pilots."

"Won't they be drowned by then?"

His cheeks pink like raspberry ice cream. "They're a kind of whale."

"Do they fly?"

"In their own way."

Mrs. Butters' busy hands turn out a warm sock. "Huey will see you safe home, now."

Sadie takes one hand and Huey the other and we set sail. The big night speaks in rustles and hoots asking for a song to light the road home and we oblige.

Her eyes they shone like the diamonds
You'd think she was queen of the land
And her hair hung over her shoulder
tied up with a black velvet band

THREE

I know about letters that get folded into pockets.

Auntie Mary's braid paints my cheek as she leans over the couch to my hiding cave. "What's the trouble?"

"Are you sending me back?"

"Auntie Elsie just wanted us to know that Jacquie's okay."

"The bustard?"

She hands me a tiny square. "She had a boy." The picture turns circles in my hand. I know it takes a while for hatchlings to feather-up, but this situation looks more like a baby than a bustard. Auntie lifts her soft self into the corner. "He's gone to live with a nice family and Jacquie still managed to pass her year."

"Jacquie has a baby?"

"I thought you knew."

"Auntie Dolores said she had a bustard in her."

"She was using an unkind grown-up word for a baby."

I remember the Montreal stress day that made my hair frazzle like a ready-to-spit porcupine. Jennah lifted the tablecloth and talked upside down. "Come on, sis. Let's make like butter and slide on outta here."

Jasper suspected it was a lure, like the *here kitty kitty, come get your tuna* that'd turn out to be a distemper shot in the bum, but anything was better than the horrification happening around me.

At the corner shop, Jennah bought a nickel's worth of penny candy. She sacrificed a whole Pixie Stix and I dusted my tongue with the puckery powder. A straw of lime emptied into her mouth and Jasper laughed at her sucked-cheek fish lips. The "J" Appletons are head-swivelling pretty with yellow hair and bluebird of happiness eyes. "H" Appleton is brown and grey like Daddy.

"Jennah, you're a secret fairy, right?"

"A secretary."

That must be just as good because with her first pay, Jennah bought me a ball, Jillianne a skipping rope, Jory a rainbow hair band, June a writing book, and she gave Jacquie a satin-eared bear. She bought herself a bunny-fluff blue sweater.

I looked up to Jasper riding in the wave of Jennah's sunshine hair. Two lighthouses signalled under the blue sweater. Before a boy zeroed in I asked, "What's the trouble with Jacquie?"

"Grown-up stuff."

"Is Daddy still in the river?"

"Deep-sea fishing, sis." We climbed the steps to the library. Jennah smiled at Scotty as he opened the door.

"When is Daddy coming back?"

"Go find a book. I'll meet you here at two o'clock and we'll go for ice cream."

Ice cream, too? It's Armageddon, Jasper.

I walked to the counter. "Excuse me, ma'am. I'm looking for a book about . . ." I hushed my voice, ". . . bustards."

The library lady peeked over her glasses. "Would that be greater or lesser bustards?"

With all the wailing going on I knew the situation was big. "Greater, ma'am."

Ten times through the book and I still couldn't figure how such a thing had happened. Bustards were long-necked, pea-eyed birds, not even common to these parts. How one got into Jacquie's belly was a Jesus-landing-in-Mary mystery.

"Is Daddy ever coming out of the river?"

"He's not coming back, Ari. He died." Auntie Mary smells like sun-dried pajamas as she snugs against my back. "Tell me what you remember about that day."

"Just . . . throwing Jinxie her ball. Daddy called, 'Hairy, my fairy.' From far off he saluted like in our hero soldier game— then, he . . . fell and Jennah screamed and screamed."

"Do you know why?"

"Because June's Icee exploded all over her and Daddy fell in

the river. Scotty wouldn't let me go save him. Then policemen
came and gave Junie a big grey blanket 'cause she was so cold
and we rode in the black car even though our blue one was right
there with all our groceries in it. Jennah said Daddy went fishing.
He didn't, did he?"

"No, sweetheart. When you get a little older I'll tell you everything I know. It's too big a weight for a little heart."

"Is . . . he burning forever?"

"Why do you think that?"

"Auntie Dolores said the Devil got him."

She hushes my hair. "I know there've been so many bad
things. Can you remember one thing that was good?"

"Nothing."

"I remember your daddy playing the piano and singing 'Oh!
Susanna.'"

"His made-up songs were best."

"Can you sing me one?"

My voice wobbles like a calf on new legs. *"Ohhh, Hariet, get
your chariot. We're going for a ride. Now, Jory, don't worry, you can
come along . . ."*

"What else?"

"When Auntie Dolores said if I didn't shut the hell up about
Jasper she'd flush him, Daddy said to pay her no mind. He said
only little girls with magic in them had seahorse friends."

"Where's Jasper now?"

"Riding Hoover's tail."

"You know what I believe? Hell for your daddy isn't burning.
It's knowing he hurt his precious girls."

"Can I stay here with you, forever?"

"If forever was mine to give, but your mummy has taught me
two things."

"Mummy teaches things?"

"Everyone teaches us something."

"What did she teach you?"

"That things never stay settled for long and from somewhere deep comes the strength to find the sunshine wherever you land." She sits up. "Come see something."

I hoist my weary self onto the sofa. Auntie Mary opens a treasure album to a smiling picture of her and Auntie Nia by the shore holding a bundle.

"You have a baby?"

"That's you. Grandma brought your mummy here for a rest before you were born. Mrs. Butters caught you in this very house."

"Shhh, listen."

"To what?"

"Jasper's sing-spinning all colour happy."

FOUR

The side of the overturned skiff curves like a half-opened eye. From underneath I watch Jake hurry a silver fish twitching on the sand back into the ocean. I tuck into the shadows when he calls, "Ari!" Still, he discovers my hiding place. "Ari? Your aunts are worried stiff. Why'd you run off from school like that? Dr. Quinn?"

My knees hide my head.

He sits close, his niceness warming my shivers. "I near ran screaming when the Missus took me for fillings."

"You did no such thing."

"Did." He tugs on my braid. "The freezing needle was a stinger but that was all it hurt. Come back now. We'll make everything right."

Auntie Mary snatches me from Jake's delivering hand. She scolds and scolds, then scolds more. "Don't ever scare us like that again. All this foolishness over a dental check. I'm making an appointment for tomorrow. Now, get to your room and stay there 'til you're told."

Auntie Nia comes and sits her blue-jeaned self on my bed. Her white hair, pulled into a ponytail falls like a question mark on her white blouse.

"Sorry, Auntie."

"I'm not cross. I understand how you feel about dentists." Her tongue slips her teeth out then back in. "How have you managed your checks before?"

"Whenever the dental lady came to school I hid."

"Tomorrow, we're taking a trip."

"To Dr. Quinn?"

"He's too much a monkey. My dentist is walrus kin. Believe you me, you don't want to lose your teeth. I found out too late how to stare down my fears."

"You're never scared."

"Oh, Mylanta, child. Only fools are never scared." Her steady hand lifts my quivery chin. "Some say the eyes are the windows to your heart. I think the mouth is like the door. It's so hard to open your door if unwanted guests have ever visited." She gathers me close. "No shame in being afraid, but lioneagles muster their courage and fly right into it."

On the long drive Auntie Mary is soft again. She tucks a bucket by my feet since I lost breakfast on the Skyfish path. Auntie Nia stops at every rest stop along the way for my cramps.

Dr. Little is more a caramel walrus than a chocolate one. She lets me sit on Nia's knee for the first look. "All I'm going to do is shine a light and have a peek. Just imagine you're opening for a big bite of your auntie's cinnamon buns." When I open she smiles. "Well, who'd have thought I'd see a treasure chest open to beautiful jewels. You've been taking good care of your teeth."

"Jennah made us."

"Will you come over to my chair and let me have a closer look?"

An orange cat curls where the seat dips for the bum. "Could Swish stay?"

"He might. Usually he likes to give my friends plenty of room for the daisy spin." She presses a button and "Pop Goes the Weasel" plays while colours spin up a giant glass tube ending in a spray of happy flowers bursting out the top. "Hop up on the chair and you can press it anytime you need a break and I promise I'll stop before the daisies pop. Okay?"

From the ceiling, saucy faces look down, sticking out tongues. I only have one small cavity and a grinding-down situation on my back teeth. After everything is done, the ceiling faces laugh at me. Dr. Little pats my hand. "How're you doing, Ari?"

"It was nothing much at all."

"Nothing much? You growled at the devil and he ran like a terrified chicken."

I hear Jasper crying. Seahorses never cry. I press the button and pop go the daises.

All the way home Auntie Mary looks out the side window, then goes to bed without supper. My bed has wrinkles and the whole house feels wobbly. Jasper pokes, *Go and say sorry for all the fuss.* Their beds must have lumps, too, because they're empty. I'm scared I've lost my aunties until I catch whispers coming from the sunroom. I know I shouldn't be stealing a listen but my feet won't move.

"If he wasn't already dead, I'd kill him myself."

Auntie Nia sways Auntie Mary in a hush-hush. "Don't let what went on in the past rob us of the joy we have with her right now."

"I don't know how to help her."

"All I ever needed to get through was love from one solid person, and creative work."

FIVE

Daddy hated his job at the bank, and the one at Desjardins, and especially the one at Bombardier. He'd come home, landing like a bruise on all Jennah's shining of the house. He and Mummy snapped and snarled like chained dogs until the brandies soaked in.

At Skyfish, Jasper watches as I careful-wrap a set of mugs and make change from a twenty. *Too bad Daddy never got to play at work like we do, eh, Jasper?*

One hundred and fifty-two dollars grows in the Bank of Nova Scotia from the sale of Ari-Fairy Chimes. Four of my pots sit on the wabi-sabi shelf, priced one-fifty to three dollars. Wabi pots are beautiful in their wonkiness. When Auntie's muck-wet hands circle mine, the pots come out full-moon round but when she sets us free the pots fly where they please. Now that I'm near being a ten-year-old, grade four graduate my pots hardly ever fall flat.

Auntie Nia watches as I roll clay bits into beads. "Are you making birthday presents again this year?"

"Hope everyone likes them." Last birthday I suspected the trains were rerouted to India or the postman had bubonic dysentery until Auntie Elsie sent a letter saying she thought of me every time the breeze sang through the chimes. Grandma sent a clown card with one dollar. That was all I heard from the west and it was enough—almost.

"What would you like for your birthday?"

"Pardon?"

"A gift? What could Mary and I get that you would like?"

"What did you get when you turned ten?"

"My Grandma made me a new dress every birthday. The year I turned ten she broke her wrist so Granddad took me to Sydney to buy a dress. We came home with a set of wood chisels."

"That's what I'd like."

"Are you brave enough to ask the wood what wants to come out?"

"I like wood people. Will you teach me how?"

"First, we're going to make Sadie a dress for your party."

I pick a purply-blue piece with white daisies from the fabric trunk. Auntie Mary looks like an African princess with pins lining her lips as she fastens the pattern in place. "Your grandma taught me to sew."

I careful-cut around all the paper pieces. "How come she didn't teach Mummy?"

"She did. She taught all of us to cook, sew, and sing."

"Mummy can sing?"

"She and Elsie sang duets. They won competitions all the time."

Nia shows me how to match the pieces, then bends willow-like over the old Singer. She guides my hand as the machine makes cha-cha-cha music. "Now stop at the end, move this knob up, and reverse a few stitches. Ari?"

"Mummy can sing?"

23

Sadie wears her new frock to a toe-tapping Skyfish party. Jake fiddles near as good as Huey and keeps my feet clogging until the moon pulls all of us home. On the way out he kisses my cheek. "Birthday best, Ari. Come out on the boat tomorrow if you like."

"Can I be first mate?"

"Always."

Auntie Nia latches the door then stretches out in the middle of the yellow floor. "I'm getting too old for this."

I lie beside her. "Only thing you're too old for is foolishness."

Mary fills in the empty side. "None of us is ever too old for that."

"Auntie Dolores said you're both short on beans."

"What did she say?"

"That you've got less beans, but I think you're full of them."

Auntie Nia cages a laugh in her throat 'til it bursts out like a jungle full of happy monkeys. Mary laughs like one of them is tickling her. She blots her eyes with her sleeve. "Oh, my land."

Chuckles settle into the weathered old bones of the roof. "How come you called this place Skyfish?"

Nia turns her moonlit head. "You ever see a fish swimming in the sky? We wanted to live where impossible things happened. After the war we turned this place into a studio with our own four hands."

"You were in the war?"

"Patrolled the home shores. That's a story for another night."

There's a shiver to the grass and a haunt to the ocean's hymn as we push on to the house. Auntie Nia scatters handfuls of corn. "We love you, Ari Appleton."

"We do at that." Auntie Mary stops to take in the size of the night. "If the tides change for a time, don't be afraid. She knows where you belong."

"Who? The God of our Mothers?"

"Aye." There's a kitten-cry in auntie's throat. "She'll be painting the grass pretty tonight."

"Are you sending me back?"

"Never sending. But sometimes, no matter how tight the hold, storms take."

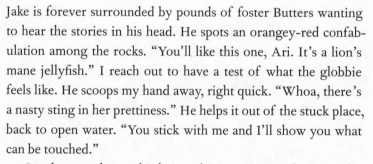

SIX

Jake is forever surrounded by pounds of foster Butters wanting to hear the stories in his head. He spots an orangey-red confabulation among the rocks. "You'll like this one, Ari. It's a lion's mane jellyfish." I reach out to have a test of what the globbie feels like. He scoops my hand away, right quick. "Whoa, there's a nasty sting in her prettiness." He helps it out of the stuck place, back to open water. "You stick with me and I'll show you what can be touched."

Sea drops gather on his hair and Jasper goes exploring in the little jewels. "You ever see a seahorse, Jake?"

"In these waters they're as rare as lioneagles. But you might catch sight of one if there's seahorse blood in you." He arms me to my feet. "Let's go see what we can catch for the Missus."

I never worry my aunties will run errands and forget to pick me up like was known to happen with regularity when I was a one-*r* Hariet. Supply runs to Halifax land me with the Butters for sleepovers beside my best-ever friend. Huey and Jake send songs up to the loft, making me heart-happy—most of the time. I poke my head down through the ceiling hole. "Jake Tupper, don't you be playing 'Farewell to Nova Scotia.' It's more than a tired body can take without blubbering." He looks up, leaning his cheek to his fiddle and asks it to play 'Tura Lura Lural' just for me.

The Missus calls up, "Says your prayers now."

Sadie murdalizes my hand. "Don't say it, Ari. Not the die-before-waking part. It gives me shivers and my eyes won't stays shut."

Just say prayers like me:

> Now I'm going off to dream
> Of lovely places I have seen.
> If I should dance before I wake
> I'm sure to get a fish from Jake.

Only the god-listeners hear "*kiss* from Jake." Sadie would never laugh, but too many foster ears fill this house. She arrives soft on my shoulder. "Make one special for me."

> Um . . . let me think . . .
> Sadie's going for a ride . . . on . . .
> on eagles' wing and ocean tide.
> If she should sing 'til morning come
> Then we will see a pretty sun.

"You must be the smartest poem maker God ever borned. I sure hopes they don't come and takes you away like times before. The Missus says it's a mortal sin the way they ripped you from Mary."

"What?" *Now I'm mixed up in my head. Hope the soup stays off the bed.*

"I heard the Missus telling Lizzy Harmer that your papa said you could stay but your mum came and took you away. Hey, I worked out a poem."

SEVEN

The scarred wooden box full of chisels is hidden under my pillow. I read the note in the moon ribbon, *Ari, my child, to teach things I know and have her teach me back. Nia.*

My head burrows under the covers. *Jasper, they're sending us back.*

Hide us.

The air ices my skin and the lingering smell of burnt grass mixes with the salted air. My nightie licks up dew as I wade through August grass. The summerhouse glows firelight-soft; the aunties' shapes knitting into one on the other side of the screen. Auntie's sobs slap the shimmery night. "I can't bear this again. I . . . I . . . I'll die without her."

"I know, love. I know." Auntie Nia hushes the black. "We'll get through. Somehow, we'll all get through."

Jasper shivers in my middle as I back away. I tuck my quivery self between the apple bushels in the shed and wait out the long darkness.

From a dream a muddled-headed moose snatches me for dinner. "Let's get you warmed up."

"Auntie? Where's Auntie Mary?"

"Sleeping in the summerhouse." She snugs me on the sofa with a downy plump. "I see you found your chisels."

"I don't like night presents."

"Why?"

"Night before Daddy . . . went away he put a war ribbon on all our pillows. Jennah threw them in the stove. Burned them all up."

"Is that what you keep in the little bottle you brought?"

My head nods to my knees. "Jasper told me to."

"Smart little seahorse. You know, it's ashes that make my hydrangea so full of blooms."

"Did I live here before?"

"You stayed for your first year until your mum got on her feet. Then for some lovely months when you were two."

"Mummy sure has troubles with her feet, doesn't she. I'm leaving, aren't I?"

"She's moved to Toronto near your Grandma and wants you home."

"I want to stay with you."

"Skyfish will always be your home. Even if there are times we have to be apart."

My "No" has the sound of the far-off foghorn.

"My mummy died when I was little. My father worked for the railroad so he brought me here to this very house to live with my grandparents. Look here." She lifts the lid of the trunk to ribbon-tied bundles. "He put treasures for me in letters. And living here, they were good years. When I turned twelve, there was no school past grade six, so I went to live with relatives. Aunt Pru was nothing but thistles and Uncle Gene was forever looking for something up my skirts."

"Auntie Nia?"

"I hated it there, but I always knew this place was home and I'd come back. Sleep now and tomorrow I'll give you your first lesson in carving and tell you how each dark place I've lived has given me treasures."

"Can I sleep with you?"

"I'll sit by your bed 'til dreams find you."

Auntie Elsie and Jory come to take me back. Just as Skyfish has smoothed and shined me, Jory has been edged by Auntie Dolores. She shares my bed, leaving no room for Cork or Wabi.

I listen to hushed voices in the kitchen. "I agree it would be best, but it's not up to me. Theresa pitched a fit when it sunk in where Hariet was."

Nia snorts. "Took her twenty-two months to bother to find out?"

Auntie Elsie says, "I'll find a way you can keep in touch."

Mary's snuffles scramble me out of bed and into her arms. "Everything's okay, sweetheart."

Nia untwists my shoulders. "Remember, Ari, there is a treasure hunt ahead. For now, go get your ashes."

I return with the little bottle and under the full moon we plant a linden tree. "Sprinkle the ash around the tree and water it in. The roots will drink it up and it'll become part of the tree." Auntie Nia claps dirt from her hands. "Now, come see what we made for you."

They made me a treasure box for the hunt with a carved lion-eagle flying toward the moon. "It's made of a Skyfish tree that will go with you." Mary's eyes are ocean-full. "And we'll always be looking out for you. I promise."

Jory follows me for all the goodbyes. Jake crooks his head from under Huey's broke-down Buick. "Off on your adventure, then?"

I give him a book. "This is for you."

"Our world, eh, Ari?" He hugs *The Sea Around Us*. "I'll sure miss you."

"You will?"

"You're the best first mate I've ever had."

His grease-mucked hands have me feeling fiddle music in my toes until he looks past me to Jory. Buttery hair melts on her shoulders. Her fourteen-year-old chest is near spectacular. She's as beautiful as a lynx. Next to her, I'm a gerbil with stressed fur.

I heavy-foot inside for the terrible farewell. When I come out, Jory surfaces from under the hood of the Buick with a giggle and eye flap. "Bye, Jake. Ever so nice meeting you."

"Bye, Jory." He sad-smiles at me. "Write me, Ari. Okay?"

He gets bigger as the distance grows.

"He's really cute. Too bad he smells like fish."

"You shouldn't get that close. He has smallpox, very contagious."

"Bet he doesn't have *smallcocks*. Did you see the size of his feet?"

Just like that, Mrs. Butter's "Farewell to Nova Scotia" lemon loaf sours in my belly and lands on the road.

EIGHT

I rummage my pocket for a hankie and pull out a note. *Find the treasure, Ari, and bring it home.*

"I see you're still a big baby."

"Hush, Jory." Auntie Elsie passes a tissue. "Feeling things deep doesn't make you a baby."

I find my knitting and clack along with the train.

"Did Mary teach you to knit?"

"No. The ladies at Wednesday Knitting and Prayer Society. 'There's no heaviness that busy hands can't make a little lighter.'"

"You sound like an old cow, but I dig the scarf. Make one for me: orange, purple, and red."

"Lord, Jory, that would be awful."

"No, Auntie, you should see when the sun spills those colours on the ocean."

Anticipation of Jinxie's half-flopped ears and wiggling bum eases the missing—a little. I make my way to Mrs. MacLaren's and knock. She dries her hands on her apron. "Why, Hariet, look how you've grown. Jillianne's gone to the store. She'll be back in a lamb's shake."

I'm near bursting for Jinxie's licks and leaps. I whistle. "Here, girl."

"Oh, Hariet, didn't anyone tell you?"

"What?"

"Um . . . Jinx fell in love with a handsome farm dog and moved to the country."

Who would believe that Mrs. Iris MacLaren, president of the Catholic Women's League could be a pants-on-fire liar? Running on cement isn't near the joy of flying over red dirt and Aunt Dolores' house doesn't have the sweet cedar corners of Skyfish. The scratchy chair and warty gold curtains hide my blubbers. Aunties come into the parlour for a sit. I'm not stealing a listen; everything just falls into my ears.

"Don't you break that. It's going straight back to where it came."

Jory says, "I'll have it. It looks like peacock feathers."

They're talking about one of Auntie Mary's prettiest pots. The day it came out of the kiln she shook her head, saying, "Wish I knew how I did that."

Elsie says, "Dolores, she sent it as a kindness."

"I'm not having anything of hers in this house."

"Oh, would you give it a rest. She's your sister and she's never done anything to you."

"I know what she is."

"She and Nia are just business partners."

"Right. Jory, where did everyone sleep?"

"Alls I know is I got stuck with Scari and the stinkin' dogs."

The drapes ripple with the opening of the door. "Where's Hariet?" Jillianne sounds as spring-light as I remember.

31

"Thought she was with you." I can almost feel Auntie Dolores' spit-spray. "That child is never anything but trouble, too much of her father in her."

They all rumble into the kitchen and I slip outside to mourn Jinxie under the yellow-leafed pear.

I discover a note in my PJs. *Ari: A little treasure from Emerson. "What lies behind you and what lies before you are tiny matters compared to what lives within you." Aunties M&N*

Kitchen whispers replace ocean lullaby. The sofa is zippered in plastic and every fidget sounds like a skiff rubbing against the docks. When the phone rings, I Jesus-wish for it to be Aunties M&N wanting to say goodnight. Auntie Dolores sounds thistle-in-her-panties irritated. "She's moved to Toronto. No, you cannot have her number. She's not interested in seeing her."

Auntie Elsie asks, "Who was that?"

"St. Mary's. Seems Vincent's mother is on her way out. She wants to see the girls."

"Maybe you should let Theresa decide."

"No sense stirring things up. The sooner that family is wiped off the earth the better."

"Hush, Dolores. Little pitchers have big ears."

Over the years I've heard gallons of whispers said after too many tips and sips. *I'll wager that last one is the only Appleton of the lot. Look at them, then look at her.*

I know the way to St. Mary's. Mummy went there often for major conniptions, so I navigate my lone self there on the bus. On the ride I remember a Nana, soft as velvet. She was a let's-eat-ice-cream-from-the-carton nana until Granddad showed. Everyone steered clear when Granddad tipped the bottle. Except June, she'd turn sour-faced disgusted and let him know she thought he was poop. Granddad would swell like a mean-genie, screaming, "Get that look off your face." Once he knocked her right off the chair. Her face blossomed like a red cabbage but she never did change her look.

Nana looks a hundred years older and eighty years smaller. The nurse cranks up the bed-head. "Mrs. Appleton, your grand-daughter is here."

"Hariet?" Her breath is puffier than Mrs. Butters' after ten jigs.

"Hi, Nana. Not doing so good, eh?"

"She winds easy, but her wits are all there. Talk to her."

Her face shines happy with all my tellings. ". . . and Huey has a boat. This one time a humpback came right out of the water, crashing down so hard I got soaked to the skin."

"You're Vincent's mirror reflection. He never did all those terrible things they said, did he?" Her eyes turn the colour of air when the coldest fog moves in and her face is crumpled like a letter started but tossed away because of mistakes.

I pat her needle-stained hand. "Sometimes I hear him singing. I know it's him because nobody made songs up like him."

"Bring the nurse."

"I'm right here, Mrs. Appleton." Grandma's finger asks for her ear. She whispers and the nurse leaves.

"I better go, Nana. They'll be missing me."

"Wait."

The nurse brings a little envelope. "Your nana wants you to have this." She slides an emerald diamond ring onto my palm.

Nana pushes out words. "It was your great-great-grandma's. I always wondered how I'd choose which of you jewels to give it to."

"I'll remember you whenever it sparkles." She smells like Hoover after a roll on a carcass when I kiss her cheek. "I planted a linden tree looking out over the ocean for Daddy. When I go back home I'll plant one for you. What kind would you like?"

"A willow."

"Where have you been!"

"Buying wool for Jory's scarf."

"You can't just go wandering off on your own."

"Oh, hush, Dolores, when hasn't Ari Appleton navigated life on her own?" I smile at the sound of my new name said out loud in Montreal. Auntie Elsie examines my bag. "You're right, Ari. These colours will be fun together."

"Is Jennah here yet?"

"She and Roland are coming for supper."

"Who's Roland?"

Jory looks up from her comic book. "Her dorkbutt husband."

"Jennah's married?"

"Knocked up and tied the knot."

I tuck in the corner with my Skyfish pillow. Jinx is gone, and Jennah is tied in knots. There will be no promised flower-girl dress and pink sweetheart rose-ring for my hair.

Jennah has disappeared somewhere under puffed cheeks, swollen belly, and thick ankles. Roland takes the comfy chair and spits, "Christ, Jen. You smoke this whole pack? Keep your grimy paws outta my pockets."

"There's a pack in my purse."

"Get 'em. Grab your Uncle Gordo and me a beer while you're up."

All the lights are off in Jennah's hair. I push the hassock up to the chair for her swollen feet. "I'll get it."

34

"Thanks, sweetie. One for me, too." Jennah fingers the clay beads around her neck and gives me a wink-smile.

"Can I say hello?" She nods and I whisper to her mounded tummy, "Hi, baby. I'm Ari. Do you have a seahorse in there with you?"

Uncle Gord slingshots me to the couch with a tug on my waistband. "You're blocking *Candid Camera*, ya pea-brained Newfie."

Roland scratches his balls and goofy-laughs while Jory pesters him for a dollar. He holds it in one hand and slaps her butt with the other. "Fetch me a beer for it."

I take my plate to the kitchen and pick up the towel. "Thank you, Auntie Dolores."

"The dishes your job at Mary's?"

"We all pitched in. Even the dogs gave a tongue."

"You have your own room?"

"Shared with the dogs."

"You sleep in with them when you were scared or anything?"

"I wasn't much scared there."

"Mary and Nia—"

Auntie Elsie pinches her words, "Dolores, I said let it be."

Down east I learned a thing or two about fishing. "We were like the Three Bears: Auntie Nia liked her bed hard. Auntie Mary liked hers soft. And my bed was just right."

NINE

I study the backs of Uncle Marvin's and Auntie Elsie's heads as he drives us to the train. There's just niceness inside them, like a pair of good dress socks. Auntie Dolores and Uncle Gord are a pair of stinky gym socks. I wonder if they found their matches or made each other that way. Mary and Nia are warm handcrafted highland woolies, and Mummy is like the bin of odd socks kept atop the dryer. Even with Daddy they were a mixed unpair.

Auntie Elsie peeks over her shoulder. "You okay, Ari?"

"Jennah didn't find a very good sock, did she?"

"Pardon, honey?"

"Nothing." I climb up the metal steps and sink into the velvet seat.

September pictures from a Toronto-bound train aren't near as good as October heading east. Auntie Elsie squeezes my knee. "You want a soda?"

I want my aunties and my pups, my school, and Jake. "What happened to Jinx?"

Jillianne finds her tongue. "She bit Toby and Auntie Iris said she couldn't have a vicious beast around the boys."

Jinxie was more a peaceful rug than a dog.

Jory slathers on pink lip gunk. "Toby's a demon-spawn. Likely poked the old girl in the eye with a fork."

"Hush." Auntie Elsie loads Jory's hand with Chiclets to stick up her mouth. "Uncle Gord took her to a nice farm."

"Right, the Triple D: Dead Dog Dirt-nap farm."

"Jory Appleton, that's enough. And where did you find that top? It's too small."

"Snitched it out of Scari's bag. It's radioactive."

"It's what?"

"It's batik," I say and swallow down my inside tears.

Auntie Elsie brings Jory back for the tenth time. "Sit and don't move a muscle while I see to lunch."

"What if I have to whiz?"

Auntie Elsie never yells but her, "Just—sit," stings like a wallop on each cheek.

Jory thunks her feet between Jillianne and me. "This place is a freakin' gold mine. Old chrome-dome up there gave me two bucks to cop a feel of my tit and I've pocketed at least twenty cigs."

"Auntie Nia says smoking is bad for you."

"Auntie Nia says smoking is bad for you." Jory thinks her making-fun voice is smart but she sounds like a dolphin crying.

Auntie Elsie brings tuna sandwiches and little cartons of milk.

"Did you know tuna can grow over ten feet long and weigh hundreds of pounds? Jake told me that."

"Then how do they fit them in those little cans? He's one of them pea-brained Newfies." Jory kicks my shin. "Hey, that geezer by the door will give you five bucks if you let him pet your pussy."

"Jory Appleton! Let's hope your new father can put some decency into you."

I scramble out but my belly ups before I reach the toilet. While surveying the mess in the aisle, shiny black shoes come into view.

"Sorry, I'll clean it up."

William Walrus in his brass-buttoned suit buries it in sawdust. "Don't fret yourself, little miss. Happens all the time."

"They're taking me from my ocean."

He crouches low and lifts my chin. "Every shining jewel comes from a crushing it never knew it could survive. There's good waiting for you. Old William sees it. Go wash your wee face."

Auntie knocks. "Hariet, come out. People are waiting."

I march to my seat, snatch the pillow from under Jory's head, and dive into it, face first.

"Your mummy wanted to tell you herself. I hear he's a very nice man."

Jory lobs a wad of something that thuds on my shoulder. "He owns a store. We're going to be rich."

TEN

Every Thanksgiving the Appleton girls posed jewel-pretty on Grandma's steps. June always snorted, "Nothing like Appleton Lie for dessert."

Jasper and I study the framed prints marching up the wall. The first ones picture just Jennah. Then Jennah holding June. Then, Jacquie sits on Jennah's knee and June beside her. Two years later Jory is added. Two years after that, Jillianne. Then in 1953, I'm in the picture, looking the little troll at the end of a line of golden fairies. The picture for 1961 is absent but 1962 hangs there—without me. I finger the empty step. *Not that I wanted to come or anything, but did no one notice they were an apple short, Jasper?*

Thanksgiving 1963 Mummy marries Len Zajac. What does she see looking at the picture of her girls lined on the steps for the occasion? Jennah is the kind of puffed that would have Mrs. Butters propping her in bed with herbal tea and no stress. June's hair has died, been murdered black as black to match her shadowed eyes. Jacquie is puddled in pounds of chips and Oreos; her face pocked like all the tears have burned holes into her white skin. Jory is buried under cherry lips and green shadow. Jillianne could be on Mars or in Florida, her disappearing stare is anywhere but 36 Leyton Avenue. And me? I kind of shine.

Mummy laughs at *I Love Lucy*. She fusses over Jillianne. When I tell her I read grade seven books and draw like a child prodigal, she looks at the coffee stain on Grandma's rug. "You get that from your father." When I ask if I can go back to my school in Pleasant Cove, she looks past my shoulder. "That's no place for an impressionable girl."

Len Zajac buys 47 Leyton Avenue for his new bride. He paints the yellow brick the brightest blue God ever thought up. Jory helps herself to the bigger room with silent Jillianne. June makes a cave in the basement pickle room. I excavate a corner of Jacquie's room. She's messier than the aftermath of a maritime storm; every corner is piled with books, cookie bags, bar wrappers, and nothing-to-wear battles with clothes.

The greatest trauma of my situation comes from having my bed aside the newlyweds with only a thread-thin wall between. Sometimes, when I slept at Sadie's we'd hear Huey and the Missus whispering sweet, "Gets over heres and butter me toast." Their cries were like whale music. Now, I hear the headboard bump-bump-bump against the wall before Len moans three times. Then Mummy skeedaddles into the shower, staying until the hot water turns cold.

Out of the houseful, Len stresses me least. He makes settling into the new of this place softer. When today, the wailing, big as the Atlantic, started up everywhere around me, he was the only one who didn't say, "This is not for children's ears." He took me to the lake and told me that the president of our neighbour country had died. He gave me a starry paper flag to place in the quiet waves. He said his name was John Fitzgerald Kennedy, JFK, and all that needed doing was to honour him by being, Just, Friendly, and Kind. Jasper thinks Len would be a good president.

At one time he may have had hopes of being handsome before growing the kind of tall that curves your shoulders to protect your head from doortops. No matter how much he eats, no flesh covers his golf ball elbows. Long shirts would help but he always wears plaid short-sleeved ones and black pants that shine a little. He smiles, a lot, showing pointy teeth, a little too long and turning sideways. Whenever *Bonanza* is on Mummy sighs, "Doesn't Little Joe have the most perfect smile?"

Every week Grandma hands me a letter from Aunties M&N. She makes tea while I read it to her.

"They're coming for a visit after Christmas!"

"Don't let your mother catch wind of it."

"Why doesn't Mummy like Auntie Mary?"

"She thinks all her troubles are Mary's doing. Even the devil in your father." Grandma measures biscuit ingredients. "Your mummy was fifteen when she met your daddy. He was near twice her age, but pretty as Jesus and could charm gold from granite." Grandma flours the counter and pats out the dough while I peel potatoes. "They were swallowed up in the other until he caught sight of Mary. One look at her and Vincent could see nothing else. Here's your mummy, this golden princess, and Mary Catherine, plain as brown paper. Mary wanted none of him which made him near crazy." She rolls out Granddad Appleton's trouble with the drink and his knocking blocks off. "That mother of his coddled him something terrible."

"Cuddled?"

"Coddled."

Like an egg, Jasper?

No, I suspect it's like diddling under his pants.

Yeah, sounds like it.

"Your father went to church five times a week and twice on

40

Sunday, as if the Almighty could fix up that mess."

"I thought God could fix anything."

"In my seventy-some years I've never seen Him show up and fix a damn thing. It's up to us to make what we make." Grandma hands me a bowl of beans to snap. "When the war started, Mary Catherine volunteered right off. Your daddy followed her to the enlistment centre. He came back from war cracked worse than most."

"So Mummy hates Auntie Mary because Daddy liked her?"

"Oh, I shouldn't have told you all this. Some things are not for children."

"But they get loaded up with them anyway, don't they?"

Grandma's flappy-skinned arms swing like hammocks as she reels me close. "Dwelling on things does no one any good."

When Huey Butters fixed boats he stripped the wood bare and replaced the rotten bits. He said a hundred coats of paint would never hide what's underneath. Aunties M&N were never one bit squeamish about peeling back layers and opening my underhurts to the sun.

"M&N are good, Grandma."

"You don't have to be telling me that. Every grey hair on my head is from your mother and father." Grandma scurries to the hall as the borders come clomping in. "Mind your boots. Don't be tracking in muck on my clean floors."

I tuck my letter into my treasure box behind Grandma's sofa.

My squeeze sends her steadying on the coat rack. I say, "It does a body good to have another woman to talk to."

"Off with you now."

As I cross the street I hear Applegeddon rising inside our house. It's report card day. Our beside-neighbour tackles the snow on his sidewalk. "Afternoon, Mr. Hawthorne. Could I do that for you?"

"For a nickel?"

41

"Visiting Sparky suits me more."

He passes me the shovel. "Whenever you need time with Sparks just come on over."

I glance up the street to see Len sauntering along, hands in pockets, whistling. When he's out in the open I see the giraffe in him as he walks and takes in the sky.

"Evening, Ari. Looks like we'll have a white Christmas." His words rumble around his peach pit. The flavour of his voice isn't as sweet as down-home talking but there's something like warm cookie in it. He listens to the house. "Some trouble?"

"Report card day."

"How was your term?"

"All A's except for PE. I turned every folk dance into a clog."

"Come to the store tomorrow and pick out a reward."

The door slams as Jory bolts, red-faced and riled down the street, saying the F-word to us as a hello and goodbye. Len grabs a shovel, too, and we work until not a single snowflake remains on the walks, then with no other choice we go inside.

Mum stiffs as Len kisses her cheek. "You're late. I can't be expected to do everything around here."

"We were just clearing the walks, Mummy. Mr. Hawthorne has a bad knee so we did his, too. You look pretty with your hair like that."

Even after all the troubles, Mummy is beautiful, all willowy long and curvy. Hair, like butterscotch, with threads of gold waving like the ocean at sunset. Her eyes are bluer than the forget-me-nots in Auntie M&N's garden. "The girls need a father. Jory missed more school than she showed up for and Jacquie's not even trying."

Len examines the report cards then starts up the stairs to try and reach Jacquie buried under her blankets and burdens. "Ari, go wake up June for work."

June won't be sleeping. She'll be reading angry books or writing gut-ripping poetry like,

God is a squirrel
hoarding nuts
in his fat cheeks,
twitching his bushy tail.
Ordering
from his great oak, 'Fall on your knees.'
I stand . . .

She works at joints in the Village where poets and musicians sing about freedom and love and establishment bastards. I sniff before knocking. If I smell something like a sweet summer bonfire, she'll be more wooly-grey than black. "June, you want me to make you a sandwich before work?" The room is cloudy when she opens the door. She's wearing the T-shirt I made her: black with bleached moons and silvery star beads.

"Go scope out the escape route. Flick the light when I can get past the Gestapo."

June has taken a vow of silence until the Oppression of Women ends. Mummy always growls, "If you don't talk I'm going to rip that tongue out of your head and make you talk."

She also pretends not to eat, in protest of war and poverty. She started talking to me one day when I brought her a plate of Auntie M&N's survival cookies, imploring, "June, don't starve to death before you bring about world peace."

She squeezed her eyes over the top of her book so that her eye-paint looked like two prunes staring at me.

"*Silent Spring*. Is it about the sea, too? I read *The Sea Around Us*."

"Bullshit you've read Carson."

"Jake read it to me."

The sweet herb smoke in the air that day made her rubbery easy and hungry. "These aren't bad."

Since then, we talk poetical stuff while making T-shirts for

Malik the drummer and Crystal the sometimes singer with the band.

But what I love most is her smiling a real smile when I say, "You're a treasure, June, like a black diamond."

ELEVEN

Back in 1959 I tried digging a tunnel to North Cuba. I fell asleep in the hot sun and woke under black dew. While running home, Jasper helped me sort my trouble. *Tell them you were kidnapped by a kangaroo that thought you were her lost joey.* I snuck into a sleeping house. Daddy draped the couch like a tangled blanket. Mummy curled kitten-round on the mat by the toilet. I covered her with a towel and went to bed.

Len's the kind of daddy who goes hunting for missing daughters. He brings Jory home door-slamming mad and Mummy ends up screaming at Len. The wall beside me is glass and I see Len facing the wall and Mummy facing the door and they're under blankets of ice. I turn to Jacquie. "You, want me to tell you a story?"

"I'm seventeen for Christ's sake."

"What's your baby's name?"

"It's not mine." Minutes creep through the dark, moving moonshadows from the closet to the foot of Jacquie's bed, until she says, "Chris . . . so it would fit if it was a boy or girl."

The name spoken into the space between us twitches like a firefly and I hear how Jacquie has wanted and wanted to feel *Chris* on her tongue.

"It was a boy."

She pops up on her elbow. "How do you know that?"

"Auntie Elsie sent a picture. He had a shimmer of gold on his head and one hand, no bigger than Jinxie's paw, stuck out from a blue blanket." I wait. The silence feels bigger than the dark so I wade into it. "Mrs. Butters lost her three kids. In her life she's cared for dozens of fosters. Huey says nothing has brought them more healing. The family that has Christopher feels that, too. You did that for them."

"Did he have five fingers?"

"Four fingers and a thumb."

Len says, "Jacquie, come with Jillianne and Ari to the store. My Uncle Ignatius taught math in the old country. Until him, I thought square roots grew boxwood trees."

Jacquie groans in a tickled way and trudges along with us. Len's store is a universal disappointment to Jory, a-dozen-hankies-for-a-dollar kind of place, with bargain-this and dis-count-that, green coveralls and workboots.

Babcia is a granny who pinches cheeks and feeds us down-home good tastes. Uncle Ignatius has stories and a strong belief in a ten-year-old working. I sit by the cash, ringing through purchases. "Morning, ma'am. Will you be needing thread to embroi-der those towels? Look at this one, the prettiest shade of blue ever seen." Len smiles as the lady picks out yellow and green, too. "That will be two dollars and eleven cents."

"Go pick a treat, Ari." Really, Len wants me to help Jillianne who's wandering around kind of helpless. She'll come across something like toothpaste and start humming, *You'll wonder where the yellow went when you brush your teeth with Pepsodent.* I stay put because jars of beads are lined up like gumballs under the glass-faced counter, paintbox colours in all shapes and sizes.

Len picked up cartons of them at a fire sale. I string a line of turquoise and purple with black spacers.

"What are you doing there, *corka?*" Len's *daughter* makes me think about giving *papa* a try on my tongue.

"Painting daisies on the middle bead." I blow it dry, placing it on the counter so I can ring up purchases for Molly Harper's mom. "Hi, Molly. Your hat is spectacular." Molly is ahead of me at school and already wears a bra to hold up grape-size boobies.

Her mother explains as I ring up socks, ribbon candy, pocket knife, and a key chain. "Just a few last-minute things to stuff stockings."

"Excellent choices, ma'am. That will be three dollars and seventy-six cents." Molly tugs on her mother's coat to whisper in her ear.

Mrs. Harper asks, "Is that necklace for sale?"

"One-of-a-kind love beads. Handcrafted from imported woods. Sale price, today only, one dollar." She hands over a buck like it's nothing.

Len's mouth gapes with wonderment. When they are gone he says, "Ari, make more."

As hours pass the strands pile on the counter. Len asks, "Did you sell two more?"

"They'd go even quicker if we made a window display. Auntie Mary says presentation is half the sale."

"Do it." Len never complains, but things aren't easy feeding all the Appletons, and business has slowed with the Shoppers World opening on the Danforth.

Upstairs, Jacquie looks a little less pressure-puffed. Uncle Iggy's wheelchair is crammed up to the table. I kiss his bristly face. "Ah, my little Arishki. Not afraid of a man with no legs?"

Jacquie snips, "Appleton girls are more afraid of men with three legs."

Babcia cackles like a happy bird and hugs Jacquie from behind.

"How'd you lose your legs, Uncle Iggy?"

"The war."

"My aunties were Wrens, intelligent operators keeping the enemy from invigorating our shores." I empty out an old carved box. "Babcia, can you make me a sign? Handcrafted Groovy Love Beads, one dollar."

Len surveys the window as Babcia ripples sapphire satin under the box and arranges necklaces like a pirate treasure spill. "Come, *corka*."

Fat flakes float like parachutes past the street lamps. The road stretches out whisper-quiet and I leave off my mitten to hold Len's hand all the walk home.

On Monday, Molly Harper's older sister comes to Pennyworths and buys three strings of beads. Before day's end, every last one has sold. By Tuesday the jars of beads line the windowsill of the blue house. Everyone is stringing. Jory has a flair for *far-out* combinations. June's are particularly poetic and Jacquie paints little doodads better than I ever could. It makes a body believe a glorious Appleton revampment is possible.

Mummy counts as June stuffs a dozen into her bag before heading to work. "Don't take what you can't sell."

June's silent stare is like a slap. Mummy lifts her hand to return it. She's out the door before the smack.

"They'll be gone by morning, Mummy. The Village is a happening place and love beads are a hot commodity." I don't tell that June sells them for two bucks and pockets the profit.

Len receives some headboard-thumping forgiveness for going to the school and arranging for Jacquie to retry her math exam. She got a seventy. Actually, she got a sixty-nine but Mr. Mathers gave her a bonus mark for improvement. And over Christmas, if she writes a spectacular essay on *Catcher in the Rye* and one on WWII she'll get her English and history.

47

We're cider-warm and popcorn cozy with Ed Sullivan's really big Christmas *Shoe* playing on TV when a cab pulls up with Jennah and baby Dean. Mummy effervesces like her Alka-Seltzer. "Give me Grandma's sweet boy."

I'll forever love Len for seeing Jacquie falling overboard into the frigid ocean and diving in after her. His "Well" comes out more like, "*Vell*, Theresa, seems we've set up a house too small. Jacquie and Ari, could we give our guests your room and have you stay with Babcia?" Jacquie's feet hit her boots one-two quick and she's gone.

Mum claws Len's arm. "Why did you do that to me? You knew how much I was looking forward to having all the girls together."

"Jacquie would've escaped somewhere. To the store is better than returning to her darkness. Let her mourn her loss a little, then I will bring her home."

Mummy near spits, "What losses does she have to mourn?"

Jillianne turns up the TV. Jory navigates Mummy to the sofa and brings her a sherry. Jennah sits close, resting baby Dean on her lap. "Len's just making room for the rest of us. We'll have our days together. Just look at this little fellow. He has your colouring, don't you think?" Jennah chins to the bottle. "One for me, too, sis."

The atmosphere around Mum clears a little. "Where's Roland?" she says.

"Working 'til Christmas Eve. I couldn't wait for Dean to meet everyone."

Len gentles my shoulder. "Come."

I want to tell Len that he's a treasure in my collection. I want to say sorry for the Appleton burden. I want to hug him for going and finding Jory. I want to tell him that he makes all the missing feel smaller. But all I say is, "How'd you meet Mummy?"

"She was the prettiest customer to ever walk into Pennyworths.

She bought a big box of Borax and I offered to carry it home for her."

"That was a nice thing to do."

TWELVE

Roland shows up Christmas Eve and Armageddon rages through 'til Boxing Day. Seems Jennah caught him with some skirt-hoisted chippy. When yelling turns to smack, smack, smack, Len chucks Roland out by the neck-scruff, brings home a second-hand crib, and hauls Jacquie's stuff to the store.

Sleeping on the couch gives me a front-row seat for the screaming Jory-fits. When she sneaks in after midnight the hall light flicks on. "Where have you been?"

"All-night prayer meeting."

"Did you take money from my purse?"

"I didn't take squat from your fucking purse."

"Jory, please, do not talk to your mother like that."

"Fuck you. You're not my fucking father."

Mummy yells, "Get up to your room, now!"

Jory cupboard-slams through the kitchen.

Jennah stomps down the stairs with Dean screeching in her arms. "Does no one in this house have a fucking brain in their head?"

I slip down into June's empty pickle room. The cement damps my bum and the door ices my back. *Jasper, when Aunties M&N come, we're going home.*

I hang over the couch, head between the curtains. Mummy scolds, "Hariet, don't you have anything better to do than gawking out the window?"

Jory smolders in the chair. "She's waiting for the lesbos."

The taxi pulls up in front of Grandma's and my feet land in my boots.

Mummy blocks the door. "What? Who? Mary?"

"Please. Let me out."

"Go to your room."

"I don't have a room." I bolt out the side, across the street, and into my aunties' arms.

Mummy's housedress is half-closed and her slippers soak up the slush. "Hariet, get back to the house—now!" She yanks my ear, twisting it in the way that gives a body no choice but to follow.

"Theresa, you're hurting her."

"Don't you dare be interfering with my child."

Mr. Hawthorne watches from his veranda and I run from the disgrace to the pickle room. Len finds me hours later. "*Corka*, don't cry."

"Can I go with my aunties?"

"How would I bear life here if you were to go?" He holds me on the outside like Jasper does on the inside. "I will work something out. I promise."

June has been gone for nights and nights and the pickle room is the loneliest place I've ever stayed. Somehow she knows, comes home, and snugs up behind me, her hair falling like seaweed over my shoulder. "Bloody assholes, eh, Ari?" She lights a rolled smoke, sucks on it a while then holds it to my lips. "Here, it'll make everything bad seem small."

"Auntie Nia said cigarettes are bad for you."

50

"It's not a cigarette. It's good for you. Like spinach." I cough and sputter. June's voice steadies me like when she taught me to ride her bike. "Slow down. Don't be afraid." I'm in a boat. She sounds water-soft. "You think I'm pretty?"

"Like the moon in a night sky."

"You look like Daddy. Did he fuck you?"

"He . . . took me fishing."

"Right, fishing. For fuckin' worms, eh."

"I hate worms." The air swirls in soft waves.

"He just finger-fucked me. I bit his ear, hard. He never touched me again." She snuffs up snot. "Fucking fucker." My head bobbles as she bolts up and cranks the radio. "Ohhh, I love this song." She loud-sings, "Here in my deep purple dreams . . ."

My eyes sink to the bottom of the sea, opening after a long drift. Radio light glows in the damp dark. June sits on the floor, fussing with her arm like the time Dr. Herbert helped himself to my blood. "June, are you sick?"

"Wish I'd never bit him." She crawls back into bed. "Don't get fucked up like me, Ari."

Mummy's feeding Dean his morning bottle.

"Please, can I go over to Grandma's and see Auntie Mary?"

"They've gone."

I slam on my boots and march across the street. Grandma pats my stressed hair. "They left. They didn't want to cause trouble. Go back home and get a coat on. It's ten below."

I head home, not for the coat but to pack. Mummy stands in the door. "Put that suitcase away and get cleaned up. Len needs you at the store for the January sale."

"I'm heading east."

"Look how easily they left. They don't want a rag like you."

"I hate you. I hate you. I hate you!"

"Well, you'd have to be more than sewer gas for me to mind about that."

I shove my life savings into my pocket. *June and me will get our own place. We don't need any of them, Jasper. First Len's getting a boatload of my mind for breaking his promise.*

The Pennyworth's over-the-door bell gets a dollar-full slam. Babcia stands at the cash.

"Where's Len?"

Her eyes point upstairs.

Mary's reaching arms are the first thing I see. "Oh, Ari, I've missed you."

"I thought you left."

Auntie Nia stretches her bear arms around me. "We just didn't want you caught in a battle."

"Take me home."

Len crouches low. "They'd go to jail if they took you. They will stay here this week. You come after school. I'll see what I can reason with Mummy, okay, *corka?*"

Len negotiates a week of sleepovers at the store by saying that I annoy Jacquie out of bed better than anyone and she needs a fresh start for school.

Aunties M&N help Len with his store troubles. They know what's selling in New York and San Francisco and they get Len jumping on the Toronto market. The upstairs turns into a peasant-skirt, tie-dye, headband, fringed-bag factory. Polish relatives come and go with more handwork than is seen in two years of the Wednesday Night Knitting and Prayer Society gatherings. The love bead arm of the operation continues at the blue house. Downstairs the store is divided in half—Aquarius Boutique to the right, Pennyworth's to the left. The only place in town where you can buy a patchwork vest and toilet paper in one convenient location.

My headtop connects with Aunties M&N as we paint the new sign. Auto paint doesn't sparkle like sea glass but we make do. Auntie Nia admires my star. "Beautiful, Ari. Do you have art at your school?"

"I got ninety-nine percent. Miss Glenn said she would've given me a hundred but creation should have room for growth."

"And what treasures have you unearthed?"

I tell them about visiting Nana Appleton and teas with Grandma and about black June, but leave out the smoking situation. I tell them that the school librarian put a star on a shelf that says, Ari Appleton read all the books on this shelf and recommends *The Secret of the Hidden Staircase*. "And I have a borrowed dog named Sparky."

Auntie Mary takes my brush. "How are things with your mummy?"

"She's still short on nerves and seems Len or me are always murdering her last one."

"Before we head home we have two surprises. Your mummy has agreed to let you go on vacation with Auntie Elsie this summer."

"Where?"

"Your mummy didn't ask. And Elsie didn't say, but . . . did you know your cousins have never seen the East Coast?" She winks. "Len, we're ready for the next surprise."

At first I can't make out what Len has cradled in his elbow nook. It looks like Babcia's rabbit-soft, very-cold-day hat until its sleepy-eyed head lifts and I swear my puppy smiles at me. "But Mummy won't let me."

Jacquie pats him. "I'll take care of him here at night for you. What will you call him?"

"Zodiac." Because all the goodness of the heavens is in him.

THIRTEEN

Jennah wakes me singing "All Shook Up." She makes oatmeal while she irons my dress. The kitchen sparkles and Mummy's hair looks like seahorse tails pinned with bobby pins.

"Morning, Mummy." Her eyes stay closed as she sucks on her cigarette. Jennah tips whiskey into two teacups. "Len said that's not good with her pills."

"Just taking the edge off things, sis."

I brush the ash sprinkled on baby Dean from Jennah's cigarette and kiss his downy head.

Jennah is a go-getter. She went out and got a good typing job with Hydro and a new boyfriend named Wilf. He has a belly and an empty hair spot on his head but he has a big Chevy Biscayne and calls Jennah "princess" and at work people call him *Mr. Ferguson, sir.*

I help trundle Dean over to Grandma's before school. She heaves a big put-out sigh until Jennah leaves. "Imagine two dollars a day for looking after this lamb. She better keep her legs closed with this one, though. You know what they say about buying the cow."

"What?"

Jory stumbles crusty-eyed from Grandma's parlour. "It's the sixties, Gramonster. She's not getting knocked up until she sees if there're any better bulls to bleed."

"You get yourself cleaned up for school or out looking for a job or you'll not be spending another night in this house."

Twenty dollars floats onto the table. "Got me a job."

"Where?"

"I don't give the milk for free."

I head home to collect my books and see June ralphing on the juniper before she heads in and downstairs. Mummy is mining for aspirin at the back of the kitchen cupboard. "Pick up Jillianne's homework from school. She has a sore throat."

"Is Len gone?"

"To Buffalo to pick up stock."

Seems Len travels further and longer to find inventory he used to get downtown. I take Pepto to June. "You okay?"

She scarfs half the bottle and rolls over with a lit joint in her hand. I pry it away, cover her with a quilt, and take the edge off Ari Appleton before putting out the light.

On Sundays Mummy fusses because Wilf Ferguson comes for dinner. Doesn't matter that he's twice Jennah's years because he's triple-good as Roland. When his sainted mother died she left him a house and insurance. A big diamond glitters on Jennah's finger and a little bump might be growing under her dress. Mummy checks out the window. "Hariet, go tell Jory we're waiting on her."

Grandma reminds, "See she turns off the lights."

I go in the always-open kitchen door. Moans call my eyes through the arch to the parlour couch. Jory's breasts shine like Mrs. Butter's best china cups and the boarder's big hand doesn't care if it breaks them. Light spills from the window over her shoulder like honey. As he licks up her sweetness I back out of the house, standing between the water meter and the budding peony, before trudging around to the front door. The girl who finally opens the door to my endless knocking has a waterfall of blonde silk pouring over her red T-shirt and a smudge of pink under her lip. "Jory, lunch is ready. Make sure to turn out the lights."

The Appletons are fathoms from glorious revampment, but we're picture pretty in new dresses for Cousin Zara's wedding.

Mummy checks her updo in the mirror. I say, "Oh, you're prettier than the bride," but really I think Jacquie is loveliest in a sapphire empire that makes her pearness look like the most delicious fruit ever tasted.

My dress, darkest pink, sings like the wind through the aspens when I dance. I never knew Polish polkas and down-home reels were first cousins or that Len's bones stretch long so they can hold all the music in him. Next to Len, my best partner is Uncle Iggy. Things can be done with a wheeled partner that can't be spun any other way.

Len drags a boy, almost as tall as him, over to Jacquie. "This is my cousin's son. He has been trying to gather courage to ask you to dance." Jacquie smiles and all the other hopefuls are plum out of luck.

I help myself to Cousin Alphonse. He isn't much of a dancer but he seems right proud that I peeled him off the lonely wall. I'd give Len every dance but he's sashaying Mummy around the floor in his handsome-suit and Mummy is moving like a Rockette. Uncle Petros tries to cut-in but Len quicksteps her away and Mummy laughs out loud, and it's the best treasure I've found yet.

FOURTEEN

As the calendar flips, May 1964, '65, '66, I wonder if Mummy has any memory of expelling me from her womb. She doesn't see me turn eleven, twelve, thirteen . . . she doesn't see me at all. I travel through my dark places, my book now over-fat with treasures, finding only one from her. Given accidently, but a treasure nonetheless.

For the most part Grandma's boarders are a plague, except for Mr. Fountain, a collector of rare coins, stamps. He buys and sells things, keeping favourites for himself. Precious coloured bottles line his windowsill. His eyes near the same green of the perfume bottle he gave me on my twelfth birthday.

Every Monday I helped Grandma change the beds. If there had been a thousand washdays he'd still not run out of stories from his adventures. The day he asked, "Do you know why there's nothing for me to buy on Mondays?"

I stuffed a pillow into its case. "Why?"

"Because I'd lose seeing something rarer than a Double Eagle." At twelve my breasts were not much bigger than silver dollars but he handled them like the treasures he kept in boxes. He'd slip out, "I love you" before unzipping and pulling out his swelled-up thing.

Jasper always tugged me to pick up the dirty sheets and answer Grandma's yell for the laundry whenever his weenie weaseled out.

One Friday, we had a half day at school and Grandma was at bridge. I wanted to see him without other people around. I imagined he talked to spirits and made papier mâché masks. I tiptoed up the stairs, and sounds like warthogs grubbing came from his room. My mother's legs twisted around him like pale snakes. His bum had two red pimples, ready to pop white pus, and likely I was the only person on earth who would ever know they were there.

Now, I change the beds on Saturdays.

When school lets out, Len loads me on the train with the kind of love that hurts to see me go. Mum thinks I go to Auntie Elsie's, if she notices me gone at all.

Homecoming to Skyfish is a sapphire strung on a year of pebbles and pearls. Aunties M&N and I walk the shore, beginning so early the sun is little more than a far-off promise. We gather discoveries then climb the rocky slope back to Skyfish with a new day ahead. In their hands I learn to shape clay and wood; the world, too, I suppose.

In my thirteenth summer, Jake notices the rising tides beneath my shirt and the wild spirals of my bum-length hair. Sometimes on our seashore rambles he helps me from a rock, keeping hold of my hand longer than needed but shorter than wanted. We walk through questions until we find a place to hope or sit, reading book after book to each other.

"Each species has its own ties to others, and all are related to the earth." He looks up from the pages of *The Sea Around Us*, gazes across the Atlantic then at my tanned face. "It's not as much a tie as it is a freeing with you."

"Feels more like a seeing."

"How'd you mean?"

"Everything is so big here, the sky, our ocean, these rocks sit atop each other to fit in all this solid earth, but I never feel invisible, especially with you. Not like back there, crammed right up to Mum. She's more likely to notice a chip in her nail polish than me." My head nests on his shoulder; his cheek floats over my hair. "You've always seen me. And even in all your shape-shifting I see you."

"You think I'm shifty?"

"You're sea mist and solid rock, music and silence, gentle warrior, sorrowful joy, a story written on water, impossible to read but easy to know."

"Your words could make that washed up kelp believe it was a dolphin."

"I'm not shifty. I call things what they are."

His eyes turn northeast, toward The Rock.

"You ever hear anything from your mum?" I say.

"Nah. Nia tracked down an uncle. Apparently she was last seen headin' to a place called Pensacola in some guy's fifth wheel."

"Your sisters?"

"Went with." He springs up like a jack-out-of-the-box. "Let's go check on the puffins."

Summers always end with a Skyfish party and Jake fiddling, music dancing out of every muscle of his seventeen-year-old, hard-work body. He takes centre stage. "Here's a song for the prettiest girl to ever come to this shore." Sweat-soaked hair hides his eyes but not the flush on his cheek as he sends a lonely waltz up to the rafters.

At the threshold of the goodbye we linger, his two fingers connecting with mine, a gentling of hair away from my face and a small kiss, not on my cheek, but on my lips.

I lie on the after-party floor with Aunties M&N. I don't tell them the Appletons are falling from the tree or that Mum disappears for days and comes back shaky. I tell them I wrote my hero essay about them. I tell them I'm safe with Len. I tell them that the day I turn sixteen I'm coming home, and they say my room is waiting.

Aunt Elsie travels with me from Montreal to Toronto so she can visit Grandma. "Did you have a good time?"

"These summers mean more to me than I can ever say."

"For as long as I can swing it, you'll have them."

"Mrs. Butters told me Aunties M&N wanted to keep me as a baby. What happened?"

"Your mummy despises Mary."

"How could she?"

"It's just her way. Mary's age put her three steps ahead of your mum. It twisted her to see Mary win at anything. Your grandpa and Mary were best buddies. That twisted her even more. Theresa expected everything but did nothing. She could never be wrong. Never said sorry to anyone for anything. And stubborn, oh, my Lord. Maybe we let her get away with too much, but it was so much easier than battling with her." Elsie straightens. "Listen to me going on. Please, don't repeat any of that. How are your sisters?"

"Jennah married another Smashus Clay."

"What? She shouldn't put up with that."

"Jennah wheels and deals more than puts-up-with. 'If you smack me then you owe me something really big.' Seems to be working. The last clocking got her a shiny red car. Besides she's preggers again. It better be a boy this time or Wilf will just plant another one."

"Jennah is too smart for that."

"Brains don't mean much when your heart isn't screwed in right."

"And June?"

"Wish I knew. I haven't heard from her in over a year. But Jacquie was top of her class at business college and she's met the softest boy."

"Oh, it does my heart good to hear she's found some happiness. And how are things with Len?" The world blurs into ribbons of green, dotted with cows and trees and churches. "Ari?"

"What's worse? Being tolerated or hated?"

"I don't know."

"Being invisible or despised?"

She shrugs.

"Len's so kind and decent. Having him for a stepdad has been a lucky break for all the Appletons."

"Your mother . . ."

"She's screwing him over."

"Your dad got her so turned around with men."

"He turned us all inside out, passed on his brains but made us heart-stupid."

"Except for you."

"Only because he checked out before completely excavating my soul."

"It does no good to talk of these things."

"Of course it does. Why do you think Jacquie's not stuffing herself with cookies faster than Mr. Christie can bake them? Because Babcia understands. When she was Jacquie's age soldiers raped her. She had a baby that her father ripped away. She doesn't know if he threw it in the river or left it alone in the woods. Babcia and Iggy help Jacquie unload all the shit and flush it."

Now Elsie's looking for a way out the window.

I nudge her knee. "But most of the time a kid just needs someone like you who makes them believe in good."

"You didn't say how Jory and Jillianne are faring."

"I'm thinking Daddy got more of their souls than anyone knows."

FIFTEEN

Jacquie wears an ivory silk dress and a small feathery spray of pearls in her hair. She crowns my head with a wreath of baby's breath. "There. My beautiful maid of honour."

"I know you're happy, but are you scared?"

She picks up a bouquet of calla lilies. "I'm too full of hope; there's no room for fear."

Just Len and I go to City Hall to stand up for her and Franc.

There's an after-gathering at Chan's Garden. Jennah can't come because yesterday she popped out twin boys: Dakota and Dylan to go with stepbrother Dean and sisters, Darcy and, God help her, Diamond.

June doesn't even know that the cracks in Jacquie's life have turned into the most exquisite wabi-sabi creation. June just disappeared like in stage plays where they say *fade to black*. When Jasper asks where she is, I dream her up in Paris writing poetry by the Seine, not slumped in some alley with a needle in her arm.

Sometimes, I wander through Yorkville looking for June in the coffee houses. I stuff a ten in my pocket in case I catch sight of Jory tucked in a doorway. She lives with her new "family" in whatever pad they can find to crash in.

Jory promised she wouldn't miss Jacquie's wedding, but she's usually so spaced out, she misses entire days. She says her life is a blast, but when it turns cold she knows I've left a key in the shed and an extra blanket in the pickle room.

And Jillianne is AWOL: always wasted of late. Just as well, she'd likely pitch a fit, and some sweet and sour pork along with it.

Grandma keeps asking, "Where's my purse? Dolores, did you turn off the iron?"

"I'm Ari, Grandma. I checked the iron and your purse is on your lap."

Len lifts a glass of Champanade. "Jacquie, your mother and I are so proud of the beautiful woman you have become. Franc, cherish her always."

Jasper twirls on a strand of Jacquie's hair, singing, *Real love, love reel, heel-toe, hearts-heal.*

Len and I call the back steps the de-apple-ized zone. It's Jillianne that sends us running for cover these days. She just called him a fucking polack when he asked about money missing from his wallet.

I bring his jacket. "Let's collect Zodiac and go to the lake."

"Tell your mother we're going."

"She's sleeping one off. You had no idea what you were signing on for, did you?"

"You and Jacquie make it all worthwhile." We walk and talk our way to the water's edge, then sit on our bench. "Do you know where your mother went today?"

A bar, a back seat, or a bed are the most likely bets. "No."

Len leans forward, his big hands capturing his head, elbows sinking into his knees with the weight of it. "I brought her lunch but she wasn't home. She said she went to the police station about Jillianne's shoplifting, but I took care of everything last week."

My hand opens on his back, fingers painting it with a little hope. "Let's point the truck east and not stop 'til we hit Skyfish."

"Your grandmother needs us." His hand turns mine in his, tracing the little half-moon scars left behind by strappings from Reverend Lowry. "This summer, we'll all go to the Expo, then a little further so I can see your ocean."

SIXTEEN

Mr. West tells me to wait after English class. He's a new teacher, young and hopeful.

63

Saturday, I saw him on the boardwalk in tight jeans, his ass filling out the seat like water-rounded rocks. It was the most spectacular thing I'd ever seen until he turned and I didn't know what to take in first, the chest under his white T-shirt or the dimples when he smiled. He lifted his sunglasses to his forehead. "Hi, Ari. Do you live around here?"

"No, I just come when I'm missing the ocean."

"That's right, you're from the East. I cycled the Cabot Trail four years ago, before starting university."

Jasper did the math. *Finish high school at eighteen or is it seventeen in the west like it is out east? Three years university. One for teacher's college. Twenty-one? Twenty-two? Not too old.* "You probably pedalled right through my front yard."

He crouched and patted Zodiac. "Beautiful dog. Does she do any tricks?"

"*He* does one spectacular trick."

"What's that?"

"Makes people feel better."

"I'll keep that in mind on a bad day."

I backed away, my hair was hippie wild and the tie-dyed tank showed off tits better than Jory's at thirteen-and-a-half. "Um, I've got homework. My teacher's a real pain if I don't get it done."

He laughed big. "See you Monday."

Now, I'm summoned to his desk. "Yes, sir?"

He pulls my essay from the pile and looks smack in my eyes. "Did you write this?"

I check it's mine: "Filling Uncle Iggy's Shoes." I say, "Yes."

"Did someone help you write it?" I can't decide if I'm proud or hate him. He reads my words out loud, "It's a phantom shoe, but I see it running away with his imagination. It's a winged shoe and his body can't keep pace with all there is to create. It's a magic shoe that kicks a paralyzed girl, propelling her forward on her road. It's a marching shoe that war did not silence and it echoes in hollow hearts, pumping them when they can't beat alone."

I turn and walk out.

"Ari, wait." He catches me in the hall. I snap my arm away. "I didn't mean to upset you. Please understand, some of the concepts seem beyond your years."

"Some kids live in adult worlds. They should have warned you about us at teacher's college. I have to get to work."

Zodiac runs to greet Mr. West when he enters the store minutes before closing. I say, "Red pens are on the far wall, *sir*."

He looks up from his commune with Zodiac. "I was hoping your dog could do his trick."

Len comes to lock up. "Evening. Can I help you?"

"This is my teacher."

"Is there a problem?"

"No. Ari is an amazing student. I just came to ask permission to enter her essay in a literary contest."

"Ari would be honoured. We'd all be proud."

"No way. A couple of hours ago he didn't believe I wrote it." I move to count the till.

"*Corka*, do not be hard. Many times I cannot believe what you've done. Was it the shoe story?"

"Yes."

"Would you like to meet Uncle Iggy?"

"Uh . . . yeah, I would."

He traipses upstairs to share poppy seed loaf with my Zajac circus. I try to ignore him when he returns to where I'm hanging shirts. He examines one that looks like a tiger exploded on it. "Very cool."

Len collects the receipts. "She made that, too. Pick one if you like."

"Will you forgive me, Ari?"

"I guess we're cool." I point to the foil-wrapped packet in his hand. "Babcia sending you home with cabbage rolls?"

His dimples come out with his half smile and he actually quotes *my* words by heart. "'No matter his shoes are empty. The silver ocean rolls him to the table and there he feasts on losses until the whole world is full.' Ari, it really is brilliant. If I've discouraged you from writing, then I shouldn't be teaching."

He leaves, but my imagination keeps him close. There may not be any thumping in the room beside mine but my curious hand is exploring under my candy-striped sheets and fireflies spark in my head.

SEVENTEEN

Mum washes down soul-numbing pills with whisk*tea*. She doesn't seem to hate me as much when she's hanging out with Martians, but then again she doesn't notice dog shit on her shoe, either.

Len calls up the stairs for the fiftieth time. "Jillianne, up now!" The only times she makes it to school is when Mike Fudge, aka The Candyman, has treats.

Mum says, "Let her be. She was up late."

Len fights with the sleeve of his coat. I help him with the tangle. "I have a lead on some T-shirts and scrap leather in Windsor. Wait on me and we'll walk Zodiac together." He leaks out the door, descending the street with no whistle and no head to the sky.

I rummage behind the condiments. "Where's my lunch?"

Every night Babcia makes me a paper-bag feast, the most delicious part being words that Uncle Iggy writes on the folded-down flap. The bag is crumpled on the floor, only my quote remains from Jillianne's midnight raid. *The voyage of discovery is not in seeking new landscapes but in having new eyes.—Proust*

The bag quotes have made Miss Standish and me sort of friends. She singled me out one history class when I passed one to Nick Potter. "Miss Appleton, stand up and let us all hear what is so important between you and Mr. Potter."

I read, "Do not follow where the path may lead. Go instead where there is no path and leave a trail."

She snatched the bag from my hand. "Who wrote this?"

"My uncle. I mean Emerson, ma'am."

"And you thought Nicholas needed it?"

"I usually pass them on at lunch but he had basketball." The class oooed and Sharon Murdock, his girlfriend, wanted to punch-slap me the way girlie-girls do.

Miss Standish squashed the teasing by going to the first desk, first row. "Tom, give me any words that inspire you." Silence slipped from desk to desk until she reached Nick. "Mr. Potter?"

"Only those who risk going too far can find out how far he can go. T. S. Eliot."

Nick's black hair hung shaggy around his always-tanned face. He was as cute as he was smart and if I didn't love Jake and Mr. West, I might love him.

After school he waited by the fence. "Hey, Ari."

"Sorry about the mess."

"It's not so much a mess having the coolest girl in school pass you notes."

I scanned the situation: jeans tucked into beaded mukluks, Babcia's festival-of-the-Ukraine sweater and ribbons, like a tambourine tail, weaving through the hair braided over my shoulder. I had me pegged more as freak-of-the-universe.

"You want to hang out?"

"What about Sharon?"

"We broke up."

"I have to get to work."

"You work?"

"Design and sales."

"Cool."

"And weekends I wait tables in the Village."

"No kidding?"

"Yeah, the Riverboat. I showed up so much looking for my sister, her boss put me to work."

I figured there was no harm scoping out my options while in exile from the East and waiting for Mr. West. My smile dislodged him from the fence and every after-school since then Nick walks me to the store. And at the beginning of every history class, Miss Standish opens her hand for the bag.

Maybe having a little hope in the minds of tomorrow make teachers a little less grumpy today. However, having Nick as my almost-boyfriend has set Sharon and her demon followers plotting human sacrifice.

Mum spilling tea pulls me away from crucifixions to baptisms in 90 proof spirits. "You okay, Mummy?"

Her eyes search for something. "When did your hair get so much gold in it, Hariet?"

"It's not near as pretty as yours." I kiss her cheek. She swipes it off with her sleeve. "We're getting low on bead strings. If you feel like making a few, supplies are by the TV. I'm going to check on Grandma before school."

Grandma answers my knock. "Dolores, when did you get here?"

Even before she calls me Dolores I can tell it's a bad day. At night, I lay out her clothes so she knows how to get dressed. Today, she started at the wrong end. I wonder how long it took her to get her pantyhose over her dress. Her substantial cotton panties and white brassiere add the crowning touches. "Come on, Grandma, I'll get you outside-in."

I slide into my spot just before "O Canada." I offered my own Lord's Prayer on my dash to school, *Our Father, loafing in Heaven, my Gram can't remember her name. Your kingdom come and shake up my mum before she screws over Len. Give me today my daily bread, 'cause my sister stole my lunch. Lead me into temptation behind the portables and deliver me from dumped Sharons. For mine are the hormones and the flowers and the stories. For Thursday. Amen*

Mr. West folds his arms as the class snakes out the door headed for math. "Third time this week you've been late, Ari."

"You ever had to deal with a naked granny, sir?"

"Can't say that I have."

"Well, maybe until you do you could cut a fellow human some slack."

The whole Appleton structure is precarious at best. But I catch some good breaks: a cheering section in the east, a few blocks south, a store crammed with Zajacs, and a Mr. West nodding me off. "Fair enough."

Lunchless, I head north to check on Grandma then home to scarf down a sandwich. Mum descends the stairs with her first button to second hole as I spread the mustard. "Hariet, I wasn't expecting you home 'til dinner."

"Jillianne ate my lunch and Gran was right squirrelly this morning."

Some goon looking like Mr. Clean's ugly brother tries to move his hulk down the stairs without them squeaking. "Hariet, this is Officer Irwin. He just came to talk some sense into Jillianne." Sweat curdles on a bulby nose that might've once been used as a pincushion. I reach for the knob as I back toward the door. "Hariet?"

I head for school but Jasper needs the store. Zodiac and the workroom wall me in safe. When Jacquie turns on the light I'm sitting on the floor, back to the wall. "Ari? Why aren't you in school?"

"Everything's going to fall apart."

"I'm amazed it's held together as long as it has. Look at it this way, when it collapses, you'll either land here or with M&N. I'll call the school and tell them you have cramps. Uncle Iggy needs help beading fringe for the bags."

"But Len . . . I . . ."

"Len knows he never really had her. As long as he has you he'll be okay."

When Jacquie hoists me up I see she's turned both solid *and* transparent. "And you," I say.

"Who would've thought you and I would be the pick of the Appletons."

"I'm scared for Jillianne."

"I'm scared for you if you think it's your job to save any of them. She's drowning. She'll only pull you under."

"But, you were drowning."

"Yeah, but I wanted a hope to grab on to. I don't think she does."

After school Jacquie lets Nick into the workroom. He watches me dipping a T-shirt. "You feeling better?"

I nod.

"I could help you with what you missed."

"I'll muddle through it later. It's the Christmas rush."

"Oh."

"You any good with your hands?"

"What?"

"Len gives me a buck fifty a shirt. Two for the fancier ones. They'll sell like the wind up until Christmas. I'll split the profits."

"Sundays are out, but Wednesday to Saturday I could." He holds back my hair as I smooth a dry shirt out on the press. "Careful you don't catch it."

70

You'd think after the day I've had I wouldn't be interested in kissing a boy, but feeling his chest against my shoulder makes whoring mothers very unimportant. I lift my face and he gives a scared kiss. I turn for more because I like the feeling that spreads from his lips to my belly.

He holds my baby finger. "Sharon's having a party next Friday. You want to go?"

Jasper pushes. *Say yes. We like parties.*

Boys like messing under T-shirts more than making them. I'm four shirts to one ahead when Mrs. Potter drops by to see where Nick is working. Nick looks ready to hurl Babcia's perogies at the maternal invasion.

Mercifully, my tits aren't flapping under my tank top, which sometimes happens after hours of pressing shirts. I look Amish in my apron and head scarf.

"Nice to meet you, Mrs. Potter. It sure has been a blessing having Nick's help." Somewhere between kisses, Nick mentioned that his parental units were über-Christian.

Nick's bowels can be heard clamping when Mrs. Potter says, "Perhaps you'd join us for church on Sunday."

I look to Len, as salesman-savvy as they come. "Papa?"

"If your chores and homework are done, child."

She leaves, reassured her son is keeping company with Ari Ingalls from Little Store in the Big City.

Nick is silent as we saunter to Sharon's party. "Listen, if having me over Sunday is such a horror I'll contract smallpox."

"It's not you. My parents are just way too much parents."

"Yeah, well my dad's fish bait in the St. Lawrence. Life's a bitch. Actually, my mom's the bitch."

Compared to a down-east party, this one's a dental appointment with Cheesies and orange Crush, make-out music, and an ex-girlfriend who is Gestapo-clever. A turn around the indoor-outdoor carpet to "If I Fell" is nice until Sharon says, "Your turn, Ari. I pick Randy for you." She pushes us toward a closet. "Ten minutes."

Randy is the boy most likely to skin a live cat. Before she can shove us inside I do-se-do out of his clutches. "No thanks."

A chicken-in-the-middle-of-a-wolf-pack frenzy ensues as Randy nabs my arm and the Sharon Supporters sweep me toward the closet. It becomes clear why women go for the tall guy and not the little weenies. Nick unravels the fray with big pushes and arm twists. "Ari doesn't do anything Ari doesn't want to do." He reestablishes his stud standing on our way out. "And *we* don't need to hide in a closet to make out."

He places his coat over my shivers as I throw up fluorescent orange crap on Sharon's lawn.

"Thought I heard you down here. Ari, are you crying?" Jacquie ratchets up my chin. "What are you on?" Her voice echoes and her pale hair hangs like broken feathers. My knees swallow my face as she slides down beside me. "What did you take?"

"Some shit Malik gave me."

"What?"

"Yellow sunshine." The world cracks and I'm cartwheeling into the deep. "It's so dark."

"Don't start this, Ari."

"I'm on the other side of the ride. I'm sorry. I just wanted to be anywhere but here."

Laughter sprays through her nose. "Well, that's a round-trip ticket if I ever saw one." She snatches the blanket from the bed and pulls my head to her lap. "Does Len know you're here?"

"At-the-store here. But not screwed-up here. Please, don't tell him."

"Won't have to. He'll sense it in his soft bones." For a long while she strokes me like I'm made of kitten-fur. "How was the party?"

"Come Monday, my cool status will be back to freak. They all saw how much I hate being locked in a room."

"Mum sure screwed us up, didn't she?"

So many times growing up, a keyed room was Door-a the Babysitter. When sisters we're locked in with me I didn't hate it so much, but I despised when just Jasper and me waited out the long days and nights. Peeing my pants 'til I was empty. My tongue turning to sand in my mouth.

"We never had a home, but Mum always found a room." Jacquie washes a rain of tears from my face and holds a hankie to my nose. "Come get to bed." She struggles to her feet, her nightie floating around her growing belly like maritime mist.

"Whenever I was inside Door-a, Jasper would paint a sister-house. June was the solid walls. Jennah, the windows. Jory made the roof and Jillianne the floor. You were always the yellow door." We stand face to face. "I know it was you who stood between them and us whenever you could."

EIGHTEEN

Forest church and ocean sanctuaries suit me better than solid pews. When the pastor commands, "Bow your head and close your eyes," I lift mine, eyes full-wide because, in the dark, a line

73

of jewels stretch out, biggest to small, and I remember Daddy picking the shiniest to take to lunch after church.

Mr. Potter looks in the rearview. "Did you enjoy the service, Ari?"

Jasper mutters, *It tore our guts out.*

"Yes, it was very nice, thank you, sir."

Mrs. Potter asks, "What were you writing during the service?"

"The Christmas music inspired the seasonal poem we have to do for school."

"Oh, let's hear it."

"Um . . . it needs work."

Nick nabs it from my hand, chewing his lip as he absorbs it.

Unholy Night

God,
rewind two thousand years,
send your daughter down to earth,
exalt her
princess of peace
let the world feel her
worth.
On silent nights,
unholy nights
she falls
on her knees
for men believing they are king
and she was sent to please.

"Ari's an amazing writer." He whispers in my ear. "I'm so sorry about Sharon's party."

"We hear you're giving Nick a run for first place."

74

"Not hardly, Mr. Potter. He trounces me in math and science."

A dog looking like a hairy slipper with legs comes yapping to the door, near crazy from the smell of pot roast. Nick's mother hangs up coats and slips on an apron. "Nick, let P.P. out back."

Nick turns the colour of green dye mixed with yellow. "It's short for Powder Puff."

We sit at a fancied-up table. Every bite of beef comes with a milking for information. "Do you have brothers and sisters, Ari?"

"Five sisters, ma'am."

"Five! Older? Younger? What do they do?"

"Older. Jennah was an executive with Hydro but she felt being home with her kids was more important. Um, June's a writer . . . living in Paris. Jacquie's a businesswoman. She runs the family business. Jory is a . . . a therapist. And Jillianne's . . . studying to be a pharmacist."

"How is it your name is Ari?"

"It's my second name. So many J's got too confusing."

"What's your first name?"

"Um . . . Jewel."

"And what would you like to do after high school, Jewel?"

"Be a potter, ma'am." A post-nuclear horror descends. "No, not a *Potter*. I mean a clay-and-kiln potter. Summers I study with an artist on the East Coast."

"Sounds like a wonderful little hobby. Nicholas is going to study medicine. And his little friend Sharon wants to be a nurse."

Perfect, after she gouges out your eyes she can put a Band-Aid on them.

Shh, Jasper. "It just gives me income to put away for university. I'm going to become . . . a marine biologist. Work on the declining whale population. There's a fine ecological balance affecting every creature down to the smallest bit of plankton."

Lies carry me through until Nick walks me home. "Sorry

about the inquisition." I shrug. "Did your dad really drown saving a dolphin trapped in a net?"

"Something like." I veer from the blue house to Grandma's. "See you tomorrow."

I'm discovering that grannies who can't remember why they got a spoon from the drawer remember stories they're not supposed to tell. I press for information before the elevator stops going to the top floor. Things move a little when I get her dressed and make tea. I prime the old memory as we fold laundry. "It was spring, wasn't it when Hariet was born? You took her to Mary's, was it?" So far I've unearthed that Mum was drinking sloppy, Daddy was drinking mean. Before I was born the sisters got doled out and Grandma loaded Mum on the train to Skyfish.

"Mile after mile, Theresa worried at her nails, saying, 'Vincent will have his boy and we'll be a happy family again.' I knew by the way she was carrying that another girl was coming their way and all I could think was the only safe place for the babe was with Mary."

"Mummy must have been so disappointed."

"When wasn't that girl disappointed? Such a bonnie sprite was given to her, weighing, I'd guess, less than a five pound sack of sugar. Mary coaxed in special formula and that tall one, Nia, walked her through the crying nights." Grandma journeys back fourteen years. "Mary Catherine called the wee thing Joy. She was near frantic one day when Theresa took the baby for a walk. Hours passed before this big man came with Joy tucked in his arm. He'd found her on the shore. We thought Theresa had drowned 'til she was discovered anchored at the Legion. After that it was decided that Joy would stay with Mary."

"How come I—she didn't stay?"

"Did for a time. When Vincent came to take Theresa home, Mary gave him five thousand dollars for expenses and they both went off no trouble. A year later they returned. Said God had

told them they weren't to leave a child in moral corruption."
Grandma salts her tea with fat tears. "Mary and Nia loved her so."

Jasper, I want to unknow this.

But, Ari, we found our "J" name.

NINETEEN

Egging an Appleton can never come to any good. Sharon and
the SS (Sharon Supporters) attempt an ambush. Sharon gets a
head-butt in the gut and a yolky dollop scraped off my coat and
shoved into her mouth. The rest yelp as my backpack thwacks
them good.

I figure they've squealed on me when Miss Standish tells me
to report after school. She chins to Nick. "Mr. Potter, close the
door on your way out." She opens her calendar book, taking
out the "Unholy Night" poem. Last time I saw it, it was with
Mr. West. "Ari, is everything okay at home?"

"Pardon?"

"With your stepdad?"

"It's fine."

"Ari, women don't have to accept the atrocities anymore."

"Maybe women don't, but a kid has as much leverage as
mashed potatoes."

"Maybe I should talk to your mother."

"You've got it all wrong. The only one messing with me is
her."

"What do you mean?"

"Please, can I go? I'm going to be late for work."

"All right, but I am someone you can talk to. About anything."

Heart kicks can be hidden but not eye mist.

She tucks my poem in a gilt-edged leather journal and hands it to me. "Writing this good merits a special book. You have a good holiday."

Mr. West has Nick cornered by the front doors. I take the rear exit.

Nick catches me a block from the store. "Hey, what gives? You in trouble?"

"What's that supposed to mean?"

"Nothing. Standish hauled you in. West was acting all paternal with me."

"What did he say?"

"Blathered you were special and I'd better treat you with respect."

"Just what we need, more friggin' parents."

In the storeroom, Nick kisses me too hard and fumbles under my shirt in response to his gift: an iridescent silver-blue dragon painted on a black T-shirt. My new charm bracelet jingles as I say thank you to the rise under his jeans.

"Wish you could come to Florida with us."

Appletons are not the kind of fruit that go south in new RVs to visit grandparents with winter prefabs. "Bring me a shell with the sound of the ocean in it?"

Shelves at Aquarius empty as fast as we fill them. Len lets Mr. West into the storeroom to see me.

"Oh, for pity's sake, don't you have your own family to bother?"

Len scolds, "Ari, show respect."

"Sorry, *sirs*."

Len excuses himself to the rush in the store and I continue to block and fold T-shirts.

"I came to say sorry for sharing your poem with Miss Standish. I should've asked your permission. I just didn't know what to make of it."

He's wearing jeans and a black leather jacket and I still love him more than Nick. "Didn't know teachers needed to ask permission."

"I'd say we have a special obligation to. You didn't write about holly and bells like the other twenty-nine submissions."

"I was in church. It always makes me pissy."

He laughs like a regular person, and he teases Babcia when she brings coffee. "I was hoping for more of your cabbage rolls."

I rummage through my pack and hand him a brown-paper-wrapped gift.

"What's this?"

"Your reading of *Papa Panov's Special Christmas* sucked me into the merriment." It'd taken maybe a dozen tries before getting the T-shirt the way I imagined: tawny geckos climbing over his shoulder, down his back, disappearing in the rocks and crevices under his jeans.

He carefully unwraps it. "Wow, this is so much better than the fruitcake and cologne. Don't tell anyone I said that." I really want him to take off his shirt and try it on. "I'm heading to Winnipeg for Christmas. Can you pick out two for my sisters?"

"How old are they?"

"Sixteen and eighteen."

I throw off my apron, strictly because my T-shirt shows my latest creation. *Liar, liar.*

Shut it, Jasper. "I perfected a butterfly. As fast as I put them out, they're gone."

"They're gone?"

"Give me ten minutes. I'll press up two and stitch on the beads. Go pick out belts and fringed bags and you'll be the coolest brother ever."

79

To keep him longer, I wrap each in butcher paper, fastened with a gift from Aunties M&N, a giant sun-seal with the words, *Aquarius Boutique, Designed by Ari*. I add raffia bows with little star beads on the ends. His thirty dollars slides into my pocket, not the till.

"You really are an astonishing young woman, Ari. I hope you have a wonderful Christmas."

When I was six, Christmas snuck up without Mummy even noticing. Daddy came home from working in Calgary. As he cooked up the last of the Red River Cereal he told us about a wartime Christmas. December 23, 1943, he'd watched his two best buddies blown to smithereens. Wet cold had seeped into his joints and he no longer picked crawlies out of his provisions, just wolfed them down, bugs and all. On Christmas Eve families all over Europe opened their doors to soldiers. He just had to close his eyes and he could still feel the warmth of the fire, taste the savory stew and sweet cakes, and hear carols sung low and soft. He slept on a dry floor with a pillow under his head and a blanket tucked under his chin and woke to a whole day filled with the absence of war.

On this 1967 Christmas, Jillianne's present is a trip to Montreal for time away from her nothing-but-trouble boyfriend and time with I'll-straighten-her-out Auntie Dolores. Jory phones from San Francisco, says, "Life's a blast" and "Let's give peace a chance." The apartment above the store shimmers with candles, cedar garlands, and sugary angel-wing cookies. Mummy says, "Isn't the tree the prettiest you've ever seen?" She sparkles in a sweater Len bought her from Holt Renfrew. Grandma knows it's Christmas and that I'm the littlest Apple. Jennah and Wilf come with Christmas-happy kids and Jennah drinks to joyful not messy. Zodiac helps himself to the space behind my legs as Jacquie tucks me in on the sofa. In my hand is an ocean-smoothed stone, shaped like a heart, sent from Jake. I have strep throat and Babcia spoons broth into my mouth.

Best of all, Len plays his guitar like a gypsy by a fire. He and Uncle Iggy sing the kind of songs that make gold-bangled, peasant-skirted ladies twirl under stars. Mummy's eyes glitter and she doesn't pull away when I feather-scratch her arm. "This is the best Christmas ever."

Day after Christmas, Private Appleton returned to war. Day after New Year's Auntie Dolores brings Jillianne home and Grandma's life becomes a terrible battle.

TWENTY

Grandma's mind re-enters at the worst times. She knows her things are being sorted and pitched and the *Rooms for Rent* sign now says *For Sale*.

I plead for mercy. Len offers to take her into the blue house. But Auntie Dolores says Sunny Crest is best.

Watching Grandma have her life eviscerated is how I imagine Daddy felt seeing his buddy's guts hanging from a mulberry tree. I put my temporary brain-blip down to the stress of it all. How else could I be so careless as to leave my treasure box of letters behind the sofa?

Nick comes home with me after school to help move the heavier stuff. When we walk through the door, Mum has Nana Appleton's ring pinched between her fingers. "Where? Where— did you get this?"

"Nana gave it to me."

The backhand my mother delivers doesn't hurt near as much as Nick witnessing I'm the spawn of a stark raving Froot Loop. Theresa Appleton has never been much of a hitting mom. She's more a turn-the-back, I'm-so-disgusted-I-can't-stand-to-look-at-you sort. Not so today.

"Your father gave it to Mary. It was always Mary."

"No, I went to see Nana at the hospital before she died."

"How could you do this to me?" Her hand claws up a wad of letters. She pitches them into the fireplace.

"No, Mummy, don't!"

She whacks, whacks, whacks at my head with the metal dustpan, caterwauling like a demented hyena, then abandons the pummeling for my three years of everything-is-going-to-be-okay letters from M&N and dumps them into the fire. My treasure box follows them into the hungry flames. I go after it. The metal bits stick to my hands and my singed hair smells like a three-day-dead gopher poked with a stick.

"Ari!" Nick pulls me outside, plunging my hands into the snow. Blood drops falling from my head bloom like poppies on a new canvas. I turn shivery. I want to sleep.

Our neighbour Mr. Hawthorne appears. "Go get Mr. Zajac," he says to Nick. "Tell him to meet us at the East General." He has strong hands and his car seats are made of soft leather like Mr. West's jacket, and sometimes Auntie Dolores is soft.

"Let me see, honey." She turns my hands as Mr. Hawthorne drives. "You'll be okay."

Mum stays in the waiting room reading a 1963 *Woman's Day* while Auntie Dolores takes me in to the exam room. Dr. Paulin stitches a gash over my eyebrow. "What happened here?"

"We were cleaning out my mother's house, burning old papers. Hariet came home from school and tried to rescue some old letters we didn't know she wanted."

"Her face?"

"She . . . she hit the andiron or something in the scramble."

"Or something?" He looks at me. I shrug.

"Hmmm . . . well, elevating the hands will lessen the pain. Keep ice on her face and keep the dressings clean and dry. Here's a prescription for pain and antibiotics. Have her see her doctor in two days."

I get queen treatment, plumped on Babcia's bed. Even Zodiac is allowed up. Jacquie pokes her head 'round the door. "Nick is downstairs. Can he come up?"

"Tell him I moved to Bucharest."

"He has red carnations."

"Tell him I died and he can release them to my ashes drifting in the lake."

"He has your box."

I hoist up my thirteen-and-three-quarter years of charred flesh. "Brush my hair?"

Nick saved my box and maybe I love him more than Mr. West, but never more than Jake.

"Ari, you okay?"

I bite back my lip-quiver.

"I was saving these for Valentine's but thought you might like the ocean right now." He opens the treasure box to two small conch shells, side by side. He kisses my forehead like I'm dying of consumption. "I'll bring your homework after practice." He opens the door and stops. "Your mom's out here. You want me to stay?"

Save me. Get me out of here. "No."

Why the bloody hell did I get put in the room without a window to jump out of? I burrow into Zodiac's fur as the volume cranks up. Jacquie says, "Just go and leave us the hell alone."

Len says, "Just give her a couple of days, Theresa."

"If I have to call the police, I will." Mum's voice has that teetery shrill where I'm never sure if she's going to break something or down pills.

Officer Irwin hoisting me over his shoulder and parading me through the store flashes before my eyes. I make for the chair in the living room, snap up my legs, and hug a cushion in front.

Maybe Mum pictures that, too, since she sits almost calm on the coffee table. "Hariet, please understand, the shock of discovering Mary has been pursuing you behind my back was devastating. She's always taken everything from me. She's an evil, evil person. She corrupted your father."

I hold back the *bullshit*. "My name is Ari."

She dabs a dry tear. "Breaks my heart to hear you say that. I gave you your name."

"All you gave me was a misspelled atrocity."

Her fake whimper makes puke pool in my throat.

"I want my ring. Nana gave it to me."

"Mary has hurt me so much, it tore my heart out just looking at it. I threw it away."

Liar, liar.

"Auntie Mary could never hurt anyone. The only one hurting you, is you! You're a . . . a . . . deceiving jellyfish." I never bother much with crying but sometimes the forty-days-and-nights flood explodes.

Auntie Dolores snatches up the ringing phone like she owns the place. "Hello? Who is this? Mary? How'd you get this number?"

Mummy spits her words. "Len, you've deceived me, too?"

Jacquie nabs the phone. "I gave it to her. You've nothing to say about me talking to her. Hi, Auntie. A mess. The bitch had a tantrum, gave Ari a shiner, and in the tussle Ari's hands got burned."

Mum grabs the extension in the kitchen. "Mary Catherine, if you ever contact Hariet again I'll have you arrested for corrupting a minor. No letters, no phone calls, no visits. Have I made myself clear? If I catch wind of you going behind my back I'll send her where no one will ever find her." She slams the receiver down, picks it up, slamming it again and again—and again. "Len, you have her home by the time Dolores and I get back from Sunny Crest." World-done-me-wrong blather follows her down the steps and out the door.

Len takes the phone from Jacquie, talking in the deep mumble that makes it hard for a blubbering person to get the scoop. He hands me the phone.

"But Mummy said she'd have her arrested."

"She said nothing about you talking to Nia, besides no one here is going to tell."

I muck up my bandages with snot. "Auntie?"

"How's our girl?"

"I'm good."

"We're coming for March break, though right about now I want to march in and break that woman."

"Jacquie would if her belly wasn't so big."

"Just think, there will be a new baby. I'm sending you a book. I'll send it to the store."

"No. Better not risk it. Love you. Bye."

Len takes a cool cloth to my face. "Feel better, *corka?*" I nod. "Uncle Iggy will help you with your studies. Don't want you falling behind."

Iggy knows when to fill my head with numbers and when to stuff my heart with hope. He writes a note for my empty box. *What has gone before and what is to come is a small thing compared to what is inside you.*

"This is the first note M&N sent with me. I found it in the pocket of my PJs."

"See what you remember, *corka?* See what is inside. You are the holder of the treasure. When I came to this country I came

85

without my Katarina, my sons, or my legs, my pockets were empty, just like you, not even gotchies under my trousers. But no matter what was stolen from my past or my future, never could anyone take the love between us."

Many times, Iggy shared the horror in learning that his family had been taken to Belzec and the sorrow of never finding a trace of them. Uncles with no legs and broken hearts never get enough hugs, and whenever I give them, *I* always feel better.

TWENTY-ONE

Mr. West crouches by my desk, bewildered and über-sympathetic. "Are you sure you're up to being at school, Ari?"

I hide the stitches that make me look like a half-surprised meerkat under my gauzed hand. "I'm fine."

"How's your grandmother?"

"Great, if hell is your idea of a good time."

"Don't worry about keeping notes. Nick can use the Xerox and copy his."

Next day, I almost make it out the door before Miss Standish snags me. "Miss Appleton, come in and close the door."

I stare at the shit-brown tiles. "I'll be late for English."

"Mr. West will cut you some slack."

"Really, *really* don't want any slack right now."

"Fair enough. I just want you to know I'm here if you need help with anything."

I raise my eyes but not my messy cheek. "Could I use your address for someone to send me letters?"

"It wouldn't be appropriate for me to be passing letters to a student."

"Then I guess you can't help me."

"Who?"

I paw at the door to get it open. "Why do you care?"

"Because it must be pretty important for you to have asked."

"My aunts. They took me in when . . . after . . . forget it."

"Ari, how did your hands get burned?"

"I . . . just wanted my letters from them."

"Your aunts are a help to you?"

I nod and bite my cheek, hard.

"Go to the post office and set up a box."

"A kid can?"

Miss Standish walks over and opens the door. "If you have a social insurance number and can afford a couple of dollars a month."

It feels like the kind of plan that might get Mr. West thinking about asking me to the theatre. After all, mature women have their own post office boxes. I decide twenty bucks should cover all contingencies and leave enough to treat Nick to fries. I pass the teller my bank book and withdrawal slip. The machine schleep-schleep-schleep-schleeps. Maybe Nick beats me in math but I have enough number-smarts to know that four thousand seven hundred and eighty dollars minus twenty doesn't equal insufficient funds. "I'm sorry, this is a mistake. I haven't made any withdrawals since last summer and I made a three hundred dollar deposit just after Christmas."

"The balance is nine dollars and seventeen cents."

"Unless I missed another stock market crash, this is wrong."

"The money has been withdrawn, Miss Appleton."

"Nick, can you go get Len?"

College, Expo 67, a trip to Paris to look for June passes before my eyes as the manager produces a stack of cheques. Another teller says, "This isn't Hariet Appleton. She has blonde hair." I study the practiced signature. The one I made look so Picassoesque.

"Can I see some identification?" I produce all that a thirteen-year-old has: my library card. "Have you been in a fight? Is this your signature? Are you Hariet Appleton?"

The floor turns rubbery. How will Jillianne survive prison? When not acting the Tasmanian devil she's a wide-eyed doe in the morning mist. I sit hard on the bench contemplating my five years of work up in smoke. *I hope it was good shit, Jillianne.*

Len arrives out of breath. "Some trouble, Ari?"

"Big—Hiroshima big."

Officer Irwin does Mum a favour. Two cops nab Jillianne on the street, cuff her, and deliver her home, scared shitless. I sit, picking at the flaky scab on the heel of my hand. Underneath, it's the colour of bubblegum and I can't remember ever getting that colour on a T-shirt. Len sighs, lead-heavy. "Theresa, she needs to be charged, held accountable for this."

"You make her sound like a murderer."

"This was not five dollars from your purse, ten from my wallet. It was fraud and a theft of thousands, stealing that showed no conscience for her sister."

"Hariet was careless leaving her chequebook where Jillianne could find it." My hand stings from a big hunk peeled from my baby finger. "She's just acting out. Don't think she doesn't see how you favour Hariet."

"She would get guidance. Learn discipline and rules. She'll be dealt with as a minor, receive extra help."

"That's what her family is for. Hariet, Jillianne is sorry. She'll work and pay the money back. It's settled."

Jillianne never says sorry, never really looks at me. She's sweet, the kind of sweet that comes from summer smoke rising from the pickle room. She's subdued, the kind of subdued that comes from emptying the whiskey bottles. She's quiet, the kind of irritable quiet that comes from a TV overdose. And she's restless. The kind of restless that comes from missing a boy who hurts you hard and bad.

Tony, the good-for-nothing-boy is not so willing to pass weed through the cellar window without something for him. Mum stashes her pills and booze in the cartons of Christmas decorations. Len's wallet holds only a note: *Jillianne, I love you. Please let me help you.* Grandma and her borders are no longer plums for picking and Ari Appleton has nada. Jillianne hits bottom, and the cesspit where everything that has been carefully buried oozes up.

Miss Standish doesn't look up. "Did you want something, Ari?"

"Um . . . you said if I needed help . . ."

She puts down her pencil but gives me the mercy of looking at her papers.

"I . . . I have a friend who has some troubles . . . drugs and stealing mostly . . . she . . . this stuff happened . . . and . . ."

"How old is she?"

"Sixteen."

"Your sister?"

I nod, pushing down the Niagara behind my eyes.

"There's a treatment centre for women, Springwood, just north of Toronto. If I arranged something could you get her there?"

"I'll stuff her in a Hefty bag and tow her if I have to."

Jacquie looks like she swallowed a watermelon whole but still she waddles up the stairs and into the tiger's cage. Len and Franc wait in the hall ready to net Jillianne if she runs. I sit on the stairs, to keep my options open. Jacquie sounds Nia-wise. "Jillianne, no matter what you do, no matter how hard you try to blast it out, it's still there. Daddy betrayed you, stole from you. I don't want to lose you. I want this baby to know his Auntie Jillianne."

The squeaky kind of cry that you don't want to let out but just has a mind of its own, leaks out of the room. From my perch on the stairs I study Len. The wall holds his weight, tears puddle in his eyes, and I can't remember what my dead father looked like in the light.

"Franc and I checked out a beautiful place with really good people to talk to. We're taking you there."

Mum comes out of her bedroom, huffing like a train speeding up. "What are you doing?"

"Getting Jillianne some help."

"Do you know what those places are? Making you rip open your guts while everyone stands in judgment."

"So let them. They'll judge Jillianne as heroic for surviving."

"I'm so sick of all of you feeling sorry for yourselves. You girls had more than most, and your father . . ." The hesitation is all Jillianne needs to topple Jacquie onto a mountain of clothes, bolt past Len, over me, and scramble out the door. By the time we right Jacquie and reach the sidewalk, there isn't a hint of which way she went. We head all points on the compass, searching for days until Jacquie goes into labour. Len and I keep looking, but Jillianne doesn't want to be found.

TWENTY-TWO

The street outside the window greens. A robin pair builds a nest in the housing of the burned-out porch light. Mum sits squashed on the sofa, struggling for half an hour to put four beads on a string, the shake in her hand about a five on the Richter. Her voice falls like a spider on a single thread, "I'm going out to look for her."

I know exactly where she's going as she draws her lipstick way off course. First, she'll check out the Zanzibar. There she'll find Officer Richard Irwin having a drink after work. Then she'll search his pants.

"You need to stay here," I say, "in case she comes home. I'll go look in the Village."

"I have to get some air."

"Then go over and see the baby."

"I will." She focuses on the vase of flowers behind me. "I should have made her go with Jacquie."

Every trip to Yorkville, I see more people losing and finding themselves. People know me here. I'm the Riverboat waitress who will sell you the shirt off her back. It's not a slutty thing like Jory, just a marketing strategy. Weekend hippies have parental cash in their pockets and I always have a tank top under the merchandise.

I navigate between tables and ripe bodies. "Hey, Bernie. Have you seen Jillianne around?"

He hands two mugs over the counter, nodding me to the table in the corner. "Lose another sister?"

"Yeah."

"Haven't seen Jillianne. But Malik is back. He ran into June somewhere out west."

"Really?" I button my coat. "Thanks. See you Friday."

"Bring more goods."

"Count on it. I've had a major financial setback."

Two doors down and two flights up I find Malik in his usual crash pad. He resembles a half-dead sheepdog. "Hey, kid." He opens his arms from his mattress on the floor.

I like dogs so I fall in. "Bernie said you saw June."

His yawn sends hair-curdling breath across my cheek. "Yeah. In a commune in Coombs. Hardly recognized her. She's a blonde."

"Is she okay?"

"If you call eating granola and living with some organic tree-hugger okay. She has a kid."

"She does? What?"

"Girl, I'd guess with a name like Spring."

"Did she ask about me? Did she send a letter?"

"Don't remember much. They grow grade-A shit." He lights up, inhaling deep, exhaling memories of June. "Her hair looked like melted butter." He holds the joint to my lips and I take the edge off Ari Appleton.

The baby snorts like a pig at Jacquie's breast. I snivel at the end of her bed.

"It sounds like she's found a good place, Ari."

"Why doesn't she write, send me a postcard, a call . . ."

"Haven't you ever wanted to walk away into something brand new? Leave everything Appleton behind, like it never happened? Daddy wrecked June bad. He coaxed her to the river that day. 'Please, Junebug. Don't you betray me, too.'"

"Daddy thought you betrayed him?"

"I told Dr. Herbert it was him even though I promised I wouldn't. I had to. I saw the way he looked at Jillianne, and . . . at you."

"Junie thought Daddy didn't love her."

"He didn't love any of us. He stayed away from June because

she pushed back. But that day she told me that he begged her to go with you to the river."

"Why?"

"Because his game was over, he was caught, and he wanted to gut someone. Why not her and Jennah and you. She said he smiled right at her, pulled out the gun and *bam*! Her T-shirt, her hair . . . all spattered red."

"Jennah said her . . . Icee exploded."

"He . . . rained blood on beautiful June on purpose."

"I'm unplanting his tree."

"Don't. Plant five more for the six sisters that grew up strong." There's light around Jacquie, lightness, too. She isn't pretty anymore. She's beautiful, like a dolphin leap. "Dry your tears. He doesn't deserve them."

"They're for June."

"You know why we called the baby Arielle? She's the Angel of new beginnings, and somehow you manage to do that no matter what."

"You've done that more than any of us." I crawl up to her side to finger Arielle's velvety head. "I hope she has June's hair, not mine. Did Mum come over to visit?"

"No. But Nick called looking for you."

"Yeah, it's prayer meeting night." The only night his parental units aren't hovering.

I walk to Nick's after closing. I'd skip it, but I really need the hug. We're only moderately bad. He has the fear of God in him and I don't want anyone in my pants. He's an okay kisser and he touches my boobs like they're eggs he's scared will break. The first time I slid my hand under his jeans he came faster than the watered-down catsup at the diner. Now, he moans low and sweet for five, maybe ten minutes.

Tonight is one of those holding and hugging nights, it takes him longer to de-stress, six forty-five to seven ten. He flushes the toilet paper. I do up my bra. The rec room is cold so he gives me a sweater and pulls a fat fisherman knit over his head. While he makes hot chocolate, I find *My Favorite Martian* on TV and get out our math books. And that's how his parents find us, summing not cumming. It's an hour and a half before their usual return time. "Uh . . . Mom? Dad? What are you doing home?"

"Your mother had a headache. Nick, what are the rules about having friends over when we're not home?"

"Sorry, Mr. Potter. With all the grandma trouble I got behind in math."

"How is she?"

I pack up my books. "Last time I saw her she called me Ethel and whapped me for stealing her purse."

"No need to go now. I'll make some popcorn."

"No, thank you. I've got a ton to do. Don't be mad at Nick. He was just too nice to say no when I asked for help."

"I'll give you a lift."

"Our springtime poem is due. Walking helps me write it in my head."

TWENTY-THREE

The words, "Ari, wait," strain my thin nerves. "Where's your spring poem?"

"I'm still working on it."

Mr. West extends his palm. "It's due today." More and more he has this way of crawling in through my eyes. Most days I feel older than him. Today, things teeter a little more equal.

"Words that make you or anyone else uncomfortable shouldn't be rewritten for pleasantness."

"You haven't even read it."

"Knowing you, in one way or another it'll be messy." He takes it from my hand, adding it to the pile. "Can I ask what the trouble is with Sharon?"

"Nick is going around with me. So that makes me the enemy. I've been called worse."

"Can't imagine what."

"Try Hariet, a misspelled Hariet."

"Unique and gifted people always get picked on. Take it as a compliment."

"Yeah, I'm all aflutter."

I admit, I didn't like seeing *Ari is a Slut* painted on the front door of the school. Though, because of it I may have found my first girlfriend since coming to Toronto, Rhonda Pace: the don't-mess-with-me Westside Story kind of girl, with a boyfriend who owns a car, a father with money, and a dead mother. A year older than everyone else because she travelled in the Far East. An exceptional story if nothing else.

When the principal walked into class this morning, steel-face pissed, asking, "Does anyone know anything about the slander defacing our school?" Rhonda spoke up.

It may have been kindness, bravery, or the fact that she needed a smoke and we'd been told we'd all have to sit through recess. "Sharon Wilson did it." All heads swiveled to Rhonda. Sharon protested innocence with Scarlett O'Hara flare but Rhonda yanked down the velvet drapes. "Don't believe me. Ask Mrs. King at the variety. She saw, too." With that, Sharon dissolved into a confessing heap and the wheels of grade eight justice were set in motion.

Now, on my walk to work, in one side of my head I'm designing a fringed bag with a silver cobra and green bead eyes as a thank you. In the other brain-half, I imagine Mr. West sitting in a leather chair in his apartment by the lake reading my poem and I want to disappear.

Black June Yellow June

Before Spring
He
forced summer,
saturating early June
dark August green.

Then, *dis*graceful fall
turned June
October red.

She bled,
leaves dropping
like monthly courses.

Acid winter
snowed deep on
the last day of June.

After Winter,
it looked like death,
those long black branches
of a winter wood.

But roots dug deep into black earth,
where she found the sun, weeping yellow leaf,
giving birth to
Spring.

TWENTY-FOUR

The shore ice cracks, shifting into open-mouthed leviathans. Len lifts his eyes from the grey lake to the thread-thin sun. "Quite the week."

Nia provides a top-up of coffee. "Aye."

I link my arm through Len's. "I sure get all the lucky breaks."

Mary snugs a little closer against the March cold. "Lucky?"

"You're here and Nick left for Myrtle Beach before he could see the ambulance haul Mum off."

Mum downed all her pills with a whiskey chaser. It seemed a reasonable option after the police called to say that Jillianne had been arrested for break, enter, and assault.

Nia checks the time. "Len, we should go."

I watch their lean frames begin to wade away through the slush. "I don't want Jillianne to go to prison."

"This is serious. She's going to be prosecuted." Mary sighs, "Maybe this is what she needs to turn her life around. Sam Lukeman is the best. He'll help."

Where did Jillianne go? Sweet, silent, pleasing Jillianne, broke into a house with her horrible boyfriend Tony. It isn't so much that she stole, but she also kicked an old lady and put her in the hospital.

"I want to come home with you."

"Your mother is in no state to reason."

"But that's how I got shipped out all the other times."

"Maybe if Len could get custody we could take you."

Jasper pipes up before I can shut him. *Len would come, too, right, Ari?*

"It's enough you're here right now. Can we go break Grandma out of Sunny Crest? You should hear her roommate,

Gladys, reliving her bingo days. I swear, twenty-four seven it's B-6, O-74, N-37, G-52. It's enough to drive *me* squirrelly."

Grandma has a four-day vacation from hell. Sometimes she knows us, sometimes she doesn't, but she has a smile on her face and her purse in her hand.

Lucky for Jillianne, Officer Irwin kept previous troubles off the books. Tony is going to the big house but Nia's friend Mr. Lukeman holds some hope for Jillianne. He sits at the table downing Babcia's baking. "She'll be tried as a juvenile. Given it's a first offence I'm confident we can negotiate treatment, probation, and restitution. But she's going to have to deliver a no-bullshit promise to straighten out."

Auntie Mary asks, "Can I talk to her?"

"I'll arrange it."

"Me, too?"

"You're too young, Ari. But Jacquie, I think it would really help if you saw her. And Mr. Zajac, she's convinced you hate her but if—"

"I'll be there. Whatever she needs."

Mr. Lukeman is keeping his expenses to bare bones but Len still forked over seven hundred dollars.

"Will you smuggle in a letter from me? In a cake or something?"

"How about we try it in a chocolate bar."

Miss Standish has a sunburn and passes out oranges to the class. "What did you do on March break, Ari?"

Sister arrested. Mum netted and hauled. Covert Aunt visit. Sprung a granny from hell. Changed diapers on a new bum and a very old bum. Made a hundred and fifty bucks tossing shirts at the Riverboat . . . "Nothing."

98

"Ari Appleton, you're never up to nothing."

"I learned a new batik technique."

A little blue box sits on my desk with a silver shell for my bracelet. *Missed you so much. Luv, N*

Sharon and the SS want to remove my eyeballs and bury me in an anthill but Rhonda scares them shitless. Her, "Hey, Appleton," this morning has me thinking she might be in the market for a friend, but she always splits before I can discuss my Sadie O'Shaughnessy shortage.

Babcia's perogies dance a polka in my belly as I approach Rhonda's door. The fact that inside, dogs bark like ravenous wolves reassures me somehow. I like dog people. She answers the door, holding back two boxers, shaking their back ends like Elvis.

"Can they have a cookie?"

"What? You're a Girl Guide?"

"No, I came to give you this." I hand her a paper-wrapped present. "I just happen to have Milk Bones in my pocket."

"Knew I liked you, Appleton." She squeezes the package. "What's this for?"

"For getting Sharon out of my teeth. She's like a wad of tinfoil."

"Ditch the coat and the llamas."

I survey my boots. "I believe they're caribou."

She rips off the paper. "Whoa, groovy bag." She introduces a boy, midbite into a hamburger, as her boyfriend, Tyler.

He talks with his mouth full. "Shirt's cool, too."

I have on a Picasso batik, which I remove and toss in his direction.

"I can keep it?"

"Good advertisement. Tell people you got it at Aquarius on the Danforth."

"What if I said I wanted your tank?" I turn to see a McCartney-cute, brooding artist standing in the kitchen arch. He has a book in the cross of his arms, *The Adventures of Augie March*, dog-eared like he might actually be reading it.

"Then you'd have to come to the store and I'll give you one."

"Ari, my brother Chase. Chase, Ari."

"Chase Pace?"

"Really, it's Cecil, but if you tell anyone I'll have to cut out your tongue."

I go right for his ear, whispering, "Mine's really Hariet, and that's a spectacular book."

"Where's your store?"

TWENTY-FIVE

The Appletons are still fathoms from revampment. Jillianne is incarcerated. Jory has some guy colouring her in with permanent inks. Since the birth of Arielle, Jacquie is having mind-twisting headaches. June is still running, and Jennah moves slow as she walks up the stairs.

"Are you okay?"

"Silly me, I fell off the deck. So what do you need for your date?"

"Well, it's Easter Sunday so I'm thinking an extra-holy look."

"A white dress will do it and I have this precious mauve cashmere sweater."

The Potters add sections to the dining room table to accommodate the multitudes. Nick's brother, Dennis, home from Queens follows my plate setting with cutlery. "So you're Nicky's chickie. You sure don't look like any fourteen-year-old I've ever met." His finger creeps down my side like a spider.

I contort away. "Well *you're* acting like all the ones I've met."

"Easy. Nicky said you liked a good time."

"He also said you had brains, so I guess he lied on both counts."

Mercifully, I'm seated between the uncle whose dentures slip when he talks and the aunt more interested in eating than digging into my life. Two hunks of ham land on my plate. It's the colour of ham that makes me gag. I camouflage it with potato while answering questions about faith in Jesus, life goals, and my opinion on Pierre Elliott Trudeau. Nick asks, "You feeling okay?"

I shake no.

Mrs. Potter sees Nick stab the meat off my plate. "You don't like the ham, Ari?"

"Everything is so spectacular. I kind of filled myself up. How do you make these biscuits so fluffy? I'll have to get the recipe."

"Hope you have room for apple pie."

Dennis licks his fork. "Speaking of apples, you wouldn't be related to Jory and Jillianne Appleton, now would you?"

"Yes, they're Ari's sisters. Do you know them, Denny?"

"Yeah, I *know* them. Heard Jillianne's gone into law."

"Pharmacy, isn't it, Ari?" Mrs. Potter starts stacking dishes.

"She changed majors, ma'am. Are you finished with your plate, Uncle John? Aunt Nora? Grandma Potter?"

You'd think with all the people around I could steer clear of Dennis the Menace. He blocks me in the hall then bulldozes me into the bathroom. "So Nicky picked an Appleton tart."

Trapping an Appleton in a locked room with ham in her stomach can never come to any good. "Let me out."

"Be good and I won't say a word. I just want a little of what you give Nicky."

"Get the fuck out of my way."

"Ooh yeah, a dirty mouth, too."

Usually I hate the ease with which my belly expels occupants, but I don't mind the ham hurling onto the big swine.

"You bitch."

I scramble out, exit the house, and hurry down the street.

Nick nabs me halfway around the block. "Ari, what's the matter?"

"Me . . . my family. We're freaks and losers."

"I love you. I don't care what anyone says." As much as puddles can be directed, he directs me, not to the blue house, but to Zodiac and Jacquie.

She sits me near Iggy and plunks a basket of Arielle's nappies between us. "Get folding. I'll make tea."

"Once Dennis tells the Potters who I am Nick won't even be allowed to talk to me."

Jacquie says, "None of them have a fucking clue who you are. How could they? You're from the ocean deep, they know nothing but floating around in a pretty little swimming pool."

"I don't want to be an Appleton."

Iggy folds a nappy with military precision. "You have emerged from Hariet into Ari. There is much more to come, *corka*. The clay of you is the most beautiful I have seen."

"To the Potters, I'm just dirt."

And so my first great love ends. Likely, he wants to be Romeo, but the parental hammer squashing the grad trip and basketball camp is just too weighty. He leaves a quote on my desk. I wonder how long it took him to find the pathetic thing. *Let us no more contend, nor blame each other, blam'd enough elsewhere, but strive in offices of love, how we may lighten each other's burden, in our share of woe.* —Milton

    My heart is breaking that I cannot see you anymore. Nick

Miss Standish asks, "Is that today's quote?"

"Yeah."

"Well let's hear it."

Nick stifles a moan as his head sinks to his hands.

My brain wades past the casualties floating near shore to my boatload of treasures. I pull one out; "Twenty years from now you'll be more disappointed by the things you didn't do. So throw off the bowlines. Sail away from the safe harbour. Catch the trade winds in your sails. Explore. Dream. Discover. Mark Twain."

TWENTY-SIX

May arrives, kicking winter to distant memory on its way in. I turn fourteen. Aunties M&N send a rock tumbler, addressed to Joy White and signed by Wabi-sabi. Sadie and the Butters tuck in notes to save on postage, but Jake spends the nickel and sends his own. Miss-yous weave through scribblings about jigging 'n rigging, and this one ends with fourteen xo's shaped into a seahorse.

    Jory comes for dinner because she knows there will be cake. She weighs maybe ninety pounds, has a tattoo of a dove from shoulder to hand, and is a bona fide Jesus freak. I help her make a passel of shirts that say things like *Jesus is my drug, Rock 'n' Roll of Ages, Let the Son Shine In*. Her church replaced the holy wine with divine pot and they have communion a *lot*. She believes in *free* love now, but says it never hurts to pass the collection plate.

Nick shows up; walks right into the workroom. "I wanted to give you this." The familiar little blue box slides across the press. "I didn't get the chance on Easter and I know it's your birthday."

"Give it to Sharon."

"I don't give a fig about her. She just keeps my parents quiet." He picks a tiny cross off the white cotton. "It's for your bracelet. Like a secret vow between us. We could meet in the shed in your backyard."

Jasper pokes, *Maybe Hariet would, but no Lioneagle cowers behind fertilizer.*

"Do I look like a garden shovel?" I fold an eagle batik. "Beat it before anyone sees you slumming with me."

"Ari. I love you—"

"Yeah, yeah, yeah . . . help yourself to some socks for Sharon's bra on the way out."

Jasper and I always perk up after a long soak in the old claw-foot tub. I dress in my gift from Babcia, an embroidered peasant blouse that folds like a waterfall.

Len floats up behind, smiling at my mirror reflection and fastens on a necklace. "Happy birthday, *corka*. It's the closest I could find to a lioneagle."

A fine silver chain holds a gryphon. "Thank you, Papa."

Sometimes, I believe in *maybe*. Dreamy thoughts, like maybe things will work out between Mum and Len. She's come to the store, and in the evening window light she watches as Jacquie arranges the dozen love beads she just brought in. She's sober and picture-pretty in a navy dress that Len bought on a trip to the States. The clatter of the bell has her moving in an easy step to the side without any wobbles as Chase walks in.

"So, you finally came for your shirt. Take one, get dinner free."

Babcia calls for store closing.

"We're having *piecʒen siekena-klops*."

"Say what?"

"Meat loaf. And it's my birthday so there will be quadruple-decker cake."

Chase has been apprised of the whole bushel of Appletons and thinks my life poetic, song material even. The Paces are their own can of mixed nuts and welcome a little fruit in the mix.

A fresh audience makes Uncle Iggy dance in legless grace. Jory breaks bread with us sporting DIG GOD across her braless boobies. Babcia scolds Len for feeding Zodiac at the table then throws him more scraps. Mum stays and is full of nods, not shakes as Chase talks politics and anarchy and save the planet. Arielle sucks on my shoulder as I look at Len and the smile between us is maybe the best thing I've ever known.

TWENTY-SEVEN

"Ari, wait." Mr. West has on a black leather tie and he looks so good he ties my stomach in two half hitches. "I need your consent for the grad trip."

"I've seen Montreal more than I care to, sir."

"You'll be our tour guide. I'll see you're roomed with Rhonda."

"Len can't spare me from the store."

"It'll be a disappointing grad trip without you. Let me talk to him."

"No, I'll see what I can arrange."

I fork over seventy bucks when I'd rather have a root canal with a pocket knife. Two days before the trip Rhonda busts her knee surfing the hood of Tyler's car. I climb on the bus and see a seat with a sign pinned on it, *Reserved for Harriet Scariet*. I stare at Nick. Out of all the brilliant quotes within my grasp I spit out, "*Et tu, Brute?* And there's only one r."

"What?"

"You spelled it wrong" I plunk beside Margaret Mink, the only person lower than me at Oakridge. And so begins a three-day descent into hell. The soulless rhymes are blackfly annoying: *Hariet scariet big fat fairiet. Harry scary no one will marry.* As the miles pass, the song inside my head, *Hariet, get your chariot we're going for a ride*, becomes eardrum-piercing and I wish Sharon could out-chant the ghost of my father. Miss Standish cranks around. "Sharon Wilson, do I have to remind you that you are on probation?"

"Least I got probation, not hard time."

I hope whatever Nick got for exposing my nuclear waste was worth it.

I anticipated a *Lord of the Flies* trip and so I borrowed Chase's *Lord of the Rings*. There's nothing I can't do while reading: walk, piss, eat. At the comfort stop, Nick offers a chocolate bar. "I'm really sorry. Sharon promised she wouldn't say anything. Ari? Please don't hate me."

I turn the page and re-board the bus.

At the hotel I'm informed that my bunkmates are Margaret, Bernice, and Trixie, the three wusskateers. Randy Crawford whispers in my ear, "What say you and me have a little fun." I catch sight of the joint in his hand. Taking the edge off would be bloody spectacular, but Randy would never betray Sharon, so I know plans are in the works to mess with me. I'm safer cuddling up with Trixie Lizaro, aka Lizard Girl.

One minute into the room and Margaret whispers, "Don't

tell it was me who told, but I saw Randy put something in your pocket and I heard Sharon tell Wendy that they're going to get you expelled."

I conduct a top-level security check of my person and backpack right down to my sanitary pads. Margaret looks on in awed wonder. "You have monthlies?"

"Two years now."

"Wow."

I locate a joint in my pocket and a small baggie in my pack. I flush them, then pull a Sherlock on every crack and crevice. "Margaret, you are the queen of cool. I'm forever in your debt." She fingers my bag of handwork as I reload my stuff. "Want to make some love beads?"

I don't mind sitting on the bed, eating everyone's food stash, and making crafts. Kind of like the loser cabin at camp that actually likes making macaroni jewelry boxes. I'm expecting the thump on the door, but the bunkmates have forgotten and their beads go flying.

Mr. West, Mr. Thorpe, and Miss Standish stand in a row. Mr. Thorpe knows I'm trash and is salivating to prove it. "Miss Appleton, we've received a report that you have drugs in your possession." I step aside so the hall gawkers can have a better look.

Miss Standish says, "Ari, step into the bathroom. We need to check your pockets."

I give over my sweater, then my jeans.

"Ari! Into the bathroom, please."

I remove and toss my T-shirt.

"Ari, stop this."

Ever since I was eight I pick only the nicest underwear. This pair has orange stripes and fits my butt perfectly. "You want me to bend over?"

Mr. West turns to the window. Mr. Thorpe sounds like he has raw liver caught in his throat. Miss Standish nervous-shakes no.

"I did discover some dope planted on me. I flushed it. Maybe you should ask the person who squealed how exactly it got there." Mrs. Standish puts my sweater over my shoulder. Mr. Thorpe breaks up the freak show in the hall. I pull on my jeans. "I'm going to my aunt's."

Miss Standish says, "Ari, you can't. You're under our supervision."

"Do you know how long I have to work to earn seventy bucks? I don't need this shit." My roommates, Tweedledee, Do, and Don't, quake at swearing in front of a teacher.

Mr. West makes for the door. "Bus tour. Downstairs. Fifteen minutes. That includes you, Ari."

Miss Standish can be a yeller but I've never heard a raised word from Mr. West. Sharon and Randy sit on the bus while the rivets vibrate and the rest of us wait outside. Then Mr. West exits, fake-chipper. "Okay, load 'em up. Mount Royal, here we come." He forces a smile at me. "Enjoy yourself, Ari. No one's going to bother you."

Oh, Mr. West, how little you know about a woman humiliated.

Silence blares as we trudge around the city but I admit, at supper, we four losers have a spectacular time. No one at the other tables know why the waiter is flirting with me but it's because he's Ian MacLaren, one of the MacLaren boys. His brother, Toby, manages the place and we get the biggest complimentary sundaes God ever sanctified. And the cherry? Ian, a rugged first-year McGill student, gives me a hug as we leave. "Bye, Ari. You have my number. Come along, too, Maggie and I'll hook you up."

Mr. West waits for a hidden moment. "Fun's fun, Ari, now hand over that number."

"Relax, sir. I grew up with them. He was just helping me mess with the SS." I scrunch it up and toss it.

The room-to-room phone calls start at ten with whispery warnings, "Someone is going to die . . . oooh . . . beware."

"Yeah, you are, you bleedin' weenies."

The call sends Bernice digging for her breathing medication and Trixie for her psoriasis cream. I slide the ringer down then stuff it in a drawer, squashed under pillows.

Trixie squeaks, "What if someone calls and they think we've snuck out?"

"Then you'll instantly be cool without having to do anything bad." She sleeps, dreaming of the possibilities. Her liniment smells like Mrs. Butters and that's enough to take the edge off.

No tour of Montreal would be complete without Notre Dame. Whenever Mum was working on revampment, she'd bring us for a dose of our Catholic roots. The music still echoes in my brain, *Thou canst save amid despair. Safe we sleep beneath thy care.* Mum would breathe in the notes and lighten a little. Those remembrances soak in, leaving me waterlogged and foot-heavy. Not the best way to meet the river. Most good memories of my dad are here: watching boats, taking turns making up stories about what they carried and where they were going. "It's loaded with jewels for the Princess of Siberia."

"No, pet, all the jewels in the world are right here with me."

We'd walk Jinx, eat greasy fries, fish off the pier, never catching a darn thing except once when Daddy snagged a pair of glasses. "Oh, dear, I've taken a dolphin's spectacles." He tossed them back. "Sorry, mate, didn't do it on porpoise."

Mr. West fetches me lagging at the rear. "Move it, Ari. Picnic ahead."

"I'm not hungry."

"Come on, don't sulk."

I know better than to leave myself wide open, still I do. "My father died here."

"Another one of your stories?"

The *fuck* stays tucked under my breath but he feels it as I smolder away, walking right into the trap. Randy corrals Nick as he yells, "Ari, go back." His, "Don't . . ." gets swallowed by a scuffle. To my right, on the water's edge two sticks, tied together form a cross. A fake ear and a plastic gun lay puddled in catsup. A cardboard tombstone reads:

Mr. Appleguts
RIP
Ripped In Pieces

The scattered petals of some fading bloom, like bits of ham staining the rock, knife me more than the rest.

The small Hariet in me stares. The lioneagle backs away without a single sound, without a single feeling. Not even breakfast has permission to move out of my gut. Teachers yell, commanding me to come back, but only a one *r* Hariet would give any of them another thing.

I know hours have passed by the light moving in the stained glass when Mr. West moves in on one side of the pew and Miss Standish on the other. I hug my knees tighter to my chest. Mr. West touches my shoe. "Ari, what went on back there?" Silence. "Was that about your father?" Peaceful, quiet. Only the occasional soft cough of a pew receiving or releasing weight. "Ari, please, it will help to talk."

Air snorts through my nose. Jasper pinches. *Shhh, don't give away that we hear, we feel.*

Miss Standish says, "I know Nick betrayed your trust. I promise whatever you tell us will not be repeated, to anyone. Aaron?"

Mr. West says, "I promise."

I warm somewhere in my core. His name, Aaron, is a little like mine.

Miss Standish removes some of her teacher clothes. "You

know why I'm so drawn to you? I used to wish my father would kill himself. He drank up every bit my mother worked for. All any of us ever got was a whack. My sister and I looked like the cat spit us out. The name that stuck with me was Smelly Belly." Her arm slips around my shoulder. "I understand what you've been through more than you know."

A small voice leaks out. "When I was eight, I could believe my dad drowned saving something or someone. Now, I close my eyes and see June's yellow hair and white face speckled with him. He stained her because she didn't love him right."

I let Miss Standish pull my head to her shoulder. "How so?"

"She fought back."

"And do you think you loved him right?"

My hand, it's always my hand I see, small in his, being pushed in his pants to feel worms and fish guts and naked moles, always peppered sweet with, *There's Daddy's little sweetheart.* Quiet words slip out of my mouth, "Jacquie had a baby."

I don't know I'm crying until Mr. West gives me his handkerchief. "I know."

"Not Arielle. Christopher. My nephew-brother."

"God . . . Jeeesus."

Miss Standish sighs, an anchored sigh. "Does Nick know that?"

Lucky break that so many secrets stayed down deep. "No, but he was there when the fire thing happened and he saw my mother freaking out. I suppose Mrs. Applenuts in a straightjacket is next."

Mr. West straightens switchblade-like. The anger in him feels Jesus-and-the-money-changers big and I'm scared.

"Aaron, stay with Ari. Let me go back and talk to them."

"Please, let me go to my aunt's. I know the way. She'll see me home."

"Aaron, can you take her and make sure it's okay?" Miss Standish leans into my ear. "I've taught for twenty-seven years and you are the one gem I'll remember most fondly. After I'm your teacher, I hope to be your friend." Her shoes echo like the aftershocks of "Ave Maria."

Mr. West folds into a rubbery bewilderment, his big hands swallowing his face. "Is your aunt's a good place?"

"Whenever we got farmed out, I used to hope I'd land with her. Until I got sent East. Pastor and Mrs. Lowry were the worst."

"Why?"

"They'd switch my legs every morning as a warning not to be naughty." My fingers uncurl, stiff with memory. "Then strap my hands at night just in case they missed something."

"My dad couldn't get through a spanking without turning it into a playfight. My mother thought withholding a cookie was harsh." My whole cheek fits in his hand as he catches a fat tear with his thumb. "Was your spring poem about your sister?"

"I'm told her hair is yellow again and she has a baby named Spring. Wish I could see black June's hair yellow again."

"I can't imagine never seeing my sisters again." We sit church-quiet and spirit-close. "I better take you to your aunt's."

"Can I have a minute for my face to unpuff?" He pats my foot while we listen a sweet while to the music of silence.

TWENTY-EIGHT

Escaping from Sunny Crest fills Grandma's dreams. When you're a wilted old lady hogtied to the bed, options are limited. Auntie Elsie stays on after bringing me back to Toronto and it's a comfort knowing she's with Grandma. It frees the body for the burdens at home. The heaviest being how Len has greyed under his eyes.

Jacquie folds and refolds Arielle's nappies. "Mum was gone the days you were away and she's bad jittery again."

"Oh, forgodsake, I swear I'm gonna slug her." I gather my books. "Tell Len I'll be to work by three thirty."

Nick is waiting by the ball diamond before school. "Ari, I really am so sorry."

"Just shut the fuck up. Stop talking to me, and about me."

"I never meant—"

"Well you did, and it stinks."

I walk into class and a size forty-two in a thirty-eight suit, with yellow teeth and a plaid bowtie demands we sit.

The intercom comes on; sounding like an SOS from a leaky submarine. "Mr. Fffruger, ffflease send Fffari Fffappleton to the fffoffice."

An apology from the SS, maybe? A refund for my troubles?

The principal, Miss Standish, and a man I don't know stand in the small office. Mr. West sits forward, examining his shoes. Mr. Barrett directs people to chairs. "Ari, there have been some very serious allegations about the grad trip."

"I swear, sir. I never had any drugs."

"We received reports that on Friday you ran off."

"Yes, sir."

"Why?"

"It was the first time being back where my father died . . . I just needed to sit in the church."

"We understand that you were not in your room on Friday night."

"I went to my aunt's."

"Did Mr. West go with you?"

"He walked me there."

"And?"

"He left. My aunt brought me home on the train yesterday."

"Did you go back out and meet Mr. West later?"

"What? Pardon, sir?"

"Did you meet Mr. West later?"

"No."

"Can your aunt verify that?"

"Yes, sir."

"Were you alone with Mr. West that day?"

"No, sir."

"What about when Miss Standish left you?"

"There were Holy Fathers and praying ladies."

"Did Mr. West at any time touch you?"

"Wha ... geeze ... no!"

The man I don't know says, "Perhaps Mr. West and Miss Standish could wait outside." The walls and ceiling close in. I stand.

"Sit, Miss Appleton."

"No ... I ..."

"This won't take long."

Miss Standish says, "Either I stay or you call her parents."

"We're just trying to get the facts here." Mr. Barrett taps his notepad. "West, please wait outside and close the door."

"There's nothing closed-door to tell. He was nothing but Amish with me. He patted my shoe and gave me his hankie when I started blubbering and that's all."

"Have you ever seen Mr. West outside of school?"

"No, sir, or ... yes, sir. He came to the store to ask my father if he could enter my essay in a contest—and once he patted my dog at the lake."

The man I don't know says, "I thought your father died."

"Len's my stepdad."

"Why would anyone make these kinds of allegations?"

"What allegations?"

"That Mr. West is perhaps over-involved in your affairs."

"Oh, for pity sake. Are there no teacher courses on girl-spitefulness? Sharon hates me and Mr. West blasted her for torturing me."

"There's nothing more?"

"Nothing, Mr. Barrett. I swear."

At this point Miss Standish pipes up. "This is absurd. As I said, Mr. West was about to go back and speak to them over a cruel joke about Ari's father. I thought it better he cool down. I made the decision to have Mr. West deliver Ari to her aunt. There's been no impropriety whatsoever. The hours Mr. Thorpe says Mr. West was absent from his room, he was back in the church, talking to me." Miss Standish guides me to the door. "If you want to interrogate Ari any further, I insist her stepfather be present, but it's that brat you need to confront."

Jasper mutters, *These are our educators? Heads of cabbage have more brains.*

I stop where Mr. West is perched outside the office. "I'm really sorry, sir. Appletons are more trouble than they're worth."

His inner animal leaps with some splashy defiance, likely the first of his life. "Then you're big trouble Ari Appleton because you're worth more than the moon, sun, and stars."

The recess bell rings and I escape. At lunch a police cruiser sits smugly out front of the blue house. I contemplate the gun in Officer Dick's holster slung over the chair and wonder what colour his balls would make spattered on the green wall. I press on to the store for some Arielle-elixir and lunch with Len.

"No school, *corka?*"

"Forgot my lunch."

"Come see what I have hot from London, for your graduation." He unboxes a work of fashion art.

"Holy perogies, it's the grooviest dress ever." He soaks up

115

my hug and I haven't the heart to tell him I'd rather be boiled in borscht than go to graduation.

After lunch, I sideways glance from *Pride and Prejudice* and see Mr. West back behind his desk. After class Miss Standish stands cross-armed at her door. "Miss Appleton, you are not to leave without signing out. Where did you go?"

"Home."

"There was no answer when I called."

Her Mum was in handcuffs.

Shut it, Jasper. "Store-home. Here, smell Arielle's spit on my shoulder." I study the geography of her face. "Is everything okay?"

"It's all sorted."

Three days later when the familiar flllzzz-tap-tap-tap erupts over the PA, my stomach flips. "This is Mr. Barrett, your principal." He always clarifies that fact. "Graduation is just over three weeks away and with that it's my great pleasure to announce Oakridge's top grade earner and class valedictorian . . ." Nick puffs in his seat. He should. Despite being a lily-livered-secrets-for-sex whore, he's served this school well. "Ari Appleton."

Oh, just cut me deep and throw me to the sharks. "Sir, I withdraw, abdicate, and herewith decline."

"You can't. It's school tradition." Mr. West looks at Sharon. "Words are powerful. They can destroy or build bridges. Start wars or end them. We will all benefit from your wisdom with words."

A pall of silence descends. Not even Rhonda can deflect the death stares landing like arrows on their mark.

The intercom rarely comes on after "O Canada." It annoys me right squirrelly when I'm summoned to the office. Perhaps I'm to be made Queen of Oakridge. My first role as her majesty will be to ban the SS from high school. Jacquie and Franc stand there, wobbly and pale as porridge, and I know Mum has washed down too many pills.

"Ari, Len's had a heart attack."

He's white and too silent but I know he knows I'm here by the way his hand curls when I hold it. I ask the doctor, "Is he going to die?"

He says, "The first twenty-four hours are critical." The nurse says that visiting hours are over. Jacquie says nothing when I slip between the lockers and the heavy door to wait for unseen moments when I can sit with him.

He won't leave us, Ari.

We won't leave him, Jasper.

In hospital, night sounds echo, coughs to clatters, whispers to cries, footsteps to fear. Len's breathing echoes hope.

Nurses coming and going mark the long hours, twenty-four, twenty-three, twenty-two . . . I move the chair and the night stand so I'm one quick step to the corner and to my hiding place behind the heavy window drape. One nurse hums whenever she comes in, the war tunes my dad always sang.

That's the Nightingale song, Ari.

The world upside down. Streets paved with stars. I remember, Jasper.

I hold my breath as the nurse tugs the drape to block the street light outside the window. "You rest, Mr. Zajac. Morning will come."

She's nice.

Mum didn't even bother coming. A tail of music follows the nurse out the door, fading into the pale hall light. *The aunties said Mum had a beautiful voice. You ever hear her sing, Jasper?*

Never a note.

I take up my seat beside Len, resting my hand on his heart. "You're my real papa."

There is a blanket over my shoulders and sunlight fanning across the bed when I lift my head. The humming nurse is checking Len's blood pressure. She elevates his head a little more, winks a smile, and leaves.

Len is as chalky as the pillow and the distance between us feels more than I can't bear. While I swab his lips I beg the god of endings not to take the man who makes me believe there's good in the universe. When I tuck the blanket under his chin I ask the God of our Mothers to have mercy on daughter of Len. His eyes flutter open and I whisper, "I love you, Papa."

Twenty-four hours pass and the doctor says, "He's holding his own."

The humming nurse returns for the night shift, leaving two packets of oatmeal cookies and a cup of steamy tea on the windowsill and a blanket on the chair after she checks on Len. Noises beyond the room make him twitch. "It's okay, Papa. I'm here."

Forty-eight hours pass. The doctor scans pages of test results. The way his head nods signals hope. He looks to Jacquie. "Will his wife be in later?"

"Depends. Are we talking life or death?"

"Life, I believe."

Jacquie's fingers comb through Len's stiff hair. "Then, I doubt it."

By day three he's sitting up, eating lime gelatin, and I obey when he says, "Go home and sleep, *corka*. That's what I need to feel better."

Mum is AWOL: Adulterating With Officer Letch, so I move over to the store. I hear Chase's voice and Jacquie saying, "She's sleeping."

"I'm awake."

Chase comes up the stairs and sits beside me on the couch. Something is stirring between the fruit and nuts, something sweet like Cadbury. "How's your dad?"

"The doctor says it was a mild attack and he'll be okay."

"That must piss off your mom."

"Insightful, Chase Pace. Jacquie caught her looking for Len's insurance papers. She didn't even come to the hospital."

"Bitch." Chase tames my confusion of hair. "Speaking of bitches, Rhonda says Nick's mom is going ballistic about you being top mark. She started a petition."

"Against me?"

"She thinks English and art marks should weight less because math and science are harder and more important."

"What they really mean is that garbage shouldn't represent the school. Pass me the phone." I dial the familiar number. "Hello, Mrs. Potter? This is Ari Appleton. My father's sick and I won't be at graduation. Nick is the one who should be valedictorian anyway. I'll have my sister call the school and let them know. Thanks. And I still would like your biscuit recipe. Bye."

"Had you pegged as a scrapper."

"If I've learned anything as a potter it's, some pieces you fight for and others you release to the scrap pile. I just don't care."

Graduation Thursday, Len is home and doing well. He asks, "Can I at least see you in the dress?" It has an indigo top that hugs my almost spectacular boobs, falling in scarf-sheer layers through every radioactive colour of the rainbow, stopping inches above my knees.

Jacquie says, "Let me try something with your hair." She makes it look like a party with little flowers spiraling through.

Then, lord a t'under, knock me over with a puffin, Aunties M&N sneak up the stairs. "You think we could at least see our girl graduate?"

I turn to Jacquie. "Where's Mum?"

"With that creep, Irwin. Trust me, your graduation is not on her radar." Jacquie takes sparkly slippers out of a shoebox. "She couldn't even tell you what grade you're in."

Good, right, Ari?

Yeah, bloody spectacular.

Three wheelchairs line the back of the auditorium: Uncle Iggy in one. Grandma, spit and polished in the other, and a third in case Len needs it. Nia and Mary stand, cameras poised. Jacquie and Jory, who mercifully cast off her *Rock it Lord* T-shirt for a peasant dress, sit together.

The hoots and cheers from the fruits and nuts are embarrassing, but I like them when I collect the art and the English awards.

Nick moves with practiced grace through his speech. He's a bit heavy on sappy quotes, but not bad at all.

Mr. West approaches the podium to close the ceremony. "Before we end tonight, it's my privilege to present one last award. Ari Appleton, come to the platform, please." My legs turn squidish. I can't remember what's in my stomach, but it's doing a mazurka. "This year I submitted a piece to the National Literary Competition. Ari's essay, *Filling Uncle Iggy's Shoes*, took first place in the junior essay division." He passes me an envelope and a book. "Ari wins a one hundred dollar cash prize and her work has been published in this anthology. I'm hoping Ari can find her way around some of her words for us tonight."

Mrs. Potter smirks at my locked-jaw. *Jasper, spit something out, please.* "Um . . . recently, Mr. West said, 'Words have the power to hurt and the power to heal.' I'm lucky because for every hurting word that has happened my way I've received libraries of treasured ones. This one is from my aunts: 'I'm not dirt. I am clay. And I can make something spectacular out of it.' And from my teacher: 'I'm more worth than I am trouble.' Tuck these words in your pockets, believe them in your hearts because they're true for every person here. Especially this gem from my Uncle Iggy: 'When life takes your legs, fly.'"

After chairs are stacked, backs patted, punch and cupcakes served, Mr. Barrett announces, "In Oakridge tradition, young men of the graduating class find your mothers, and fathers, find your daughters for the first dance."

If I never have another thing in my whole life I don't care. The music of Len's heart beneath my ear is more beautiful than "What a Wonderful World" playing on our slow turn around the floor. "Enough partying, Papa. Let's go home. I need you for a long time yet."

"Stay for the party. Chase said he would see you home."

Seems I spoke too soon about never wanting another thing. I want the twisting and shouting in the coolest dress, with the cutest boy this side of down-home Jake to never end.

I'm not invited to the after-party at Sharon's but Rhonda and I get taken to the Red Barn for burgers and shakes, then to the bowling lanes where I throw gutterball after gutterball in ugly rented shoes and the prettiest dress, and it's maybe the best time I've ever had.

TWENTY-NINE

A fragment from June's poems stays with me, *What say those lines written on white flesh? Appleton cry, Appleton cry*. All the sisters have stories on our arms, spidery threads where we tried to work out the mess inside. That grade seven summer when M&N discovered them on me they drove me to a mucky deposit of clay. We painted our naked bodies like earth spirits and danced like African queens. I asked, "Are you mad at me?"

Auntie Mary imprinted a soft red hand on my cheek, smiling the kind of smile that looked more a sadness. "The earth is stained with the blood of women."

Auntie Nia plopped a great blob of mud on my head. "There's great kindness in you, sweet girl. Don't forget kindness to the one we love best. Ease your pain, but gently."

After that I never felt much need to add more blood to the earth, just a greater longing to touch it.

Every week we visit Jillianne at the court-sanctioned treatment facility. Three weeks ago, Jacquie saw the closed books, Jillianne's empty face, and the fresh cuts on her arm. Jacquie charged straight into the muck and wouldn't let go until Jillianne spilled that some social worker named Tom was messing with her. By the end of the week Jacquie had wrung the world inside out with lawyers and reporters and investigators. Anyone important got earfuls and dire threats of holocaust proportions if they didn't get our sister out of that place.

They moved Jillianne to Springwood. Jacquie brings books. My gift is a batik phoenix to wear and Len's offering is employment doing handwork.

She fidgets with the beads. "Is . . . the lady that I . . . is she . . . ?"

Len takes her hand. "She has recovered."

"Could you ask if there's any way I could write and tell her how sorry I am?"

"I'll ask. Even if it can't be sent, it would be a good thing for you to write."

When we are about to leave she asks if Arielle could come for a visit, and the air feels fish-jumping magical.

Summer of sixty-seven, everyone in Toronto is looking for tie-dye and love beads. Upstairs, Babcia and Iggy turn out fringed bags and belts like horny rabbits. It's a lucky break when the occupational therapist at Springwood calls to ask if there are more opportunities like Jillianne's work for some of the other women. An especially lucky break for Len, because he's done like dinner.

Chase leashes Zodiac and I nab Len for a double dip at the Maple Leaf Dairy. We walk to the house to pick up the mail. Mum has cleared out her stuff and moved in with Dick Irwin and all the sisters are gone. "Len, don't you think it's about time you sold this bruise? June and Jory are likely never coming home. When Jillianne gets out, she can share my room at the store."

Chase asks, "What's with the blue?"

"When we met, Ari's mother said she would like it this colour, so I painted it for her."

"My dad's company could sandblast it in a day for cost. It'd sell better."

"Arrange it, please. We'll put it up for sale when we return from our trip."

"Just say you'll never get rid of me."

"You, Ari, will always be my *corka*."

Len's cousins, Sabina and Otto, take over running of the store. Aunt Dolores takes over Granny duty. Jennah promises to visit Jillianne. And we're off for the month of August. Our minibus is loaded like the Beverly Hillbillies, except instead of a rocking chair we have a wheelchair and instead of a banjo there are two guitars and a concertina.

Never in my fourteen years on this earth did I know a body could laugh so big. We sing and dance our way through Expo 67, filling passports and bellies. Then, day's end, from Babcia to baby, we're baptized in the hotel pool. Once Uncle Iggy plunges into the warm water there's big trouble getting him out, not because he doesn't have legs but because it's the closest thing to flying free he can remember. I sit, legs adangle watching Jacquie on the pool steps sparkling in waterworks from Arielle's excited hand-slaps. Franc kisses her cheek, whispering something in her ear and she leans love-happy into his chest. Len splashes up beside me. "Having fun, *corka*?"

"Best time ever."

"Your friends are good company. Would you prefer Chase go with you to Mary's? I know a young girl prefers the arm of a young man."

Len and I are planning to take the train east while the bus heads back to Toronto. I slip down into the water and link arms with him. "That's just what I'll have."

"Are you and Chase . . ." He pauses. As he hunts for the word, I steel myself against hearing the word *sex* come from Len's mouth. "Are you . . . courting?"

How to explain what's going on with this guy and how much I like it? "He's more of a soul man than a skin guy. He's looking for a woman to have an existential experience with."

"To what?"

"A meeting of the minds. It kinda works for us."

Len absorbs the passing August pictures as we ride the train through Quebec. "So beautiful. I've been in Canada over twenty years and this is the first I've really seen it."

"You ain't seen nothin' yet."

"Did you see your mother before we left?"

Does anyone ever see my mother or understand why she spit out a diamond to chew on a hunk of donkey shit? "She came by to see Arielle, shakier than a Parkinson's ward. Jacquie couldn't even let her hold the baby. She pocketed twenty bucks from me then turned around and asked Jacquie for more."

"You and Jacquie work hard for your money. Don't give her more to destroy herself with."

"The crap gene pool I come from scares the liver out of me."

"When I look at you, you are so unlike your mother that I can scarcely believe you are her child. And what I know of your father I despise. But I despise not a single hair of you, so you are far removed from any likeness to him as well." Len smiles down as he stands. "Babcia says you were created by the fairies and dropped as a surprise, a surprise for me." He extends his hand. "Lunch?"

On all my train trips I've never sat in the dining car with white china and linen and tea in little pots. A boy sits at the end of the car. These days, I always notice when there's a boy. He's a college type with a bit of travel bristle on his tanned face and he's studying me. My jeans fit tight and my birthday blouse from Babcia folds like a waterfall. My braid falls past my bum with party spirals coiling around my face and I know for certain if I wanted a kiss I could get one. But lunch on an August train with Len fills me better than a thousand cute boys.

Having Len at Skyfish brings all my constants together. We walk the shoreline, tasting, touching, smelling, and we return, always, to Skyfish. As Len turns clay on the wheel, Mary's head tilts, echoing the graceful arc of a pot. "You're a natural at this, Len."

"My heart beats without trying when the clay moves under my hands."

I look up to the clatter at the door and the step dance in my chest begins. Jake drops his delivery and reorders his hat-hair. "Ari Appleton, how is it you're prettier than last summer?" He catches my leap, swinging me full circle. "Coming to the bonfire tonight?"

"Better get permission from my old man."

He sets me down, wipes his hand on his pants, and extends it to Len. Len doesn't know what to do with the muck on his but Jake helps himself to a shake anyway.

Mary, Nia, Len, and I saunter through blonde August grass toward a great orange sun that is hurrying off for a swim in the ocean. It hits and in unison the women say, "Ssszzzttt, ahhhh." Len's guitar rests on my shoulder and already cells in my body are jumping with the music rising from the shore. An hour in and Len is blended like another Butter into the beach band.

A half-dozen boys buzz around Sadie. She's an auburn-haired, green-eyed mermaid and the kind of friend who lets you know you're worth a trillion boys. Those of the female persuasion have set their compass on Mr. Tupper. A girl has to be prepared for competition when it comes to a fine-bodied fiddler. He looks across the fire to me and it's hard saying what I see back, like defining what's reflected in a churned ocean. Gold peppers his sandy hair and questions so load his eyes I can barely tolerate settling in his gaze. His sweetness makes my teeth ache and the salt in him burns my tongue. Music pours out; still, I know desert silences stretch inside. And his face is shadow-light, full sun meeting dark night.

When Len and Huey settle into some starry lullabies, Jake puts his fiddle down and disappears behind a rock. Annie

Crawley follows and I feel a dying just east of my centre. But ocean wind carries his voice back to me. "Jesus, Ann, can't a man piss in peace?"

Jasper stretches for a look at what's taking so long. *He's at the shore washin' his hands. Here he comes. Here he comes.*

He abandons his fiddle, anchoring himself on the log just over my shoulder, close enough that his fiddle fingers can play a tune on my hair. I sense navigational questions: Move starboard? Turn the boat around? Hold course? Everyone yawns and heads toward home. Auntie Mary tosses a quilt our way. "Put out the fire, safe."

I can never tell with the aunties. Bonfire or lust fire? Likely both.

Jake asks, "You cold?"

"The ocean's creeping in. You?"

"Some."

I open the blanket over the log. "You taught me that two bodies wrapped in a blanket produce more than two-hundred watts of heat." He smiles; sits. I settle between his legs, pulling the blanket and his arms tight around. "My best adventures have always been with you."

His cheek settles on my headtop. "What's the best?"

"Maybe the puffins on Bird Island." My face lifts to his. "Or maybe this very minute."

I've never felt Jake scared of anything, but he swallows down some terror and looks at the fire. "You like Toronto, Ari?"

"When I'm sixteen I'm coming home."

"I know I'm coming on eighteen and you're just turned fourteen but when you're ready . . . if you ever wanted . . . I'd be waiting."

"You mean it?"

"Who else could I ever be waiting for?" He must be teasing but I feel an *I love you* in the way he holds me close.

I climb into bed between Mary and Nia, holding onto every sweet minute we have. Auntie Mary strokes my hair. "Ari, what if you could come here for high school?"

I snap up. "Really?"

"Elsie says you shouldn't be around that man your mum's with and Len's worried she'll decide you can't stay with him. We hate to uproot you again but if Len could get guardianship would you want to come here?"

"I want to come home so bad. Could Len come, too?"

"He could come and go as much as he pleased. We all just want you settled."

Wabi and Cork mine their way up the middle of the bed between us, and I sleep, dreaming of maybe.

Nia whispers through the early morning grey, "Go get Len."

I creep in, gentling his shoulder. "Come, Papa. Be tip-toe quiet." August's end has deer thinking about hungry winters and a half dozen of them come for a juicy McIntosh. Nia flashes a picture when a brown-eyed lovely lets Len touch her nose.

He smiles soft. "Who knew heaven was a train ride away."

The mouth-watering smell of cinnamon buns and coffee arrives before Auntie Mary does. The deer know her by heart and don't startle away. They like Len, too, even aside from the apples on his lap and the corn in his pockets. I hear a treasure before it disappears into the doe's ear, "After my *corka*, you are the most beautiful thing I've ever seen."

I love watching Jake fiddle on stage but this girl wants a dance. All I get is a cheek-peck when he leaves. Last night I asked Auntie Mary if I should love him so much and she said the two of us were like putting clay to the wheel and she thought something spectacular might come of it. She did tell me not to hurry the piece but the wind was in my ears by then.

Len has turned in and Mary, Nia, and I are finishing up our end of a summer's lay on Skyfish floor. "Nothing is ever as good as being here."

"Maybe we can get you back before school is too far in. Let's to bed now, there's a long journey ahead."

As Nia pulls the door closed Jake jumps out of Huey's truck. "Just came back for my fiddle."

Mary laughs. "First time that's ever happened. Pull the door tight behind you."

I wait, just to make sure the door is locked. A sad smile tugs on the corner of his mouth. "So, write, okay?"

A girl can't make things any plainer than a finger on a button, a wetting of the lips, and an eye wander in his hazel-wood. I tip-toe up to his lips. They're wind rough and his breath peppermint sweet and he softly takes the want from my lips as I help myself to hope on his.

On the train back, I tuck under Len's wing, our reflection caught against the whirring miles. "I often saw the giraffe in you but I had to get you to a place where you could spread your wings to see the other half."

"And what did you discover?"

"Who I inherited my eagle side from."

"Your Jake said he would help me if I opened a store."

"My Jake?"

"Imagine a Papa's joy, releasing his precious seahorse into an ocean of kindness."

THIRTY

Every oppressed eighth grader dares to dream, believes really, that high school will be a better place.

"You're trying way too hard." Jacquie pops off my headband. "Lose the skirt. Wear your jeans, a black tank, and moccasins." She tames my nervous hair. "Always have a book so you can look like you don't care if you're alone. Something mysterious."

I rummage through the pile Chase keeps feeding me, picking *The Stranger* by Camus.

"Perfect. Now, just drink breakfast. If you hurl you don't want Froot Loops floating in it."

In the back seat of Tyler's car on the way to school Chase gives me his ring. "How about you and me take this place on?" I slip it on my silver chain because in Toronto he's my safe harbour.

The hierarchy begins before entering the building: coolest arrive driving their own coup, next down, a friend with wheels finds you worthy enough to ride in their car, next is the bus, then walking by yourself, and near fatal is climbing out of a parental car and having mummy yell, "Sharon, sweetie, you forgot your lunch."

Sharon's looking a little bromidic, wouldn't you say?
Positively insipid, Jasper.

The *table* situation is the ultimate test. Minor niners are barely allowed entrance to the cafeteria and can only survey the possibilities that lie ahead if they survive. Harvard hopefuls, prefects, jocks, druggies . . . have reserved spots. Then there is the table everyone aspires to: the cool kids, rebels with a cause, say the right thing, wear the right thing. If they play an instrument it's sax or drums. Their sport is football, the really tough positions like linebacker. They're on student council to fight for world peace and organic French fries in the cafeteria.

In a spectacular table-turn I discover that Chase is the emerging king of the school, positioned in the cafeteria to move up the ladder to the supreme cool table.

Skipping the bottom rungs may not be fair but walking past my former tormenters hand in hand with Chase is a double chocolate sundae, with Ari on top.

Casualties line the hall, the small, the dorky, the bespectacled limp in tatters; and it's only second day. Margaret Mink collects her binder and its guts spill across the floor. I gather up flotsam while Chase mops up the jetsam. She mirrors a kitten plucked from the drink. "Chase, this is my friend Margaret. She saved my life last year."

"Hey, Mags. I'm running for VP. You want to be on my campaign team?"

She slides her glasses up her nose and nods.

"First meeting, Thursday at three ten. Student council room."

Margaret buoys, floating off to face the horrors of the girl's change room.

"For that, Chase Pace, I'm making you the coolest campaign T-shirts in the history of politics. I better go and make sure they don't hang her by her undershirt."

On the home front I feel a little like Margaret. Scared, wanting to avoid certain halls.

The un-blued house sells quick. Len whistles at the profit. "I can smell the ocean air, *corka*."

Mum has the balls to show up with Officer Dick holding out a hungry hand for half. Mum's always been a looker, which has gotten her a lot of mileage and maybe too much forgiveness. Tonight, she wobbles in on spiky silver sandals. Her exposed skin, and there's a lot of it, is tanned like a brown leather sofa. She's permed her hair big, either that or a bleached poodle has exploded from her follicles. Her black skirt is so mini I fear there's no room for underwears underneath and her boobies perk in an itsy-bitsy yellow tank top. I'd laugh if I didn't feel so belly-sick.

Dignity curtains Len's exposed heart-ends. "Theresa, if you're saying you want a divorce, I understand. We'll meet with our lawyers to discuss a fair settlement."

She folds her hot-pink lips. "The house is half mine. Just write me a cheque and we can be done with it." Len would hand over the dough in a minute if he didn't know Mum would be back in a week for more.

"No, Theresa. I'm sure Officer Irwin will agree it's better to settle things legally."

Irwin sucks in his gut and adjusts his pants.

Mum teeters in daily. Horrifying, mortifying really, to have a mother acting my age. Yesterday she had on a black bra under a pink fishnetty thing. Irwin keeps sending her over with demands for her share of the Zajac empire which has inflated to Rockefeller bigness in his eyes.

Len tosses me my backpack. "They just parked down the street. Go out the back."

"Is it okay if I just stay at Rhonda's?"

"Make sure you get your homework done."

Things are turning into a big mess. According to the law Len doesn't have to give Mum much of anything. The store is in Iggy's name, always has been. Len owned the house before they married and he'd paid for it lock, stock, and peril. Money from its sale is in Iggy's account. Too bad Officer Dick and his Dickhead Chick have clued in that Len wants me and they decide that incarcerating me at Dick headquarters is a way to make him settle up.

Having a home away from home as freaky, if not freakier, than the Appleton Asylum is almost comforting. Chase's dad suits up for big business every morning, but he gets down and funky at day's end. LSD is given like communion, but for me it's a ticket to hell. Life on my outside is a bad enough trip. Put demons in my head and I've nowhere left to go. Everyone smokes pot like cigarettes and believes sharing is spiritual. I'd hook Jory up with Mr. Pace, but a hippie chick already shares his bed. He's cool with Tyler helping himself to Rhonda as long as his "Mr. Love" wears an overcoat, dozens of which, by the way, fill a bowl by the front door.

The first time I slept in Chase's bed a twist and shout played in my gut until I figured the existential love thing out. All the edges were off as we sat on a cloud-big sofa. Chase played with my hair and pulled my ear to his lips. "Lay beside me tonight, Ari." I followed him, thinking it was what a girl had to do to keep a man like him. I got down to my underpants, blue with a yellow sun on my bum. His hand stopped mine as I lifted my tank toward naked skin. "No, I like this." My body tingled when he curled up behind, pulling me as close as two bodies could be. "Tomorrow I'll read to you. Tonight I just want to feel your heartbeat." I'd heard that one before but he really did seem more interested in the music under my skin than the tit between my heart and his hand. *Rubber Soul* played on the stereo and I fell asleep.

As if just holding each other equals a big insufficiency, we keep what we do under the covers a secret, just for us to know, but he's lonely for me to be there and his arms soften the continued unravelling of my world.

THIRTY-ONE

Poseys. Who picked that name for Nazi torture? The nurses splay Grandma on the bed with posey restraints around her ankles and wrists. Chase isn't squeamish like most boys. He thinks Grandma's fissured face is a treasure map and death is a rapturous journey. I think it's worse than discovering the hotel room you booked is the lower level of an outhouse. The nurses let Chase play "Blowin' in the Wind" because Gladys stops yelling Bingo numbers whenever he sings.

I untie Grandma's shackles. I don't care if she plows head-first over the side of the bed. It would be better than this. Len comes around eight. "Ari, you go with Chase. I'll sit with her until Dolores arrives."

Chase hands Len the guitar and kisses my cheek because he knows I'm staying.

Len strums, calling gypsy angels to the room and I help myself to the spot beside Grandma. Not a hint of floury goodness remains on her hands. "Did you know Grandma taught Auntie Mary to make those cinnamon buns?" Grandma's hands are a mess of mauve worms and they're cold. "Do you believe in heaven, Len?"

"I believe there's more, but I'm not sure what that means. I can't swallow that death is the last chapter this creative life writes. Nor, that grief is how love ends. I believe we die to be reborn into another's life."

"I feel like I've been born a hundred times and not one of the births is quite my own."

"I understand that."

Auntie Dolores pokes her head around the curtain. "Hariet, you shouldn't be on that bed. It's unsanitary. Len, get her home. She has school tomorrow."

"Hi, Auntie Dolores." I hug her big. "I'm so glad to see you."

"Look at how tall you've grown."

"Babcia's cooking."

"Go on now. I'll sit with her."

"Don't let them tie her back up."

Aunt Dolores smiles, a mercy smile. "I'll hog-tie the nurses before I let that happen."

I kiss Grandma's used-up tissue cheek. "You have no legs, so fly—be born again."

The night is September cool. Len's hand warms my shoulder. "May I take my best girl on a date?" We walk to The Goof, the local diner with the burned out "D" in the Good Food sign. Over grilled cheese and chocolate milk we listen to "All I Have to Do Is Dream."

"So, are we needing to have a talk of the birds and bees, *corka*?"

"You know how just being with Zodiac is the best medicine in the world? Chase is my Zodiac."

Len's forehead ripples with brain confusion.

"You can relax. Our relationship is metaphysical." We talk over brownies and "Heartbreak Hotel" about opening our store. Len and I come to a silence, like passing under a bridge in a rainstorm. I hear the red vinyl seat squeak under my bum and smell a fresh pot brewing. Brownie icing stretches over my tongue and my neck hairs startle-up as I feel someone at the big window. I look past the painted words: *Hot Breakfast $1.50* and see my young Grandma looking in, smiling, then moving on.

The wallop of shit-pureed-sausage-'n'-egg-disinfectant at Sunny Crest is replaced by flowers that don't know that too much sweet is as good as a stink. No one told my mother that neon green and cleavage are not the best choice for a funeral, or that messy tears are best spilled when you've chosen waterproof eye-gunk.

Everyone is smoking. Jasper coughs, *Guess no one's read the report that smoking fast-tracks you for Resthaven's mahogany bed and worm breakfast.* There's a tree out back where a girl can catch a breath of air and remember a Grandma who knit red mittens, never forgot a birthday, and talked to me woman to woman.

"Len said I'd find you out here." Mr. West hands me a hankie. "Sorry about your Grandma." A funeral situation that sends Mr. West back my way means I can take a hug and he can give one. His arms are full of the hush-hush comfort that makes a body feel lighter. He whispers into my hair, "Miss Standish is inside."

I've grown taller. Our faces could meet if he leaned down two inches and I stretched up one. "Would you like to meet Aunt Mary?"

"East Coast Mary? I'd love to."

Long, long after he's gone, maybe still now, I feel the heat of his hand on my back as he gentled me back inside.

Auntie Dolores says, "Jennah, you've done all right for yourself." It's a big house, filled with big payoffs. Jennah keeps it perfect for Wilf. The kids sit quiet and good. Dean, just turned four, serves 'round a plate of cocktail weenies.

I lean against the fence surveying my sister-house. Jennah is dressed like Grace Kelly. Her face resembles Auntie Dolores' Royal Doulton ladies and the glass of her eyes glistens exactly like Mum's; well, Mum's before the eye-gunk situation. Jillianne, out on a compassion pass, tucks herself small on a chaise, staring at sky-reflections in the swimming pool. With her hair cropped short she looks like a newly hatched bird, scared to fly. Jory has another tattoo, a butterfly, the antennae curling round her eye and she has a swelling belly under her peasant dress. Franc slips his dark glasses on Jacquie and smoothes the headache lines from her forehead.

Auntie Nia sighs over my shoulder, "Jacquie's migraines still bad?"

"Getting worse."

"What does the doctor say?"

"The tests all say she's fine."

"A good roll in some red mud would do her a universe of good. You hear anything from June?"

"I send postcards regular to Coombs hoping someone knows her and will pass them along."

"Quite the collection of wabi-sabi pots you girls are. Let's see if I can't get some decent food into Jory while I'm here."

I cozy up to a shrub when Uncle Gord moves in, sizing me up with greedy eyes. "Well, look at you, Hariet. Who'd have thought you'd turn into a fashion model." I wish I'd gone for the Amish cover instead of the Mary Quant look. "Give your old uncle a hug."

I back away, searching for escape and find Auntie Mary right behind. "Come get something to eat." I'm not much of a cry-baby but fat tears surface anyway. Auntie M catches them with her sleeve. "What is it?"

It's the smell of an uncle touching my bum, sliding a hand under my shirt, beer-breath mumbling, *Nice of Vincent to break in his girls for the rest of us.* It's Jory waving ten bucks, *Look what Uncle Gordo gave me.* But I say, "I miss Grandma." Now, it's a giggling mother with maxed-out hair draped over Officer Irwin's arm.

Auntie Mary navigates me through the intoxicated mourners. "Let's get Len to take you home."

Bob Dylan, grade-A shit, and pressing campaign T-shirts may not be a proper way to spend Grandma's funeral day, but it makes the hurting edges less razored and makes Chase's reflections on death more poetic. "Babe, all this energy's exploding into the universe, like this nuclear love bomb. Can't you feel the love drifting over all humanity?"

I am feeling it until Jacquie thrusts her head around the door. "Hide. Stay put 'til we say."

We shut everything down, grab all evidence, then burrow into the centre of some stacked boxes. "Sh-sh-sh. Stop laughing." He piles T-shirts under our heads. "Sh-sh-sh, you're safe with me. What the fuck are we doing?"

"Don't know." Like a punch, exhaustion hits and I'm more tired than I've ever been in all my days on this earth.

We listen to voices through the vents. "She's coming home with me until you pay up."

"She's not here."

Mum's spiky shoes stab each step to the upstairs. A few minutes later, they needle the basement steps. I pull Chase's right hand over my mouth and his left over my heart to muffle the cannon bangs. Purply light spills in as the door opens, then yellow light pours down from the switching on of the bare bulb over the workbench.

Officer Dick sniffs. "What's that smell?"

Jacquie is as smooth as Arielle's bottom. "Hemp fibres, from pressing the T-shirts."

Detective Dick sleuths. "This press is hot."

"Babcia was pressing stock. Ari isn't here."

"Where is she? We'll pick her up."

Right. He'll feel you up.

Oh, Jasper. He's dirt, dirt, and I'm gonna be mud.

"Likely a walk by the lake."

Len says, "No, Sunny Crest. She's taking some of the flowers over to Gladys."

Jasper, why hadn't we thought to really do that?

Tomorrow we will if you're not incarcerated.

138

Mum shrills like a stressed loon. "I'm not being swindled out of this, too."

"For Christ sake, Mum, no one swindled you out of anything. Sunny Crest was expensive. After the funeral and plot, that's all that was left."

I surface for air as the enemy retreats, wondering why a mother who becomes so absorbed by her men has let none of Len's goodness soak in. Chase whispers, "What was that about?"

"They likely thought money was coming from Grandma."

"What's that got to do with nabbing you?"

"I'm leverage to pry money out of Len."

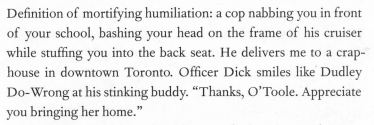

THIRTY-TWO

Definition of mortifying humiliation: a cop nabbing you in front of your school, bashing your head on the frame of his cruiser while stuffing you into the back seat. He delivers me to a crap-house in downtown Toronto. Officer Dick smiles like Dudley Do-Wrong at his stinking buddy. "Thanks, O'Toole. Appreciate you bringing her home."

Two junior Dicks stand gawking on the beat-up porch. Mum opens her arms. "Hariet, thank God you're here."

"Don't touch me, you bitch."

Officer Dick backhands my face, hard. "Watch how you talk to your mother. Get inside."

I calculate the odds: one drugged-out mother in sparkle flip-flops, one beer-bellied cop, one doughboy, and one barefoot stoner against one long-legged, pissed-off girl with twelve blocks at most to Yorkville. These Royal Canadian *Mount-me's* are not getting this woman.

I bolt to the Village, peel through the Riverboat, taking cover behind the condiments in the storage room. Crystal follows me in. "Shit, Ari. What happened to your eye?"

"Satan and his spawn are after me."

In Yorkville sympathy runs big for those oppressed by establishment bastards. "I'll get some ice," she says.

Bernie comes in with Crystal. "What's the trouble, doll?"

The whole done-wrong drama spills out.

"Crash upstairs long as you need."

More dropped-out humanity wanders around my hideout than pores on Officer Dick's nose, but still I feel alone. I miss Zodiac and Chase. Most of all I miss Len. Oh, and I miss clothes. Not for me. Jory brought me stuff. But some crashers take their clothes off and can't remember where they put them. Now, I'm no prude but no matter how I look at giant slugs flapping free I can't see pretty. In the past, I've kept my eyes closed whenever a weenie came out, but now I'm having some good ganders and I wonder if, under their jeans, Mr. West and Jake dangle like these guys. Steve catches me looking at his package and the thing stands up, points right at me. I hope it doesn't mean anything too weird that I think the chicks are nicer to look at—tits perk but they never point.

Jory brings my books. I rub the love child growing in her belly as she preaches salvation. "At the meeting last week, Pastor prophesized that this baby will help bring peace to this broken world."

"Maybe the kid could help Len negotiate my release." Which can't happen soon enough. No one here messes with me but sometimes an unwashed person, lost on their way back from taking a whiz helps themselves to the other half of my mattress mistaking me for their love child.

"Sorry, Ari, thought you were Cheyenne."

Chase shows up at eleven unable to wait until tomorrow to see me. He's taking me home tomorrow for a civilized sit-down. Auntie Nia's lawyer friend, Mr. Lukeman, came and took a picture of my face at its rainbow finest. But my living with Len all boils down to money. Mr. Lukeman has drilled into Chick of Dick that she gets next to nothing, seeing as everything belonged to Len's family and she did the adultering and the leaving. Len has agreed to sacrifice half of the proceeds from sale of the house in return for ironclad custody of me.

"It's looking like you'll be able to live at the store and go back to school."

I clutch at Chase's arm around my body. "I'm scared to go back. I'll be the freak of the school."

"Being picked off the sidewalk by police and going missing for a week has elevated you to ultra cool. Besides the school VP has your back."

I turn as the love symphony plays around us. "How about my front?"

"I have your mind and spirit, Ari. That's ultimate connection."

"Can I at least have a kiss?"

He kisses my eyes, my nose, my cheeks, then catches my lips in a connection that's nothing like Jake's. "I love you so much, Ari."

"Love you, too."

Mr. Lukeman finalizes the divorce details. Thirteen thousand dollars will be sacrificed in exchange for custody of me. As soon as things are signed Len and I are heading east.

Mrs. Russell hands back my character study for English. "Fascinating piece of work, Ari, but it was supposed to be a non-fiction piece."

"Oh, Mrs. Russell, I really wish it was fiction." I tuck *Naked People* into my backpack. "The guy with the belly swag is still giving me nightmares."

"The ones without clothes are colourful but the parallels you draw to spiritual nakedness are profound. The Dick is metaphor, right?"

"Well, I suppose if I'm using an enormous Dick to connote a giant asshole, then yes. He's the one who had me nabbed and hauled off to Crapdom."

"I'm really going to miss your contributions to the paper. When will you move?"

"Barring disaster, next week."

THIRTY-THREE

Len hands me my sweater. "There won't be many more nights this perfect before we leave."

We love harvest moons and late-October's bite. At the water, we sit on our bench, contemplating the moon-painted road crossing the lake. "Is it hard to change your name? I'd like to be Ari Joy Zajac."

"You could marry cousin Alphonse."

"I was thinking, daughter of Len."

He nuzzles my headtop with his cheek. "You are Ari Zajac by love. Though, one day you will be Ari Butters."

"Jake's a Tupper."

"He's a Butter at heart, and you are bread to him." His smile lifts me. "Come, *corka*, there is school tomorrow."

Len walks with his head up again. Whistles, too, but his hands aren't in his pockets. One holds mine, the other Zodiac's leash as we walk along the boardwalk. He stops to take in the evening stars, drops the leash, and grabs his arm. "Len?" His grip tightens on my hand. "Papa?" He crumples to his knees pulling me with him. "No, please, no!" I scream, "Help. Someone help! Call an ambulance." People run, doing what helpers do.

His head rests under my heart as he breathes out, "With you was best time I ever had."

"Don't leave me, Len, please. Papa, don't leave me." His hand never lets go of my arm as our world ends.

As people shift, even the pews remain silent. I hear, "Len's daughter, Ari, would like to say a few words." Aunt Mary releases my hand and a girl with my legs and hair, rises—black shoes on red carpet, up one step, two steps, three . . . past lily and freesia, all trying too hard to lay their thick sweet over the sadness. It will be my first words in four days. I'd stay in the silence forever but this is the only moment I have to say to the hundreds gathered that I love Len.

They push you too soon to get things done and buried. I'm still on the splintered wood of the boardwalk, holding him, believing somehow, he won't leave me. I stare at a trail of ivy spilling over the polished oak, talk directly to it for a while. "My papa believed that each day lived moves us closer, not to death

143

but to rebirth; each birth connecting us to the past and opening up more love, more becoming. I'd look at his face in the moon-spill of our walks and wonder how many times he'd been reborn to have become this extraordinary person of quiet kindness and goodness. Six daughters. He took on six daughters and never once, with all the trouble we could be, did he raise his hand or voice. He just loved us. He loved me." You feel it when the freezing starts to come out. I squeeze back blood from invading the frozen places. "My first day in the blue house I sat scared on the back steps. He came with ginger snaps and milk and sat down beside me. I asked, 'What do I call you? Daddy?'

"He said, 'Start with Len. Papa is a name to be earned.'" I wait, swallowing hard, swallowing, swallowing . . . Franc, shy Franc climbs to the platform; rests his hand on my back as I catch a breath. "At sunrise last summer we had breakfast with a gathering of deer. A beautiful doe gazed at Len when he said, 'I am honoured that you would eat from my hand'. . ." The ice breaks, I crack. "Papa, I'm honoured you called me, *corka*, daughter. Your family taught me to fly with no legs. Now *you* must show me to how live with half a heart here and the other half reborn with you . . ."

Mr. West touches my shoulder. "Ari, you and Zodiac are coming with me."

Len painted my wall blue because we loved the ocean. I've lost sight of the shore, drifting for days, I think. My voice comes out thin and brittle. "Did they sort things out?"

"They're upstairs talking."

I haul my rumpled flesh into a sit. "Did Auntie Mary call you?"

"I called. I've been worried about you since the funeral."

Voices escalate upstairs, again. I rest my head on his shoulder. "My mum thinks she owns the store. Told Babcia and Uncle Iggy they had two weeks to get out. Mum's loading horror on their pain and sadness. Every night I hear their tears raining down the walls. I can't stand it."

"They won't have to move."

"Mr. Pace says she might have the right because she and Len were still married."

"Mr. Lukeman is on his way over. He wanted you on the East Coast before he opened Len's will, but Miss Standish's place will have to do."

After Mum's screaming tantrum last night my backpack is stuffed, ready for running. I follow Mr. West out, stopping for a minute to listen. Aunt Dolores sounds like Grandma. "Oh, for Christ's sake, Theresa, stop being so bloody self-centered and think of Ari for once in your life. Let her go with Mary."

"And let her ruin Hariet's life like she has mine?"

"Your pathetic life is your own doing. Yours."

"Richard and I need her here at the store."

"She needs stability and fresh air and school. And God knows she needs some peace, especially from that horse's ass you've saddled yourself with now."

"I'm her mother."

"So you finally figured that out. Well then, stop acting like a spoiled brat and give the child what *she* needs for a change."

Aunt Dolores means well. But she'd have more luck reasoning with a rutabaga. "I can't remember, did Mum come to the service?"

Mr. West gentles me out the door. "I didn't see her until the reception."

"With Irwin?"

"Alone, sober, and acting the widow." Zodiac helps himself to the space behind the seats of Mr. West's jeep.

"Miss Standish won't mind him coming?"

"She loves dogs."

Life sure gets jumbled for a kid middled in a money grab.

Auntie Mary doesn't belong on the sofa in my teacher's living room drinking tea from a china cup.

Mr. West touches my elbow. "I'm only a phone call away if you need me." I reach back for his hand and he takes mine like Len did when I was scared. "Everything is okay."

Miss Standish is likely older than my mother but gets more graceful the longer I know her. She leads me to a chair. "How'd you like to stay here until things get straightened out? I'll arrange home school and you can just have some peace."

"Auntie Mary, I can't go with you?"

"The custody agreement wasn't signed and your mum's going to be angry about the will."

"Why?"

"The business goes to Franc and Jacquie. Everything else, apart from a few bequests, goes to you."

"Then give it to Mum and let me go with you."

"It's in a trust. Except for an allowance, it can't be touched until you're eighteen."

My pillow smells of lavender. Out of respect for the lace, Zodiac stays on the rug, but his soft fur is under my hand.

"Night, Ari. Call if you need anything."

I want Aunties M&N. I want Chase. I need Len. "Thank you, Miss Standish. I'm good."

"You think you might call me Belle now that we've moved on to being friends?"

"It's a pretty name."

A body should sleep good in such a quiet place, but nightmares land me in a corner with porcupines throwing needles. "Ari? What's wrong?"

My voice sounds like metal vibrating. "If I die does my mum get the money?"

"It goes to Arielle, I believe."

"What if he kills Arielle?"

"No one's going to hurt you or Arielle."

"He'd think nothing about knocking my head off, and Arielle's so little. It'd be nothing more than wringing a kitten's neck."

"Mr. Lukeman will sort it out. Come, I'll set the kettle to boil."

I sit, cracked, leaking. Mum sees only a golden egg as Mr. Lukeman reads the will. Len's notes have me thinking he suspected a rebirth was ahead. The fact that he wasn't afraid makes me a little less scared. A thousand dollars for Jennah: "Just because you're precious, not because I'm sorry." A thousand for June when she's found: "Embrace Spring. You are new and good." A thousand for Jory: "One man on this earth wishes nothing more than for you to see your incalculable worth." For Jillianne: "Your restitution has been fully paid. Begin anew knowing you are my cherished daughter." Jacquie and Franc receive the building, business, and expense money for Babcia and Uncle Iggy. "Jacquie, could I have been blessed with a more perfect woman to become mother to my family? Only goodness has ever come from you."

I'm back at Jillianne's note, thinking about the gift of starting anew, and all I want is one more walk with Papa's hand in mine. Mr. Lukeman talks profits and insurance, house sales and savings. "Ninety-eight thousand will be held in trust for Ari."

"Is there a note?"

He hands me a box. Inside I unearth Len's best pot, saturated sea green and blues. "Ari, *corka*, my spirit child. You are the richest of clay. As you create, know I am in the earth, the sea, and sky, and your hand and heart will always connect with mine. Papa."

Two seats away, Mum quakes, ready to blow. I slip into Babcia's room, secret my treasure inside her trunk under the special-day linens then hide behind the door. She erupts, "What about me? What about our deal?"

"The divorce proceedings have no relevance now. Nothing had been signed. Mr. Zajac's will is ironclad."

"Hariet is mine, so that money is mine."

"Except for a small allowance it can't be touched for three and a half years. I'll be managing it on her behalf."

"I'm her mother. I'll manage it."

"You have no say in the matter, ma'am."

"Richard, do something."

"Now, listen here, the widow is entitled to her fair share. This is the address where the kid will be staying. Have the expense cheques sent there."

Jacquie says, "Mum, you can have the expense money. Let Ari stay here, near her school."

I don't know what's flying out there but an Armageddon of smashing erupts. "You . . . you and that filthy little bitch. First you take your father from me with your fawning and flirting. Now, Hariet steals what's mine from that spineless excuse . . ."

I scurry out the window, down the fire escape, peeling along the alley, over fences, through prickly shrubs. I locate Belle's key from under the patio stone, stuff my gear into my pack, and fly to the basement. My choices end in small spaces: the furnace room, laundry room . . . I opt for the crawl space under the stairs.

I have Len's soft flannel shirt under my head and the arms of his lanky sweater hugging my shoulders. I fish out my Pennyworth's flashlight and stack of condolences, re-reading the one I always turn to.

I walk the shore, more restless than the waves. I'd let my imagination run these past months as I scoped out spots for Len's store. I saw us as a family.

I was sitting by our log this morning thinking that for me family is only a wish that will disappear the moment I reach out. And right then an eagle walked by, just like that. Wings tucked in, like Len's hands in his pockets. It stopped and gave me a look, eye to eye, I swear. A whole book, with unwritten chapters was in that one look, an exhortation to hold onto hope. I half expected him to leave behind a feather for me to continue the writing of our story.

If I could find a way to come and hold you through this sorrow I would. More fosters arrived yesterday—twins, the most cantankerous pair I've ever come across. They only quiet when I fiddle so I can't leave the Missus.

Len was like Huey in his softness, don't you think? When my dad drunk himself off the boat it was more relief than a sadness. Just imagining the time when I'll have to let Huey go makes me wonder how your heart isn't falling to pieces. If love can keep it beating then you'll be okay, because I am sending that to you every minute. Jake.

I fold the letter. *Papa, I want to go home. Please, I just want to go home with you.*

I drift until sounds snap me awake: dishes clinking, the phone ringing, kettle whistling, and then a pounding at the side door and a police-big voice, "We're here for Hariet Appleton."

"She's not here."

"We'll have a look if you don't mind, ma'am."

"Help yourself."

They clomp around like the goon patrol. How they miss the jackhammering of my chest pounding under the stairs is a Jesus-strike-them-deaf mystery.

"You hear from her, call this number."

"Why? So Officer Irwin can smack her around? She's a good kid who's just lost her father. Leave her alone and go do what the taxpayers pay you to do."

"This is a serious matter, ma'am."

"Don't be the fool. She a fourteen-year-old honour-roll student. Now get out before I call the chief of police." Then Miss Standish's voice comes again, softer now, "Mary. Any luck?"

"No, I hoped Zodiac could track her down." Nails clickity-clack down the steps and I pray the fuzz have retreated because Zodiac is scratching at the crawl space door wanting Len and me to take him for a ramble.

THIRTY-FOUR

Jennah sets the table with her prettiest china. "I'll get things signed, sealed, and delivered before the petit fours."

"Why does she want someone she hates?"

"To stick it to Len like she thinks he stuck it to her."

"He was only ever nice to her."

"She rewrites everything in her head. Somebody's always done her wrong." Jennah folds the linen napkins into a crown. "You lay low. It's easier getting her mind off the meat when it's in the freezer." Jennah cuts lemon squares with the exact same hands as our mother. She's like Mum down to the wave in her hair. The difference is, Jennah owns every bed she's made. I don't know what she does about the beds that aren't her making, but last year, in her pool, she taught me to scream underwater and she's really good at it. She fills a crystal dish with cigarettes.

"Thought you quit."

"Smoke keeps bees from stinging." The old truck pulls into the drive. "Take your book into the den. Jacquie and I'll handle this."

November cool skitters in as Jacquie arrives with Mum. She sounds like an old barmaid full of other people's smoke and troubles. "Where're my sweet-D's? Grandma's brought candy."

"They're at playschool. Um, hello. I didn't know you were bringing a guest, Mum."

"This is Richard's girl, Ronnie. She wanted to meet her new sisters."

Frig, Jasper, the Dick's planted a snitch. I settle into a leather chair, more interested in the story unfolding in the dining room than in *Wuthering Heights.*

Fifteen minutes into the cucumber sandwiches Jennah says, "Do you like pinball, Ronnie? There's a machine in the rec room. Plenty of chips and coke behind the bar."

When the basement door closes I creep down the hall and peek into the living room. Jacquie sits quiet, pushing against the pain in her head with her palms. Mum's right eye folds into her face as she sucks on her cigarette. "That one's a firecracker like you, Jennah. Could you spare a twenty? I'm a little short until I get this money mess straightened out."

"You know, Mum, I bet we could finagle a cash settlement from Mr. Lukeman if you'd give Wilf and me custody of Hariet."

"What kind of settlement?"

"Maybe the thirteen thousand originally worked out in the divorce agreement."

"That's not cutting it now. The penny-pinching bastard. All I did without because he said he had money troubles when he was sitting on a gold mine. As his widow, it's my estate."

I swear I'm going to pitch her in an urchin stew.

"Let's not talk about money right now. I never realized how hard having kids was until I had my own. With all your struggles, all your hard breaks, you made sure we were okay."

Who's she talking to, Ari?

She's just catching flies with crap.

"And look at us, Mummy. I've got this lovely home. June's travelling the world. Jacquie's a businesswoman. Jory's doing the Lord's work. Jillianne's taking a design course. And Hariet was top mark last year. She's been moved about more than any of us. Let her stay put at the store for high school."

"I'll have to ask Richard."

"He has nothing to do with this, Mummy. Think of Hariet."

"She's never thought about me, has she?"

"How can you say that? She's a bundle of kindness, especially to you."

"Me? The way she was always climbing over your father? And don't think I don't know what she was up to with Len. That Mary ruined her."

Jacquie starts hissing, "You—how? You are—"

Jennah clenches her words. "Shouldn't you be getting back to Arielle? Wilf will drive Mum home. Take the package in the hall with you." Jennah fills Mum's cup with whiskey. "Well, for all the trouble she's caused, let's get her out of your hair once and for all."

"So she gets what she wants and I get nothing? Again?"

"You'll get thousands if you give over custody. But if you take her, all you'll get is a thorn in your side. You need to take care of yourself."

"He's laughing at me."

"Who?"

"From the grave, laughing, laughing, laughing . . . Well, last laugh is on him."

I don't know why I want to hear more but I want to hear all of it. Jacquie pulls me out the door. "The fucking stupid, crazy freak. Come on, Ari." Jacquie's firm hold lands me in the old Ford. It still holds Len's shadow and a little of his scent. "If you dare take to heart one word that bitch says I swear I'll pitch you in the prickle hedge."

"Has she always been this loony?"

"She's always soured at anybody having anything more than her." Jacquie's tears muddy her words. "Len was so good to her. She can't even trouble herself to say his name."

"I don't want Papa's name on her lips."

"I hate her. I fucking hate her. The blind bitch doesn't see anything, not even herself. Christ, she looks like a used-up whore." The truck clunks into second then grinds to first.

A penny pokes out from under Jacquie's shoe. I remember it flipping from Len's pocket when he pulled out his keys only last month. *Jasper, how can he be gone?* "I wish her heart had been the one to stop."

Jacquie pulls onto the road. "She'd have to have one for that to happen."

I'm hiding in a two-bedroom bungalow afraid to answer the phone or flush the toilet in case things are bugged. There's no work or school or family, only Zodiac insulating me from the gaping Papa-shaped chasm.

At the preliminary hearing Mum is toned down in an Audrey Hepburn getup and Marilyn Monroe hair and Officer Dick is polished and ribboned like a war hero.

The negotiations have me thinking that judges are dumber than dirt. Not clay dirt, dirt-dirt. Everyone has a mouthful to say but no one asks me a friggin' thing. Then, it's against the rules for me to stay with anyone who loves me until the judge decides who loves me best so they're plunking me in a foster farm until the reports are pondered.

A lady seizes me, loads me into a black Lincoln, delivering me to purgatory. "The Guthries are close to your school and two of our most experienced caregivers. You come from a big family so you won't be lonely for brothers and sisters here."

"What kind of a friggin' stupid child protector dumps a kid with strangers when she has perfectly good relatives of her own?"

"It's for your own good."

"You've never personally had the pleasure of being fostered, have you?"

"I have thirty years' experience."

"Oh, for pity sake. You could hold a snake by the tail for a hundred years and never have a clue what it's like to face the mouth end, *ma'am*."

A major curl of red paint looks like the front door is sticking out its tongue. The rest of the clapboard has a bad case of eczema. The piss stink throws me back to life with other butt-whacking fosters, except I sense here the parental units will have trouble figuring out how to open a Cocoa Puffs box. I don't know how many foster kids they keep, but they have two blood sons, Donny and Doolie, and a little cross-eyed girl named Donna. At least the J's show a little imagination.

Given the spectrum of possibilities, I get a spectacular break. Daddy Guthrie's dick is incarcerated in yards of belly flab and he's welded to the La-Z-Boy. By law, they have to provide me with my own bed, which they do: a rollaway cot on the back porch. I'd freeze, toes at one end and tits-to-nose at the other if they gave a rat's whisker about me. But as long as they get their government lettuce and the occasional cabbage roll, we're square. I tell them I'm going to the library to study. Ermmaline scratches her butt in consent. When I come back with perogies she sends me out for more, encouraging my studies 'round the clock.

After school I work at the store, eat Babcia's body-good cooking—which she does all day and sometimes through the night, like somehow it keeps her sad heart beating. I soak up my dog and the people that miss Len as much as I do, pass through the Guthrie's, drop off a toll, escape through the back door, landing in Chase's warm bed.

A hearing happened today. I wasn't invited. Afterward, Auntie Mary's hair looks more a stress than a party. She repeats, at least five times. "Things will be okay, sweetheart."

"What happened?"

Water collects in her eyes. "Your mum said some things that cast doubt on whether I could be a suitable guardian."

I know it's the Nia love, a thing that can't be talked about or said is true because God and country declare it an abomination. "When do I get to say what the situation is?"

"I'm not sure you do."

"Can you tell Mr. Lukeman I need to see him?"

Chase sits on the bed singing a song he wrote about his love being longer than my hair. I smile at the snow leopard in him, knowing that, with me, he feels almost happy being a creature with unique spots. Weeks ago, I gave the seduction thing another try, snuggling up birthday-suit shiny behind him and kissed his back. He scurried out the end of the bed. "Jesus, Ari. Why do you have to go and fuck things up between us?" At first, water gathered for a pathetic girl-cry but then the laughing started and wouldn't stop tickling me. He started, too. "What are we laughing at?"

"We're both so fucked up we don't need to fuck. We're fucking perfect for each other."

Tonight, he climbs over and kisses my knee. "How's the letter coming?"

"I'm thinking it doesn't matter what I say. No one is going to listen. You want me to write on the sofa so you can sleep?"

"I'm reading *War and Peace* and you're writing it." He comes back with hot chocolate and rippled potato chips. "Let me know if you need an ear."

I crunch while composing, I hope, an epic of Ben-Hur magnitude.

Dear Right Honourable Judge: I count back and there are eleven, that I can remember, places I've lived. I was most afraid travelling alone to Aunt Mary's, but there I met the mother every child should have, but rarely gets. Three pages of blessed times with M&N flow out, written with all the wholesome churchiness I can resurrect on paper. *Leaving there was the hardest thing I faced in my ten years on this earth. But here I met Len, the father every child should have, but rarely gets.* Pages capture the Zajac years. *I've watched my mother through a whisky-pilled haze for as long as I can remember. The times she surfaced, hope ran big. I don't hope anymore because it makes her sliding back under hurt less.* Though it could be an epistle, I leave her failings on a single page. *You must decide where I'll live, and ice is creeping under my skin with the thought that no one will hear a kid's voice. After all, what do we know? I know my mum has stood before you in her Grace Kelly suit and Officer Irwin in his brass-buttoned finery saying that they only love me. It's a lie and I know the truth. If you're a fair judge, the kind that stands with a blindfold and weighs the evidence you will ask me the answer before you decide. Sincerely, Ari Appleton.*

What you wear when you stand before a judge is important. Hippie look, too rebellious. Minidress, too slutty. Peasant skirt, too Amish. "Jennah, you've got to help me get this right."

She dresses me in a navy pleated skirt, navy tights, penny loafers, and a white bunny-soft sweater set. Len's necklace for strength and a fat braid down my back. "Go get 'em, sis."

Mr. Lukeman takes me to a place in downtown Toronto that confirms that judges are kings of castles and kids merely dirty rascals. "What do you have in the box, Ari?"

My voice sounds like Chase's high guitar string in the echo-y hall. "Evidence."

A lady shows me into a big room, looking on the inside like Grandma's coffin did on the outside. "Sit. Judge Learner will be with you momentarily."

I place the box on a brass-nailed leather chair, then journey around the room looking at travel treasures nestled beside the judge's important books. A door I didn't know was there appears. A man in white shirt and suspenders clears his throat like a tommygun. I wish I'd sat like I'd been told to because I top him by inches. "Sorry, sir. I was just admiring your vase. Is it from South America?"

"Costa Rica."

"It's spectacular."

He cracks, just a little. "Sit, please. I have to be in court in an hour."

"Yes, sir. I appreciate you giving me this time."

"Your letter was compelling. So, state your case."

I'd hoped for a little butter-up small talk first but you don't mess with a judge on a schedule. "Auntie Mary wants me because she's good and wants to give me a safe home. Officer Irwin wants me so he can keep an eye on the money until he figures a way to get it. And my mother wants me out of spite."

"Spite?"

"She hates Auntie Mary and knows nothing will hurt her more than seeing me hurt. And she's angry at Len and wants him to suffer in the great beyond by seeing me suffer here."

"That's a rather jaded view of your mother."

"You get that way when you've been the misspelled Hariet at the end of a string of jewels your whole life."

Air puffs through his nose like a dog sniffing for clues. "What's in the box?"

I lift it onto his blotter. "It's not a bribe, sir. I just want you to see what a kid who believes she's dirt becomes when she has a Mary and a Len who show her she's clay."

He lifts out the pot, turning it, the colours of sun and ocean mingling like tears. He stops where a phoenix is emerging. "This is magnificent. Where did you get it?"

"I made it, thanks to Auntie Mary's hand guiding mine. There's only a small window where the clay is soft and pliable and the spirits inside can be coaxed out."

"I can't accept . . ."

"I'd say any decision-making judge should have at least one reminder along with all these books that he needs to look for the Mary in a kid's life and hurry them there before the clay hardens."

"Miss Appleton, by law there needs to be compelling—overwhelming evidence to supersede a mother's rights to her child."

I tell him what I know of my birth.

"She came back for you, didn't she?"

"You know what she said to my aunt when she took me from her?" I can hardly let the words into the light. "She spit it right into Mary's face, 'You love her, mind, body, and soul, don't you? Well, live knowing that that's how much I despise her.'"

"You can't know that."

"Mrs. Butters was there, so was my Grandma. Even if they hadn't told me, I've felt it my whole life."

"It's hearsay. I need facts."

"In my letter are pages of facts, and my sisters, aunts, and teachers have given you the goods. If I have to get messed with before you can do what's right," I stand, "then Mr. Bumble is right, *the law is a ass*."

Judge Learner commands silence with a few shots from his throat. "This decision has not been an easy one. While the law states . . ." Yards of blather and humming before he gets to admitting that his hands are tied and I'm the property of the Dicks. "I strongly recommend that the child's schooling be considered and that she be permitted to continue at Birchmount by staying with her sister Jacquie Zajac during the week. It's remarkable to me that in light of so many losses and stressors, Miss Appleton has maintained a B average, a position on the school newspaper, and two part-time jobs. She's an articulate, accomplished young woman. After reviewing the facts, it's the opinion of this court that this is in great part due to the influences of the Zajacs and Mary Trembley. I have found no evidence of moral impropriety and am hereby ordering that . . ." I look up, heart thrashing, porridge churning, "that the minor child be permitted to work after school and weekends at the family store and that she spend the months of July and August with her aunt."

The small victory feels pretty close to the best of my life.

THIRTY-FIVE

The fact that Auntie Mary gets something throws Mum into a whisky sour. Lawyers, Mum, Dick, Jacquie, and I gather in a room. Mr. Lukeman begins, "In accordance with the judge's recommendation that Ari remain at her school I propose that she stay with Jacquie."

Mum is riding something new, and whatever it is it's making

her not so much jittery as sharp. "Let me make this clear, her name is Hair-eeee-ittt. Secondly, there's nothing to discuss until her going to that pervert is off the table."

"That was Judge Learner's decision and is not part of this discussion."

"She's never going there. We'll take it to the Supreme Court if necessary."

"This is family court, Mrs. Zajac. Besides, are you prepared to incur legal expenses for a challenge to the judge's ruling? Mr. Daniels, inform your client that legal aid would not be available for that kind of action."

"Piss on him. We'll hire our own lawyer. We've got money coming."

"You do understand the trust is untouchable? Even if something were to happen to Ari before her eighteenth birthday, it would pass to Arielle Zajac, you could not access it."

"Hair-eee-fucking-it. How fucking stupid are you?" She looks at me. "Too good for the name I gave you? Get in the car—now."

"If you're not prepared to abide by the terms of custody then Ar—Miss Appleton will be returned to the Guthries and another court date will be set. And I assure you Judge Learner is not a patient man."

Mum stands. "Richard."

"Let's hear the deal first, Theresa. How much if we let her stay with the sister?"

"Excuse me?" Mr. Lukeman cranks his head. "Nothing. The allowance goes to her guardian wherever she'll be living."

"Fine, pack your bags, kid."

Jacquie asks, "How much would they get for expenses?"

"Based on meals will often be at the store with the Zajacs and that Ari works and pays for clothes and incidentals, they'd be entitled to two hundred and twenty-five per month. And that's a generous calculation."

"Mum, I'll give you two-fifty if you let her stay with me."

"Now what kind of a mother would let her child live on the street, 'cause Missy, that's exactly where you're heading."

"Give it a rest. You can't touch the store. You can't touch the money. Now, do you really want to lose *your* sisters, your girls, and your grandkids over this? We've all had it with you."

Jacquie has been holding her tongue for my sake but the "crawling all over daddy" remark lit a fuse and it's nearly reached all the sewer gas. "You move our sister into that house and you lose everything."

Mum coils tighter than I've ever seen her. "You girls, you've never had anything but—"

"Shut the fuck up. What we had was a vacuous bitch who traded her heart for a bottle, her brain for pills, her conscience for men, and her girls for what? A few stinking bucks? You are the most pathetic—"

Mr. legal aid tilts a file that lifts a clipboard that topples a jug half-full of water. He sums up while mopping up. "The child's placement with the Guthries is in effect until December thirty-first. The parties have until then to settle on the terms. Mrs. Zajac, I strongly suggest that you follow the court's recommendations."

I've always counted on a certain civility, a ladylike load of shit with Mum. Now we have us a Mrs. Hyde situation. She says, "Fuck off," giving him the finger, and clicks out.

I want to stay at Birchmount High so bad my bologna on rye is performing a lead-footed mazurka in my gut. I cling to Chase like a chicken headed for the block. He lifts my chin. "Go get everything sorted."

I start with phys. ed. I've missed twice as many classes as I've attended. My teacher looks up from tying her sneaker while perched on a basketball. "I really need a pass, Miss Mitchell. The

Board won't give me permission to live out of the area and go here if I'm failing any subject."

"I know you've had a tough term, Appleton, but I can't assign a mark for PE based on two essays." She picks up another basketball so easily it's like her fingers are sticky. "Even with giving you perfect they're still only forty percent of your mark."

"I've jumped through legal hoops. Does that count?"

"Three marks. You need a fifty for a pass."

"I've balled my eyes out."

"Five marks."

"I bent over and kissed a judge's ass."

"Seven marks."

"I outran a cop and two teenage boys over twelve blocks."

She falls off her basketball laughing and I end up with a charitable sixty-three.

Next stop is the newspaper office. Mrs. Russell sighs at my resignation, "Ari, you'll be back next term."

"Even if I am, I'll have over an hour travel each way. Between work and school you won't get much out of me."

"Let's wait and see."

The school secretary calls on the intercom, "Excuse me. Is Ari Appleton there?"

Mrs. Russell pushes the button and leans into the speaker. "Yes."

"Her sisters are in the office."

"Here she comes." Mrs. Russell turns back to me and worries, "Is everything okay?"

"We're taking Jillianne out to celebrate graduating her design course."

"Oh, isn't that lovely. Go, have a wonderful time."

I don't believe in cosmic bullies plotting Applegeddon. We're just chemical reactors: rotting, decomposing . . . and we're susceptible to worms and the like, but today feels like one of those seed-sprouting green days in the dead of winter.

Jillianne and I snuggle in the little half seat as she shows me her portfolio, plump with costume designs. "These are spectacularly electrified." It's my first glimpse of what dreams have been tucked under her scared-bird feathers.

"Auntie Dolores got me a job with Théâtre du Rideau Vert."

"Wish you were going to be living here."

"I miss Montreal, and it'll be nice living with Auntie Dolores."

Jacquie laughs, "Better get her back to Springwood. She's crazy."

"No, Dolores wrote me every week. We talked about stuff and . . . Uncle Gord is gone."

In unison we say, "What?"

"He left her for some young thing."

Jennah near spits. "Good riddance. I hope she got the house."

"She outsmarted him out of almost everything." As Jacquie parks the truck in the lot of the Jesus Is The Way Tabernacle, Jillianne asks, "When's Jory due?"

"Next week."

We mount the stairs, Jasper spinning with revampment anticipation. He circles the drain when we find Jory surrounded by prayer-pleading parishioners. She's wet-hot, eye-rolling, blood-soaked, and dying. Jennah roars, "Get back! How long has she been like this?"

"Two days." They blather about God protecting.

"Fucking assholes." Jennah plucks blankets. "Jacquie, bring the truck to the front. Ari, get her head. Jill, her feet. "

I stay in the back warming her best I can as we rush to the General.

At the hospital they whisk Jory away and it feels like days before a nurse retrieves us and takes us to her room. Half-doped and her belly half the size she stares at the frosted window. Jacquie follows the nurse out. When she returns, her face answers all our questions.

Jory whimpers, "Please, Jesus, I want my baby."

Jacquie pushes her head between her palms like pain is something she can squeeze out, then hightails it back out of the room. Minutes later, voices escalate in the hall, "What do you think you're doing? Stop, or I'll call security."

Jacquie's voice cuts like glass. "Have you ever had one snatched away without so much as a goodbye?"

"No, but letting them see . . . it just makes things harder."

"You've no clue what harder things wait."

As Jacquie rounds the curtain Jory's arms open, reaching for the swaddled bundle. His lips sit like a tiny blue heart on his perfect face; lashes make little golden smiles on his closed eyes. "Why, Jesus? Why? He's cold. He so cold."

We curve around, baptizing him with salt tears.

Whatever path brings Auntie Dolores to Jory's hospital room gives me faith, not so much faith in God as in a goodness that runs in the veins of women. She comes quietly around the curtain. "Oh, Jory, I'm so, so sorry." She near lifts Jory and the baby into her arms. "Honey, I'm so sorry."

"He's cold, Auntie."

"See what I've brought." She rummages her carry-all, unearthing a layette, wool changing colours through every radioactive shade of a rainbow. "When I saw Elsie knitting it, I thought what else would do for Jory's baby?"

Jacquie takes the baby. "Do you have his name?"

"Jet."

"Perfect, perfect name. Ari, fill the basin with warm water." Jacquie lays him on the bed and unwraps the gift while singing a lullaby, half in Polish, *The sky is coming through the dark night . . .* Jennah helps Jory sit up so her finger can reach his hand, tiny fingers curving like a conductor inviting music to the room. "Jennah, I need your lipstick." Jacquie coats the bottom of Jet's foot with Peach Passion and imprints it onto the little flannel blanket. The second foot comes out mirror perfect. Auntie Dolores helps her do the hands. Jory cradles the soft blanket while Jacquie towel-tucks Jet under her wing, washing his pale violet body. He's like dressing a stiff porcelain doll, but bundled in the gift he looks like he's been baptized in a paintbox.

Jory clings tight until Auntie Dolores says, "Give your angel a kiss now and let me take care of what needs to be done. You sleep."

Jory releases him to me. "Do you like his name, Ari?"

"Jet. A glint of light in the sky, disappearing, but when it does you know it's gone to some magical far-off place."

THIRTY-SIX

Jory is a grief rock star, a suffer-the-little-children beacon in her church, ministering to wounded humanity. Apparently, a dead baby is all part of God's wonderful plan to make Jory a witness to His Glory. *You ever think God's an ass, Jasper?*

The one who cries a Niagara is Jacquie, which, by some magic, waters down her headaches, even washes them clean away some days. She looks up from playing peek-a-boo-patty-cake with Arielle. "Good luck tonight."

"Thanks."

Jennah's picking me up for dinner at Chan's Garden in a last-ditch attempt to negotiate my freedom.

Big Dick, Chick of Dick, and three junior pricks sit at the table. Ricky-Dicky Jr. is a greasy-headed stoner. Dick two, Todd, has Mr. Chan counting his losses at the all-you-can-eat buffet. But it's spawn three that has me quivering like a chow mein noodle. She's a size fourteen stuffed into a size-two white sweater dress over black underwears. In front of the Dick she smiles a sweet looking-forward-to-a-life-of-familial-bliss smile. When they look away, her Cleopatra eyes needle through me: "You're dead, bitch." And that's not the worst of it. On her hand sparkles Nana Appleton's emerald and diamond ring. My ring.

Wilf uses his big business voice. Jennah cajoles. No deal. They turn down three hundred and fifty dollars not to have me in favour of the two hundred and twenty-five to take me.

Mum blots her mouth, "Hariet, won't it be nice to have a sister to share a room with?"

I search her face for a molecule of humanness and realize I'm barking up the wrong species.

A small package arrives New Year's Eve: a ring, three square stones, a black diamond with white diamonds on either side. "Ari, this was my grandmother's. I was going to give it to you on your sixteenth birthday but I think you need it now. Treasure hunts in dark places are perilous journeys. Nia." The envelope contains pages of down-home blessings from everyone. I read and reread Jake's note.

> Last summer-end party, Huey pointed his bow at you and said, 'That lady is the ocean's gift to you. She'll keep you dancing all the days of your life.' I already knew the truth of that. I've known it since we were kids. What I know too is that you, Ari, are the music. With you is the one place I feel truly home. Jake.

Me, too, Jasper. I want to go home.

Everyone has gone to a New Year's Eve dance. No one wanted to but Jacquie hoped a dose of Polish goodness would lighten Babcia's grief a little. She's always worn black, mourning the loss of many loves, but since Len's death darkness weights her tiny frame. Jacquie thought it might do me some good, too, but just imagining toe-turning Polish music makes my lungs cave in on my heart. I hold Arielle tight, breathing through my last hours at home and looking at a year ahead without Len in it.

I pack light: Skyfish pillow, feather comforter, book, change of clothes, toothbrush, and, of course, a switchblade. "Don't cry, Jacquie. It can't be any worse than that camp where they aimed to scare Jesus into us."

Franc drives me to the craphouse armed with slide locks and a deadbolt, promising to find me a corner of the house to call my own. He searches high and low. "The cellar is floor to ceiling moldy boxes, vermin droppings everywhere."

"How about the attic?"

"Squirrels I'd say, maybe bats. It's not well insulated either."

Turns out there isn't even a broom closet to call my own so I'm stuck on a rollaway in Devil Girl's satanic cave. The whole house smells of mouse piss and stale smoke. Load-bearing grease holds up the kitchen walls. Not a speckle of arborite can be seen past the debris on all surfaces. The cleanest spot in the whole house is the giant cage belonging to a bedraggled parrot named Cunt. A six-year accumulation of shit in the bird's cage stands as the proudest accomplishment of the Dick's life.

"Did Ronnie get you settled in?"

"I'm really putting her out, Mum. Please, please, let me stay at the store."

"Her name's Veronica, but she prefers Ronnie." A cigarette smolders in the ashtray as she lights another.

I wave a hand in front of her face. "My name is Hariet, but I prefer Ari."

"You know, Jacquie talked Len into signing over the store to her. Now she's turned Jennah against me. She's another Mary; took your daddy away from us, then Len. I knew what she was up to when he moved her over to the store. Mark my words, Richard will get us what's ours."

"What do you mean—"

"Oh, here's Richard. He's bringing a New Year's treat."

The smell of pizza sucks everyone into the kitchen. Officer Dick lands the box atop dirty dishes. His eyes turn to slits when he grins. "Welcome home, Hariet." A pizza sliver remains in the box. The Dick roars, "Todd, you fat cow, bring some of that back."

I say, "I ate before I came, sir."

"You'll eat when I say you eat."

Todd lumbers in with four slices stacked on his arm. I pick up the inch in the box. "This is more than enough."

I prefer the waffle-butt I get from the overturned milk crate to whatever I'd get from the stained sofa. While Mum drinks dinner, smoke circles her head like a maritime fog and I marvel that a pretty blue house with Sears catalogue furniture and a gentleman bringing roses was not enough. The first bite refuses to go down. Todd happily rescues me when the Dick goes for another beer. Ricky scarfs down his share, grabs his ratty bomber jacket, and splits. Ronnie pours herself into an orange jumpsuit that bellbottoms out like square-dance skirts around her ankles. "Daddy, I need a ten for roller skating."

He opens his wallet, doling out a five. "That's the bottom of it."

Mum negotiates the Bailey's to her cup. "Hariet, give Ronnie a five."

"Sorry, the banks were closed today."

Mum coils, ready to spit. A rap on the door untwists her back into the chair.

Ronnie answers, her sugary voice sounding like she's in heat.

"I'm looking for Ari Appleton." I leap when I hear Chase's voice.

"No one here by that name." Ronnie backs him in the direction of the rink.

I shoot out the door, and spring off the porch into his hug.

Commandant Dick roars, "Get the hell back in this house!"

Chase follows me in, thrusting his hand out to the Dick. "A pleasure to meet you, sir. Good to see you again, Mrs. Zajac. Forgive me for dropping by uninvited but I didn't get a chance to see you at Christmas." He hands Mum a mega box of Pot of Gold. "Could I have your permission to take Ari out for a walk?"

Mum checks in with Dickie for her answer and I sense a thumb lowering. "Um, maybe Chase could treat Ronnie and me to roller skating."

Mum says, "How about you, Toddie? Would you like to go, too? Like a double date."

Ronnie launches my coat at me. "Brilliant. That would make you my date . . . Chase, is it?"

Todd doesn't move, just readjusts his sweatshirt making it clear that unwrapping the chocolates is exercise enough for him.

"Home by midnight or I'll have the cops out after you." The Dick snorts at his joke.

I cling to Chase like he's floatable debris around the *Titanic*. He burrows his face into my neck. "Jesus, I miss you so much already."

"Puking Christ." Ronnie yanks my braid. "You dare tell the old man I wasn't at the rink, I'll gut you in your sleep." She turns her palm to Chase. "Gimme the admission."

A bargain at three bucks to get rid of her. Her bellbottoms follow her around the block. "Charming," says Chase.

"What am I going to do?"

"Everyone can be bought, you just have to figure out what their currency is."

"What's your currency?"

January coats make it hard to hug but his holding reaches right down to my centre. "Acceptance," he says.

I do love him, with every defined and undefined molecule. "Well then, Chase Pace, consider yourself sold. You up for music?"

"If we go to the Riverboat Bernie's going to put us to work."

"I'm going to need all the cash I can get to keep Mum and Ronnie in line. Poppyseed loaf ought to do it with Todd. The other two, I haven't a clue."

The Riverboat is always sardine-packed, but never more than when Sonny Terry and Brownie McGhee play the tiny stage. Something about the blues makes my body slow-fire. I drop off orders while drinking up sultry notes. "I don't want no cornbread, peas and black molasses . . ."

Chase says, "Ari, it's eleven thirty. We better go."

When I peel off my apron Bernie moans, "No, doll, you're not bailing on me."

"Sorry, Bernie, a big Dick with a gun set my curfew. Can I leave something in your safe?"

"No shit."

"Just some running money and a ring."

He opens the office safe. "Could you work the rest of the week?"

"I'll try to swing it."

The wah-wah of Sonny's harp spills through the open door and Brownie is crying, "Hooray, hooray, these women are killing me . . ." I drop my necklace in the safe, too.

Chase and I make a Cinderella dash toward midnight, rosy-cheeked and laughing. We land at the crapdoor of the craphouse with minutes to spare. Dick opens the door. "Where's Ronnie?"

Shit. Jasper, we forgot to write a story. We step in slow. "Um . . . at the rink . . . a friend of hers fell, wham, right back on her head. Ronnie went with her to the hospital. We didn't know anyone there so we went and put in a shift at the coffee house."

"You best be off." His chin lifts to Chase. "Streetcars don't run all night."

"I have my dad's car up the street, sir."

Mum rallies off the couch, messy and stained, in nothing but a slip; panties on the floor by the coffee table. "You kids have a good time?"

"I got some good tips. Mummy, would it be okay if I went back to Scarborough with Chase? I have to be at work by seven to get ready for the January sale and I'm not sure if the buses run that early."

"I told you, you're not staying with Jacquie."

"Chase's father is home. He lets me crash in the guest room." I fish out what looks like a weighty crumple of tips.

Mum looks over my shoulder for permission. The Dick snaps up the five bucks. "Come Monday this galavanting stops. You understand, missy?"

"Yes, sir."

Uncle Iggy told me about a time when he was hauled in for interrogation. He'd witnessed neighbours taken, never to return. After he'd been smacked around they let him go. To this moment he remembers the sound of the door closing behind him, the red brick under his feet, the taste of blood on his lip, tucking his sons into their beds, and laying with his Katarina. I know it can't compare, but deliverance on the first day of 1968 feels like the sweetest moment I can remember.

THIRTY-SEVEN

Sunday night I run out of excuses to be somewhere else. After living in grace and mercy, I can't survive here. Leaving school is a sacrifice I'll have to make. Jory's church gives me the best options for hiding. I plan my escape while excavating the kitchen counter. Ricky opens the fridge, surveying the missing mould and debris. "Hey, Hairy, you do this?"

"Lose a friend?"

A smack would have surprised me less than, "It's nice. Thanks." He helps himself to a Coke and my lunch for tomorrow then leaves for his night job. Thankfully I had digested Uncle Iggy's quote on the lunch bag before he took it.

Todd is smoldering in his room after a pummelling by the Dick. Ronnie reanimates off her bed and squeezes into staying-out-all-night gear. Best break of the day: the Dick comes into the kitchen in uniform. He's desk sergeant on nights for two whole weeks. As soon as he leaves, I'm gone. He nabs the ringing phone. "Yeah. Christ, don't start again. I don't give a fuck if he's suicidal. Half hour and he's on my doorstep, or I'll have him picked up and you won't get him at all." He slams the phone, then he sends seeds flying as he shoves the cage housing the mimicking bird. "Shut up, you stupid cunt." He sits at the clean table. "Where's your mother?"

"Sleeping."

"What's to eat?"

I sacrifice Babcia's meat loaf and give a sanctioned escape a try. "Would it be okay if I stayed at Chase's tonight so I'm not late for school?"

"You're here to get Mikey up and ready for school."

"Who? Todd?"

"Todd can get his own fat ass out the door. Not that he ever

172

does." Meat loaf tries to escape his overstuffed face. "Make coffee. Fill the thermos. I'll take a sandwich of this, too." The chair grunts as he moves to answer a knock.

A woman's voice begs, "Please Rick. You can see him on the weekend."

"You had him the whole bloody holiday. Mikey, get your ass in here." I peek down the hall to a dragged-out replica of my mother standing on the porch with two little hands clinging to her skirts from behind. The Dick growls. "Mikey, now." A willow-fine boy, seven at most, forces himself inside. His face is waterlogged from pleading not to come here.

I walk down the littered hall and crouch. "Can I help you with your coat?" He stares at the salt stains weeping around his boots.

The mother asks, "Who's this?"

"Theresa's kid. Get off, now. "

"Bye, Mikey. Mummy loves you."

Dick swings the door closed and cranks up Mikey's chin. "Hey, kid, Santa good to you?"

He gives a mandatory head nod before dragging his yellow suitcase up the stairs. The Dick hauls on his coat. "See he's up and ready for school by seven thirty."

"But I have to leave by seven to get to school."

"Then see it's done before you leave. You'll earn your keep around here one way or another. You hear?"

"Yes, *SIR*."

Sayonara, Infected Roach, right, Ari?

Precisely. I lock the door and follow the sound of Todd's tirade. "Get lost you puking maggot."

Mikey backs into the hall and crumples in defeat against the wall.

"You share a room with Todd and Ricky?" He sighs as I help myself to the spot on the floor beside him. "I have to share with

Ronnie. This is the worst place I've come across yet. You hungry?" He shakes no. I check my watch. "Well, it's only six thirty. You have any books?" His head folds to his knees. "Go get your PJs on and teeth brushed and I'll show you my pictures."

He stays committed to his silence but obeys, then makes himself a little too comfortable on my cot. I open my photo album. "This is my dog Zodiac. Len is . . . was my stepdad. This is us at Expo. And these are my Aunties M&N. Wish I could live with them but the judge says a mother has her rights no matter how big a butt-head she is." I look for his face. "Don't tell her I said that, okay?" He settles on my pillow. He looks small and cold so I start to pull up the comforter. "Do you wet the bed?" He shakes *no*. "Because my Babcia made this feather wonder and I don't care to get piss on it." I tuck it around his chin and collect my album. "Bye, Mikey. It was nice meeting you." His small hand clutches my sleeve. "I gotta go." He tightens his hold.

Jasper pinches. *He's scared, Ari. The Dick's gone.*

"I'll just be down on the couch."

Jacquie wakes me in the workroom. "Ari, go upstairs and sleep."

"I've got an essay to finish and a test tomorrow."

"Iggy fleshed out your notes and I've typed it up."

I stumble up the stairs. Iggy is propped on the couch to give his pressure spots a rest. We hold each other a lot these days. His arms always give *my* pressure spots a rest. "Thanks for the essay."

"'Tis okay. Go sleep, *corka*."

In what has to be less than a minute Chase rattles my shoulder. "Time to go, babe."

"No. Please."

"This is the first place they'd come looking." He mops up my nose. "If you need to run, I'll go with you."

"How can I leave Mikey alone in that anus? I've just got to

174

unearth a spot for him in the boys' room. That couch is like sleeping in a cesspit."

"Come on. We'll give the kid every boy's dream room."

Chase's loads his car with groceries, clean laundry, and camping gear. Jacquie gives me my essay. "We're going to get an A."

"Can you osmote biology into my head?"

Chase hands over study cards. "I'll have the key points infused in there by the time we reach Main Street."

We shuffle around clutter at the end of the upstairs hallway and pitch Chase's pup tent, complete with air mattress, sleeping bag, flashlight, and stuffed bear. Mikey scurries in and from that time onward we hardly ever see him.

Week two has me believing I might survive without running. Ronnie stays out prowling most nights. I leave for school before the Dick and Dickette get up in the morning and they're gone in one way or another by the time I get home, except for Ricky who I think hangs around waiting for a lunch, or maybe for the quote on the bag. Today he's on the February-cold front steps finishing his smoke. I hand him a bag and he stuffs it in his coat.

"Who writes these words on the bags?"

"Uncle Iggy."

He recites yesterday's jewel. "Whatever you believe you can do, begin it. Action has magic and power in it."

"Come to the store Saturday and you can meet him and see my wall of Ig-gems."

"Do you think he could—"

Mum opens the door, looking more nice than slutty in black pants and a sweater. "Hariet, come on in now. Mikey needs help with his homework." Ricky turns the green of her tight V-neck when she kisses his cheek and then wipes the lipstick smudge with her licked thumb. "Have a good shift, sweetie."

I two-step over the hall debris. "Your hair looks nice up like that."

"Richard likes it down and wild."

I only remember a mum as a skin stretched over a man's expectations and by an odd turn she seems most comfortable in this empty-headed bimbo suit. Sometimes I hear real happiness in her laugh when the Dick smacks her butt or squeezes her tit before stepping out for a big date at the Zanzibar.

She makes tea for me, her hand playing a little with my hair as she watches over my shoulder. "You listen to Hariet, Mikey. She's as smart as they come."

I hate her saying these things. Utterly despising each other works best for us. "Mum, you're getting ashes on the paper."

Todd's internal clock signals time for a snack and *The Red Skelton Hour*. He plows through the kitchen, loading up before landing on the sofa. "Todd, is it so friggin' hard to put the lid back on the peanut butter?"

"Fuck off."

"I bought it, and you can't have any more if you don't put it away."

"You gonna to stop me?" He gives me the finger and the parrot caterwauls fuck-aw, fuck-aw.

Navigating the Dick's shift change is perilous. I sleep with one eye open because Ronnie's a girl-bully, the kind who would cut your hair or draw satanic symbols in permanent ink on your forehead while you sleep. On the nights when the Dick fouls crapdom I can count on her rummaging my pack after the nightly, *Oh, oh, oh yeah, Theresa, Jesus F Christ, you filthy little bitch, oh baby, fuck, yeah baby* . . . coming from the master Dick room. She pockets the two-buck devil-appeasement offering left for her before hoisting her heft out the window. I watch her escape route in case I ever need to make a fast exit.

Spooky how quickly life in crapdom becomes routine. Even the Dick-sanctioned padlock on the pantry. When I asked if I could lock it, Dick licked his lips over the pleasure of screwing Todd out of gobbling all our grub. His sheer glee made the whole plan sour, so now I leave a bag of Fritos by Todd's TV spot as a sorry-for-being-vengeful.

Hardest to get a handle on is what the Dick wants with me. He's just finished a screaming match with Mikey's mom before she took him for the weekend. Now he obliterates the kitchen window as he hunches red-faced over the sink. Ronnie wiggles in wearing a neon green minidress so short I can see her butt swags. "Daddy, I need a ten."

"Then go out and fucking earn it you lazy bitch." He pulls out his wallet, throwing a five at her and I wonder what she has his balls clamped in. His attention turns to me. "Has the kid talked to you?"

"No."

"You're supposed to be helping him with his homework."

"I do. He works out stuff easy on paper. Um . . . I have to get to work."

"Starting Monday you be home by six." His finger is bulbous like his nose. "And you get that kid talking."

"But I work 'til six."

"Home by six or I'll fix it so you have no work to go to at all."

"But . . ." In just one step his cheesy nose touches mine and his breath smells of salami and egg. He pinches my arm in a way that makes me want to blubber out loud. "Yes, sir." I slide into my coat and out the door.

Ricky laughs as I smack, book first, into him. "Good reading?"

"*King Lear*'s not my favourite but I've got a test."

He peers past my shoulder. "How's the home front?"

"The usual, one's passed out the other is pissed out."

"You want to get something to eat?"

"If you come to the library first. Apparently, the polar ice caps warrant a five-page blather."

He trudges along to the library then buys me pizza.

"Can I ask you something?"

"Shoot."

"What does Ronnie have on your dad?"

"Nobody knows. Not even Ronnie." The coke rumbles in the bottom of the glass. "They were having it out years back; Ronnie said she'd seen what he did and was going to tell."

"What did she see?"

"Nothing. He just has a guilty conscience. Likely it was him who threw my mom down the stairs."

"Where is your mom now?"

"Holy Cross."

"I'm guessing you don't mean she's a nun."

"Fertilizer. The fucker moved Todd's mom in before the ground settled. Then there was Lucille, what a piece of work she was." He has a sweet, sad smile. "Mikey's mom was okay. When she was clean."

"How come your dad gets Mikey?"

"Laura has problems, the worst of which is my old man. He pretty much takes what he wants." He swirls the melted ice in his glass.

"I have to get to work so you better hurry up and ask."

"Ask what?"

"Whatever it is you wanted to ask me the other day."

"Can't a guy say thanks for the lunches without wanting something?"

"Rarely."

THIRTY-EIGHT

I'm on my knees at Aquarius reordering bottom shelves when Ricky cruises in.

"Hey. Did you come to meet Uncle Iggy?"

"Yeah . . . no . . . okay, I did want to ask you something." He pulls out a fat envelope. "Can you help me fill this out? It has a bunch of questions. And I have to study for this aptitude test."

I peruse the papers. "You're joining the army?"

"I want it so bad I can't shit straight. I could get papers to be a mechanic."

"We'll make it so poetic they'll beg you to join."

"You can't tell. Dad would kill me."

"Wouldn't he be proud?"

"He got booted out. Nothing would screw him more than me getting in. One day, when I'm a sergeant or captain, I'll march into the station in uniform and give him a royal salute. Until then, I'll protect you."

"Well, all I can say is having the Canadian Armed Forces on my side can only help. Iggy will help you study 'til you've got the book down by heart."

Chase drops Ricky off at the house with me and kisses me light and sweet. "See you tomorrow, babe. Take care of her, Ricky."

Mikey catapults out of the house in stockinged feet, plastering himself to me. "What's wrong?"

Ricky says, "Think maybe he was scared you weren't coming back."

"No such luck, Mikey, you're stuck with me. You have a good weekend with your mom?" He shrugs into my belly. "Let's get inside before your feet freeze."

I step over the pantry door lying on the front lawn. In the two days I've been gone things have faded to yuck. There isn't a clear inch on the counter to set anything down and the air is smokier than Pompeii. Dick rumbles from the never-used dining room, "Girl, get in here and show some manners."

Mum and Ronnie are cheerleaders for a big poker game. I stand in the door while the Dick directs his cigar to the lineup, "Murdock, Norman, O'Toole, Jonesie, this is Theresa's youngest." O'Toole, the cop who snatched me from school and frisked me for concealed weapons, winks. The cigar directs me to the kitchen. "Get up some snacks."

I have two options in this prison: make a break or put in my time and hope for time off for good behaviour. I slap bologna and mustard on stale white bread. "Ricky, go hide our lunches."

Mum wiggles in to tray-up some beer. "Isn't this fun?"

"Yeah, a real blast." I plop the stack on her tray and make for the stairs. "I gotta study."

O'Toole finishes zipping-up on his way down from the bathroom. "Hey, sweet thing. You like movies?"

"No."

He backs me toward the rail. "Well, what do you like?"

"People who wash their hands after using the bathroom."

He moves to incarcerate my hair when Todd pushes through like a tsunami, opening the way for me to escape. He winks as he goes by. "Gotta piss."

Never again will I withhold food from Todd.

Just when I think I have the situation figured out, the wind shifts. I don't mind coming home a little earlier because Ricky hangs around before going to his night job and things are a little flirty between us. Just eye-wanders and leaning close when watching TV.

The Dickhead storms in more miserable than usual, snatching my *Fahrenheit 451* out of Ricky's hand. "What the hell are you doing?"

"Reading."

"Fucking liar, get yourself to work." He turns his sights on me. "And you are finished at that store."

"Why?"

"Because I fucking said so."

"The judge said I could."

He comes at me with the back of his hand.

Ricky steps in, taking it right across his cheek.

"Don't you be interfering with me, boy."

Ricky explodes, backing the Dick up with his chest, raging in his face. "You the big man messing with a little girl. You gonna push her around like you did Mom? Leave her the hell alone or I'm telling everything."

"Get out of my sight. Fucking ingrate." An ashtray launches from his hand dinging the plaster before landing on the heap of boots.

I fly outside, following Ricky in my bare feet. "Ricky, wait."

He turns, walking backwards. "Get back in the house."

"But he's gonna murder me."

He lets me catch up and flicks off a butt caught in my hair. "He'll leave you alone for now."

I touch the dribble of blood on his lip. "I'm sorry."

"It's nothing."

"What are you going to tell?"

"About pockets I know he picks. I gotta go."

"Are you coming back?"

"I'll see you tomorrow."

My frozen feet tell me I need to be better prepared to run. Mikey shivers on the steps. I pat down his cowlicked hair. "Everything's okay."

Mum hovers, hip-handed pissed. "Don't you mess this up for me, Hariet."

Shut up you stupid, stupid bitch. "What the hell am I messing up?"

"Richard's just doing what I asked. You being around Jacquie is making me a nervous wreck. I want you away from that store."

"Too bad. I have legal permission."

I stomp up the stairs to find that Ronnie has barricaded me out of the friggin' room. The Dick clods up to the landing, lifting me off the floor by my braid. "I don't give a rat's tit what some pansy-ass judge says. I can make things happen, all your pretty life up in smoke." His teeth manipulate his lit cigar into my ear, bubbling the skin, melting wax. "You hear me?"

Scorching pain forces half-digested supper out of my gut.

He releases my braid and my knees buckle into the vomit. "Clean up that shit."

Maybe the scabby mess in my ear keeps me from hearing the warnings. I go to work all week with my nose held high, all I can-to. Three a.m., Sunday, Chase and I drag ourselves home from the Riverboat to find that Armageddon has hit the store— windows smashed, Aquarius cleaned out, everything stolen down to the last love bead and the Pennyworth side of the store trashed. Jacquie's inside clutching Arielle.

"Where's Franc?"

"He went to the hospital with Iggy."

The earth jellos under my feet. "Why?"

"It's so hard getting his chair up the stairs. He's been sleeping down in your room. The police think he heard a noise and called out. They beat him up, bashed his head bad."

"This is all my fault."

"It's Mum's and no one else's. There's not a day she doesn't phone saying I'm going to get mine and she's getting hers."

"Where's Zodiac?"

"Upstairs. Chase, will you take Ari and the dog to your place? We're going to Sabina's."

"Who's taking you?"

"The police."

"Let them take Babcia. You can't let the police know where you are or the Dick will know, too."

"Where are we supposed to go?"

"They won't think of Miss Standish. She said anytime I need to I can just let myself in."

Franc is hunched over the stretcher. His face gives away that things are really bad. I don't ask. I don't want to know that someone else is leaving me. Not my living word who feeds me more than what Babcia stuffs in a bag. I just lay my head on his chest whispering all that he means to me until only silence remains.

Nurses unhook, turn off, cover up.

Franc strokes my head. "Come, Ari. He runs. At last he runs."

THIRTY-NINE

Miss Standish has a backyard with a high fence. Winter damp seeps from the wooden bench through my coat. Jacquie arrives with a blanket and sits. We gather in a long silence. "What you said today was beautiful. He really could dance, couldn't he?"

I nod into her soft shoulder.

"Iggy couldn't make it to the toilet anymore. He was so ashamed having Franc or me clean him up. And the pressure sores were eating him away. A hero of two wars would want to die in battle. He died fighting with the only thing he had left, his voice."

"How will I survive without it?"

"It won't ever be gone. Will you write out his quotes for Arielle to have?"

"I'd like to." I mop my nose on my sleeve. "He wants to go home, so his ashes can be closer to Katarina."

"We know. Franc is going with Babcia. It'll be nice for him to see his parents."

"You and Arielle have to go, too."

"I'm not leaving you here with them."

"Babcia needs you. She needs Arielle to keep her broken heart beating. I can't protect myself if you don't go where you're safe. Threatening you is how they get me to dance whatever friggin' thing they want." I link arms with my sister-friend. "Imagine, Jacquie Appleton going on a plane to Europe."

"What about the store?"

"Len only left it to you so you'd have a future. His heart would break again if it ended up costing you that future. Sell it to Uncle Otto. He'll give you a fair price. Then when you come back, Franc can restore houses like he's always wanted."

Sometimes hope is a thing felt through a head on a shoulder. "Are you sure? I know what Aquarius means to you."

"Otto and Sabina love me. I'll always be welcome."

The lake heaves like my belly. Ice monsters rear, open-mouthed, swallowing wave after wave. I've done some hard things. Shameful that this feels like the hardest of them all.

"Ari? Belle said you needed to see me." Mr. West touches my

shoulder. "What is it?"

"Miss Standish said you were driving to Winnipeg on March break. That day, at the church in Montreal . . . you told me your parents were soft."

"They are at that."

"Miss Standish said there's a pond and fields that go on for miles."

He turns me and holds tight my shiver and tears.

"Please—take—Zodiac—with . . ." Snot is getting all over his beautiful jacket.

"No, you need him here with you."

My fingers are stiff-cold as I take a white envelope out of my pocket. He looks inside to see the hunk of Zodiac's lovely golden fur. "This was under my pillow after the robbery. If Zodiac drowned in your pond chasing after a duck I could bear it, but if his throat was cut to teach me a lesson, I'd be done trying."

"Okay, I'll take him. Let's go to Belle's and get you warmed up."

"I'm staying out of sight until Jacquie and Zodiac are safe. I'll just go."

"Where?"

"I should go to school and see if I can't salvage something from this term."

"It's six a.m. Come to my place and I'll make you something to eat."

"No. I don't want to get you in trouble. I'll hide at Chase's."

"I'll drop you."

He puts the heat on full blast and pats my hand between gear shifts, not in an improper way, but a more-worth-than-trouble way.

"Drop me at the back of the plaza so I can cut through the yards. Chase is being tortured, too. He's gotten two tickets this week."

"For what?"

"It's open season on Ari Appleton supporters."

"Ari, this just isn't right."

"What do you suggest I do? Call the police? If Zodiac and Jacquie are safe then he won't have as much to plague me with."

His eyes connect with mine. "Meet me at the lake Sunday after March break, around ten, and I'll let you know how Zodiac is doing."

In the newspaper office Mrs. Russell rustles my shoulder. "Ari, you're going to be late for history."

I push myself away from the old Underwood. "Thanks. I just needed a few minutes."

"Girl, you look exhausted. Are you eating?"

"Everything sits like curdled liver in my gut."

"Things okay at home?" Her polished nail taps a headline, "Seen But Not Heard," in the latest edition of the *Examiner*. I glance down and read: "Sometimes the only thing in your control is your own tongue, the choice of whether to speak up or shut up." She says, "What's going on, Ari?"

"Honestly? I don't know. It's like the Dick has zeroed in on all the things keeping me afloat and is puncturing them one by one." My chest heaves, but I keep the floods in. "I have to go."

"Come back after school and we'll talk."

"I can't. I have to go straight home."

"You're not going to work?"

The tremble of my lip pisses me off. "The store's been sold."

"Where's your sister?"

"She's going away for a while."

"Another loss, Ari. I'm going to make an appointment for you with the school counsellor."

"Talking isn't going to change this. Um . . . I can't afford to miss this class."

Franc and Jacquie invest the money from the store into two broken down buildings in the Village. Tomorrow they're leaving for Poland with Babcia, and most of Uncle Iggy in a jar. A little ash is mine for when I plant his oak beside Len's maple. Franc will return the buildings to splendour when they come back to Toronto and Jacquie will open a new and improved Aquarius.

Strange, seeing Jacquie walk into the Riverboat. "Can you take a break?"

"Bernie, can I take a break?"

"Sure. How many beautiful sisters do you have?"

"I'm taking five minutes for each and you can figure it out."

Jacquie scoots me out the back door, down the alley, through a gate, and up a fire escape to a tiny third-story nest, cozied with familiar things from the store apartment. "Jacquie, wha— What?"

"Franc set up everything under a holding company so no one knows we own it. The café and apartment downstairs are rented, but this is yours if you need a place to run to. Franc made it safe with bars and reinforced doors."

Len's pot graces a shelf and Babcia's warmest feather comforter covers a full-sized bed. My favourite reading chair looks liquid gold in the soft light of the lamp.

"There's only a hot plate and a bar fridge and if you bend in the shower you might get stuck, but it'll be dry and warm under the covers."

My books line a bookcase and my box from Auntie's M&N sit atop. A sign hangs in the little kitchen nook:

The Eagle's Nest
A place for Lion around.

"It's stocked with food that will keep. You could hole up here for weeks if needed." Jacquie raises the trunk lid at the end of the bed. "Your letters and Iggy's bag quotes are in here. We've set up a post office box. I've given everyone who needs to know the contact information. These are your keys. Belle has an extra set."

I jump, hugging her so hard we tumble onto the bed, feet kicking like I'm five and got a princess castle for Christmas. "This is the most spectacular thing ever."

The Dicks expect me to crash at the Riverboat on weekends, so no one is even looking for me. Chase discovers a toaster and kettle. "Breakfast, coming right up."

I believe heaven must be something like this: a friend, a featherbed, a cup of tea, a book, and . . . feeling completely safe.

I just about Old Faithful the tea out of the fat blue mug I'm holding when a phone rings. "I have a phone?"

Chase puts on his Queen of England voice, "MacArthur residence. Oh, hi, Jacquie. Yeah, right here."

I take the receiver. "Jacquie, I had the best sleep I've had in six months. Do I know how to pay a phone bill?"

"It's taken care of. Just promise me you won't tell anyone other than Chase and Belle about the place."

"That's an easy promise to keep."

Jacquie pries Arielle from my arms, replacing her with a plush toy retriever.

"Jacquie, thank you."

"It's from Mr. West. Tell me you'll be okay."

"With you safe I can rage, rage against the dying of the light."

A minute less of goodbyes and they would've made a clean getaway. The Dick pulls up and Mum steps out dressed in a fun-fur jacket slung over a leopard skin leotard. Jasper cowers. *Where's the SPCA when you need them?*

Dickprick growls at me, "You were told not to come here."

"I was told not to go *in* the store. Is it a crime to say goodbye to my sister?"

Jacquie lengthens. "What the hell do you want?"

Franc scoops Arielle from Jacquie's arms, handing her off to Aunt Sabina.

"Just came to see how the repairs are going on my store." Mum looks up at the chic new *Sabina's Boutique* sign. "What's this?"

"The new owners picked their own name."

"You sold my store?"

"Why is it so hard to get something into a head that's completely empty? I sold *my* store. Now we're off on a trip around the world and you are never going to see your granddaughter again, you stupid, useless bitch."

"You've never been anything but trouble." Mum inches up to Franc. "You know she fucked her father."

"No, her father raped her and you allowed it to happen and that makes you the lowest person on this earth. You don't deserve a single one of your beautiful daughters and you were never good enough for my uncle." Franc spits on the sidewalk then insists Jacquie toward the waiting car.

"I thought I couldn't despise anyone more than Daddy, now I just feel sorry for him for having been married to you."

Dick moves forward and Jacquie takes him on.

"Don't say one word, you murdering bastard. Once the police track down your thugs, how soon do you think it's going to be before they point a finger at you? Iggy's murder is on you. I hear cops get the royal treatment in prison."

Mum's fun-fur bristles. "That's my money. I earned it."

Jacquie screams while Franc tries to fold her into Uncle Otto's car. "All you've ever earned is a place in hell!"

Chase pulls my arm, "Come on, Ari. Now."

"No, we have to keep the Dicks from following them. I need Jacquie on that plane."

"They're not going anywhere on those tires."

I look back at the puddling rubber under the Dick's car. "What did you do?"

"Guess the construction crew should've cleaned up better."

Morning light casts bars across the floor and this is a room I love being locked in. I climb over Chase, make tea, and sit in my very own chair with Mr. West's note.

> Ari: You are the most courageous person I've ever met. I admire your spirit, grace, and tenacity. Knowing you is a privilege and caring for Zodiac is an honour. He will be cherished and loved until you're ready to take him home. Aaron West.

I sip the fragrant tea, realizing that if I don't factor in all that's happened or think about the mess waiting outside the door, I feel wholly happy.

Four o'clock comes and Chase returns me to crapdom. "Let me off at the end of the street. Dick might shoot you."

"That'll make me look guilty. I'm going in to see what the situation is; I want to be there if you need to run. Besides, I have peace doughnuts."

Mikey launches from the house like a flying squirrel. Ricky leans on the porch rail.

"Am I going to be murdered?"

"They're both sleeping one off."

Chase asks, "Are you here for the night, Ricky?"

"Yeah, night off."

Things continue to improve when Ronnie exits the house in the fluffy concoction Mum sported yesterday, masterfully accessorized with white go-go boots, black fishnets, and a hot-pink mini. Officer O'Toole pulls up and she hops in. "Don't wait up, losers."

Chase hands the double-dip bribes off to Mikey. "Keep her safe, buddy. See you tomorrow, babe."

Piss, vomit, bird shit, all the really homey fragrances welcome me when I enter crapdom. "Jesus, Ricky, what happened here?"

"A seizure and a fit. What happened yesterday?"

"They found out Jacquie sold the store and left the country."

"Was your stepdad really rich?"

"He just worked hard."

"Is it true he left you a whack of money?"

"Believe me, there's no gold mine. Just a pile of lead anchoring me here."

Todd sniffs into the kitchen. "Hey, Hari." He nabs a double chocolate, a vanilla, and a fruit-filled doughnut.

"You want me to make you a sandwich first?"

He puts back the sugared raspberry. "Sure."

"Just let me excavate the counter."

The Junior Dicks watch in rapt wonderment as I make grilled cheese. "Is your homework done, Mikey?"

He shrugs.

"Finish it, then we can play Go Fish." Mikey loves the game because he can talk with his fingers, though, it gets messy when asking for a card that has no numbers.

By the time the Dick spills down the stairs it's hard for him to get pissy confronted by such domestic bliss. He downs a handful of aspirin with swigs of Pepto. "What are you eating?" Mikey lifts his plate and the Dick scarfs the remaining inch.

I offer, "You want one?"

"Two. Wrap one to go."

Jasper dances. *Glorious days, he's going on nights.*

While we're playing Go Fish the Dick dives under the kitchen faucet and scrubs his bristled head with the dish towel. He flicks excess water in Mikey's face. "Damn it, scaredy-mouth, just say 'nine' for fuck sake."

Mikey puts down his cards to hold up nine fingers.

Ricky says, "Yeah, I got a nine."

"How about a tenner, Ricky? I'm a bit short."

"I'm clean out."

I retrieve the tips I have stuffed in my pocket, offering them with the sandwich. "Will three bucks help?"

He pincers my arm while nabbing the bills. "You think you're so much better than us, don't you?"

"I'm just a kid. In my almost fifteen years on this earth I've learned that we don't get the betterment on grownups, no how, no way." *Dirt-dumb stupid bastard.*

He throws four doughnuts in a bag and leaves us in peace. The call of *Green Acres* proves too much for Todd to resist. "Mikey, go get ready for bed and then you can watch it, too."

Ricky hangs around, drying likely the first dish of his life. "You are too good for us, Ari."

"Auntie Mary says we're all the same clay. The elements make us different, but we're all still lumps of clay. It's up to us what we make of it. You're going to make something spectacular out of yours." He rests against the counter making us almost exactly the same height. His eyes are double-dip chocolate and his hair the dark brown of forest earth. I know by his application form that he'll be eighteen on June 10th and will, I'm certain, become a soldier boy. "Can I write to you when you go?"

"That'd be nice. And a picture for my wall?" The finger-circle on my belly makes my underwear heat up. Motor grease and car dirt colour the creases of his hand and I one hundred percent like the feel of it on my one hundred percent cotton shirt.

Can there be anything more romance-shattering than the sound of one's pathetic mum hurling chunks from both ends? Yes—having her walk into the kitchen in a bra and baggy-bum panties with her flesh looking like a mess of lumpy oatmeal. She grabs the Pepto and shakes pills into her jittery hand. Eye goop leaks down her cheek. "I thought you left me. Everybody leaves me." She downs a palmful of pills, and a corner of my head and half of my heart hopes it's enough to kill her.

FORTY

I fill my warmed spot in the bed with the stuffed Zodiac, shower long to rid my hair of smoke, and dress warm. "I'm going now. I'll bring lunch back."

Chase yawns, "Love you."

I navigate the Sunday-quiet streets, arriving on the board-walk by the lake early enough to drink in some quiet time with Len and Iggy before Mr. West shows. The sky sags with steely clouds. I fold head to knees, warming inside my coat to keep my nose from turning red.

"Hi, Ari. Did I keep you waiting?"

"Waiting here is good. How's Zodiac?"

He sits close. "My parents were more excited about him than about seeing me."

I shuffle the pile of offered pictures. "He looks spectacularly happy."

"My mother has never let an animal on the furniture, but there she was calling him away from my dad to curl up beside her."

"Your family looks nice."

"There's no arguing I'm a lucky man." He holds my mittened

hand. "Zodiac told me that he'll be happy there, so you can rest your heart."

"I don't know how to thank you for this."

"I've lived a life in black and white. Yours is an unending adventure in Technicolor. Having your dog means we'll have to keep in touch. Let's set a date, third Sunday of every month we'll meet here and I'll give you updates."

Stripping the store out from under Jacquie had been the focus of Dick and Chick of Dick's combined twenty brain cells. Frightening, terrifying really, to see the bitterness set in as hope slips through their mismatched hands. It's finally sunk in that the store is gone, Jacquie has flown, and there's nothing legal or illegal they can do about it. Plan B: Step up the squashing of Hariet Appleton.

They have just over one year until I turn sixteen and can get the hell out. Minus a summer out east, that doesn't leave much time. Dick is a wily bastard, I'll give him that. Isolate the prey, easier to mess with them.

He sucks some day-old pork chop out from between his yellow teeth. "We're transferring you to Jarvis. You start Monday."

"The judge said I could stay at Birchmount."

"Well, I say you can't."

He can't torture my dog or my sister so I go to school as usual on Monday. I go Tuesday. Wednesday Mrs. Russell nudges my shoulder. "Ari, Mr. Hamilton needs to see you. Would you like me to come?"

I seize her hand when I see O'Toole, in uniform, outside the office. "I want my lawyer." We zip past him and close the door behind us.

Mr. Hamilton looks up from his papers and informs me that I have to leave.

"But, sir, the judge said I could stay."

"It was a recommendation, not a court order, and your parents are adamant." He itemizes their trumped-up charges. "They're concerned that your grades are dropping and they want you closer to home so you can help with your stepbrother."

"Mr. Hamilton, Ari lost her father, her grandmother, and her uncle this year. Not to mention the robbery and her sister leaving. That she's in school at all is a miracle let alone that her lowest mark is what? A sixty."

"A sixty-three. And I lost my tiny nephew and my dog, too, sir."

"Oh, Ari." Mrs. Russell moves in with too much poor-little-thing in her eyes and I bite hard on my inside cheek.

"Ari, I have no authority in this."

"Could you call and ask the judge?"

"I'll assist in any way I can but for now you have to go with the constable outside."

"No, sir. I'm not getting in a car with him."

"Ari, you have no choice." Mr. Hamilton nods through the glass.

The Tool ambles in. "All set?"

"Ari, go with the officer. We'll help you get this sorted."

"No, sir. I'll go to the school on my own and he can arrest me if I don't."

The Tool reaches out to incarcerate my arm.

"Don't touch me. Article 72, subsection five of the criminal code states that a female has the right under law to request the presence of a female officer at all times and can refuse transport if said female officer is not present."

"Don't make me carry you out over my shoulder."

"Refusal will result in disciplinary action and a fine of ten thousand dollars."

Mr. Hamilton stands, "Mrs. Russell, I'll cover your class.

Drive Ari to Jarvis Collegiate and deliver her records. Officer O'Toole, you can follow if you wish, but I think it would be in the best interest of the child to allow her a quiet admission."

"I have my orders."

Mr. Hamilton lifts the receiver. "What's your superior's number? I'm sure he'll find this arrangement agreeable."

"Fine." O'Toole backs out. "Just see it's done."

"Thank you, sir." I say. "That one has very sticky hands, and unfortunately, if you do want to talk to his superior officer on this particular mission it would be my mother's undercover cop."

Mr. Hamilton scratches his substantial hair. "Is that true, what you said? About the criminal code?"

"A complete fabrication, sir. Women have about as many rights as a potato slug."

Chase is on the hit list but the Dicks have no clue that mind-spirit love thrives on existential angst. He'd already taken up Iggy's mantle of finding me a quote a day, tucking it into the cracks of my old locker like sacred prayers offered to the Wailing Wall. Now that I'm banished from Birchmount, I find them tucked into my coat pocket or stuck to a telephone pole on my walk to school.

The Dick tries to get me fired from the Riverboat with threats of raids and harassment. Crystal told me Bernie stared him smack in the face and said, "Don't push me, you wormshit. You don't want my high friends in your low places. One call and every rock in your life will be turned. Even your hemorrhoids won't have a place to hide."

The Dick's pursuit loses steam when he needs a five and Mum is whining for a ten. Until they can figure out how to squeeze the golden egg out of me they'll pluck me, one feather at a time.

On Saturday, Aunt Sabina lets me use the workroom in the basement of the store. I leave half the shirts with her, loading the rest in a shopping bag.

Navigating the fire escape to my nest is tightrope-tricky with all the rations she's sent along.

Picture this: just nearing fifteen, tucked on my chair, drinking tea from a pudgy orange mug, and eating Sabina's raspberry-filled *paczki*. "Turn Turn Turn" playing in the background while I sew crystal beads on shirts, my Anne Frank assignment for school germinating in my head.

Saturday night at the Riverboat my tie-dyed creations peel off me as fast as I put them on. I sell them for eight bucks and most say "keep the change," from a ten. The band, a folk-rocky group with a little down-home flavour, has me jumping, and Shawn, lead singer in the band, has his sights on me being his bum warmer tonight. He's too much of a wake-up-with-a-different-girl-every-day guy for me, but he's also too music-full to be ignored. He kisses the mic. "Usually I'm the one tossing a shirt or two, but—" his guitar points to me—"tonight, I want that one." The crowd whoops as I peel and toss. He drapes it around his neck. "Girl, this one's for you—'Wild Thing' . . ."

I show off, catching body grooves around the room, because Ricky has stopped by tonight. When he leaves he kisses words into my ear. "I have to get to work. I'll see you tomorrow." He stays on my ear saying nothing and everything, then sponges up some of the salt sweat on my neck.

Three breaths away from sleep Chase pulls the hair away from my ear. "Ricky likes you."

"He makes life with the Dicks a step up from living in your standard rectum."

"Stay as untangled from that house as you can."

I turn toward him. "I have a choice? By law I'm anchored to that ship of ghouls. Besides, I wouldn't mind some kisses."

"Help yourself. Just don't forget it's darn near impossible to run with your pants down." His hand paints my face. "Just two and a half months and you can head east. I'm pulling for some summer lovin' for you and Jake." He closes my eyes. "Dream on that."

I surface in the small attic in my friend's arms. He groans at my escape. "Where're you going?"

"Anne Frank is calling me."

"Grab my book, too. We'll read together. And maybe hot chocolate. And Sabina's doughnuts."

"Anything else?"

"Can you piss for me? I'm too tired."

The featherbed captures us for hours. Through the barred window, the tail of a jet dissolves into absolute blue. "Anne was my age when she wrote this. I'm supposed to write a diary for an assignment, a curtain-opened week of my life. I don't think I know this new teacher well enough to barf up my truth."

"If you can't pen the truth then don't bother writing anything." Chase lifts his face to meet mine. "Is your new school okay?"

"Not so new. It's the oldest in Toronto. When I walked down the dark halls, I heard Auntie Nia say, 'Find the treasure.'"

"Have you found any?"

"My art teacher, Miss Burn, has potential. And Jasper gets all awhirl when it's time for English, but I've decided not to care. I'm just going to be one of the bricks and just watch, not feel anything or know anyone."

FORTY-ONE

Do I get, "Miss Appleton, may I see you?" more than any other kid on this planet?

I approach Mr. Ellis' desk. "Yes, sir."

"Just checking in. A change of schools during the third semester is never easy."

"Like a rolling stone."

"Pardon?"

"I keep a bag packed."

His eyes line up with his smile. "Your teacher from Birchmount tells me I can look forward to some brilliant writing."

"You talked to Mrs. Russell? Do teachers take a blathering oath or something?"

"Meddling is an optional course but I did my thesis on it. Purely selfish on my part. School bores the hell out of me. Do you need an extension on the assignment?"

He seems like a "worked late on my novel and didn't have time to shave" teacher. His hair is the black and white that puts him somewhere in the middle between the beginning and the end. Under his elbow-patched jacket, his shirt is punctuated with ink dots. I'm trying hard to hate everyone here but when he read aloud from Anne's diary today I got sucked in by the little catch in his voice.

"I'm not up to capturing my war on paper, sir. Can I just write an essay on the book?"

"Miss Burn says you're a gifted artist."

"She said that? Sheesh, am I the staff room freak topic?"

"Better. You were dinner table talk." ·

"You and Miss Burn?"

"Going steady for over thirty years now. Just so you know, we're annoying buggers. I'd like you to try the diary. An artist with a palette of words creates extraordinary things."

"Nicely said, sir. Can it be fiction? Like imagining I'm Anne."

"I want personal observations. An honest, unedited slice of your life."

"Do you have a supply of Pepto?"

"A case of it came with my grade nine teacher's kit."

"Who will read it?"

"Just me."

"I've heard that before. Spilled my guts only to have them stuck on a flagpole before God and country."

"Did you start writing with the rest of the class yesterday?"

"I gave it a go."

"Can I have a look?"

"Do you have a dog?"

"A hound. Bunny. Why?"

"Generally I trust dog people." I hand him my spiral notebook.

Monday, April 8, 1968 ~ Rising

Left-behind holes are bigger on Mondays. They're shaped like the sound 'corka' makes on my tongue and the windrush of legless flight. Spring sun is thin, barely wringing in the day. Devil girl—black-rooted, emerald-fingered, raccoon-eyed—dream-twitches under grey sheets. Her nipple, squished beneath her arm stares at me as much as to say, "Help, I can't breathe." I kill the alarm before it blares to avoid "fuck off" being the first words I hear today.

Under the hall light with the burnt-out bulb is the waiting spot for the throne room. This is the holy hour when all souls seek sanctuary, no, maybe deliverance. All I want is to wash off the reek of smoke and stale lives. Duchess of Dickdom is puking behind the closed door.

It's what I'll remember most about her when she flushes the last of her life down the toilet. The sound of retching is, I think, my earliest memory, back when Jasper and I were tiny seahorses swimming in the dark sea. Her distant whine still needles after fifteen years, "Christ, if I'm pregnant again I'll kill myself." A man, far off, answering, "If it's another bloody girl I'll save you the trouble . . ." Well, bloody girl I am, eh.

My leg hairs shiver as April's cool slips in with the opening of the front door, hurrying up the stairs ahead of The Soldier Boy. The third step squeaks under the weight of his filthy sock. The seventh step coughs. My white panties and undershirt blush pink from heat. He passes closer than needed in this narrow space and not close enough; one dirty finger tracing the scalloped lace, two fingers lagging behind on an inch of belly skin.

Empty, the Duchess opens the door, blind she passes. Blue silk kisses my arm. The brown stain on the back of her slip is an exact map of Italy. I review—in 1527 the Germans and Spaniards invaded Italy . . . I'm ready for my history test on the Renaissance.

Hungry Boy sleeps on the sofa, mouth open baby-bird wide. Turning off the hissing TV sends him chewing air and reshuffling his knotted shirt. I invite him to school with me but he mumbles something like "my ovaries are infected." It's as good an excuse as any.

Silent Child sits at the table with his porridge balanced on a crumb-lined pizza box. The sound of me saying no to Frosted Flakes "Eat your oatmeal," makes me an old prune. Silent Child claws the air in defense of the flakes and I tell him that Tony the Tiger doesn't really think they're great and Mr. Kellogg is a big fat liar.

Ratty sneakers and go-go boots mound up together

as the Big Dick ploughs open the door. This wind is colder, like winter knows him by heart. Misery follows him in. Flakes ping an unwashed bowl like iced-rain hitting a window. The box teeters on the counter-clutter, spilling onto the worn linoleum. Menacing police-issue shoes crush, crush, crush as he milks and extra sugars the mountain of cereal. With the *Daily Star* captured in his armpit, bowl in right hand, lukewarm tea in the left he pushes his bulk up the stairs.

Silent Child and I exit night, lock the door, and enter day while the house sleeps.

Mr. Ellis closes the book, slow. "Shit."
"Sir?"
"Holy shit."
I pull.
He tugs. "Let me give it another read."
A good yank gives me ownership and I back to the door.
"What's wrong?"
"Some things aren't safe on paper."
"You have to write the rest of it with the same honesty."
"If I'm murdered over this it'll be your fault."
"Fair enough." His pen misses his pocket, adding a blue squiggle to his shirt. "Is Jasper your brother? He's the only one you name."

"I don't know you well enough for that one." I retreat a few more steps. "Let's just say he's the only one who has never left me."

Cooking is easy when everything goes into a big pot with Mrs. Butters' secret flavourings and plays together for a few hours, yet the Little Dicks always seem astounded. Ricky steals a taste, licking his lips slow. Todd needs a small bowl before dinner. I navigate a sample toward Mikey's mouth but he clamps shut. I crouch low. "Mikey, it'll be okay. How about you and Ricky go get crusty buns to go with the stew." I button his jacket. "I know some better ways not to hurt so much. Will you let me show you?"

His skinny arms seize my neck and my hands hold him soft around the get-over-here bruises and the I've-had-it-with-you smacks.

Mikey's teacher summoned the Dick to discuss the zippered mouth problem. Now he returns slamming mad. "Where's that fucking ass-wipe?"

"He went with Ricky to get some bread." I dole out a beer. "Can I say something, sir?"

"Can I stop you?"

"Well, you've got more than a hundred pounds of muscle over me, and a belt, and a gun."

Ricky filled me in that it drives the Dick squirrelly that he thinks he's spawned dumber-than-dirt offspring. Hope ran big for Mikey. His would be the report card the Dick would finally be able to shove in his own father's face and say, "See what a smart kid I made?"

The Dick stares at me and does this soothing thing, rubbing the bristles of his head back and forth, back and forth. "What smart-ass thing do you have to say?"

"I know you think that I think I'm smart, but who I really think is smart is Mikey. Trouble is he's as mule-headed and steel-willed as you. Stupid people spout off their mouths. Think of the guts Mikey has to take the whippings you give him instead of just giving in."

"The little shit's going to fail grade two, for fuck's sake. They're bringing in the bloody school shrink . . . he's stupid and nuts."

"What else does he have to bargain with? He can pass and he can talk. You just have to give him a good reason to."

"And what would that be? He's not living with that loser mother."

"You're the cop. Negotiate with him."

The door opens and the breadmen trudge in.

"But for certain, a whack will just make him dig in deeper."

Maybe the Dick is a grain above dirt-dumb. He separates his thoughts like he does the carrots from the stew, setting the ones Mikey won't like aside. "Your teacher says you're good at math and she liked that project on butterflies. She thinks all your subjects are good but she can't pass you if you don't do the talking pieces. She says you might be a good reader but how's she going to know if she doesn't hear it, eh?"

Mikey dips his bread and eats a little.

"Sometimes your old man has to negotiate with a bad guy. I give a little, he gets a little. Maybe if you start talking at school we can come to an understanding here. Can we give that a try, kid?"

Mikey raises his head, coming as close to a nod as he can.

Mr. Ellis helps himself to the chair beside me. "Are you hiding?"

"I prefer libraries to cafeterias."

"Can I see Tuesday's entry?"

"I decided not to do one." He deflates, like I've just squashed his imaginary friend. "Oh, don't get sulky. I wrote one, sir. You just make me jittery."

"Yeah, I make myself jittery." He taps his pencil. "Do you want to be a writer?"

"An artist, I think."

"I'm going to fight Mina for you."

Ari, an English and art teacher are fighting over us. Give it to him. Give it.

Jasper makes me slide my assignment over. "I swear, you betray me and I'll never write another word."

Tuesday, April 9, 1968 ~ Staying Awake

There are memory noises in this decrepit house: coughs
and creaks, groans and shudders. All the houses that
have kept me, slept me, have written their own songs.
Skyfish was ocean lullabies and goddess whispers.
Aquarius: spring wake after a long winter.

There's a room inside me, northeast of my centre,
where I store all the old sounds. Jasper taught me how to
get back to some places and escape others by travelling
through time and space. Seeing that distances keep
forcing their way into my life, it's perhaps the best gift
he's ever given me.

Jasper tells me, too, when to sleep and when to stay
awake. Anne knows what I mean. I'm talking to her in
my head, comparing where we find ourselves holed up
and where we've been. Anne isn't where she wants to
be but she's hearing a lot of music in the small annex.
When I tell her there's just noise in the craphouse she
wants to slap me. She could, too, there's that much
spunk in her; and a smack for complaining would be fair,
considering the way things turned out for her. I sense
her smile, the way girls do when there's talk about boys.
"Hungry Boy is a fart on a tuba. Soldier Boy is like drums
that vibrate through your bones. But, Silent Child is
the moment the conductor lifts his hand and the theatre
holds its breath for the first note. See? There's music in
the craphouse, Ari."

She's wise and I want to hear her voice but the
warning squeak of the third and seventh step hushes
her. Like me, she knows about listening for the footsteps
in the hall. The Tool stops outside my door. In wake-
dreams, I see through doors, Tool's bulk, shoulder to

shoulder, tip to toe, his hand thinking over the brass knob. I hear his thoughts, "Just one look at her sleeping. Just a touch there, and—there." His foot shadow turns, leaving behind a line of light below the door. Toilet flushes. I catch the hiss of his fly zipping and his descent on the stairs. His black Camaro starts up, bullying away the quiet on the two a.m. street.

Anne says, "Now there's music."

"What? The Tool leaving?"

"The toilet. You never think of it as a sweet sound until you're not allowed to flush."

Maybe there's a lot of music not heard until it's gone.

I talk to invisible people and I hear voices. Every word said is kept in a room inside me, another one, slightly west of my centre. Jasper never lets me throw out a single one. He says the dirty, rotting words are good fertilizer. Before I sleep, Anne wants to know which jewel in the room is my favourite. I pick three because she's waited out the dark with me. These treasures shine even on a moonless night: I'm not dirt; I am clay. I'm more worth than I am trouble. And my newest gem that warms me, centre of centre, Shit—Holy Shit.

My book closes like a sleepy eye. Silence. I hear Auntie Mary's voice, "Back away from the heat, Ari. You have to wait and see what comes out of the kiln." I take my book and head to math, noticing things without sound: the patchwork window light covering the hall and how the jock's big high-top looks beside the beauty's black patent slipper. The sweet stink of overripe banana leaking from the cafeteria. The classroom door sanded smooth by arm-brushes that no longer remember it was once a great oak. Cool boys sprawl, one leg perched on the seat in front to hold their size and confidence. Pretty girls sit straight, shoulders back.

Most hunch, hiding, sleeping, brooding . . . I open my book and write "Wednesday, April 10, 1968, Sitting." A girl, hair the colour of burnt umber against paper-white skin places a plaid-wrapped toffee on my desk. "Hi, I'm Natasha. Is it true you moved here from Russia?"

What story are we in, Jasper? "Um, I'm not at liberty to say. It might endanger what's left of my family."

"You want to come over to my house after school?"

I negotiate words around the sticky candy, "Have to pick up my brother."

"Saturday you could come."

"I work."

She wrinkles her nose and her freckles bunch into tiny flowers. "Well, Nat, how about lunch tomorrow? My treat."

I want to hate it here. Sulk like a mistreated dog through-out my high school years but I fit in. Jarvis has more kids with fucked-up lives than any school in the burbs. You get credit for the torture situations, not murdered for them. Even volleyball holds promise. Being tall, I can block things, and all my teacher had to do was lift the ball in front of my face and say, "This is the head of the person who has screwed you most." Turns out I can smash and serve, and I swear I leave a dent on the floor when I spike. The teacher says she's going to call the Dick and get permission for me to play the final games with the junior girls' team and I wish her luck.

Second period art has Jasper sucked right in. Miss Burn returns my sketchbook. "Excellent work on perspective, Ari." Three shiny stones: turquoise, amber, and black sit atop the book. "Ellis asked me to give you these in return for the gems you gave him." I turn the smooth stones over in my hand. I like what's come from this kiln. "Any chance I could read what has him so worked up?"

"He swore an oath of secrecy."

207

"He hasn't told me a thing and he's pretty smug about it."

"Yesterday's piece inspired a sketch, too, so maybe—"

"Let me see, let me see."

I dig out the notebook, turning to a double-page ink drawing of the nest inside the attic. A forest in a room. Mary-deer rolling cinnamon buns. Nia-bear carving wood as she sits in my chair. A whole ocean inside the sink. The rafters opening to the sky, and Uncle Iggy flying to the fiddling seahorse.

"What is this place?"

"Where I really live."

"A dolphin and a tiger in a bed?"

"It's a snow leopard. It's hard to get it right when I'm drawing so small."

"Is that a giraffe and a lion in the oven?"

"A kiln. We're just hanging, solidifying dust into life."

"The only colour is the yellow door."

"From my perspective, there's always a yellow door. Sometimes it's right in front of you, other times you have to travel great distances to find it, but there's always one there."

She flips to the words.

I snatch the book. "Those are for Mr. Ellis."

I catch Mr. Ellis before lunch. "Thank you for the stones, sir."

His hair looks like an untended lawn, full of a whole universe down at the roots. I place my book on his palm. "Just so you don't get jittery, the teacher isn't you. Not that I don't think you're cool, but this one saved my dog."

Wednesday, April 10, 1968 ~ Sitting

I've grown too tall to be small, yet I'm too full of
questions to sprawl out my long length in confidence,
and I'm too full of strength to cower scared over my
desk. How do I sit? I bend a little, willow-like, I pour

over books a little ocean-like, and I always float a little too dream-like . . .

Mr. Ellis glances up, searches my face, but I'm not scared of him peeking at my inside rooms. He returns to the page for a long, slow read to the end.

. . . In the nest there are no teacher-can't-love-me rules. Here West meets East. Existential Love warms me for now.

Anne asks, "Where's Jasper? I can't see him."

"Look close. He's always the opening from nowhere to somewhere."

He looks up, shaking his head at me. "I haven't a clue what half of it means, but I feel it, I see it, and on some level I understand it completely. How are you doing this?"

"Just letting the voices in my head bleed through my fingers. You can let Miss Burn read it. But nobody else."

"Why, Ari? Your writing should be read."

"You ever been interrogated by Children's Aid for something you wrote?"

"Can't say that I have. Have you?"

"My seventh grade teacher got all Amish about an exposé I wrote, 'Granny's House of Weenies.' I had to sit down with Sigmoid Freud for twelve weeks. Could have been out in two but I had no idea that 'Of course, don't you?' was the wrong answer to, 'Do you hear voices?'"

"Did it help any?"

"Scared me more than anything. He poked at the bruises in the Appleton bushel and told me my rosy attitude was a big fat lie. Apparently, I'm really sad and angry. I do give despair a good try now and then, but it's exhausting."

"Maybe Sigmoid should've read between the lines of your essay." His head tilts kind-like. "Putting weenies on a page is a great way to lighten burdens. And just so you know, I hear voices, too. A guy named Rochester is my best friend."

Next to seahorses, the ancient turtle is my most loved spirit and I sense a kinship ahead between Jasper and Rochester. I start away to collect Mikey.

"Hey, I couldn't find Jasper either. It would help if I knew what I was looking for."

"Guess I'm writing a mystery."

A sock puppet named Screed covers Mikey's hand. His teacher made it for him to use as a friend who can talk for him and now his silence is slowly unravelling. So far he has fourteen stars for whispering through Screed, things like "seven" or "may I go to the bathroom," or "thank you." I promised ice cream as a reward.

Ricky meets us on the sidewalk. "It's not safe to go in. The old man's pissed."

"Why?"

"Ronnie got picked up for shoplifting again. Laura's bailing this weekend, and your mom couldn't account for her whereabouts this afternoon. The old man thinks she was fucking in exchange for shit. Wait here. I'll tell him we're going for groceries."

While I lighten my bag of its books and pile them up onto the porch I hear volcanic lava spewing out the door. I hurry away from the molten shit with Mikey in tow. Things must be really terrible when Todd comes huffing along behind Ricky. I consider going back and trying to talk him down but I'm not up to explaining another black eye to anyone. Mum has two legs and can walk herself out of her own mess, and if she's murdered, then I'll try to find an inch in me to be sad.

Over hamburgers I learn Todd just turned seventeen. "I thought Ronnie was seventeen."

Ricky plays with a pickle speared on his straw. "Dick's dick was busy that year."

Mikey pulls my braid and Screed whispers, "Where's Mikey's mommy?"

I nudge Ricky under the table with my foot. "Screed wants to know why Mikey isn't going to his mom's this weekend."

Ricky sucks up the dregs of his coke. "Easter is a busy time in the restaurant business. She's making some overtime cash. Ari and I will take you somewhere tomorrow. Okay, buddy?" Mikey eats up while I drink a little from Ricky's eyes.

If I ever want a conversation with Todd it will have to be over something other than eating. Grocery shopping gives us the very thing needed. Outside the store, a winter-coated German shepherd is tied to a pole. It has a sinister smile. I back away but Todd offers a lick of his hamburgered fingers and within thirty seconds he performs a deep knee bend, diving face first into the dog's neck.

"You like dogs, Todd?"

"I had two before we moved to hell." He struggles to his feet. "The bastard put them down."

"I know what that's like. My neighbour promised to keep my dog for me. They said she bit their kid. Jinx was so gentle she'd say sorry to her food before biting it." I brush his knees. "Where did those other two go?"

"Inside the store."

"Come on, before they pick out ham for Easter dinner. I can't tolerate it."

Todd's cheeks plump with a rare smile. "Me either."

Upon return to crapdom we see that the loons are exiting the roost. Ronnie heads out, slutted to the nines. Mum clicks down the stairs in (leopard skin capris, plunging backline sweater, inch-thick makeup), her hair a mop of wet spirals. "Richard and I are going for a drink before his shift. Hariet, can you spot me a five?"

I give her a ten because I want her gone. By some miracle she finds room for it in her pinch-tight bra. "Night, kids. Not too late. It's a school night."

Don't they celebrate Good Friday on her planet?

Ethanol and ether but no Easter, Jasper.

Ricky and I slow dance the groceries away. He says, "I forgot places are closed tomorrow. Where could we take Mikey?"

"We'll go to Aquarius and make stuff. Why did his mom really bail?"

He checks the living room then backs me into the pantry. "She's strung out again. My old man's a magnet for fucked-up broads. Sorry, I didn't mean. . ." A strand of my hair coils around his finger until his palm holds my cheek.

"You get no argument from me." We're out of sight and a little out of mind. His lips hover mint-breath close and I wonder when he brushed his teeth and wish I'd thought to brush mine. He's James Dean beautiful and I have to have one kiss before he gives his life for this country.

He whispers, "I should get to work." It only takes a small stretch to touch his lips. I steal a small, scared kiss and he gives me back a long, confused holding. "I have to go."

Jasper pinches. *We love Jake.*

We're not giving him our heart. Just testing our other parts to make sure they're working.

Thursday, April 11 ~ Absorbing

How long before where we are becomes who we are? Do dirty lives leech into our marrow? Change our molecular structure? "Anne, who would you have become if there had been an afterward?"

Todd enters Devil Girl's cave with a mug of hot chocolate for me. An act of humanness I didn't know was in him. I guess kneeling before a shedding dog was all it took for his heart to feel full enough that it was safe to give something to someone else.

"Thanks, Todd."

"*Fort Apache* is on the late show. You wanna watch it?"

"I'd like to but," I fan my notebook, "homework."

"Sure. Night."

About midnight, O'Toole brings the Duchess home. Giggles, moans, "*jesusfuckingchrist*," ooze through the wall.

I know where Devil Girl keeps her stash. Taking the edge off would mercifully open the room behind my left eye that is soundproof and soft-walled.

Jasper smacks me. *How does that make you any different than her? Todd's with Mikey. Let's get out of here.*

Pack over my shoulder. Out the window. Across the roof. Long legs easily reaching the wood box. Through the overgrown backyard. Over the fence and down the lane. When volleyball finishes I'll run track because tonight not even the wind can catch me.

I climb into my nest, turn the water hottest-hot, open my pores, and absorb, just absorb . . . the quiet, the fragrance of lavender. Cocooning in my bed I drift toward dreams of turning pots with my Spirit Father.

Anne would've been okay because that kitty inside her was really a tiger.

Right as usual, Jasper.

The Dick's sedan is parked out front. If he's already conducted a bed check I'll have given away the sneaking out route and my window will be nailed and barred. I breathe deep, walk down the street, and in the front door. The Dick glares down the hall.

"Morning, sir."

"Where the hell have you been?"

"Sunrise Mass."

"What time did you go out?"

"Umm . . . around five?"

"What time did your mother get home?"

"Ah . . . before eleven."

He grumbles like he has cabbage gas. "You watch the kid this weekend. Your mother and I have plans."

"But I work—"

"Then you damn well better figure something out."

"Can't Todd watch him?"

"If the kid was a TV." He fart-laughs through his nose.

"Can I arrange a sleepover at my friend's house?"

"I don't care what the fuck you do as long as you're back here to cook after Mass on Sunday. There'll be five extra for supper. Put a turkey on."

"I don't know how to cook a turkey."

"Fucking learn."

At the corner of Jarvis and Dundas, Mikey, Ricky, and I pile into Chase's car. As we pull away I close my eyes and see a girl peering through a small attic window who in two years never got a minute of escape.

I'm sorry, Anne.

The city puts on its reverent face for the sacrificial lamb hung on the tree. A green striped awning hangs over empty fruit shelves. A thin man in a thin suit opens a car door for a solid woman and two plump girls. The Clock Shoppe's sign is turned to closed.

April 12, 1968 ~ Good Friday?

Jasper likes riding on the dashboard. He always has.
Windows looking back made me too sulky to be with. He
takes in the empty streets and asks, "How do you think
this Jesus thing is working out?"
　　"Hard to say. It sure turned out terrible for Anne."

Chase moves his sweater to let me get closer. "You okay?"
　　"When the Dick said he and Mum had plans I got a little
hopeful, like maybe they had friends or were going to hear some
music."
　　"What are they up to?"
　　"The owner of Club Top Hat gave the Dick a coupon. Their
big plans are getting loaded in Scarborough for a change. How's
it possible to get so abandoned on the inside?"
　　"As species evolve they lose what they don't use." He nudges
me. "And some evolve through loss."

A day of creating at Aquarius makes for a good Friday. Ricky
surveys balsa aircraft coming together under the engineering
expertise of seven- and eight-year-old boys in the yard below,
then lifts his head to the hint of green on the treetops. I climb out
the window to the fire escape. "What's up?"
　　"I hardly got to know Iggy, but he was the kind of guy you'd
want for your grandpa. He didn't have to help me study, but he
did anyway. I wish I could show him this and say thanks." Ricky
pulls an envelope from his pocket.
　　"Did you get in?"
　　Trying to hold his smile in makes it spill out his eyes. We
teeter in a hug, then our faces tilt, locking us in a happy-scared-
desperately-want-you kiss. His lips travel to my forehead; his

215

arms pulling me closer, closer. "Sorry, I shouldn't have done that to Chase."

"Chase is okay sharing me in kisses. He's just not open to tanglings that will keep me, or you, in the craphouse." We unwind and watch Otto struggle with the old Ford in the yard below. "Last night I knew I'd suffocate if I had to stay there. It'll kill you, too." I trace the grease-etched lines on his hand. "You shouldn't love anything here that will hold you back from the adventures waiting."

He searches my face. "Too late for that." I help myself to another kiss because up here among the trees it seems like what we should do. *Ricky and Ari, sitting in a tree* . . . His kiss comes back with a tiny bit of tongue, not sloppy Paris France kissing, just a little Mount Royal, Quebec. He pulls away from the kiss but not from me. "Don't you love Chase?"

"We love each other completely, so we're completely owned and completely free."

"Huh?"

"Can't be explained. Just don't weight yourself down with shame about a kiss."

"Think I better show Otto how to get that heap purring." I watch him down the steps. His ass has nothing on Mr. West's, but his shoulders are fine.

Sabina packs a Good Friday feast. The afternoon warms and the airplanes are ready for test flights. Chase hands Ricky a rolled up kite. "This will do it. Let's go fly her."

"Do what?"

I push Ricky toward the loaded truck. "You'll see."

When we're at the lake, I sit on the boardwalk, further along but still the same boardwalk where Len left me. The hurt tangles with Mikey's laugh as he launches spitfires in the wake of his spirit cousins.

Chase holds the unfurled kite while Ricky prepares to sprint. I have a feeling it's catching this time and Iggy will see what Chase painted on top: *Iggy, I got in. Thanks, Ricky.*

"I miss you, Papa." I search the sky for *my* message.

"Come eat, *corka*." Sabina extends her long-fingered hand.

"Auntie Bee, will you teach me what the frig I'm supposed to do with a turkey?"

"Tomorrow. This day is for worship."

"How do you worship?"

"When the sun falls we will dance along with the fire."

Saturday morning the old Ford returns with twenty-one fresh-killed turkeys. Twenty for the St. Vincent de Paul and one for me.

Sabina and I walk to the market with her basket cart. We circle the aisles in the dance of feastsecrets passed from one generation to the next. She pushes my wallet aside. A holy offering to me.

The air smells like apples as we saunter home, and my memories taste sweet.

Saturday, April 13, 1968 ~ Offerings

Before the craphouse, when I lived among my spirit family, the Duchess called the Bee a witch, not a bitch witch, a spell kind of witch. Watching her weave, hearing her bracelets tinkle like chimes, tasting delicious old-world secrets passed down from her *Babcia*, made me long to be a witch.

When the Bee's pockets bulged from her hard work, the Duchess called her a Jew. I thought I'd like to be that, too; after all, it was so close to a Jewel and I'd longed to be that for as long as I could remember.

"During the war we lived months on turnip soup and black bread." Sabina lifts her face to the burnished trees. "But on special days Babcia would miraculously surprise us with a little sausage or cake. And, there would always be enough for anyone who stopped by."

Jasper swings in my hair. *I want to be like Miep who shared everything she had with Anne and the others. I wish there was a war so I could.*

We're in combat with the Dick.

Yeah. Maybe making a kid feel safe is the best battling.

From all the poppied fields we've tromped, Jasper, I have to agree.

I have a list of what goes on when. The bird has to be in the oven by eight and it's nearing seven. Chase yells down to the basement, "Car's loaded. Let's go."

I rummage through the racks of old Pennyworth's stock, filling two bags before returning to crapdom. By the time the Dick stumbles in at nine, turkey aroma fills the kitchen. Ricky is peeling potatoes and Mikey, carrots.

The Dick rumbles, "Where's the others?"

"Mum's pulling herself together. Todd's getting dressed and Ronnie's comatose."

He grunts up the stairs to launch Ronnie. Ricky smiles at me. "You look real pretty, Ari."

I turn to his glance over my shoulder and whistle. "Pretty snappy, Todd. Told you they'd fit."

He pulls a navy blazer over his white shirt and grey pants. "This was nice of you."

Mum feels her way into the kitchen looking more like a stewardess than a Church Street hooker.

Shaved, showered, and in a suit, the Dick is still an ugly Dick. "Is she still not outta bed? I'm going to fucking kill her if

218

she doesn't get her ass to church."

Ricky herds Mikey and me toward the door. "We'll walk and save seats."

Easter miracle: Todd passes on a second breakfast to come along. We snag a row when the masses change Masses, playing rock-paper-scissors to see who has to sit beside "The Hood, the Sad, and the Ugly." Ricky loses.

One minute to spare and looking like shit squashed into my kitten sweater, Ronnie plunks into the pew, followed by an unexpected Tool and, just when I think my definition of scum can't go any lower, his broken-down wife with a rounded belly and one saggy-diapered, grey-socked toddler collapse beside him. We squish down to accommodate the Duchess and I wonder at a God of lightning bolts who doesn't fry the pecker of a creep sitting in *His* house with all his little fucks all in a row.

Twenty minutes in and I wonder why *someone* isn't helping the mother at the back with her three squalling kids. Jasper bites my ear. *Hey, Ari, we're someone.* So I navigate over Todd. Mikey follows. We start with a game of Screed peekaboo over the back of the last pew and end with the brood being released into our custody to be entertained on the foyer steps. The littlest one, smelling like moldy bread, holds Jasper tender-like in the palm of her hand; the middle kid talks to Screed; and the oldest, maybe five years, follows the movement of my pencil. "Hey, Mikey, get me one of the envelopes over there." I tuck last night's tips and shirt sales, a grand total of one hundred and fifty-four dollars, into one. Jasper smiles as I write in my fanciest script: "For my daughter, the gift of Easter. We are born again in our children. Yours are precious. Love, The God of our Mothers."

We return the trio before the benediction just in case their mother has it in her mind to sneak out without collecting them. Mikey slips the envelope into her hand while I try to make a clean getaway.

The Dick incarcerates my shoulder as I dash toward the streetcar. "Where the hell do you think you're going?"

"Ah . . . to . . . the cemetery to pay my respects to my loved ones on this holiest of days."

"You've work to do."

"The turkey has hours to cook and everything else is ready to go on when the paper says. Todd said he'd do it."

"Home you get."

"No, sir. You can murder me but then who's going to mash your friggin' potatoes?" I walk jelly-legged away, ready for the sharp death bullet between my shoulders. Only that could stop a third-Sunday rendezvous.

My last diary entry percolates in my head as Mr. West walks toward me, blue-jeaned and leather-jacket fine. "Deep in thought?"

"Probably thoughts I shouldn't be having on Easter Sunday."

He sits close. "Like what?"

"Like, I don't think the God of our Fathers is so great."

"I wonder about real."

"You don't believe in God?"

"Let's just say I'm on a fact-finding mission and I'm open to all possibilities."

"Let me know if you figure anything out."

"Only if you'll do the same for me."

"Len and I used to talk like this all the time. Sometimes the only thing that keeps my cells from deflating is the belief that he's in the air that I breathe. And that his goodness is in what I exhale into the world."

"You're an old soul."

"More of an odd soul, I'd say." My arm rests against his goodness. "Am I allowed to ask how old you are?"

"Sure. Twenty-five."

"You ever going to get married and have kids?"

"I have a long list I want to get through first."

"Like what?"

"Last year I went to the Great Wall."

"In China? Far out, in the literal."

"This year I'm going to cross the Taj Mahal off my list."

"I just want to go as far east as Nova Scotia and never move again." I tuck up my legs as an easel for the photos he hands me. "Zodiac good?"

"You might have to move west because my family loves him." I shuffle through the pile. He taps a picture. "I used to skinny dip in that pond." We eye-lock for a long minute. He exhales a low, "Oh, God. I'm sorry."

"Please, don't be. It's nice you talk to me like a friend."

He straightens a little. "Belle told me they yanked you out of Birchmount."

"Whatever they do to me I keep catching lucky breaks. My art and English teachers make me happy, even when it's Monday and that means a full week in the craphouse." My head turns from its rest on my knee. "How come I get all the great teachers like you?"

"Once, when I was snorkeling off the Baja Coast I saw a seahorse. An explosion of sea life whirled about but I couldn't take my eyes off this impossible shape balancing on a thread of seaweed." He measures the sky. "You're like that. You attract people with that same kind of impossible magic."

"You don't think I'm crazy for trundling around a seahorse in my pocket?"

"I grew up in church, remember. People talked to imaginary beings all the time. Yours seems more rational and fair to me. If you called him Jesus instead of Jasper you'd get ribbons in Sunday school."

"Jennah says hearing voices makes me schizo."

"You're just off balance because of all the craziness around you."

"When are you going to let your inner animal out?"

"What you see is what you get."

"I see it plain as plain, bumping at all the walls inside you, trying to break free."

He turns, eyes expanding with a six-year-old's anticipation. "What do you see?"

"You have to discover it, but I will tell you it loves water, big open water."

His laugh coats a little nervousness. "That's why you get all the great teachers. You tempt them with possibility."

I check my watch. "Prepare yourself for this turn on wonderment. This morning I stuffed a turkey's asshole and now I'm going to stuff a bunch of assholes with turkey."

"Like I said, magic."

Two forty five has me home and everything cooking according to the list. An aged and shrivelled replica of the Dick sits on the sofa. "Dad, this is Theresa's girl."

His face lemon-curdles. "Look at the size of this. What are you? Six foot two?"

She just looks big 'cause you're a weenie prune.

Hush, Jasper.

The Irwin boys and I make a damn good team at getting up a turkey dinner with all the trimmings. No one has any trouble shovelling it in but me. I can't stomach the senior Dick and his constant go-round of crap: useless, son of useless, whores and sluts and bastards and losers. He calls me "the bean," "the freak"—endearments mixed with sentimental things like, "You'd need a giant cock on ya to fuck that Jolly Green . . ." The shrivelled Dick shines a whole new light on the gaping hole in the big Dick's chest. I wonder if the Dick ever heard "You're a good little boy" even once in his life.

While the kitchen team scrapes dishes the big Dick comes sniffing for more pie. "Good job, kids, that was really great."

Silence descends. We stare at one another, ready to fall on our knees at the Resurrection of Christ Almighty.

Sunday April 14, 1968 ~ Resurrection

I might hate the God of our Fathers or I might not believe in Him at all. If I'm Catholic I'm headed to purgatory to earn my way out. If I'm Protestant, I'd better prepare myself for fire. If I'm Jewish, I'm not exactly sure what I'm in for but Anne tells me I'll be returning to my ancestors, which could make for an unsettling eternity. Jasper says if I'm honest with how pissed I am with the whole mess I may just find the truth.

After Mass, I disobeyed the Dick, walked south, and sat east of West. He's brave enough to say "I don't know." He's looking at all possibilities.

On the Queen streetcar back to crapdom I stayed present in the "I don't know." I looked out the window and fell under my skin, tumbling toward possibilities. I opened the room where I turn pots with my Spirit Father. He always shows me that in the clay we are born and born again. Behind the room is a field of sea-blown grass where Mother God walks. Step through the grass and there is a meadow that folds into a dappled wood. Inside the wood is a vast ocean, inside the ocean is an expanse of heaven, inside the heaven is a star and inside the star is a room and inside the room is a chair and on the chair is a small girl, eagle wings folded tight behind her back, tucked under her bum where the feathers tickle bare legs. And in the centre of her centre is a little seahorse that says, "God of our Fathers, I do not believe you are good

and you should say how very sorry you are to Anne.
Amen."

Jasper doesn't mind the dark. He says here we see
things that disappear in the light. Watch close and you'll
see it, the tiny flicker of faith that looks inside the room
and sees outside the walls.

FORTY-TWO

Auntie Elsie has perfect pitch; knows when a note is off by a dust
mote. I have perfect pinch. I know when a touch is off or perfect
the instant it hits the lightfield around my body. On Monday, my
diary lands with the others on Mr. Ellis' desk. Wednesday Miss
Burn stands at my shoulder watching me draw a guitar resting on
yards of scarlet silk. Her palm connects with a few strands of my
hair. "Is Jasper your soul?"

I shade the space beneath the guitar's long neck. "A soul can
be lost."

She's silent, her soul touching mine, telling me she loves the
hush of the ocean and the brush of forest things, too. *Perfect touch.*

In English class Judy asks, "Have you read our Anne Frank
assignments, sir?"

"It's difficult to digest hundreds of pages of drama in two
days. Perhaps by next week. Tell me what you learned from the
exercise."

"Um . . . gratefulness for what I have."

"And the rest of you?"

Answers fly: "I have a boring life." "To appreciate freedom." "My mother sucks, too." "I hate writing." "I love writing."

"How about you, Ari?"

I feel betrayed that he's turned the heads to me and asked for an intimacy. I sort through all of it, tossing thoughts that could potentially water my eyes, landing at the end of the book with few possibilities. "In her last entry, Anne wishes she could find a way to become what she could be if people would stop getting in the way, but they're the reason she becomes even more than she ever dreamed possible."

Tim jokes, "What? Toast?"

"No, a voice for peace that transcends generations. We become what we become because of other people, and because of what we do with whatever they throw into our lives. I've never read of more messed-up people messing up a kid's life, or of more courage from people like Miep and Bep." The pages fan across my fingers. "Anne took it all and created this."

"Good place to end," says Mr. Ellis. The class folds and unfolds. "Tomorrow, there will be Frost."

"No, sir, it's supposed to be warm."

Mr. Ellis whips a sea sponge at Sean and gives me the *wait behind* chin up. A knot of eager minds wanting his attention blocks the door. I try to slip through and he soft-grabs my arm. *Perfect.* He unravels questions with answers until just him and I remain. He leans arm-folded against the door jamb. I wait for a Holy Shit or a What the Fuck? He doles out his words in little tastes. "Possibly, my memory fails me after thirty years of teaching, but I believe your assignment is the best writing I've ever received from a student. That includes the years I taught at college." His hand on my arm is a good father's you-are-a-magic-girl touch and I believe more than ever in *Shit. Holy Shit.* I turn to hide my pathetic grin and move toward gym class. "Hey, Ari. Is Jasper your Spirit?"

I walk backwards. "People turn to spirits and leave me all the time. I told you Jasper has never bailed."

"Hang on. Mina and I have a student writer's circle at our place on Friday nights. Would you consider joining the group?"

"I work Fridays."

"Where?"

"The Riverboat. Excuse me, sir, I have a volleyball to murder."

My feet never behave in the presence of rock and roll. It's the price I pay for letting the East Coast soak in through my toes. I watusi a full tray around and pony an empty one back to the kitchen. Times when I possess only my order pad, I'm an arms-in-the-air dervish, which is how I come smack up against Miss Burn followed by a clump of Jarvis seniors. Mr. Ellis dances *Idon'tgiveashit* free behind the group. He shouts, "We decided on a field trip."

I yell over bass too big for the small room. "Great place for a character study."

I catch Mina's ear and point to the bar. "That one is Soldier Boy. And there's Existential Love. How friggin' lucky am I?"

"Is Jasper here?"

"He's swimming in the pool of sweat in my bra."

At midnight Chase and I walk the herd of them outside. The cool air shiver-bumps my hot skin and Chase warms me. Mina asks, "Chase, do you know who Jasper is?"

"Intimately." Music spills up the stairs and we sway in a back-to-front dance.

"Okay. I'll tell a little story about Jasper. On one of my adventures I lived with the Woburns. A nice old pair but they had this rodent situation that got very noisy whenever the house got ready for bed. I couldn't sleep for fear some toothy rat was going to help himself to my nose. Jasper would sit on my pillow, whispering, 'That's just bunnies chewing away the wall. See there? A violet meadow and a picnic by the little brook with Jinxie and her new puppies.' He promised if I closed my eyes I'd see right through walls. He wasn't lying."

Mina connects with my ear. "Jasper is your imagination."

The song "I'm a Believer" somersaults up the stairs. I jump my way back to work while Ellis whines, "What? What is it?"

"I also met Soldier Boy and Existential Love."

"Like hell you—"

Thankfully, on the night of the big game, Mum sports a tight-sweater stretch-pants slut ensemble not the cheerleader mini. I, on the other hand, or leg as it were, am forced out of my sweats and into a slinky little regulation get-up. The Dick has embraced the volleyball thing after all. It doesn't thrill him like when Ricky played hockey, but having people think he's the parent of a kid on a sport team makes him kind of goofy—and oblivious to questions rising about the belt bruises on my exposed arms and legs.

For the most part I'm useless but I do three things really well: jump and block, jump and smash, and serve. I do that with a little jump, too, and those three things turn out to be the best way to get points. So Ari Zajac becomes a member of the junior girls quarter-final winning volleyball team which earns me a get-out-of-crapdom card on a Wednesday night with Chase and Ricky. I glance back at the empty stands. *Soon you'll see Aunties M&N.*

But not Papa.

He's here, Ari.

Life imitates volleyball—every up has a down. The day after the big game some bruise analyst dispatches Mrs. Vandervolt, child protector, to the craphouse. If I play it right, a get-out-of-crapdom card could be mine. The Dick tells her that I fell out the window sneaking out to see a boy.

"Is that what happened, Ari?"

Mikey clings to me like a terrified squid. There's been a wobbly equilibrium in Dickdom the past month or so. Whenever the Dick starts wailing on Mikey, Jasper jumps in and blocks the belt before I can even think. Then Todd, bless his big, fat heart, covers us both. We're like a set of Russian whacking dolls.

"Ari?"

I shrug.

She writes notes in her book and says she'll be back next week.

Mum coils after the door closes. "How could you embarrass your father like that?"

Her face is skeletal, her voice, shrill like a caught pig and I wonder where the pretty girl who won music medals with Aunt Elsie disappeared to. "How come you stopped singing?"

Her hand thwacks my cheek like a dead flounder.

FORTY-THREE

I wait with the tired, the poor, the huddled masses yearning to breathe free. The school secretary weighs each excuse being schlepped over the counter. "I slept in." "My dog ran off." "My mom's sick and . . ."

It comes my turn to beg mercy for lateness. I have several options: Traffic was jammed at the intersection of hall and bathroom.

Wish the Duchess would stick to substances that just make her sleep.

Me, too, Jasper.

A big Dick made me find a button that had been beer-launched by his gut and sew it back on his pants.

While he was still in them.

Shut it, I'm trying hard to forget the horror.

I had to drag a puddle to school and urge him to deliver on his part of a negotiated deal: Mikey would read aloud in class today and in return, now get this, he would *not* have to endure the trauma of Little League this summer.

The real excuse? A flowering crabapple tree shocked me. Its fragrance made the air too thick to walk through. Then the robin gathering winter grass for a nest tied me to it.

Mrs. Quinty readies to pardon or sentence. "Well, Miss Appleton?"

"Cramps, ma'am."

I question the wisdom of the poetry section of the curriculum being delivered in the spring. I'm already a nose-in-book/head-in-clouds freak. Add spring to the mix and I'm an embarrassing idiot; and in the meander through the great poets I'm rediscovering many of the lines Uncle Iggy delivered on my lunch bags. Mr. Ellis stands in my path until I smack into him. "Well?"

He cages a laugh when I sigh, "If only I yield myself and am borrowed by the fine, fine wind that takes its course through the chaos of the world."

"Nothing like a little D.H. Lawrence to stir the soul."

I travel on to Social Studies knowing that more than Lawrence has me stirred. Chase told me that Nick knocked up Sharon. A slice of me wants to call Mrs. Potter and say, "I never would've let him in my pants. Now who's the good girl?"

The whole getting in my pants thing has me a little worried. With the nights warming, sometimes Ricky sprawls on the roof outside his window. I climb out and stretch beside him. First, our hands touch, then he turns, asking for a kiss. Everything stirs in me like cream and sugar in a pot working toward being candy. I like his hand on my belly, feel a little crazy when his dirty fingers move under my bra, rolling my nipple like he turns a cigarette, but as soon as his hand strays south or his leg moves over mine, my volleyball-muscled thighs clamp and I feel more five than fifteen. He rolls back, hands-behind-head pissed. I unzip, touch him, pulling on his thing until he comes. He wipes up with what I call the hope rag: the towel, or whatever he brought out with him, hoping he'd have something to mop up. I like the after holding, the whispered, "I love you," but I don't think I'll ever like anything else. I'm scared to have him go to boot camp and leave me in crapdom but I can't exhale until he does.

The Dick has his eye on Ricky and me. He shows up all sneaky, coming around corners, growing meaner and meaner, smacking Ricky's ears. "You messing with your sister?" Smack. "You little pervert." Whack. "You're not to be touching her."

Ricky takes it, standing nose to nose. "I never touched that skank."

The Dick turns pit-bull crazy. "I ain't talking about Ronnie. You keep your hands to yourself."

"Ari's not my sister."

"No, she's your meal ticket, the way you see it. Ain't she, you greedy little shit?"

Things hurry toward closed fists. I yank the Dick's collar hard. "You big goon." The Dick lets go, rubbing his bristly head. "Don't you have enough trouble without making trouble?"

"I see the two of you prowling around."

"You wouldn't know a friend if it bit your fat, ugly nose."

Wham! His backhand smashes across my right cheek. Ricky

charges in, intercepting the next one. He explodes, backing his father against the wall. "Fucking pathetic loser."

Dick flips Ricky's arm around his back, hoofing him toward the door. "Get your fucking ass outa my house."

Ricky was itching for a fight to make his exit. In two days he will report to Camp Borden. His duffle is stashed at Sabina's. He grabs his pack, jumps over the porch rail, and whips out an empty manila envelope. "You hurt Ari and this goes to the Chief, names, places, dates—pictures, too."

If Dick's gun was handy he'd start shooting. "Ungrateful fucking bastard."

I collect ice for my cheek and sit among the weeds in the backyard, thinking about fathers. My DNA father never much raised his voice or hand to me. Maybe "little princess" is to a girl what "fucking bastard" is to a boy.

I don't care if Chase doesn't mess with me because he has no hormones or likes boys or because he's Rumi reincarnate continuing his quest for divine love. All I know is he feels like the luckiest break of my life and he says the same about me.

Up in the nest, a full moon slices through the top of the window dripping white on his skin. It's only May end but the attic is hot from a three-day heat wave. Our smoke-soaked clothes lie heaped on the floor. A fan lures cool air from the open window. Poetry comes easy when it's lying beside you.

Third Sunday, Mr. West finds me at the water's edge throwing blue wooden beads into the waves. "What are you doing?"

"It's Father's Day. Flowers didn't seem right for Len."

I open my hand to share and he whips them far.

I ask, "How's Zodiac?"

"As happy as a dog without you can possibly be."

"I hope he's happier than I am without him."

He looks past the fading bruise. "Things okay?"

"No. But only eight days left, then I can go home." I fold onto the quilt and open a paper bag. "Sabina and I baked yesterday."

"*Paczki?*"

"Raspberry and apple. Did you call your father today?"

"Of course."

"Do you love him?"

"He's an easy man to love."

"So was my dad, always singing and telling me 'round-the-world adventure stories. It'd be so much easier if he was like the Dick."

"Why?"

"Icing on the fake. Love and hate get so jumbled, it's near impossible to sort out. Do you think we have a chance of becoming something different than our parents?"

"My grandmother says I'm a copy of my Uncle Peter. If I had to choose a person to be like it would be him." He taps up my chin. "And seems to me you have an aunt that's your heart's double."

"How do you become a heart's double of someone when a thief steals your soul?"

"I believe we possess ourselves."

"You're lucky if it turns out that way but sometimes people just help themselves to what's yours. Look at Jacquie."

He swallows, never even thinking of talking with his mouth full. "Exactly, look at Jacquie. Is she anything like your parents? Doesn't she possess her own self despite everything?"

"You know if you're a virgin or not, don't you."

"Ari!"

"Oh, don't get all Amish-teacher on me. I didn't ask if you were, I asked whether you knew you were or not."

"You get Mennonite-teacher from me, and yes, I know."

"I don't remember much of my father. Can't even bring up his face anymore. I know he made me touch him and—stuff, but I'm not sure how much of *me* he took."

"Geezus. Do you have anyone to talk to about it?"

"Most turn the greeny-purple of your face just now. Jennah tells me to just let it go. At least my sisters know what to let go of." Sand slips from one hand to the other as he squints at the horizon. I turn from the tears pooling in his eyes and follow the distant line. "I'm sorry. Talking about this isn't fair."

"Don't be. You're the only person I know who talks honestly about anything. I'm just not sure I'm the person that could help you in any way with this."

"Give me an honest thought you'd like someone to know."

"Hmm . . . how about, I don't want to go home. Every time I imagine myself back there I feel like I'm drowning."

"Where would you rather be?"

"I want to teach where teaching really means something."

"Your teaching really meant something to me."

"I mean something wild like an orphanage in Peru or a mission in Colombia."

"Will you write to me when you go?"

"I don't have the guts to do it."

I smack his head, which might be the moment things really switch from teacher to friend between us. "Did you not feel your animal self jump up when you said you wanted to go? It's exactly what you should do."

I exhaled when Ricky left. Now, I can't get a breath in. I smile for the photo of the Junior Girls Championship Volleyball team but it's a pretend smile. In English, I keep my face closed. Judy spears the air with her hand. "Sir, have you marked our poems?"

233

"Not quite through the pile yet, Judy. By Friday for sure."

He reads "Sunset" by Rilke and "To Autumn" by Keats and then he reads "Chasing Dreams."

> When chasing dreams
> the curve of him
>> shoulder to hip
>>> hip to knee
>>>> knee to heel
>
> Atlantic in my bed
> He pulls from the moon to me
> to—we
> Open we lie and fear less
> without longing
> for longing or wanting
> want
> empty and full in the same beat of two hearts
> not coupling
> doubling
> leg vining around young ancient oak
> a seaweed tangle in his strong branches
> not fairy tale
> a myth lived
> while chasing dreams.

Judy asks, "Who wrote that, sir?"

"An up-and-coming new writer. Remember, tomorrow bring a favourite poem to share."

I rarely skip class but after hearing my words read by him I can't face numbers. I sit on the grass under the maple. Mr. Ellis follows me out, his knees crackling when he crouches. "Did I betray you by reading that, Ari?"

"No, sir, it was nice hearing you speak how it sounded in my head."

"You've been awfully quiet this week. Are you okay?"

I shrug.

"I near pissed myself when I read your poem. Mina did wet her pants. Do you have a poem for tomorrow?"

"'In Silence.'"

"I don't think I know it."

" . . . Do not
think of what you are
still less of
what you might may one day be.
rather
be what you are (but who?) be
the unthinkable one
you do not know . . .'"

"Author?"

"Merton."

He straightens and I look up to a man, sun-rimmed gold.

"Sir, would Mina be someone I could talk to? About messy things?"

"She's been waiting for you to ask."

They live in a tumble-jumble of books, travel totems, and comfy cushions. Messy laundry, even a no underwears situation doesn't make Mina skittish.

An exquisitely woven Moroccan rug is our island floating on my disquieted sea. "Jennah says compared to what some people live with we have nothing to complain about."

"Whining and mining have nothing to do with the other. You're sitting on a friggin' platinum mine." She heaps a plate with pizza that has peculiar things on top like goat cheese and aspar-agus. "Write it, sculpt it, paint it. But first, a review. Perspective. What wounds deeper? A mother and father's betrayal or brutality at the hand of a stranger?" She sprinkles hot sauce over her slice. "You're allowed to feel wounded by this. But, girl, chiaroscuro. Are you going to burden the piece with too much shadow or diminish it with too much light?" I pick off something resem-bling a pond leech. She slides her plate across the coffee table, which is really an old door from an apothecary store in London, and receives the wiggler. "Now, by order of the Goddess Athena, you get a clean palette from whatever your parents did to you."

"Athena?"

"She's smart and artsy. Clean palette is the operative here."

"What artist worth her salt has a clean palette?"

She thumps me with a pillow. "Metaphor. Met-a-phor. Work with me here. Clean canvas. Okay?"

"Sometimes I look at my yellow sisters and I see . . . my father, lying on top of them, crushing their light."

"I'm not saying you don't have colours to choose from, you have a spectrum wider than anyone should. You also know shad-owlight at its penultimate. Girl, the goddess here is you. You and you alone get to choose what you create on your canvas."

"What if someone throws shit on it?"

"Then it becomes their canvas, so you get a fresh one, put it on the easel, and start again." She raises her coke. "Good for you for looking straight at this and asking, 'What am I supposed to do with this fucking mess?' I mean that literally."

"Sex has to be the messiest mess there is and it's all most boys think about."

"It's important to both sides. It just takes some wisdom to navigate."

"Auntie Elsie told me my dad had a genius IQ, and look how stupid it made him. He sacrificed his jewels—and his life, for a friggin' orgasm. How fucked up is that? And my mum pitched a diamond for dung. And Mary and Nia are the devil's spawn because they love each other." My pizza now resembles Shredded Wheat. "I'm so scared."

"You know what I like about Jasper? Most kids from fucked-up families have voices that tell them hurtful lies on a loop over and over. Yours is the most fair-tempered, sane little fellow I've ever come across. I'm not worried about you at all."

"You're not?"

"Your voice tells you the truth and smacks you when you start spinning lies. The truth here is, sex is exquisite. The thing, the big thing is where you let it take you. It can be astronomically good or it can be devastating."

Ellis comes in shaking an umbrella.

"Pizza's on the counter, love. Come join us after you make tea." Her toe touches my knee under the table. "Ari, Jasper knows who you are, listen to him. You are not your father. You are not your mother. You are . . ."

"Who?"

"You tell me who."

"—A lioneagle."

FORTY-FOUR

Mum's cells had been organizing this breakdown just for spite. I don't care she's in hospital for dry-cleaning. Saturday, I'm on the train out of crapdom.

The Dick shovels in meatloaf and spits out a lemon. "Laura's in rehab again so you can't leave until she gets out."

"No . . . I . . . Todd, can you take care of Mikey?"

Peas roll from Mikey's mouth into his milk.

"No can do. I got that job at the vet's."

I'd be proud of him if I didn't hate him so much right now. A stuffed lizard couldn't be entrusted to Ronnie's care but staying is not an option.

The Dick slurps his coffee. "Laura will be out ten days max."

"No, sir. I have a court order. Mikey will just have to come with me."

Mikey lifts his face. The Dick cracks his head to one side, then to the other in preparation for the final victory-taking. "Mikey, if you ask for permission to go with Hariet you can have a holiday at the ocean."

I pray that all my stories will be enough to un-weld his tongue. Mikey takes in my face and for me, not for himself, knowing how desperately I need out, says, "Sir . . . ma—may, may I have permission to go with Ari?"

The Dick is the biggest friggin' colossal prick in the universal universe. No wonder he has two women in rehab. "Say, *Dad*, may I *please* go with *Hariet*."

Mikey stands, skyscraper-tall. "Dad, may I please go with Hariet."

"Go on, get the hell outta my sight. But don't expect a penny from me for this."

I climb the steps and knock on the sneaker sticking out of the tent. "Mikey?" I poke my head in. "Can I show you something?" I elbow up with my raggedy little matchbox that has journeyed with me for as long as I can remember. "My imagination has been the only thing I've felt was really mine. The only thing no one could touch or separate me from. Jasper's gotten way too big for this little bed. Would you like it for yours until it grows bigger?"

He nods.

"What do you call your spirit friend?"

"Ari, I think."

"Oh, we might get confused spending the summer together. How about Kira? The K from the middle of Mikey and Ari backwards. Mine looks like a seahorse. How about yours?"

"A dragonfly."

My fifth sunrise on the shore and the numbness is out, leaving me feeling everything ocean big. All the pushed-down grief breaks against the rocks. Nia asks, "What are you seeing?"

"Treasures, losses, lost treasure, found treasure."

"Which is the most stunning?"

"That absence can't distance me from my true family." Mikey comes sailing over the ridge, down the rocky slope, running, head up, arms stretched to the ocean, to the day, to possibilities. "And maybe, giving a child fearless moments is the best giving there is."

"I'm just sorry Jake is off fiddling around the Maritimes."

"It's a good turn, I think. His music makes me dance. I need this big silence with Len for a time."

My seventh sunrise I see Jake ahead on the beach. Nia releases my hold and I run smack into his arms. "Ari Zajac. There's the sunrise I came looking for."

"Jake Tupper, I've missed you more than dolphins jump."

"Hear you've come to the shore with a new man." He sets me down, smiling over my shoulder.

"Mikey, come meet my friend."

"Pleased to meet you, mate. Think you might like to come out on the boat and meet some of my friends?"

Mikey looks to me, hoping.

"Better get a sweater. It can get shivery out there."

Jake holds my hand as we walk back to Skyfish. His cheeks are sea burned and the colour of driftwood floats in his eyes.

"Are you home for a bit, Jake? Sadie told me you're with a band."

"Saturday we're playing not far from here. Will you come?"

"Any chance I might get a dance?"

With that he sweeps me in a jig, splashing us through the water. Where the music comes from is a mystery but the rocks sing. Now, I'm not a wisp but he lifts me into a twirl which lands us laughing on the sand.

"You free tonight?"

"I'll be here waiting."

Mary and I watch them go, Jake and Mikey, hand in hand, setting off to sea. "He's been so excited about your coming."

"Really?"

"The girls fall around him like autumn leaves but he says he's got his eye on only one apple."

"Why me?"

"Maybe, you make his heart sing like he makes your feet dance." She laughs. "He asked my permission to court you."

"And?"

"I warned him to tread slow. You be careful, too, missy. You've miles to dance before you bed."

Something has changed between my head, heart, and hands since I last sat at the wheel. Spirits around me and dreams inside mingle, turn. I'm in church, bowed in prayer. Jake reaches my knee before I sense his presence. "Mary's got supper up."

"What time is it?"

"Going on seven."

Our eyes mix, hazel with grey. "I've missed here. Missed you more than there are words."

"Is there no one you're missing back home?"

"This is home." He smiles like I just gave him a puppy so I give the whole litter. "And you're the only boy I'll ever be missing." My mucky finger hooks his jean loop, reeling him closer. His hand lights on the knee poking out of my hoisted skirt, sending music up my thigh. I reach, taking a kiss—it sets me wanting an ocean plunge on a scorching day.

A thousand dragon eyes wink from the circle in the sand. Jake invites me inside his coat, pulling it tight around us. "How many times do you figure we've explored this shore together?"

"More than all the sad moments we've known and a far cry fewer than I need. Wish you weren't leaving with the band."

"There's money to be made and I'm going to make it while the making's good."

"Then what?"

"Build a house. Buy a boat. Take out summer travellers to see our ocean. Mary says I'm a teacher in my bones. Could you imagine someone like me a teacher?"

"You're a teacher, a healer, a rescuer, an explorer, a builder, a musician . . . and those aren't even what you do best."

"And what would that be?"

"You're a safe harbour for wrecks, more, you see the treasure in them."

"I'll show you, Ari. I could be someone worth having."

"You don't have to show me anything, Jake." Moving chest to chest, face to face, atop him feels more like finding a jigsaw piece than a stress. "I already know I could never be at home with anyone like I am with you."

Dreams light half his face; disbelief shadows the other.

"Mary's helping me through my high school and I have eight hundred dollars saved."

"Ari Zajac can be had for a song."

He flips me to the sand. "You really snuck out of the ocean for me, didn't you?"

"I've been found out."

"Aye, it's these waves and the seahorse tails." Holding fathoms of my hair he travels the ends across my cheek and buries his face close to my ear. "That grows from the deep. I've never met anyone so unafraid to let people look straight inside their heart. I saw it, Ari. I saw my match in there."

I want to ask if it's Jasper he saw but I'll hold off 'til I'm sure what he said isn't mariner's code for liking my boobs.

We kiss and kiss and kiss and I don't fear the twine of his leg over mine until he takes it away.

Nia surrenders the painting to me after she shape-shifts a piece of driftwood. The wood has given up a face, a Huey Butters sea-weathered face, a little of Len peers out, too. "See what's coming out here. The happy pieces are nice but you give the grief-shadows room on this one."

I smile past her to Aunt Mary glowing with sweat as she examines the latest firing. A sigh skitters out of my mouth, "Wish I could paint that."

Mary towels her face. "Geez, it's bloody hot."

Nia flips the Back in Ten Minutes sign. "Race you." We scramble to the ocean, peeling clothes as we fly, plunge into the frigid water, bolting out in less than a quarter minute. Our *iced T&A* break that will set us giddy for the rest of the afternoon.

I'm barefoot and clay-mucked when a dentist and his wife come into Skyfish. "Afternoon. Enjoying your trip around the trail?"

The woman says, "Breathtaking."

The man says, "Our kids are out there with the dogs. Are they friendly?"

"As long as your kids don't bite them they won't bite your kids."

"They've been in the car for days."

"Would they like to make something?"

At Aquarius people buy my work like hungry piglets but at Skyfish the story is sold along with the creation. As an hour nears two, the Dr. and Mrs. have tea and scones and a lesson on making pottery. Madeline and Abigail construct their own Ari Fairy chimes. They leave with a carefully wrapped box of mugs and coffee pot by Mary, a driftwood crane by Nia, and a fat terracotta pot with a sea turtle bursting from the side by Ari and I know when they arrive home they will tell the story of the women of Skyfish. Not to mention we have two hundred and twenty dollars in our till. I watch them out of the drive. "All I ever want to do is this."

Mary says, "You may feel different after university."

"I'm coming here the day I turn sixteen and I'm never leaving. Jake and I—"

"You're getting your schooling. You both are or I'll skin you alive."

Nia sands a mermaid's cheek. "Don't fret. There are wonderful colleges close by."

Mikey flaps his arms around me before heading out fishing. "I'll catch you a big one for supper."

"Mind Huey, and keep your life jacket on in the boat."

I claim the wheel while Mary goes to the post office and Nia naps in the hammock. Too soon, the bell chatters. Mary pokes

243

her head in. "Brought you something from town." She opens the door and an ear-dragging hound waddles in.

"Is that—Bunny? Shit—Holy Shit." I unstraddle the seat, jumping into hugs with Mina and Ellis. "What are you doing here?"

"Don't ever write, 'Wish you were here' and not mean it with us."

"How long you staying?"

"Just for tea."

"No way. Jasper has a whole ocean for you."

On our fourth day together, Jake puts us on course to a pod of whales. Mina jumps every time he finds a fish out of water. "What kind is that one?"

"A humpback. Watch the footprints she leaves." Mina follows Jake's finger pointing to the round slicks. "She's coming up, there." It breaks the water right where he points then the dorsal fin disappears. "Get your camera up, wait, wait, and . . . click now." Mina captures a graceful lift of the humpback's tail. "That's the terminal dive. She'll be down a bit now." He scans the ocean and follows a dolphin chase.

Mary teaches Mina to turn pots while Mr. Ellis and I walk the shore.

"I'm glad you're out of Yorkville for the summer. There's a big hepatitis outbreak. The whole area is under quarantine."

"Yeah, Auntie Mary got wind of it. Took me for a blood test."

"Everything okay?"

"I'm good. Summers here save me a lot of trouble. I missed the sit-ins last year. The *hit*-ins, too."

Ellis inhales the salt air. "It is a refuge here."

"Did you and Jake have fun fishing?"

"Don't quite know how to describe it."

"Let me try. It was like a sojourn with an ascended master and a five-year-old walking into a butterfly migration."

"About sums it up. He's a rare soul."

"It's the seahorse in him."

"Are you writing here, Ari?"

"How can someone live in a poem and not write? I can write bits to Len now. Not poetical things, just missings." I toss remembering-stones for Len, Grandma, Iggy, and a tiny pebble for Jet into the ocean. "I've been keeping a diary since the Anne thing. Mina told me I should, even if I just burn them." He takes my hand like Len did and I feel the grief in it. "Mina told you everything, didn't she?"

His shrug is more an attempt to work out the ache.

"I sure burden-up people." We stop to watch shorebirds squawking over a silvery fish. "Len and I stood right here to take in this very show last summer. It was all the Appleton stress that wrecked his heart."

"I'm pretty sure I speak for Len when I say this." His hands land soft on my shoulders. "Given the choice between bliss and a life with you in it I'd grab the latter faster than that gull snatched the herring and I'd never let go."

"That Rochester is one brave spirit. He's a turtle, isn't he."

He smiles a wink. "A Western Painted Turtle."

"Should've guessed that he's colourful given Mina's attraction to you." He laughs out loud when I say, "I missed it because when I catch a glimpse, Rochester is always wearing a fedora and a London Fog raincoat."

"He loves having you around. It gets me writing."

We journey along the water's edge. "What are you working on?"

"A series of travel essays for teachers. I just wrote one about the Torrey Canyon."

"The tanker that ran aground last year?"

"Mina's roots are in Cornwall so we went to help with the cleanup. The birds were so exhausted they just let me wash the crud off them. Thousands died, but the ones released stay with me, I still can see the way they dove back into the water. When Mina told me what you've lived through, words that had wanted out for so long just poured onto the page."

"Why?"

"You're like those birds, plunging into life despite someone loading you with crap. Spectacular is what I'd call you."

My feet feel caught in an off-the-ground float as we veer toward Skyfish. "Come on. I'll show you how to coax a character out of driftwood."

Coming or going and everything in between always gives rise to down-home parties. Jake navigates me toward his band. Duncan and Robbie, the boys of Saltwind take me in with a whistle. "So, the girl is real. We thought Jake dreamed you up."

Kathleen, Saltwind's angelic voice sizes me up. "Don't go getting your heart broke."

"Pardon?"

"Jake and me are having some good fun." She winks a smile at him. "Eh, b'y?"

Jake's hands at my waist tell me she's churning up our calm ocean. I whistle. "Well, lord, Kat, you're prettier than Marianne Faithful. I might want to have a go at you myself." Duncan laughs and smacks his *bodhrán* like a period on a punchline. He corrals them and leads them to the stage. Jake leans into my ear, "I'll be playing only for you."

Jake is freer than I've ever seen him, letting his voice out now along with his fiddle. There is a haunt to it that burns and chills in the same breath. "And then she made her way homeward, with one star awake, as the swan in the evening moved over the lake . . ."

I inhale when the music picks up. It makes no difference what man, woman, or child asks me to dance, I clog, step, and heel-toe to every jig and reel. Usually, Jake's eyes close when he plays, but tonight they keep finding mine, lips turning in a quarter-smile, sweatbeads sparkling all over him. One spins on a salt-wet length of hair. *Look, Ari, it's Jewel.*

Like he's just caught sight of Jasper, he leaps off the stage, touching down inches away, chasing me in a dance around the floor, fiddling all the while.

We've barely voices left but still sing chorus after chorus, "Way hey and away we go, donkey riding, donkey riding," all the way home.

I wander over to deliver groceries and to soak up the sugar in the missus' hug. Sadie's taken a job down the coast and the house is so chocked with boys, Mikey included, I know she'll be hungry for a woman to blather with.

The Missus has had more life whacks than anybody deserves and she'll tell you about them with her story weaving as fine as her knitting, but never with a thread of "Oh look what a bloody mess."

I pick up a wailing foster and sway him in a hush-hush. "Thanks for letting Mikey bunk here. He's thriving on all this walrus love."

"Reminds me of young Jake."

"What would these misdelivered ones become without you?"

"You know it's Mary and Nia that cares for these young'uns as much as me and Huey do. They wanted so desperate to take in wee Jake but peoples that didn't knows a thing about them said they weren't suitable. Imagine such foolishness. For years, they traipsed over to the Tupper shanty, sometimes twice a day after his mum up and left, to takes him food, warm woolies, and hugs. They paid Teacher's oldest boy, Marlin, a quarter a day to picks Jake up for school and sees him safe home." She serves up more pound cake and history. "Broke m'heart when they lost you. Every day after, I went over to pulls them up. I told them that my wee ones was gone and would never comes back but that you were theirs and would find your way to your true mothers. And weren't I right?"

"I want to take care of kids like you do."

"O'course. What else has your journey been for?"

FORTY-FIVE

Ocean wind on my skin makes me buoyant and on an ancient quilt I float. I know touch, dark, and light. I know the muscle of someone who's been submersed by evil and drawn to the surface by good. Jake explores me quietly, kissing my breast, his head curving like the deer at our trough, his tongue taking a gentle drink.

Unafraid, my skirt folds back, right leg settling like a satin ribbon falling from a gift. I want, want, want the drift of his hand up my thigh, fingers breaking the lace seal of my panties, blue and silk, against my white hip. He hums because the sea is his home. I hum because water between my legs as the potter's wheel turns is my heart. I think I would let him come inside but he doesn't ask, he just plays out the song in me all the way through to a quiet smile.

His belly, hard and concave, gives room to fit my hand under his jeans. "Ari, you don't have to." And there is the difference for this girl. When I *have to*, to settle a boy down, an ugly messy thing fills my hand. With Jake, because I love him and I *want to*, I discover a whole different set of lovely parts.

When under my breath I say, "I want to see you," his pants disappear like the magician's tablecloth trick. He smells good, not funeral-flower sweet, more like salvation-clean soap. I like the velvet of his thigh skin and the coarsening of his belly hair as it moves down to his penis, like leaving the forest edge for the heart of the woods. I like his swallowed gasps and pleasure moans. And I love that he keeps his hands tucked under his head.

Almost-nineteen-year-old boys who are touched like this come quick and easy all over their bellies, and in my mind a long-ago sermon surfaces about some guy getting slaughtered by the Almighty for spilling his seed instead of getting his dead brother's wife pregnant. So sadness muddies the joy as I wonder about a God who fries a person for that but doesn't bother much about a father that knocks up his little girl.

Jake strokes my arm, "What are you thinking?"

"Do you believe in God?"

"Do you need me to?"

"I need you to talk me through the tangle. What is and isn't sin about this is hard to figure."

"All I know is you set me breathing my own breaths."

"Mary and Nia get me thinking about a creator. Len had me believing in something more. But God the Father makes my teeth itch."

"When I fiddle I feel something big like the ocean listening."

"I'm listening. Sometimes, back there in Toronto, on the loneliest nights, I swear I hear you."

"I know I have many sweet listeners, but oftentimes I feel there's only one in this vast universe who really hears me." It might be the fear-fullest touch I've ever felt when he wraps his arms round me. "Love me, Ari—please."

"Forever, Jake."

On the shore, Mikey treasure hunts with a legion of pirates. From my perch on the ridge I can see the dragonfly sitting on his shoulder. Nia helps herself to the patch on my left and Mary to my right. "Why do I have to leave here? The only conversation Mum and I have had this past year is, 'Gimme a twenty and where's the Bromo.' I wish she'd just hurry up and kill herself."

Mary gathers my braid in her fist. "So do I."

I look at her. "You never think any such thing."

She laughs like a coyote. "What do you think flies through my head when I'm whipping stones at my failure pots?"

"You should play volleyball."

"I just wish Jacquie was going to be there for you."

"Babcia is failing and she needs Jacquie; being back home has lifted a little of her sadness. I'm relieved. It scares me the most what the Dick could do to them. Ricky told me he's a dirty cop with pockets full of scum friends who owe him favours. I just wish I knew what he's planning for me. They had their eyes on the store but it's sunk in that it's gone."

"Does he touch you?"

"Sex-wise he prefers used-up old broads. He never lays a hand on Ronnie. But he smacks Mum. Takes belts to the boys. He's more into hair pulling now that Mrs. Vandervolt is sniffing for bruises." I turn my bracelet, woven from the horsehair of Jake's broken fiddle bow. "It'd be so sweet to yank out just one fistful of his."

Nia pulls my head to her shoulder. "A few more treasures to unearth then you can come home. We'll come at Christmas and stay to New Year's."

Mikey's laugh floats up as he chases Jake. "You think you might sneak Jake along? The Ellis' have a big house."

Mary says, "He'll have festive gigs right through. He's bound and determined to save for a house and a boat."

"Can he stay with me in the summer house tonight? We're not. . . you know. I just want to be with him all the minutes I can."

My fingers play over the skin the sun never reaches. "You ever notice that all of our wants and hopes fit together like notes in a song?"

"Soul music." He lifts on one elbow, his finger chasing love-happy curls away from my face. "Ari, I know there are years before we can be together. Just say you might save last dance for me."

"Is that a proposal, Jake Tupper?"

"What life is worth living without you?"

"What if your band becomes bigger than the Beatles?"

"That'd send me screaming home faster than being chased by pissed-off bees."

"What if a woman lures you with her exquisite beauty and blue-as-sky eyes?"

"Then I'd be dead because anyone more beautiful than you would have to be an angel."

"What if you're given command of the finest vessel to sail the ocean?"

"I might be late for supper, but I'd be home before bed." He helps himself to a slow, deep kiss and I discover that prime fiddlers play encores.

Once again the train is chomp-chomp-chomping up the miles away from where I came. Mikey is a puddle on my lap. William

Walrus brings him a pillow. "There, there, laddie. The glory of a train is, for every trip away, there's always a train home."

His face is so tanned against the white pillow. "I promise, Mikey, it's just the beginning. We'll go back next summer. Until then we'll treasure hunt together."

"I had the best time ever."

"One day you'll live with me there. You and I know how magic it is because of where we've been." He clings to a stuffed bear Sadie made for him and drifts off to sleep. As the August-end pictures blur outside the window I close my eyes to see M&N reading the note I've left tucked into the pocket of Mary's ratty old robe.

Aunties: Do you know who is borne of you? Who turns the world with her hand, calls spirits from wood, and leaps over the edge believing she can fly? I am the child of your love. I am your child. Ari.

FORTY-SIX

Mr. West always brings a book on third Sunday, seeing as our meeting times vary according to epilepDick's seizures. Still, I run across the park to him, as if to lessen the span that July and August created. He closes *Meditations in an Emergency* and looks up. He's changed. I'm changed. The East does that to a body. His hair is longer and he looks like his shoulders have been weighted with both wonder and despair. The Taj Mahal is crossed off his list but I suspect a boatload of new questions have been added.

Heat percolates inside and out and I remove my sweater without thinking.

"Jesus, Ari, what happened?"

I scan my arms. "Just a precious little game the Dick and I play, Assault and Buttery."

"Say what?"

"For every pinch he gives me I butter his sandwiches with vermin droppings. Sometimes I goad him just so I can spread some bird shit on his bologna on white."

He studies the mess like it's a Picasso, *Arm with Green and Purple Grapes*.

"I'm just sparing myself from becoming 'a final chapter no one reads because the plot is over.'"

"Pardon?"

I tap his book. "You haven't reached that bit yet?"

"Don't think so. You've read this?"

"Title sucked me in. The reference is to making one's self appear too beautiful."

"I don't know a single girl who reads O'Hara."

"Jacquie gave it to me. She used to read a book a week, sometimes two."

"Her headaches still bad?"

"No, she's doing great. It's like her washing and bundling Jet for Jory depressurized the hurt in a way nothing else could. It's reading Polish storybooks to Arielle that's slowing her down."

"How's Mikey?"

"Spectacular. What a time he had discovering his inner dragonfly. And, Dickie has eased off with the pummellings because Mrs. Vandervolt is right nosey about his 'accidents'. The prick just chucks him into the cellar now."

"Jesus."

"Chase got us a vermin-proof container from his dad's company. We stocked it with all the comforts of home: mattress, books, pillow, blanket, nourishment, flashlight, sweater. It's like a fort. It even has ventilation, so he can climb inside and close the lid when he hears things scratching in the corners."

"No one should have to live like this, Ari."

"And yet we do and we are not a few. You found out just that on your travels this summer, didn't you?"

His hands swallow his head.

"This will cheer you. I've taught Mikey to play Sanitary Confinement. After the Dick throws him in the hole, Mikey puts in time cleaning the toilet or the bird cage."

"That's cheery?"

"He uses the Dick's toothbrush."

His baritone laugh sounds as beautiful as the turning leaves look.

"Do you sing?"

"Did my time in choirs. Like you, church made me pissy." He scans the water. "I don't know how to process it all. The poverty in India is something I can't get out of my head, and the spirituality . . . everywhere I travel they have their story, the truth for them."

"Yeah, more and more I think this big God thing is imagination run amuck."

"My parents think it's dangerous to my soul that I went there."

I sit sideways, knees up on our bench. "It is if you let it make you sad, but not if you let all that your trip gave you soak in and mean something to you in how you appreciate your life."

He turns from the water to my face. "I'm not sad."

"Yes you are."

He half laughs. "You're right. I am. What do you suggest I do about that?"

"Sing."

"Sing?"

"Sing the song about being more worth than you are trouble."

"I just feel so . . . I don't know, heavy."

"What spectacular luck."

"Why?"

"It's like a thistle in your underwear. Who would change any-thing if they felt nice and comfy all the time? My old teacher at Pleasant Cove went to Haiti and came back ready to hurl herself off a cliff. Instead she collects broken crayons, scrap paper, old books, pencils, all kinds of stuff and sends them to a mission there. How about collecting up all the textbooks ready for trash-ing? Box them and ship them to that school you visited. They'll think Vishnu himself has arrived." He snaps out of his slump when I start singing a down-home folk tune,

> Lay hold William Over, lay hold William White,
> Lay hold of the cordage and pull all your might.

"What's that?"

"Sacred music at its best. A story about neighbours helping." Sun through the maples lights the space around us more spectac-ularly than cathedral glass.

"Can I hear more?"

"There a whole lovely story but here's the end chorus:

> Lay hold William Over, lay hold William White
> Lay hold of the cordage and pull all your might
> Lay hold of the bowline and pull all you can
> And with that we brought Kit out of Tickle Cove Pond."

"You have a nice voice."

"My dad had the voice. Whenever he sang the whole church, even the piano, softened in respect and the pews became deathly quiet. Down-home music is often a whale of a fish story but it's never a lie." I check my watch. "I have to go."

"But you just got here."

"Laura didn't pick Mikey up on Friday. I promised to take him over to see that she's okay."

"Is she?"

"She'll pull herself together enough to reassure Mikey."

"You need help?"

"Chase is picking us up. But next time Laura bails it sure would be nice for Mikey to spend some time with a shit-free person."

"Well, I'm your man."

"You are at that."

His lips tense into a sad smile. "I'll keep my weekends flexible."

"It's your heart you keep flexible, that's why you're shit-free." I reel away singing. "Lay hold Ari Zajac, lay hold Aaron West. Lay hold of the cordage and pull with your best . . ."

He calls, "Ari, I'm glad you're back."

"Third Sundays are worth coming back for. Say hi to Belle for me."

Laura meets Mikey and me at her door. She looks like a dripped-out icicle ready to break. "How're you feeling?"

Her head moves like a bobble doll. "So-so." Her hand trembles as she smoothes Mikey's hair. "Just a bit of the flu. I'll be right as rain next weekend." She steadies herself against Mikey's hug.

She looks more at the greying sky than into my eyes. "Thanks for taking Mikey along this summer."

"We had a great time, didn't we, bro?"

Mikey releases his mom and takes hold of me.

"Those chimes he made were the prettiest things anyone has ever given me."

"Next summer I'm going to teach him how to turn pots."

"Can't wait to see what I get out of that." And with that, it's over. She says, "Be good, sweetie. See you next week."

The craphouse smells like piss and bird shit despite the fact that Cunt died two months ago. My mother is wired on shit and the Dick continues to shit on everyone, so life is pretty much how we left it. Except for Todd, who lost maybe twenty pounds just getting off the couch and off to work at the veterinary clinic. He's closed the book on school but with all his experience living in shit he has a great career ahead cleaning it up.

Ricky never responded to any of my letters and in truth I'm not sad he's gone. My Fiddler has room for Existential Love but things would be way too complicated living with the Soldier Boy.

I open a letter from Jake. His poetic rambles keep me afloat in this cesspool.

> Isaac and Peter's mum finished her time and came to collect them. Oh, the joy-jumping at her arrival. They're all off to an uncle's farm over on PEI. They're such good lads, they'll do well. We're taking a gig in Charlottetown so I can stop in and give them a hello.
>
> No sooner had they left than Danny arrived. He wasn't in the house an hour before he set the Missus' best tablecloth on fire. He's a nine-year-old sorry stew. Mary and I went to a psychologist for some pointers. He said that I had insight. Imagine him saying such a thing. Anyways, he told us about Danny's dad who treated his only child worse than one would a rodent. Yes, girl, I'm listening . . . and seeing.
>
> Yesterday, I anchored the boat and stood for a while watching gold-limned clouds turn like skirts at a Friday dance. A great blue heron nabbed a fish nearby then launched like an arrow inland. I wondered if he was taking it to his mate or a lonely marsh for one. I know bounty not shared is bitter, and solid is as likely as the ocean roll under me. I know, too, that love is as much held as those clouds are. All it can ever be is a hope, or maybe something

bigger, like a belief. Right now a simple hope would keep me breathing. Save last dance for me, Ari?

And so begins our what-if game played across the miles:

"What if Nova Scotia falls into the sea?"

"Then I'll build us a submarine."

"What if an eagle steals your fiddle?"

"I'll send a lioneagle to fetch it back." I especially like that one.

"What if a giant turtle snaps off my toes?"

"Then stand on my feet and I'll dance for you."

FORTY-SEVEN

Milky grey saturates third Sunday, January 1969. I bring hot chocolate and Aaron West and I sit close. His solidness quiets the chaos that follows me from the craphouse.

Aaron asks, "How was your holiday?"

"The usual worshipping of baby Jesus with spirits."

"Not good?"

"*Come they told me for rum-rum-rum-rum.* The Dick and Duchess were more rum-soaked than the Christmas pudding. Jillianne came for a visit."

"How's she doing?"

"Loves her job. Says she can't sleep sometimes for all the ideas in her head. She's off drugs but she downs the wine like its H2-oh-no-problem. We went to Jennah's and she and Jory emptied five bottles in two hours."

"You hear from June?"

"Metaphysically. I imagined her in a cozy log cabin. Did you have a good Christmas?"

"It was fine. My sisters got the church involved making shoebox school kits to send along with the book shipment."

"Did you know your mom sent me a picture of Zodiac in reindeer antlers pulling your cousin on a little sleigh?"

"Yeah, he was the star of the annual skating party."

"Did you skate on your pond?"

"Every Christmas."

"How Norman Rockwell. Belle took Mikey and me to the Ice Capades. The kid loved it."

"What doesn't delight Mikey? He sees magic in a hike through a swamp."

"It's the dragonfly in him."

He surveys the naked branches above us. "You ever going to tell me what you see in me?"

"Doesn't work that way. You've got to meet it yourself. But stick around. You know Jasper is bound to get pushy. Especially if you keep looking for it in the trees."

He shifts. "But what if you don't stick around long enough for me to find it?" His face is so open and lost and—exquisitely sad.

"Jasper never leaves a kindred spirit behind."

"You see a seahorse?"

"Lord, no. Your animal is way too adventurous to live in the sea grass."

"You see a fish?"

"It's a voyage of discovery, not question and answer time."

"Question and answer is how I discover."

"Sorry, my craziness, my rules. Tell me, what animal do you see in your mother? Don't think just say it."

"A brumby."

"Nice horse. How about your dad?"

"A stallion."

"Your sisters?"

"Um . . . a swan and . . . a heron." He tilts his head. "And, I see a bear in your sister Jacquie."

"A mythical yellow bear. My warrior. My protector."

"I'm sorry she's so far away."

"My sister-house sure is on shaky ground."

"Well, your true home is waiting for you. Just four months and you'll be sixteen."

"One hundred and eighteen days, but who's counting?" The hot chocolate curdles in my gut knowing my freedom means leaving Mikey behind.

"And how is life in crapdom?"

There is a story in the paper about a prison escape. The guy had two months left on an eight-year sentence and he broke out. *He went squirrelly, Jasper.*

I can see it happening. We should send him a card.

Jasper and I have always been able to escape inside ourselves wherever we landed but the craphouse is so infested with vermin of every shape and kind, we can't find a crack where we can rest and regroup.

In class today, Mr. Ellis said, "It's the tiny details that make a story interesting. They connect the reader, make time and place real. Think about detail when writing your assignment."

The Tool is sitting on the red chenille chair when I return from the library. "Hi, Ari. Needin' sweet treats?"

He's exposing himself—again. *You think Mr. Ellis wants this detail, Jasper?*

I look him in the eye. "Hey, O'Toole, there's a piece of spaghetti on your lap." He doesn't flinch. His thing isn't small, it's gross and menacing and I feel like taking the hedge cutters to it. I boot up the stairs two at a time.

In my room Ronnie is snoring—on my cot, under my blankets. A storm of wadded-up TP is on the floor. I sit in the dip at the end of the hall where Mikey's tent used to be and try to study for math. Mum coughing in the bathroom sounds like she's about to deliver a lung.

Todd exits his room, sees the bathroom is occupied, opens the hall window and pisses out of it, and the mystery of the yellow canal on the roof is solved. He heads down while the Dick's voice booms up, "Hariet, you lazy cow! You think we got all night to wait for you to get supper up?" I close my book and hoist myself downstairs. He flicks my forehead. "Move it."

I feed the pigs. While cleaning up their mess, O'Toole sneaks up behind and says, "Thanks, sweet thing." His hand slips under my shirt.

I whip around and take a swing at him with the frying pan. "Keep your fucking hands off me!"

The Dick storms in from the hall. "You show my guest some respect, you hear?" He pins me to the wall by his forearm pressed to my windpipe—more, more, a little more 'til I'm sliding down the wall into blackness.

These are the details as I surface: a heavy black boot on my hair, pinning my cheek to the dirty floor. The stink of pickle juice and singed rubber. A line of ants disappearing under the stove. An empty cigarette pack propping up the table leg. A splat of old bird shit on the yellowed baseboard and the 'ta' sound of a tear hitting the cracked linoleum.

They pick up their bowling bags and leave. I pick up myself, clean up, and go upstairs. When exactly Ronnie resurrected off my bed is a mystery, but my pack has been pilfered and my cot is empty except for a greasy head-print on my Skyfish pillow and on Babcia's feather comforter is menstrual blood, I assume, since I know it's not virginal.

I go into the boys' room and tap on the bigger tent that Chase and I pitched when Ricky moved out. "Mikey? Can I camp out with you?"

He unzips the door. I crawl in and curl up in a tight ball.

"Do you want me to read you a story?"

"No, I just need some quiet to make up a story for school."

"Make it about a dragonfly and a seahorse that go camping in the great indoors, okay?"

"I'll give it a go."

He pulls his blanket over my shoulder and pats my back with his small hand.

I crave sleep but details chase me: the wretched skin-crawl of O'Toole's hands on me, how the Dick's new torture leaves fewer bruises but is scarring my soul, how my mother's complete abandonment of herself has turned her into the left-behind skin of a molted animal.

Jasper, I want to go home.

My breath catches when I hear the door open, but I exhale when I recognize Todd's wheeze and heft settling on the bed outside the tent. I drift off but snap back to attention when his bed creaks rhythmically, picking up steam like a locomotive. Todd's moans escalate with his wanking and Jasper sings "Help" to drown out the horror.

FORTY-EIGHT

Jackson Pollock slides click through the carousel. My heart refuses to slow down. The rush in my ears makes me nauseous. I slip out before the lights come on, grab my coat, and head across the field. Jasper slows me down. *Go back. I want to paint angry messes like Jackson.*

We are an angry mess.

I give Matt Talbot ten bucks and he hands over a bag of weed.

We'll miss English.

Shut up.

I like the weak sun and the February bite on my cheeks, mixed with the warmth from the fire in the rusty tin drum. I savour the slowing of my heart, the sway of the trees, and the melting of all the jagged edges. I make my eyes focus as my fellow delinquents scurry away like oil in the presence of dish soap. I turn to the shadow over my shoulder.

"Don't you have to pick up Mikey?"

"Um . . ." *Did we forget him, Jasper?* "Ah . . . no, Sabina . . . a birthday party . . ."

"Come on. Let's go." Mr. Ellis tugs my scarf.

"No, thanks. I'm just not up to any lectures."

"Well, that's a relief because I don't have any. Come on." His arm on my shoulder gentles me along. "Rough go, eh?"

"I'm caught and I'm done."

"You're in a bloody tangle but there's no way a fat buzzard can outdo a Lioneagle." He opens his car door. "How does lasagna sound?"

"I have to work."

"We'll give you a lift later and check out the music."

"What about writer's group?"

"Upstaged by a basketball game. Can you believe that?"

By the end of a shower my high is completely gone and I want to follow the scummy water down the drain. Mina has left me fluffy towels and clean clothes.

The coffee table is heaped with food. Ellis says, "Dig in."

"Are you going to bust me about the pot?"

"I'll make you a deal, just promise Mina and me no dope during school and no skipping."

"I'll promise no shit, period. It's making Jasper really cranky."

Mina impels me toward the food and forces me into a cross-legged sit on the carpet. "I'm shocked Jasper hasn't slugged you about it already."

"The Dick keeps knocking both of us off our feet."

Ellis wags a baguette at me. "That's not what this is about."

"Pardon?"

"It's not your mother, or O'Toole, or that bloody Dick."

"Yeah, it is."

"No, it's about Mikey."

"Mikey and I are allies."

"Your head is in a battle that's months down the road."

"What battle?"

"You know you have to get away from that house and you know that you can't leave Mikey behind and it's giving that bastard the upper hand right now."

"You said no lectures."

"I said *I* didn't have any. Rochester is pissed and ready for war." He hands me a plate. "Eat."

"What *am* I going to do about Mikey?"

"I don't have the answer. But when the time comes we'll all help you figure it out. Right now, something has to be done about those bruises on your neck."

"You got that right." A pinch or a fist is one thing but stealing my breath is the worst torture yet.

"Ari, you have to tell Mrs. Vandervolt."

"Hold your britches. Before you send us down that road, picture them all sober and polished up, saying these bruises are hickeys and that I'm rebellious. At least I can walk away soon. The one we risk destroying is Mikey."

Mina puts salad on my plate. "Think I'm with Ari on this one. I've heard too many horror stories from kids in the system. What does Mary think you should do?"

"I keep this toxic spill off the East Coast. Mary worries so much and Jake thinks he needs to make life perfect for me. I can't tell them that I'm imploding inside my skin."

"Nia called last night."

I try to read Ellis' face.

"She said your letters sound like Rebecca of Sunnybrook Farm trying to paint an up-side picture of Dante's *Inferno*."

"What did you say to her?"

"Well, I didn't tell her that I see you crossing the field every day at lunch. And I didn't tell her that you got thirty-two percent on your math test or that I miss your wit and wisdom in English." He lifts my chin. "I told her that Mina and I were watching out for you and would help you through."

Mina tucks in on the sofa behind me and has a go at my tangle of hair. It's a kindness that makes me bite my cheek—hard. "We have to figure out what he won't risk losing. What matters to him, Ari?"

"Len's money."

"Well, he can't get his hands on that for another two years. And he flushes money like water anyway. What is he really afraid to lose?"

"I've never been able to figure out his currency." I sop up sauce with garlicky bread. "His loves are gambling, drinking, and the torture of women and children."

"And?"

"That's it."

Ellis scrapes and gathers plates. "As screwed up as he is, he always gets himself to work. His job must be important to him."

"Yeah, he loves being a cop." I check my watch and unfold from the floor. "I really should go. Maybe getting Jasper into some salt-sweat at the Riverboat will bring some scheme up from the depths."

I review the file Ricky gave me when he left. *There's no doubt the Dick has sticky fingers but how do we pin any of these names and dates on him, Jasper?*

I call Todd at work and he agrees to give up information in exchange for me bringing him a turkey on rye. "I seen TVs, radios, booze, all kinds of shit in the trunk of the car. And you think he goes to Woolworth's to get your mum those bangles?" Todd opens a cage and takes out a pup, gives it a pill and a dose of praise. "Good boy."

"You're spectacular at this, Todd."

"Best gig ever." He moves on to the next cage. "If I see anything I'll give you a heads-up. You should get a camera and take pictures as evidence. Like on *Perry Mason*."

When I return home I catch Ronnie pillaging my stuff. "Hey, Ronnie. Looking to de-edge?"

"Fuck you. Got any?"

I have a couple joints left since making my promise to Ellis to lay off. It's enough to make her as pliable as Gumby. I get tidbits: a place on Front Street where the Dick gambles, a ruby ring he snatched off a body, loot he brings home. When talk turns to a motherlode of tie-dye last year, my neck hairs startle up. "What did he do with it?"

"Unloaded it in Buffalo."

"Did he give any of it to you?"

"Gave me a hundred bucks to stop pestering him about it."

"Oh."

"One time he gave my mom a diamond watch. She never wore it, though. Said it was too good for wearing."

"What happened to your mom?"

"They were upstairs having it out over something." She picks at a spec on her tongue. "And she fell down the stairs."

"Did he push her?"

"More like threw." Controlled puffs dot the memory. "Ricky and me were watching TV. There was no thumpity-thump, just one thud and she was there in the archway, her head turned so she was looking out the window, backwards."

"Geez, Ronnie, I'm sorry."

"It wasn't always the shits. We went to a cottage once. It was a blast. I landed a fish bigger than Ricky's and Daddy said, 'There's my girl.'"

"What did your mom say?"

"She showed me how to pan fry it over the fire. I'd never smelled or tasted anything so good." She takes a long, slow drag. "She wasn't beautiful like your mom, but she had really pretty lips. I think. I can't really remember her face."

"You have pretty lips."

"You think so?"

"I do."

Chase loans me his dad's Polaroid and already I have a wad of photos. I make sure the sedan's license plate is in view when I take snaps of two cases of whiskey and cartons loaded with boxes of Laura Secord chocolates. It's not the crown jewels but it's a start. I take a shot of the TV in the living room, Mum's ring, a shiny motorcycle in the garage, a bag of prescription drugs for a slew of people I've never heard of, and I get one of the Dick's gold watch, inscribed, *To Walter, for outstanding service, December 1957.*

On Sunday I bring back clean sheets for Ronnie's bed, too, not that she'll notice but maybe the smell of clean laundry will help her remember her mom's face. If I want more info, weed is my best option.

On Monday I nip across the field and fork over twenty bucks to Matt Talbot for a bag of truth serum. When I swing around, my eyes connect with Mr. Ellis standing over by the fence. He turns away and heads back to the school. I run to catch up, "Sir, wait. Let me explain." He doesn't stop, doesn't look back.

In English, I might just as well have skipped because he acts like I'm not even here. I wait for the class to leave but he grabs his jacket and satchel and turns off the light.

I figure Mina doesn't know because her chatter is unchanged but Mr. Ellis' silence bruises me on the inside. On Wednesday I drop my essay on his desk. "Just want you to know, sir, yours is one of the worst leavings I've ever had. I'm sorry I disappointed you."

FORTY-NINE

Mr. Ellis returns my story, only mine. He starts to speak but Aubrey and Sean get into a tussle in the hall. When he goes to break it up I head home, reading the back of my paper as I walk.

> Ari:
> I've tried to write this in a hundred ways and the best I
> can come up with is, please forgive me for being such

a pompous ass. How dare I judge you for turning to something that softens your harsh world?

Your story is brilliant, as usual, achingly tender without a hint of sentimentality, but I can't accept it like this. I'm asking that you rewrite the ending, this time with the truth, not this predictable easy out. A great tragedy has its place but it's not the right end for this dragonfly and seahorse and you know it. Mina and I are here for you, no strings. —E

"Ari! Miss Appleton!" I turn to see Mr. Ellis bolting across the field, pockets clattering, tweed jacket rippling. "Hold up, please."

I walk backwards, slowly.

"Wait, Ari, please." His breath is impressively unpuffed. "There's a note on your paper, but I just have to say I'm sorry before Rochester keeps me awake another night."

"I read it. We're cool."

"You sure you forgive me? I've just felt like shit."

"Well, this will likely put you knee-deep in it, but I need you to know that I never broke my promise to you. Not that I wasn't being scum, but not promise-breaking scum."

He stops like I punched him. "What? Pardon?"

"Getting Ronnie high helps me excavate intel from her. She steals my money and gets wasted anyway. I figured I might as well get something out of it."

"Ah, geez. I really am so sorry."

"I'm an Appleton. What else could you think?"

"I could have heard you out when you tried to talk to me. I could've given you the benefit of the doubt. I could have and should have been there for you no matter what."

"Thank you, sir. That's nice. I mean that."

"You can screw up and I'm not going to bail. I mean that."

"Auntie Nia says I don't screw up enough. That I'm too much a pleaser. That's why I gave myself permission to dope up Ronnie."

"Did you learn anything?"

"I may have some ammunition against the Dick, but it's more likely just fodder for a crap novel."

"Let me get the car and drive you to get Mikey."

"Parent-teacher thing. The Dick's bringing him home."

"Come over and have a tea then."

"Rain check. Walking stirs up my creative juices and I have a new ending to write."

His inner animal smiles. "Then come for dinner tomorrow and we'll strategize."

"If Laura doesn't bail on Mikey, it's a date."

I feel like skipping, so I do, most of the way home, stopping midhop when I see Mikey's pack on the sidewalk contents strewn everywhere. I bolt in and hear Dick's fury thundering down the stairs. "You want the ocean, well here's the ocean! He takes you fishin'? Well then go bloody fish."

I reach the bathroom just as the Dick plunges Mikey's head into a bathtub full of water. "Stop. Stop! Let him up!" I claw and pull but his lock on Mikey won't release. I grab Mum's Aqua Net and spray it in his face. His hands spring to his eyes and Mikey flops like a weighted doll to the floor.

Before I can get us out, the Dick's rage turns to me; a backhand, a punch, a lift by the throat, and then I'm down into the water. My scream is swallowed into my lungs. My chest burns. My belly jerks. Air bubbles out of my mouth. Then I'm up, gulping at air, then under again. His face above me is cold fire. From behind an arm locks around his neck and forces him back. I take in great gulps of air. Mikey is on all fours, retching.

I want it to be my mother's voice I hear, or Todd, even Ronnie, but it's O'Toole who unearths my face from the tangle of hair. "Breathe, darlin'. You're okay now." He looks up. "Christ, Irwin, what the fuck is wrong with you?"

I see the Dick's boots backing away and hear the scared animal in his throat.

O'Toole stands me up. My legs, the floor, turn rubbery. "You gotta get out of here. Dry yourself off. Get the kid changed." He mops blood off my chin. "Just go 'til he calms down."

The room spins when I bend over to secure Mikey's arm. He's like dragging a boat through sand but I sludge him into my room. Through violent shivers and eerie silence I remove his wet clothes and bundle him in my comforter. "We're okay. It's over." My right eye is swelling and the size of my lip won't let my mouth close. I hurry into jeans and layers of sweaters. "Stay here. I'll get your clothes."

It strikes me how absurd socks are as I struggle them onto Mikey's feet, but they're not optional in a Canadian February. It hits me, too, harder than Dick's fist, that my mother is watching TV. The Tool forces five bucks into my hand. "Go grab a burger. Come back after he goes in for his shift."

A burger? We want a hospital, Ari.

Mikey and I are hustled out the door with half-zipped coats and no mitts. Our wet hair turns stiff in the cold. Mikey blurs into wobbly lines as I try to focus. "We should go to emerg."

Words shiver out of him. "They'll call the police."

The distance to any of our havens is farther than my reserves. "I've got to sit, Mikey."

He nabs my hand and pulls me along the narrow space between crapdom and next door. He lifts the cover to the cellar entrance, descends the crumbling steps, pushes open the door, and scuttles into his fort. I manage to get in, but I know getting my quivery self out won't be easy. It's smaller than the single mattress, so it feels like we're in a boat. The height of it only gives me room for an angled sit. We zip into the sleeping bag and burrow under one of Babcia's featherbeds. "We can only stay until the Dick goes. If you can't wake me, you have to call for help."

271

He nods into my chest and holds on tight. The cellar is damp-cold but the small nest feels intoxicatingly warm with the lid closed. As voices expand and contract above us, Mikey's grip tightens.

I rest my head against the metal wall. "What set him off?"

"Miss Mumford said I was the best student in the class. She showed him my work."

"And?"

"He saw my hero page about Huey."

I didn't mean to fall asleep. Escaping in darkness would've been easier. A cross-hatching of pale silver lines slice through the vent holes. My first thought is that I'm failing math, the second, I have to figure out where we go from here. Mikey's breathing sounds like metal on metal. Every scrape hurts my head. *What am I supposed to do, Jasper?* I want my sisters. Jennah knows about beatings, but taking a mess to her house would knock her carefully choreographed equilibrium off-kilter and the thought of prayer from Jory's church makes my teeth twitch.

Sabina knows about war.

Mikey whimpers as I wrestle my stiff body out of our cocoon. His cheek feels white hot.

I struggle out of the box. As I squat and pee over the drain in the cement floor, mist rises from my stream. I peek at the driveway through the narrow window. The Dick's car is gone. I check my watch. If he went to work we have maybe a half hour until he gets home.

Before opening the cellar door I listen for sounds of stirring, then creep to the phone on the wall. It rings ten times before someone picks up. I whisper, "We need help."

"Ari?"

"Come, please."

"Otto will be there in fifteen minutes."

"We'll be at the corner."

Dr. Shomski is Sabina's second cousin and despite the Appleton blight on the Zajac clan he has always been kind to me. He knows I'm lying when I tell him Mikey fell in the lake and that I got banged up pulling him out, but he trusts Sabina to sort out the truth.

He whispers something to Sabina in Polish, and I ask, "Is Mikey okay?"

He rips prescription orders off of a little pad and tucks doctor gear into his black bag. "His larynx is quite irritated and his lungs congested. What concerns me more is the both of you staying away from dangerous water. I'll check back this evening."

Otto goes to the drugstore while Sabina calls our schools. She makes soft food, checks Mikey's temperature, and tucks him into bed. "Sleep without fear, słoneczko." The name *little sun* suits his small, fair head poking out from under the quilt. She plumps a pillow on the other bed. "In you get, *córka*."

A Dick defense plan feels urgent, studying for my math makeup test is an imperative, my history paper was due yesterday, today I'm missing a biology lab worth twenty percent of my mark, my hair is matted with blood and the left the side of my face is a freakish mix of tingles and throbbing. "I can't sleep, Auntie."

"Lie down. I have a poultice to take some of the swelling down." I comply and she retrieves something that fills the room with the fragrance of spring rain. She gives me a white pill then covers half my face with a gauze bag filled with cold goop.

I squeal like a piglet.

"It will hurt only for a few minutes then the pain will calm."

Jasper slides up and down my toe to distract me. *Smells like cucumber.*

"What is this?"

"Comfrey." She makes a futile attempt to unstress my hair. "Rest if you can."

"I'm sorry to be all this trouble."

"Trouble is unwanted. You, *corka*, are wanted, you are precious to me."

The little pill eases the pain but the accompanying dreams are as appealing as the "acid tests" conducted in my past. *We don't like this, Ari.*

I know, Jasper. And I'm going to fail biology.

I drift, waking over and over from Dali-like dreams—*Still Life Moving Fast. The Face of War* . . . distortions too close to my truth.

I give up and shower. As the mist on the mirror retreats I wonder where the Dick would have dumped our bodies if O'Toole hadn't needed to piss.

The poultice has not produced the miracle I'd hoped for and my face resembles a surreal Mexican sunset. As I slip into the clothes Sabina put out for me I wonder if she mixed up the pile: silky new underwear from the boutique, black tights, a soft hand-knit pullover, a peasant skirt that a peacock would envy, and one of Babcia's warmest shawls.

I join Sabina in the workroom. She scolds when I start folding the pressed shirts. "Eat before you start."

"I nabbed three perogies from the kitchen." In truth, I considered a soda cracker and just didn't want the bother of throwing it up. "What am I supposed to do, Auntie?"

"I know someone who could get you and Mikey passports. Poland would have you safe with Jacquie and out of their reach."

"I got a passport after Uncle Iggy died. I have no clue how the Dick found out but he said if I ever ran away he'd have his associates nab Jory and . . . by the end of what they'd do to her, she'd be begging for her God to take her. If that didn't bring me back he'd go after Jillianne, let a gang of pervs at her. Then he said he'd beat Jennah to death and set Wilf up to take the fall. He smiled that greasy smile, 'Then what else could Nana and Pops do but move into that pretty bungalow of Jennah's and take care of those little orphans?' He was likely just messing with me but look what he did to Iggy."

"Ari, you know that those of us who care about you cannot allow this to continue."

"No shit. But you have to help me figure out how to do that without getting my sisters murdered. Len said you were my age when you took on the Germans. He said you were the smartest cog in the Resistance wheel."

"I was a naïve girl playing a dangerous game. It was a time with few options."

"What are my options?"

"The authorities."

"I have a file of two-bit crimes and suspicions, but no proof. And look, we all know he set up the Aquarius robbery but where's the evidence? If I deliver what I have to the wrong person, Mikey and I are screwed. Mum would never back me up. If I do something that costs him his job but doesn't land him in jail, I'm dead."

"You are right. This needs to be planned very carefully." She pats the work table. "Up you get. Lie back."

"Why?"

"We need to gather the troops. No one is going to be willing to discuss anything when they see your face. Mr. Ellis for one will call the police."

I stretch out my long legs and tuck the shawl under my head. "This can't be covered up."

"All we need is a little distraction while we come up with a plan." She gets out paints and brushes and goes to work. "Just relax and tell me what you are thinking right now."

"The thing skittering around like quicksilver is that he wanted to be Mikey's hero and he near killed him because he wasn't."

"Who are his heroes?"

"People with money, power. He's a major butt-kisser around Wilf."

"Jennah's husband?"

"There's always a pissing match when they're together but Wilf is clearly alpha dog."

"Before we can diffuse this bomb we need to understand the tick-tick-tick. Is Officer Irwin a religious man?"

"He gets shined up in uniform for special Sundays and positions himself for an audience with Father Humphrey."

"How is he with his own father?"

"I've only met him once. The Dick grovelled around him like a kicked dog."

The tiny brush on my skin hurts and soothes. "What is the happiest you have seen him?"

"Winning on poker night."

"Deeper happiness."

"The man has less depth than the pores on his nose."

She dots my nose. "Then you go deeper. See him," she says, but what I see is the rage in his face as he held me under. "Or, just let your mind float."

"The police chief made rounds before Christmas. Apparently, he stopped and talked to the Dick, shook his hand, thanked him for his service. You would've thought the Queen of England had knelt at his feet. Drunk or sober, that's all I heard about for weeks."

"One thing I learned during the war is that a man's behaviour snapped into line the instant his superior came into the picture."

"Should I invite Chief Mackey for dinner?"

"Not yet."

"I was kidding."

The bell over the door clatters and Jennah's voice follows. "Sabina?"

"In here."

Her voice moves closer. "Have you heard from Ari?"

"She is here."

She opens the door and adds things up. "Holy ghost and jam. What did that bastard do?"

"Long story." Sabina stands and stretches. "Let me check on Mikey and put the kettle on."

I sit cross-legged on the table. "How come you're looking for me?"

"Mum called. Asked if I knew where you were."

Mum dialed a phone?

FIFTY

This is the Resistance ready for the battle ahead: Mina and Ellis, Sabina, Jennah, Chase, me, even my boss Bernie has agreed to make his resources available. Otto and Wilf are entertaining the kids at Jennah's house.

Ellis' despair when he hears what happened makes me believe that Len is close. He calms down, but is reluctant to support any plans that have Mikey and me returning to crapdom. "Vandervolt suspects what's going on. One call and she'd get them out."

"But where would she dump them?" Chase has a magic marker behind his ear and is assembling a flip chart. "Ari could take care of herself. But Mikey? And how long before the Dick had them returned?"

"There are any number of places where they'd be safe. My sister in Quebec would take them in a heartbeat."

Chase asks, "And could you promise he wouldn't hurt her sisters to punish Ari?"

"No." The heels of Ellis' palms push against his temples. "So what do we do?"

Sabina pours coffee. "We can't out-bully or out-muscle him, but we sure as hell can outsmart him."

"That's just it. Stupid is stupid and does stupid things. There's no controlling that."

Chase is enjoying this a little too much. "So we make Ari and Mikey too hot to touch."

"How? They are nothing to that bloody fool."

Sabina's bracelets jingle. "We make hurting them cost him what he craves more than anything."

Ellis asks, "What? Money?"

Chase uncaps his marker and writes, RECOGNITION. "He wants approval from people above him."

"And who would that be?"

"So far we've identified," the marker squeaks and it hurts my teeth, "Father Humphrey, Chief James Mackey, and William Dennison."

"Mayor Dennison?"

"Jennah knows his daughter and wife from committees. I'm on his youth council and Wilf knows him from Hydro negotiations."

Mina says, "Bill Dennison was principal at Ellis' first school. We've worked on his campaigns."

"Boooonus." Chase writes on his clipboard. "Okay, while Jennah and Ari are on their mission at the precinct we'll finalize the plan for cozying up to the mayor. Then Ari and I will go to the Riverboat as usual."

Ellis sighs, "Ari, at least give yourself a break from work."

Chase says, "No can do. Bernie is good friends with the chief of police. He's organizing a sit-down to discuss ongoing problems in Yorkville with key players. Ari is going to be at that table."

278

"To do what?"

"The Chief sees the hippies as one of Toronto's biggest problems. Ari has a lot of insights to offer."

My head ratchets up. "I do?"

"We'll go over the key points. The media will be there. The Dick just has to get wind of Ari having the Chief's ear." Chase checks his watch. "Jennah, a lot is riding on you. How do you want to handle this?"

"Give me half an hour. I'll just zip home and get myself presentable."

When she's gone Sabina scolds, "Ari, eat something."

"Sorry, Auntie, I can't face anything until this formidable pain in the ass is down to a manageable hemorrhoid."

When Jennah returns she looks more alluring than Grace Kelly in *High Society*. While she was gone Mina finished the whimsical masterpiece Sabina started on the bruised side of my face. Now luminescent dragonflies stretch open-winged over pale flowers.

Ellis says, "I still think we should give it the weekend. Let him calm down."

Jennah works her hands into elegant white gloves. "The station house is safer than Switzerland, and striking while the remorse is hot will get us a better deal."

"Remorse? The only one he cares about is himself."

"Maybe so, but I guarantee he's scared shitless about how the mess is going to sort itself out, if only for his own sake. Come on, Ari. Grab the goods."

Sabina hands me our weapons: a large box of pastries and a thermos of coffee. "You both look beautiful."

Looking pretty and offering food are, I suppose, how women armour-up for battle.

As luck would have it, the Dick has the evening shift. We march into the precinct. Really, Jennah more glides in and tilts her head to the man at the desk. "Excuse me——" She deciphers his badge and pronounces his name with a Parisian lilt. "Officer Fournier. We need to see Officer Richard Irwin on an urgent matter."

He's so mesmerized by Jennah there's no need to make an excuse for the Van Gogh on my face.

The officer scuttles away and Jennah warns, "Remember, look contrite and keep your mouth shut."

"If I could I would." I attempt to bring my puffy upper lip in line with my pouty bottom one.

She hands me a tissue. "If you can't close it at least dab up the drool so the violets don't run."

The Dick bursts through a swinging door, his coat half on, and attempts to sweep us out the door. "There's a coffee shop on the corner."

Jennah skirts around him and waltzes into the inner sanctum. The air does what it always does when Jennah enters a room full of men, it organizes into a whistle. She smiles and speaks to the room. "Nonsense, Richard. I've brought nourishment for your men." She sets the box down on some gape-mouthed guy's desk. "Dig in, boys."

The Dick commandeers us toward a grubby little office. "You've no right to be coming to my job like this."

"You should have thought of that before *your* handiwork barged into my work." She dusts off a chair and sits. "Imagine my humiliation when in the middle of a meeting with the mayor's daughter, two half-drowned, bleeding relatives show up at my door."

The chair moans as it takes the Dick's weight. "Yeah, right. Don't con a con."

"Lorna Dennison and I are co-chairs on a committee called Science in the Classroom. Domestic violence is another passion of hers. Even more so of her mother, Dorothy."

"What did that one say?" He chins to me and finally takes in my face. "Jesus Christ, what the fuck is that?"

Jennah says, "Lucky for you, it's camouflage. Ari said, very generously I might add, that Mikey fell in the lake and that she hit her face on a rock trying to save him."

"That's exactly what happened and you can't prove any different."

"Oh, Richard, please. I'm an expert at this." Jennah slops on the hogwash. "I have notarized photographs of the handprint under that paint. One we all know will match yours. And, did you know, there's new technology that can identify fingerprints from bruise patterns?"

"Bullshit. There's no such thing."

"Maybe not here, but, oh my, the things they can do in Washington. It's only a matter of paying a lab for the results. My committee work is important to Wilf and he will spare no expense to protect his investments." She pours coffee into the lid of the thermos and slides it to him. "But let's avoid all that messiness, shall we? I know Ari can be a handful, but surely we can find a more . . . civilized way to resolve these little conflicts."

"This got nothing to do with me."

"I'm sure, but let's just see if you and I can't put our heads together to keep Ari and Mikey away from lakes so that the pictures in the *Toronto Star* are of our family at a barbeque with the mayor, not in a courthouse for your murder trial."

He feigns outrage but nothing camouflages that he knows that he near killed his own son last night. "I don't give a rat's fuck about her anymore. The little bitch can get the hell out of my house, I don't care what Theresa wants; but I'm not losing Mikey."

A promise of freedom is the last thing I expect to hear and Jasper sings the alphabet backwards to keep me from being swept away by a tsunami of tears.

"If you're confident you can keep Mikey away from lakes on

281

your own, then we'll be on our way." Jennah stands as she pushes away from the table. "I'm sure once Mrs. Vandervolt gets the doctor's report she'll have a few questions for the authorities. The Chief, perhaps."

"Fell in the lake, remember."

Jennah places her hands on the table. "Once Ari is free we will all tell the truth, the whole truth, and nothing but the truth."

He turns paper-white, except for his nose. "What the fuck do you want?"

"I don't like messes. Wilf doesn't like messes. I'd like to help you clean this up."

"Fuck off."

"I'd love to." She chins to me. "Come on, Ari."

"Wait. Sit down." Jennah just stares him down until he says, "Please."

The contrition in his voice tells me we have the upper hand. Jasper strokes my frazzled heart like it's a frightened puppy. *We'll be okay, Ari. Things will get better.*

Jennah lays out the conditions, which basically boil down to, hands off Mikey and me, keeping O'Toole on a leash, and enrolling Mikey at the YMCA so he can have peace from crapdom and I can stop babysitting and spend time getting out of my mess at school. She's sandwiching it all with delusions of Dick grandeur, his stepping up as a father. When he grumps, "What's that after-school thing gonna set me back?"

Jennah says, "A lot less than it will cost you if you don't."

My gut is flipping like a Russian gymnast. "Sir, is there a washroom I can use?"

"End of the hall."

When I open the office door, cops pretend they're looking at reports. I scramble toward the toilet praying it's not occupied. Bile hurls from my belly into a scaled toilet, adding backsplash to the filth around the bowl. It makes me retch more. When there's nothing more in me to deposit I get up and scrub my hands. As I sip water from a Dixie cup I study my face in the grimy mirror. The swelling gives the flowers dimension. A dragonfly's wing appears folded in flight on my puffy cheek. Behind me, reflected in the mirror, is a magazine photo of a glossy-lipped woman with perky tits, perched on a sleek car. I turn to exit and Jasper says, *She has nice headlights.*

Shut it, Jasper. I'm in no mood.

I recognize a couple of the cops from poker nights. Norman says, "Hey, Hariet. What's with the getup?"

"I'm in a play at school. We had a dress rehearsal."

"Huh, what play?"

"Um . . . *A Midsummer Night's Dream.*"

"So what's with the doll in there?"

"Peace negotiations." There is one *paczki* left in the box and I snag it to sweeten the pot. "I better get back."

It's over before I reach the room. Jennah is all smiles as she opens the door and ramps up the volume for the closer. "That's wonderful, Richard. I'll let the mayor know you support the plan."

I step in and place the pastry beside his coffee. He looks up. "Where's Mikey?"

"At Jennah's."

"I never woulda hurt him."

"The doctor put him on antibiotics because of the water in his lungs. Worse than that, you scared him so much he's got that far-off quiet in him again."

"He needed to be taught a lesson. This all would have blown over if you'd have kept out of what doesn't concern you."

"Have the lessons your father taught you ever blown over?"

"They taught me to be a man."

"Wouldn't you rather be a hero?"

I hesitate at the door, trying to catch sight of his inner animal. It's one of those wretched, flea-plagued creatures that children at the zoo point to and say, "Ew, Mummy, what's that?" I leave him scrubbing at the bristles on his head.

On the way back, Jennah is open, like the window she's always been in my sister-house. "He's given you an out, Ari. He said you could leave right now. No one would think badly of you if you walked away from that hell. Not even that freakish imaginary friend of yours."

"What? Go east and give up the chance to hobnob with Toronto's elite?" My eyes close as my body sinks into the car's leather seat, wanting Jake's arms and the ocean's hush-hush more than anything in this vast universe.

Riverboat steam and sweat made a complete muck of the cover-up. Chase removes the last of the paint with cold cream. "Shake a leg. You're late."

"Can you please go and tell him I'm sick?"

"Aaron lives for third Sundays. Don't be selfish."

"He lives for trekking jungles and jumping off mountains."

"You're as close to that as he gets in Toronto." He forces on my coat, pulls up my hood, and twines his ultra-long scarf around my neck. "Go. Be brave."

Mr. West is sitting on the bench. I approach from behind, sit on his left, and stare at the water. "Sorry I'm late."

"I'm just glad you made it."

"You might think different when you're trying to digest your Sunday dinner on a belly full of fury."

"Why would it be?"

I turn my face to meet his. He inhales sharp and exhales a long, "Ohhh." I can't read his eyes but they never look away. "Jesus, Ari."

"I'm okay."

"Obviously you're not."

"It's set the forces for good in motion so please don't feel bad."

"It's too cold out here. Let's walk."

Once or twice I've told him about Len and me finding refuge at The Goof diner. He navigates me there without asking anything and I just plain feel lighter with him knowing I need a dose of my papa.

The waitress hugs me when we step in. "Ari, we've missed you around here. What have you been up to? Boxing kangaroos?"

"A rabid dingo."

"Your old booth is empty."

"Thanks, Hazel."

Aaron naturally sits where Len used to park himself. "Are you hungry?"

For the first time in a long time I am. "Um . . . I'd kinda like a grilled cheese. And hot chocolate—and a brownie."

"Anything else?"

"Music."

The drama is told in measured bites. Aaron offers a sprinkle of sympathy, but mostly he just frees me up.

"How can I help?"

"You mean that or is it just the thing people say?"

"Of course I mean it."

"Ellis is setting me up with a math and science whiz. If you could pick Mikey up from the Y on Tuesdays, I might have a chance of crawling out of this hole."

"What time?"

"Five? He wouldn't have to be home until seven. The kid really needs a Len in his life."

"He's lucky he has you."

"I wish he could come east with me."

"Maybe the Resistance will bring about freedom for both of you."

I clink his mug with mine. "To freedom." Our hands come

to rest so close, the hairs on his finger touch my skin. His eyes stay on my face and now I see the longing for wall-less space and his thirst for something wild and unharnessed. "Yours and mine."

FIFTY-ONE

I'm discovering that a person can be smack in the middle of a cesspool and not smell it. The Village has changed, but the stink in my world has been overpowering, masking the decay in Yorkville.

While Bernie and Chase reconfigure the tables, I wipe spots off the glasses and review the notes Chase made me. The original hippies have moved on, except for a few who can't remember where they came from. Runaways, greasers, and bikers have filled their places. Weekend hippies still migrate in for the music and drugs but day-to-day life is abysmal at best. "Chase, am I supposed to have a clue how to fix any of this?"

"You know more than you think you do. Don't worry, we've got ringers coming with the facts and figures." He turns to the sound of boots on the steps. "And here's one now."

"Jory?" We scramble into a hug. She smells like musty socks and peppermint. Having the roof of my sister-house squeezing me with all of her ninety-pound force settles my jitters.

As a crew of ambassadors board the Riverboat, attire makes the sides clear: rebels versus suits; except for Chase in jeans and a crisp blue shirt and me in black pants and Babcia's embroidered peasant blouse. Bernie makes introductions around the circle.

Greg and Suzanne from Trailer, George from the Merchant Association, Clay who is a law student, Anne from Women's College Hospital, Bill from Queen Street, Michael and Sheila from Digger House, June who is a journalist, John from the drop-in centre, Margaret from Toronto city council, Jory from The Way, Chase who is a member of the Mayor's youth council, Ari who is a student and Riverboat employee, and James P. Mackey, chief of police.

Chase takes control of the meeting. "Our goal for this meeting is to start meaningful dialogue and to come up with solutions to deal with the current crisis in Yorkville. This is not a forum to bring up past conflicts; we're here to look at how we can meet the needs and interests of the here and now. Everyone will have ten minutes to voice their perspective. Then together we'll look at priorities and identify first steps."

Really, the goal for this meeting is to position me beside Chief Mackey when reporters from the *Star*, *Globe and Mail*, and the *Telegram* come at 3:15 for a brief photo op. By reflex, I get up and help Crystal fill water glasses as Suzanne and Greg describe the work going on at Trailer, a mobile social service haven for junk-sick youth. A bleak picture is painted around the table: hepatitis and venereal disease rates, drug psychoses, the struggle to feed and shelter homeless youth at Digger House. . . . Jory describes a normal day of loading up a van with hot soup and bags of stale bread, old coats and blankets, and returning every day with kids tripping out on acid mixed with bad shit or in the heaves of withdrawal. I'd always seen the dog in her. On the outside she looks like a whippet, but inside she is a valiant St. Bernard with its rescue barrel, herding the lost to shelter. She's not yet twenty, but many call her Mom.

June talks about the broken homes and fractured lives bringing the new wave of wannabe hippies to the Village. She is a lion, and I wonder what it would be like to have a mom like her.

The councilwoman calls the Village a festering sore and Chief Mackey rhymes off crime stats: drugs arrests, assaults, prostitution . . . "It's a dangerous place and the police must take a tough stance." He looks directly at me or more at the chartreuse and mauve evidence on my face.

"I do understand your concerns," I say, "I do. My stepfather is a police officer so I know a little about the challenges the police face. I've also been coming to the Village since I was eleven and have never felt threatened." I point to my face. "In fact, getting smacked in the face by a volleyball at school has caused me more harm. The problems here are big but not bigger than the caring people around this table. A fisherman once told me that before you can catch something you have to know what you're going for." Jasper gets a little overzealous and strays from the script. "Penguins, zebras, pandas, skunks, and orcas may all be black and white but they are different animals."

George from the Merchant Association says, "What the bloody hell are you talking about?"

"Well, for starters the original hippies have migrated. Except maybe Beatle Bill and Murray. With them went a lot of goals and ideals. The weekenders come for the music scene and to score. They leave cash behind that fuels the good and the bad. The resident hippies are young, wrecked wanderers. They're using but they're not the suppliers. The greasers are obnoxious little thugs. They steal and deal and they're lousy tippers, but they've got family that would bat their ears and put them to work in a factory if they knew what they were up to. Then there are the bikers. They've got power and are supplying all the hard stuff. They're good tippers but I'm thankful folky-jazz isn't their scene because they rarely come here." I get up and help Crystal with coffee and sandwiches. "What I'm saying is you can't treat all these people as if they were the same. Some animals should just be left alone, others need to be sheltered and fed, some might have to be caged, others tamed and domesticated."

"Humph." Chief Mackey's head wobbles a little. "Astute observations, miss." I bite back a smile and he half-winks.

Chase says, "Focusing energy and resources is the only way to tackle the concerns raised at this table. Let's take a break before we look at next steps."

Chase choreographs the rest of the show with the precision of a brain surgeon.

As Jory packs up every crust of leftover food I give her the wad of tip money I have squirreled away in Bernie's safe. "Do you know how proud I am that you're my sister? Wherever Jet's little spirit landed he knows what an amazing mother you are."

"All praise is His."

"When I see God working as hard as you do I'll give Him a dose of praise but for now I'm giving it to you. Please receive it."

"Righteous." She gathers her load. "Rock on, sis."

I take a tray of cups into the kitchen and find June with her journalist's sleeves rolled up. "Please, don't trouble yourself with those."

"Nonsense. What better way to get to know you and find my story. Who is Jet?"

"Jory's baby. He died."

"The loss of a child is so sad."

"Do you have kids?"

"Two boys. Two girls. So how is it you came to be in the Village at the ripe old age of eleven?"

"I have a sister named June." I pick up the dish towel. "She was right into the scene back in its heyday. I often came looking for her."

"And did you find her?"

"Sometimes. Then one day she was just gone. After that I'd come looking for Jillianne or Jory."

"Jillianne?"

"Sister five. She got mixed up with a bunch of greasers. She's doing okay now but it was a really hard go."

"And the other two? Did they come to the Village?"

"The disorder here would have sent Jennah and Jacquie squirreling over the edge."

"What kept you from going over?"

"Up until last year there was someone I wanted to go home to."

"And now? Is it Chase?"

"Chase and I are each other's immune systems."

"Pardon?"

"Sorry, I'm trying to get caught up in biology. We keep each other strong." I stack the clean mugs. "There's just someone who needs me at home."

"Your mother?"

"Lord, no, she needs me as much as a left-behind snakeskin would benefit from mouth-to-mouth." I wipe off the condiment jars and put them in their spots. "Please, please don't write that."

"Your father?"

"Miss Callwood, it excites my inner animal more than I can say to talk to a journalist who really cares about the mess here, but there's a story that I have to create first, and right now you have to look at me and see good not trouble."

She wipes down the counter. "Volleyball can be a very dangerous sport."

"If you help me, when this is done I'll do better than tell you my story, I'll show you where salvation meets earth for lost kids."

She shakes my hand so firmly that Jasper launches like a banana out of its peel. "Deal."

"Tell your kids that Ari says they're lucky to have a lioness for a mother."

The photo in Saturday's papers makes facing Jarvis' druggies on Monday brutal. At lunch I march right over to my supplier.

"Beat it. I mean it, Ari."

"Come on, Matt. You know I'm no narc. What better way to keep the heat off us than to turn it on the Village, eh? Besides the meeting was more about how to feed kids in the Village. My sister runs a church program. I was just helping her out. I swear I'd never betray you. Say we're cool."

He stubs out his cigarette on the fence post. "Yeah, sure, we're good. Just make yourself scarce, okay. You're bad for business."

The peace at home is worth the fallout at school. The picture in every newspaper was one taken during the break, the Chief casually talking to a group of us. My mouth is open and the Chief is looking at me. The Dick asks, "What were you saying?"

In truth I was asking him if he wanted mayo or mustard on his sandwich. "Um, during the meeting I mentioned my stepfather was a cop."

"Why'd you do that?"

"To let him know I understood about the stuff cops have to do. He asked me who you were and I was just telling him."

"You meeting again?"

"In March."

"You caught up in school?"

"I'm working on it."

O'Toole knocks like he's discovered manners. "Evening, Ari. Ready to go, Irwin?"

The Dick nabs his bowling bag and the remaining hunk of pork chop off his plate. "Make your mother some soup, then get at your homework."

The Dick is taking a stab at sobering the old girl up for appearances sake. She definitely has a little more colour around the edges and a few brain cells reanimating like winter flies in a spring-warmed window.

Mikey's tent is our barracks where two battle-weary soldiers regroup at the end of the day. I zip through the math quizzes that Ralph, my tutor, gave me. "Why so quiet, Mikey?"

"The Dick asked if I wanted to go fishing."

"Yeah, the cordiality around here is creeping me out. What did you say?"

"Aunt Sabina said I needed to be like a war spy and make him think I like him, but I don't want to go."

"Far as I know, he's not big on the great outdoors. Tell him you think fishing is kind of boring and you don't really like it that much. That'll play down the Huey-the-hero mess. How about . . . you say that you always wanted to learn an action sport like bowling. Throw in that you heard O'Toole say Dick was the best. Chase and I will go to the lanes and you can bump into us there and we'll muddle through the horror together."

"You're so smart."

"Wish Uncle Iggy was here to help me with this math."

"Ralph not any good?"

"He's a whiz. But Uncle Iggy would never make me go to the Spring Fling with him as payment."

"Jake won't mind. Can I read your letter from him?"

"There's too much mushy stuff in it." Really, I don't want Mikey to read the lines of longing and the despairing hope that I'll soon be home for good. "But he misses us."

"What are you going to paint for the art show?"

"Chase says I have to do something with bees."

"Why?"

"Apparently the mayor likes them."

Jennah and Mina organized an extravaganza. One hundred works of art from student artists all over the city have been selected and displayed at city hall all month. Tonight there is an auction with proceeds going to Digger House. Mayor William Dennison has the honour of selecting the first painting as his prize. Mine is not the best, nor is it authentically me. It's more of an Audubon-style print placed where the mayor sees it every day on his way out.

The night is glittery. The Dick is in his dress uniform. Jennah managed to stuff life into Mum and fill the cracks with enough shit to hold her upright but not make her jittery. She's still beautiful in a robin's egg-blue dress and swept-up hair.

Mayor Dennison studies every piece, narrowing his choices down to ten. When he finally chooses mine as his prize, I'm not even present in the room, not my soul anyway. A replica of me smiles, poses for pictures while shaking his hand but it's all an illusion created just to make this demon, puffed-up at my side, stop suffocating me and Mikey. It's working and I'm despairing that my supporters who gave me leave to run won't now understand why I can't stay.

FIFTY-TWO

Trees, birds, people are waking in the thin April sun. Mr. West arrives with a shopping bag of clothes, laundered and neatly folded. "Mikey said you're collecting stuff."

"I am. For Jory's flock." He sits and I catch a whiff of fresh lime. "Thanks for spending time with Mikey. I've never seen him so happy."

"I think his happiness has more to do with the climate change at home."

"The Dick is like a big, goofy kid. The mayor sent me a thank-you note. The Dick had it framed and took it to work. Whenever he passes the Chief at work, he near pisses himself that the big kahuna gives him a nod."

"As long as he's treating you better."

"He hasn't so much as pulled a hair from my brush."

"I can't tell you what a relief that is, for all of us. And how's your mum?"

"She'll do anything for the Dick. He says, 'Clean yourself up,' and she sparkles."

He turns and gives me a teacher look. "Then why are you sad?"

"Oh, that's low, pulling a Jasper on me."

"But I'm right, aren't I?"

"Yeah, spectacularly low. It's the plight of kids in Yorkville, I suppose."

"You're doing what you can. It's enough that you're helping Mikey."

"I just got a letter from Jake. A foster kid that he's really close to has leukemia. He's cancelled all his gigs so the kid's not alone through it. That's real. What I've done for Mikey is set him up in a house of mirrors. It's an illusion that I know is going to come crashing down."

"Well, at least for today the mirrors are in place, and I feel like ice cream."

I test his arm. "You feel nice and warm to me."

Kind teachers and makeup assignments have gotten me out of the academic crapper and heading toward the honour roll. Miss Burn, first period, Mr. Ellis last, and smashing volleyballs before facing the craphouse makes for spectacular days. Evenings are manageable: retrieve Mikey from the Y, help him with homework, make supper, and keep the house a step ahead of health department condemnation.

Mum wobbles along, a buffet of happy, sloppy, jittery . . . but she's less often wound tight or passed out these days.

The Dick stays the course and hasn't so much as farted in our direction.

Trouble with toxic gas is it has to go somewhere, eh, Ari?

"Yeah, Jasper. It's building."

Ronnie is a champion bloodhound sniffing out clues in return for treats. Yesterday, I learned that the Dick is under investigation at work for some missing dope and his gambling situation has him owing some bad guy big money. I sleuthed around for the weed, but he would never hide dope anywhere Ronnie might find it. Today, she traded a nickelbag for intel about him tipping off some Buffalo gangster with eyes on Toronto that the cops were on to him.

The cop buddies arrive to play Texas Hold'em. The Tool is still on a leash but as the beer flows, he gets the game mixed up with Toronto Hold'er. I make sandwiches, grab my pack, and head for the door. On poker night, handing the Dick five bucks for his game always buys me a ticket out of Las Crapas.

The Dick clouds the hall, waiting for the dough. "You be back to get the kid off to school."

"Yes, *sir*."

Stupid Irritating Reptile, right, Ari?

You got it.

I see the light in the nest from the top of the alley and run. Chase has popcorn popping and hot chocolate warming and is reading my latest letter from Jake. "Jake is such a good guy."

"He's a rare animal."

"He sure has it bad for you."

"Don't get me mooning. I can hardly keep my heart and hormones in my skin for how much I want to get back to him."

"Too bad about this kid, Danny. Leukemia is a tough break."

"He's stopped all the trouble now that he knows he's going to die. Jake takes him to the shore every morning, carries him into the waves so he can feel the froth on his toes."

"You ever think about ending it?"

"After all Jasper's done for me I could never bail on him." I nestle close, fearing the answer to asking, "You?"

"Used to contemplate dying all the time until I witnessed a life spectacularly lived in chaos." He kisses my hair. "You stink. Go shower."

"Yeah, that place leaks in."

"The Dick still behaving?"

"As much as he has the capability to be decent." I strip off my clothes. "We've got him believing that he's really hot stuff. From what Ronnie tells me it's making him really ballsy."

"How does Ronnie get this dirt?"

"The Toole and Dick talk around her like she's an empty chair. So what's the plan for when it all blows up?"

"The best Sabina and I have come up with is to fake your deaths, but we're working on a less drastic next move."

No one in crapdom remembers my birthday. Odd, because it's my sixteenth and by law I can walk out and never look back. I have to report to the post office front desk because they have things that didn't fit in my mailbox: a photo album from Jacquie, a camera from Mary and Nia. Two feathers, one inky black, the other moon-white, the box tied up with a black velvet band.

Forty-five days until I can hold you. You'll have to wait 'til then for your real birthday gift. Your last letter asked, "what if I discovered you were really an otter?" Then, Ari, I'd trade the seagrass for a bed of sleek fur, take hold of your silver whiskers, and swim with unharnessed joy. I love you so much. Jake.

Chase lugs an ancient shelf up to the nest to hold our growing collection of books then takes me to Mina and Ellis' for a birthday feast.

After gorging on Cornish pasties and blowing out candles, the boys go to buy batteries for my camera while Mina and I eat chocolate cake right off the platter.

"What did you wish for?"

"Peace on earth."

No, we wished the Dick would just fucking die.

Same thing, Jasper.

I lick the icing clinging to my fork. "Did you have sex before you got married?"

"Well, given the fact that I'm *Miss* Burn, it's safe to assume so."

"Do you like it?"

"Seven times out of ten I love it."

"The other three?"

"I love Ellis, so what's two minutes going to put me out?"

"I asked Jennah if she liked it. She said, 'It's just currency, sis.' Jory lays herself down anytime, anyplace to spread the love of Jesus, and the only thing Jillianne can tolerate touching her are the covers on her single bed. I hoped for a more positive spin from Jacquie. She says every time is like being held under water. She counts through it knowing on the other side of it are a sweet holding and a lightness in Franc that gets her breathing again."

Mina's sigh wobbles her head. "Well, a seahorse can breathe under water. You'll be happy whatever place it takes you."

"Um . . . I need . . . do you have any idea how I can get the pill?"

"Say what?"

"Doctors won't prescribe it unless you're married. Jake and I are going to end up mattress dancing and I don't want to wreck our lives."

"I know a clinic. I'll take you. But don't be in a rush."

"How old were you?"

She stuffs a big bite in her mouth. "Sixteen."

I take a bigger bite. "Was it a bad thing or a good thing?"

"It became a lovely thing. It was Ellis. He was two years ahead of me in school. We lost each other for a few years around university, but when we found each other again we both knew we each just wanted the other."

"I've loved Jake since I was eight. Does that sound silly?"

"How could you not? The man can cajole a whale to wave hello. But, you might have to fight Ellis for him. He has a big crush."

FIFTY-THREE

Mikey is well-prepared to score points as the cops take on the firefighters in a Victoria Day baseball challenge. "Good call, ump."

The Dick adjusts his mask and hauls up his pants. Jasper looks anywhere but at Dick's ass and he bends, poised to call the next pitch. *Look, Ari. There's Aaron.* I scan the crowd near the water and see Mr. West toss a Frisbee. The group he's with scramble for it and a pretty blonde Barbie jumps up and down and hugs him. *Come on. Let's go play with him.*

298

He wouldn't want us around, Jasper. The thought aches through my chest and down into my gut.

Mikey jumps off the bleachers and peals across the beach. "Aaron!"

Jasper catapults me after him before the Dick catches wind of another hero situation.

Aaron receives Mikey's hug without hesitation. He smiles at my approach. "Hey, Ari. What brings you here?"

"Recognizance."

He pockets his hands. "Uh, Ari, this is Carrie."

The pretty girl seizes his arm. "So how do you know Aaron?"

"Through school."

"Oh, are you a teacher, too?"

"No . . . I . . ." I look to Aaron and the mischief in his eyes makes me stretch. "I'm a potter." I flash the T-shirt under my blazer. "And a designer."

"Oh—beautiful, really."

"Come on, West." A guy calls from behind. "You're holding up the game."

"You better hustle." I nab Mikey's arm. "Let's go, Mikey."

"Can't I stay and play Frisbee?"

"No, you're on a mission." I drag him along as I head back to the bleachers.

"Hey, Ari. See you Sunday?"

I give a high thumbs-up without turning around. "Mikey, keep your eyes peeled for the Chief. Chase says he'll show for the last innings."

"Baseball is boring."

"Well, we're playing chess."

I see Mum, her eyes closed, gummy as a serenaded cobra. "Go hurl some more shit at the Dick's calls while I take the queen out of play." She shakes off the spell when I rustle her shoulder. "Come on, Mum. Richard thinks you should take a nap." The sedan is in a cherry spot up on the grass along with half a dozen other cop vehicles. I load Mum into the back seat and cover her bare arms with a towel.

The hoots and hollers from the field have me running back for the post-game's pissing and back patting. With the Dick as ump there was never any question which way the game would go. Mikey and I pick a plum spot behind the pushy suck-up cops. The Chief shakes the Dick's hand. "Good work, Irwin." The timing is perfect as he catches sight of me. "Ari, hello. What's your call on this game?"

I weasel through with Mikey. "Great police work is all I can say."

"And who's this fine young man?"

The Dick roughs Mikey's hair. "My boy. Mikey."

"You want to be a policeman, Mikey?"

"Uh . . . yes, sir. A detective."

"Runs in the family I see. Will you be at the meeting on Thursday, Ari?"

The Dick's hand lands on my shoulder. "You bet she will. Civic duty and all."

Checkmate. Game—Ari and Mikey.

The distance from Monday to Sunday is a heart jumble. Chase doesn't untangle the mess so much as he loosens it. "So, you love Jake. You love Aaron. And clearly, you love me. Know what that makes you?"

"Scummy?"

"Lucky. You're sixteen. Your emotions are supposed to be fucked up. Go flirt and stop worrying. Aaron will never colour outside the lines. Besides, Jake's in a band. You don't think he sniffs other bitches?"

"He's a one-woman dog."

"Zodiac's heart is all yours but I've seen pictures of him taking loving from anyone putting out." He pushes me out of the nest. "Just be."

Aaron is sitting on our bench perusing this month's *National Geographic*.

"Reading your bible, I see."

He stands like gentlemen do when a lady approaches. "It's nice you get that about me."

"It's not my religion, but I think it's cool." I sit sideways, knees tucked, facing west.

His side rests along the bench back so he's facing east. He slides the magazine into his backpack and pulls out a gift, cheeks heating when he gives it to me. "This birthday warranted extra celebration."

It's a wooden box containing three sable paintbrushes. "I wrote a story in fifth grade," I say, "about going to Siberia to put tail warmers on martens who'd sacrificed their tail tips for Ari's magic brushes. These are spectacular. You'll be with me whenever I paint."

I smile reading his card.

> Ari, I'd wish you a birthday as spectacular as you are but I don't think such a thing is possible. Aaron.

My face lifts to his, smelling the coffee on his breath.

"I'd never heard anyone use the word spectacular more than you. I used to wait just to hear what would come out next."

"Jasper has always been overzealous."

"What is he pushing you to do, now that you're legally free to go?"

"He's a fly-by-the-tip-of-his-tail seahorse. Finishing my school year makes sense given that the armistice is holding."

"Then?"

"Hope runs big the Dick will be dead or incarcerated before I have to figure that out."

"Is he still behaving?"

"It's spooky. Since Monday's big game he's blathering to everyone that the Chief is going to make him a detective." I test the brush on my arm. "Um . . . sorry about crashing *your* big game."

"I'm not."

"So, Carrie seems nice."

"You really think that?"

"Yeah, I do. But, your inner animals are oceans apart."

"Astute observation. I took her to dinner once. Next date we went to a movie with two other couples, and then last Monday she forbade me to go to Kenya."

"Forbade?"

"Forbade."

"So . . . no more Carrie."

He shrugs and his face says, gone.

"Speaking of Kenya, did you get all your shots?"

"All done."

"Mikey said to remind you that you need to get some quinine and a bug net. He signed every book on Kenya out of the library."

"Tuesday I think I might pitch the tent in Belle's backyard and take him on safari."

The chatter between us weaves and floats and I rest in it, revive, refresh—but I sink back into the bottom scum as I make my way back to crapdom, realizing that Aaron and I are the closest Mikey has to a mum and dad here in Toronto.

FIFTY-FOUR

I figure it's because a turtle spirit is so connected to the earth that it feels the tectonic plates shifting before others know what is happening. Mr. Ellis zips across the field to catch up to me. "Hey, Appleton, wait up. I want to see your painting before you take it home."

"Don't give me that. I know Rochester's beady little eyes have already been all over it."

He smiles. "Mina showed it to me last night. She thought the detail was extraordinary."

"And you?"

"Ordered and still."

"It's a gift for Jennah. She loved the one I did for the art show."

"Rochester wants to know how you paint stillness when there's none in your life?"

"Things are cool. I'd tell you if the Dick was ready to blow."

"But, would you tell me if you were ready to blow?" His hand lands soft on my hair as we walk. "I think I'd rather catch you heading across the field at lunch than see you sitting under that tree, staring into tomorrow, books and lunch unopened."

"Were you in the war?"

"Yup. Got called up late. Didn't really see any action."

"My dad said when he heard that the Germans had surrendered he didn't know how to put his gun down and stop fighting. He volunteered for every detail in the aftermath cleanup because he didn't know how to go home."

"Ari, you just get on the train and go."

"All my summers out east have been a sanctioned leave from conscripted battle. Now it's me deciding to re-enlist."

"Mr. Peterson came to see me about your biology exam."

"I must've done okay because he said he was proud of me."

"You got a ninety-seven."

"Oh, bloody frig."

"What?"

"I promised Ralph that if I got above eighty I'd go with him to his cousin's wedding. My toes barely survived the spring dance." I stop to inhale a simmer of mowed grass and early roses. For the first time in weeks I feel like I could sleep.

Mr. Ellis' deep sigh surfaces me. "Ari, you are so bright and full of potential. You haven't asked for my advice but I have to give it. Move into your life with your aunts. Sixteen is too young to be a soldier."

"Tell that to Mikey."

"The Resistance is not going to stop fighting for him. It's okay for you to go home."

"Thanks, sir. That really helps." The lie stings my tongue. "I have to fly." I tuck the painting under my arm, turn, and run.

Hand-me-downs from the sisters have always been treasures to me. Whenever we got farmed out Jasper could fill out Jacquie's sweater so it felt like she was lying in bed next to me, or he could turn June's scarf into a sturdy hug. Now that the apples have fallen far from the tree and I'm more like a string bean than a golden delicious, the pickings are slim.

Jennah roots in her closet for something for me to wear to Ralph's cousin's wedding. I hold up a pretty sundress and check out my reflection. "I like this one."

She snatches it away. "You can't wear white, or black, to a wedding."

"Oh."

She smoothes her perfect hair and swipes on pink lipstick. "Come on. We're going shopping."

"What about the kids?"

"Maria picks them up and Wilf goes to the club on Fridays."

"I'll have to go to the bank."

"My treat, sis."

My dress, when we find it, is palest mauve, a flapper meets the sixties with sass. It scoops low on my back. Skin peeks through fine lace insets on the front. Jennah tames some of my hair with a sparkly clip. "The bride is going to hate you."

"We should keep looking."

"You're right about that." She snips off the tags. "I'll find something for me. And we need shoes. Then dinner."

At the restaurant, two men at the bar drink us in. I want them to go so it can be just us. I want Jennah to tell me how she grew to be so brave. "I remember a night when Mum locked us out of the house. You loaded us in the station wagon and drove us to Auntie Elsie's."

"Impossible you remember that. You couldn't have been more than three."

"And I remember you in our kitchen making crispy little pancakes out of nothing."

She nibbles up a tip of asparagus. "Amazing what you can do with rotting potatoes, flour, and sour milk."

The waiter appears with two glasses and a bottle of wine. "From the gentlemen at the bar, miss."

"Thank you. But we must decline." Smiling, Jennah looks over her shoulder and says in a voice loud enough to be heard over the tinkling music, "Mother of five and," she points to me, "jailbait."

The one resembling Rock Hudson takes off his glasses and looks right through me and I'm grateful my dress came with a gossamer shawl I can disappear under. I want to talk about Mummy meeting Daddy when she was younger than I am now. I want to ask if he was always the devil. I need her to help me sort out the voices crying in my dreams. But Jennah seldom tolerates a stirring of the daddy muck.

The waiter returns with two chocolate-drizzled whipped strawberry clouds. Jennah's eyelashes lift upwards to the waiter. "Tell the gentlemen, much better choice."

"He asked that I give this to the young lady." A business card is placed near my plate. I read, "James Smythe, Agent," in embossed gold letters.

Jennah tilts and appraises it. "Please tell Mr. Smythe she'll be in touch when hell freezes over." The waiter snorts and goes away.

"Agent? Like a spy?"

"Undercover definitely, sis. Roland had the same bloody card."

"Scuzzy-first-husband Roland?"

She punctures dessert. "He was chocolate-covered shit." A small bite slips into her mouth. "I still can't believe I let that creep into my pants."

"Auntie Nia says messing up is good fertilizer."

"I adore Nia, but no matter how you dress it up, messing up does not look pretty on a woman. Look at Mum."

"Was there ever a time she didn't? Before me?"

"God, no. It's her gift. Want to hear a case in point? Auntie Elsie and Uncle Marvin picked us up in their shiny new Buick once. It was scorching hot and they were taking us for a picnic. The men sat in the front. Little Nathan had on this precious sailor suit and kept smiling over the seat to us girls in the back. Uncle Marvin asked the songbirds for a melody. Auntie Elsie sang, "Let Me Call You Sweetheart." Everyone joined in, even June. Except for Mum who rolled down the window and sulked. We sang, "Swinging on a Star," "Mairzy Doats," "In the Good Old Summertime."

I ask without thinking, "Was Daddy singing, too?"

"If I've told you once I've told you to eternity and back, that person deserves no remembrance. Anyway, when we got to the lake we all grabbed bags and blankets. I turned back to take June's hand and I saw Mum dragging her nail scissors along the side of the pretty blue car. That perked her up for the afternoon. She was humming when we headed back to the car. She gasped like Scarlett O'Hara, 'Oh, my, look at that nasty scratch!' Uncle Marvin examined it and said he must have caught a branch. Mum said, 'Elsie, you must be devastated.'"

Elsie knew, but she has such class. She smiled and said, 'We survived the day without a scratch on any of us. It's just a hunk of metal.' Mum got all sulky again after that."

The waiter clears away my untouched dessert and Jennah asks for a pot of tea. "She's never been wired right, Ari."

"Well, the circuits are pretty much fried now."

"I always remember you trying to cheer her up."

"You know what I remember most about you?"

"Me bossing you around?"

"You singing and putting things back in order."

"You were the only one who ever seemed to notice. You'd get right tickled about a washed pillowcase. Positively giddy over a tablecloth and some jam for your toast. All you ever wanted was a home that stayed put under you." She pours tea into my cup. "Do you remember calling me Jemma?"

"You were the best ma I knew."

"So, can I give you some motherly advice?"

"Please."

"It's time for the lion side of you to rest and the eagle to fly."

"Thought you thought my spirit friends were craziness."

"Thinking a man will change is what's crazy. This civility is not going to last. I know about taming men and this one is going to start frothing at the chains. Wilf says there's talk the Chief is retiring at the end of the year, so that constraint will be gone. He's already getting cocky. Am I right?"

"Yeah."

"Keep low until school lets out, then you're moving to Mary's for good."

"He'll destroy Mikey."

"Let his mother step up."

"Like ours did?"

"We managed."

"What you did for us, who you are now is so much more than managing. You're a lioness. You were and are my strong, fierce sister. I wouldn't have survived the chaos without you."

"See, we all turned out just fine and Mikey will, too. It's not your job."

Aunt Sabina comes at me with a broom. "Ari. I thought you were a mouse. What are you doing in there?"

I emerge from the closet draped in Len's lanky cardigan. "Getting my grad dress."

"I thought Jennah bought you a new frock."

"It feels like the empress' new dress."

"You feel like a queen?"

"No, I feel naked in it." I remove the dress Len bought me from the garment bag. "This one has joy woven into it."

"You've outgrown this, I'm afraid."

"Frig." I plunk on the chair. "Do you ever outgrow missing a person?"

"The weight, the size of the loss never diminishes. But you grow more muscled so it feels lighter, more bearable to carry." She goes into the shop and returns with a simple azure shift with cutwork flowers edging the bottom. "This will suit the occasion." She tugs off Len's sweater and slips it over my head. "Two nights ago, Len was in my dream."

"A good visit?"

"I stepped outside to the patch of dirt behind the shop and it was a garden with lush flowers and water trickling down the rocks. He was strumming a blue guitar. I asked where he'd been and he said he'd been seeing the country but he was home now."

"I wish he'd come to my dreams. Mine are filled with crying: Jacquie's lost baby, or a cat, or Jillianne. Last night it was a fish that wasn't really a fish as much as it was a wolf."

She twists strands of my hair and joins them with an enamel butterfly. "Do you know what year I left Poland?"

"No."

"In 1943 an uncle arranged for me to join his family in New York. Think of what that date means."

"You left before the war ended?"

She smiles. "Your papa is home now. Go to this wedding, then east. Go to your life."

Mr. West is leaning forward on the bench, studying the ground, not the lake. His smile is forced when he looks up.

"Is Zodiac okay?"

"He's great."

"Then what's wrong?"

"Nothing. I'm just going to miss these Sundays."

"Auntie Nia would thwap you for being sad about the Sundays we won't have on the Sunday we do have." I perch on the bench. "Besides, Jasper tells me that you and I are friends for life, so we'll figure out the workings of that as we go along."

He searches the trees. "You really think that?"

"Spectacularly so. Your inner animal does, too, if you'd listen to it."

"But we'll be provinces apart."

"Lord, man, in two weeks you'll be conquering Kilimanjaro, and you see the Trans-Canada Highway as an insurmountable barrier?" I hand him an embossed leather journal. "I don't know when your birthday is but I figured this would come in handy on your adventure."

"Where did you find one with my initials on it?"

"I made it. Fringed bags are out and we've got a leather stockpile."

He reads the inscription. *Aaron West, In you is a story the world needs to read. Write it. Ari.*

His head lifts slow, cautious, like someone just peeked into a room he kept locked inside him.

I smile. "Something bumping around in there?"

His head shakes over a skittish laugh. "Enough. So when do you leave?"

"Saturday we're hitching a ride to Montreal with Ellis and Mina so I can see Jillianne, then Mikey and I are taking the train east from there."

"The Dick okay with Mikey going for the summer, same as last year?"

"He calculated his grocery savings and gave his blessing."

"I'll be looking out for him here next year. You know that, don't you?"

"I appreciate it more than I can say." I nudge him with my sandal. "But, I was sure I'd get a, 'hope you come back in September' from you."

"Seeing just the surface of the damage that house causes you," he rests his eyes in mine for one deep inhale and a long exhale, "how could I ever hope that?"

We back away from the subject and wander and talk around the world 'til we come to a silence, an ending, and we stand. He wishes he could kiss me goodbye. I can tell. "Jesus, I'm going to miss you."

"Travel safe."

"I'll touch base in September so we can figure out how to get Zodiac back to you."

Jasper is brave and pushes me into a hug. "Thank you for seeing me through all this."

He gathers my hair and holds me close. "You—are—spectacular, Ari Appleton." He releases and I back away.

"So are you, Aaron West."

There were speeches in me on why I should go. The words sit like a bowling ball in my gut because no one needs to hear them. I take a sandwich to Todd so his mouth will be full while I get it out.

He clips the nails of a prissy Pekinese. "Shit, Hari. You're nuts if you don't get the hell out when you've got the chance."

"But Mikey."

"Get off the pot. You think you're Jesus Christine? You know the Irwins managed to feed and dress themselves before you showed."

"I know."

"You don't belong in that shithole. You never did." His eyes are as sad as the basset hound in the cage behind him. "And if you don't run and never look back I'm taking back saying you're the smartest person I know."

"You've never said that."

His cheeks plump with his smile. "Not to you."

Chase fills my mismatched fancy glasses with Sprite, lights the candle, and pulls out my chair.

"Tell me honestly," I say, "is the Resistance meeting without me? Everyone is pushing me east."

He slips a fluffy omelet onto my plate. "Swear I haven't seen any of them since the mayor's barbeque."

"So are you going to tell me I should ditch Mikey?"

He smacks and shakes the catsup bottle. "Mikey had this idea of making a catsup gun. It's a brilliant idea."

"Is that code for what you think I should do?"

"Nope, there just has to be an easier way to get this stuff onto my egg."

"If it was in tubes like my paints you could squeeze it out."

His ragged notebook flips out of his shirt pocket and he skims to a blank page. "You might be on to something."

"You going to invent it?"

"I give this stuff to Zander. He does R&D for my dad. The deal is, if he strikes it rich he'll help fund my campaigns."

"You know exactly what you want to do, don't you?"

"Right now I pretty much do." He forks up a cheesy bite. "So do you."

"Really, Chase, I don't. What do you think I should do?"

"Do you trust me?"

"More than myself right now."

"Okay. Saturday you and Mikey get in the car and go. For eight weeks you play, create, absorb, dance, eat, sleep, love, and be loved. When thoughts about September come, put them in a bubble and blow them away. I'll call you last week of August and ask you a question. In your answer you'll have your answer."

"Sounds like hokey-pokey baldercrap."

"Jasper, what do you think?"

I try to put the twirling seahorse in a bubble and flick him away but his excitement can't be confined.

"Touché, Chase Pace."

FIFTY-FIVE

I leave my corner of the craphouse untouched so the stink can't follow me. "Mikey, don't pack the books you've read." His yellow suitcase is already ten inches above closing.

Todd huffs into the room. "Quick, hide."

"Why?"

"The Dick is coming up to take Mikey somewhere." I hear the squeak on the stairs and we scramble out the window and tuck up under the eaves.

"Where's the kid?"

"Um, he wanted to say bye to Laura so Ari took him over."

"Go get 'im."

"Uh, uh, they were heading somewhere after. I think they said that Mrs. Vandervolt was having a little party or something."

"Why didn't I hear about this?"

"Dunno. Mikey had a form; you signed it."

"Fucking Christ." He stomps down the stairs.

Todd pokes his head out the window. "There are two guys downstairs and O'Toole's in the driveway."

"What are they up to?"

"No clue."

"Are they in the kitchen?"

"No, the front."

"Go chat up O'Toole. Keep him away from the backyard."

I nab Mikey's hand and creep across the roof, navigate onto the woodbox, ease Mikey down, lift the door to the cellar, and we sneak in. "Keep low in the fort. I'll gather whatever I can through the vents."

A voice I don't recognize says, "A kid's good cover. Nice family holiday. Seeing the Falls and all that."

"Well, Mikey will be home soon. Tell Tino his cargo is in

good hands." Feet shuffle. The door closes and the action moves around to the driveway. I tiptoe over, swallowing a squeal when a mouse skitters across the workbench.

Mikey shiver-whispers. "What?"

"Shhh, shhh, the window is open. Don't make a peep and don't turn on your flashlight."

I'm near eye to eye with one of the thugs as he slides under the car on a dolly. He emerges. "Looks good. Let's take her for a test spin."

O'Toole and one thug drive off. I see the Dick's boots and another set, a pair of polished dress shoes. "Cross the border at meal times, more traffic, fewer guards. Stick to the third lane, the third, you got that?"

"The third, right."

"Don't flash your badge, just let it casually be seen when you show your license. Make sure the kid and your wife have ID."

"Right, sir."

The sedan returns and the guy checks underneath again. "All secure."

"Tomorrow, Irwin."

"You can count on me." The thugs leave and the Dick grumbles, "Where's that fucking kid?"

O'Toole lights his third cigarette. "It's a shit idea anyway."

"Whadaya mean?"

"You can't control what a kid's going to say. 'Specially if he's pissed about not going on holiday with that little bitch." He horks on the driveway. "I say we polish up Ronnie and Theresa, make the story that we're going over so our ladies can do a little shopping. People do it all the time."

"You got a point. You stay with the car."

Mikey is balled-up like a frightened pill bug when I try to get him out of the fort. "Come out. It's okay. They have a new master plan."

Mikey never cries but his whisper sounds like dust. "Please, I want to go with you. Please, Ari."

"I'm taking you to Ellis' and we're leaving at sunrise, I promise, but to do that we have to climb the fence in the backyard."

I deliver Mikey to Mina and Ellis and head back to the craphouse. The Dick is sitting on the front steps. "Where's the kid?"

"At Jennah's, upchucking. Ate too much at the party, I guess. I just came to get his suitcase."

Inside, Mum is up and showered. She licks her finger and tests the heat of the iron. "Oh, Hariet, Richard is taking Ronnie and me on a little holiday. Shopping, Niagara Falls, Madame Tussaud's. Won't that be fun?"

"Sounds like a blast."

"Get me my suitcase from the closet."

The little Samsonite feels like concrete as I lift it down. It's full of cop porn, "Detective Cockburner gets his woman, Undercover cop Erec Tion is on her case . . ." I dump it out on the bed and swipe off the dust with a musty towel.

"So . . . have a great time." I place it on the kitchen table and back away from the flurry, Mikey's pillow and yellow suitcase in hand. "*Adios, sayonara, au revoir*, have a nice life . . ." Mum doesn't even look at me.

Let's split.

I just wish she would—

Never mind her, I see you, Ari.

Thanks, Jasper.

Nancy Drew would get a picture of the underside of the sedan, but it's not worth the risk. I'm two houses down when the Dick yells, "Hey, Hariet."

Don't run, Ari. Play it smooth as butter.

I turn, "Yes, sir."

He lumbers toward me. "Can you spare a tenner?"

"Uh . . . I guess."

He nabs a twenty as soon as it comes out of my pocket. "Thanks, I'll pay you back on Sunday."

"Right."

Three blocks from Ellis and Mina's I step into a phone booth and gather my change into a pile. *You sure I should do this, Jasper?*

He'd get years for smuggling drugs. Then we could all stay in Pleasant Cove.

I dial 0.

"Operator. What number, please?"

"Could you connect me to the Canadian border crossing station in Niagara Falls, Ontario?"

"One moment, please." I wipe my fingerprints off the quarters while I wait. "I have that number on the line. Please deposit fifty cents."

I do and someone sounding eerily like the Dick says, "Customs."

Jasper adds a French accent to my voice. "Hello, I am sorry to bother you, and this is probably nothing but I was just in a diner and overheard two men talking. It sounded like they were planning on crossing the border tomorrow at Niagara Falls with drugs or something."

"Your name, please, ma'am."

"Uh, yes, it's . . . Madeline."

"Last name?"

"Uh . . . Real."

"Is that R-E-E-L?"

"Ah, no, R-I-E-L. Like Louis Riel."

"Who?"

The operator interrupts. "Please deposit another twenty-five cents."

It pings in and the man says, "What did they say exactly?"

"Um, they planned to cross at busy times, guards might check the trunk but they never look under the car, things like that."

"What did they look like?"

My stomach starts to roil. "Um, I only saw them from the back as they left. One was in his fifties, balding, and built like a bear. The other, was in his thirties, thinner, greasy black hair."

"Did you see their car?"

"Just a glimpse. A sedan, dark blue."

"License?"

What is it, Jasper?

Three. Seven . . . Maybe six at the end.

"Um . . . Three, seven, something? I'm not sure."

"Number where you can be reached, ma'am."

"Uh, ah—Oxford eight . . . 1222."

"Address?"

"Please deposit twenty-five cents."

"Sorry, I'm out of change." Like it's a hot potato, I hurry the handle to the cradle. *Oh, Jasper, I don't know about this.*

What could go wrong?

Countless times I've perched like Mikey, watching my world disappear through the rear window of a car. There is more fear than longing as he watches the miles being swallowed up. He fidgets with a moth hole in the pillow, unaware of the accumulating spill of feathers. I gather a handful, roll down the window, and release them. He follows their flight then looks to me. I nab a fistful of pillow guts and set them free. Mikey almost smiles. The casing is half-empty when Ellis spits out a downy bit. "You guys molting back there?"

"Ari's making a feather force field that makes us invisible to bad guys."

"Carry on, then."

When our mission is complete he settles his head on Bunny and sleeps through to Montreal.

For the first time in my life I receive the hug I've wanted from Jillianne. She holds on and I can't let go. "Some of my friends are here. I can't wait for them to meet you."

The backyard is crammed with theatre people, aged five to eighty-five. Auntie Dolores leaves her post at the grill, gives me a meaty hug then tosses me into the fun.

In this time and place my sister is called Anne, Anne Trembley. The swan in her has fully emerged, strong, graceful, and shockingly beautiful, and in this gathering of birds of a different feather she is still a solitary spirit.

Day's end, she nests beside me on the bed. "I'm glad you're here."

"Best day I've ever had with you, *Anne*."

"Unloading the 'Jilli' was like emptying rocks from my pockets." She reaches over to the bedside table and gives me an envelope. "There are still a few that weigh me down." I open the envelope and pull out a cheque for five thousand dollars. "I am so sorry, Ari. Can you forgive me?"

"Completely and utterly forgiven." I hand it back to her. "Please keep it. I don't need it."

"No friggin' way."

"Have some fun with it then. Out of all the people here today who would you love to help?"

"Easy. Marie Claire. She's on her own with two little kids."

"Tell her it's a gift from Len."

Her head rests on my shoulder. "He was something, wasn't he?"

"He still is. The only way I can bear his absence is to keep looking for his presence."

"He would bring me handwork, three or four times a week. He never hurried away. I never understood why he loved me, but I knew he did. The last time I saw him he said he wished he could have spared me all the pain I'd known, and I started to cry. He gave me his hankie and said, '*corka*, may I hold you?' In his arms

318

was the safest I'd ever felt." She wipes her nose on her sleeve. "Everyone at Springwood thought I'd start using when he died, but I just couldn't disappoint him again."

"See, he is still here."

"He's getting more solid as time passes and Daddy is dissolving." Her sigh is light. "Did you see him blow off his head?"

"It's a jumble."

"Tell me."

"Jennah says he's not worth a single thought or word."

"But I'm worth sorting through it. Some of it I just need to stare down and spit on. What do you remember?"

"Um, I think we'd just gone grocery shopping. June and Jennah were getting the bags from the trunk when Daddy came rushing out with Jinxie. He told them to get back in the car. Jennah did, but he had to butter-up June with, 'little June-bug,' crap before she'd come. All the way to river he sang one of his made-up songs to "Jingle Bells," 'Jack-jack-jack, Jack-jack-jack stabbed me in the back. She got my gun and had some fun blowing me away.'" She takes my hand and I squeeze in return. "How could it be all Jacquie's fault in his head?"

Jillianne shrugs. "How could he look in the mirror if he didn't tell himself that? He didn't blow his brains out because he was sorry. He did it because he wanted to hurt us."

"Then, for you, I won't give him the satisfaction. He didn't hurt us. He freed us."

Jillianne fires off a stream of pretend spits. "What happened when you got to the river?"

"I only remember playing on the hill. Daddy called me. I thought he was waving. Now, I think he was lifting the gun and wanted me to see him but June was in front. Where were you and Jory?"

"Jory stole Mum's cigarettes and was over at the park selling them. I was behind the sofa," she says, "hiding."

"You and I sure spent a lot of hours in sofa-caves, didn't we."

"Yeah. That day it was because Daddy was raging, raging, raging at Jacquie."

"What was he saying?"

"'A diary? A diary! Where is it, you little cunt?' His fists were balled in her face. Jacquie screamed back, 'Aunt Elsie, Dr. Herbert, the police, everyone knows what you did!' She kept baiting like she wanted him to whale on her. He saw you guys pull up with the groceries and like a light switch he turned it off. He tried to smooth Jacquie's hair. I thought he'd flipped when he said, 'A son. My son.' I thought he thought Jacquie was a boy, but I know now he was talking about the baby. She spat at him. He whistled for Jinx and went out all smiles." She props herself against the headboard and plays with my hand. "After he left, Auntie Elsie showed up and asked Mum where he was. Elsie said Dr. Herbert had called the police and they were on their way. She had on this creamy dress with pink roses on it. She crouched down to me, touched my cheek, and asked, 'Jillianne, did your Daddy ever hurt you? You can tell me anything, honey.' Mummy started hurling things. A bottle of ink hit Elsie in the head, dribbled down her shoulder but she just kept stroking my cheek."

"You don't have to answer," I fidgit with the tatting on her pillow, "but did he?"

"I've had years of spilling my guts, sis. It dilutes with the telling." Then she tells me, talking like she's watching a documentary. "There were all those years of messing with me," her arms fold to hold herself, "*us*. Putting our hands on him, making us *kiss him nice*. 'There's my little, sweetheart.' I turned ten the week before he died. I went to sleep dreaming about cake, my birthday dollar from Grandma, and Jennah's promise to take me to the movies. I woke up and—I was in his bed. He said, 'Don't be scared, Jillybean. This is what big girls do.' Then he raped me. His hand was over my mouth, keeping my scream inside. He was a ragged knife cutting me open while he cooed, 'Sh, sh, I know it hurts but Daddy's just helping you through.' He tried to cuddle me after but I started retching and ran to the bathroom."

"Where was Mummy?"

"Likely passed out on the couch. When Jacquie found me in the bathroom she knew. She locked the door, ran a bath, and got in with me. The water turned bubblegum pink as she gentled me back together. She said, 'He will never touch you again. I promise.'"

"Jacquie knew she was pregnant then, didn't she?"

"Yeah. One time when she visited me at Springwood she told me her plan that night was to kill Daddy. While she was holding me she'd planned it out. She would stab him in the heart with his war sabre, then bash his head with the iron frying pan." She climbs off the bed, nabs a bottle of wine, and returns with two glasses. I'd rather have weed but I receive the glass. "Anyway, when she saw him lying there, so peaceful, she decided death was too easy and she wanted me to see it was his fault, not mine. So, she told Auntie Elsie."

"Has Jory ever talked to you?"

"Not so much. Remember how Daddy and her played 'horsey'? They 'rode' each other, but I don't think Daddy liked her very much. Dr. Singer said that it's all about power. Jory was always too eager to please."

"Jennah won't even say his name."

"Oh, that's a whole other mess." She refills her glass. "For a long time she was Daddy's one and only. Think of how she mothered us. When he started on Jacquie, Jennah was so hurt, like Daddy had left her for someone else."

"How is it we're not all stark raving Froot Loops?"

"Maybe, 'cause someone always came along and balanced the shit with sugar." She clinks my glass. "And we had the sister-house."

"We did."

"You know what part of the house you were?"

"I never really coloured that bit in."

"You were the electricity. A spark, light, warmth. I could always find hope when I was with you."

The centre of me smiles and my head finds her shoulder. "When I landed at Mary's, I wanted so bad for you to see it was a real place."

"I'll come visit you this summer. Nia and I have become good buds."

"You have?"

"She talked to me at Grandma's funeral. Like she was reading my mind she said, 'You don't have to forgive, you just have to channel the anger into creative energy.' Every day I was hearing that to move on I had to forgive and I couldn't and I felt like I'd be stuck forever. Did you know Nia's uncle raped her?"

"I think I knew indirectly."

"And look at her. She's fire and water, steel and cloud. She sends me wisdom at least once a week."

"Are you happy?"

"I'm peaceful."

"Are you lonely?"

"How could I be? I've finally arrived at my true home."

Sunday evening Anne (sans Jilli) and Mikey splash in the pool. Auntie Dolores brings a pot of tea to the patio table. "Did you make your call?"

"Yeah."

"To Jake?"

"Jake and I are letter lovers. We abhor phone blathering. I called Toronto looking for some hopeful news from Todd."

"And did you get it?"

"Mum and the Dick are safely home from their little trip so no, not hopeful." The whole caper is told. "They decided to cross at Fort Erie instead of Niagara Falls. I swear he farts shamrocks."

"Doesn't sound like luck to me, more likely someone tipped them off."

"You mean from customs?"

"They're the only ones who heard your story."

My head slumps to the redwood table. "I'm so dead."

"Never in a million years will he think a young girl had the brains or balls to do that. He'll think it's a good cop who's on to him or bad cop looking to move in." She pours tea into a pretty cup. "I'm so thankful you're done with that hellhole."

I point to Mikey who just then cannonballs and water droplets land on the table. "But he isn't."

"Everything will come right. I'm sure of it."

"It sure has for Ji— um, Anne. I'm glad she has you."

"You girls have been through so much."

"After talking last night, I feel kinda, I don't know, guilty that they went through so much. I got off easy."

"At least your sisters had a molecule of motherly affection. Theresa went out of her way to be mean to you."

"What did I do to make her hate me so much?"

"Your dad had this twisted belief that his lack of a son was judgment from the Almighty. It's difficult to describe the hold your father had on your mother. She was just fifteen when they met. Theresa thought he was a god above all others. After she gave birth to you he severed all affection, all courtesy, all humanness. For your mother it was worse than hell."

"I never felt like Daddy hated me."

"You were the only one that looked like him."

"Please, please don't tell me I'm like him."

"He was a selfish, arrogant bastard. You are nothing like him on the inside. You have his colouring. That is the sum total of it."

Her hand reaches across the table. "You won't believe this but I always wanted you."

My head turns. "Pardon?"

"When your mum brought you home from Mary's I was smitten. You were this jabbering little button with the wildest mane and the most pleasing spirit. Theresa complained so much about her burden that I offered to take you." Her sigh moves the trees in a gentle sway. "She took too much delight in my childlessness to let go of the pleasure it brought her. I know I was a sour old prune with you. At first, I thought if your mum believed I didn't like you she'd reconsider. Then it became a way of cushioning my sadness. Before long, it was habit." Her eyes connect with mine. "I'm sorry for every unkindness."

"I always saw the alpaca in you."

"An alpaca?"

"They may spit now and then but they have eyes that soothe the soul and the softest fur in the universe."

FIFTY-SIX

William Walrus punches my ticket.

"You have any secrets for me?"

"I see a grand young man waiting at the end of the line whose heart is near bursting."

Mikey says, "That's Jake."

"And you, laddie, can let all your worries go."

"What about me?" I ask.

"For a time, little miss. For a time." William winks and moves on.

Hours in I wander to the snack bar looking for sticky food that will shut Mikey up for a while. William walks by and checks his watch. "If you don't unload that heaviness, we're never going to stay on schedule."

"This year has left me with a lot of suitcases."

He pulls out a stool. "Up you get."

I perch so that I can see Mikey back in his seat snuggled up with his book. "What do you think is worse, a dad who doesn't love you right or a mum that doesn't love you at all?"

"Can't be compared." He pours me a milkshake from a metal shaker. "Mums are your arms, they teach you to hold. Dads are your legs, showing you how to stand. That's why you're seahorse kin."

I wobble on the stool. "How's a seahorse supposed to take care of a dragonfly?"

"Just rest. Your arms and legs are coming in straight and fine and right on time." My eyes close under the warmth of his hand on my head. "Ahead is a season of joy. Let the heaviness go."

When I was little I'd watch the faithful being slain in the spirit, babbling as they were filled with the Holy Ghost. In this present moment I'm certain their ecstasy couldn't come close to being baptized by a walrus. The fierce white-hot stab of my sisters' pain explodes into a thousand points of light. My oppressors turn to ash, carried west on a strong wind. A giddiness follows me back to my seat.

Mikey watches out the window as advertisements flash by, playing billboard mash-up, "You're on your way with—the best to you each—Kool menthol—easy peasy lemon—things go better with— Brylcreem, a little dab will—Hey, Mabel, look for the Black—Heinz 57 . . . Each meadow, barn, and gap-toothed fence draws me home.

Things go better with Jake, eh, Ari?
Yeah, Jasper, they do.

Jake gets bigger as the train pulls in, white T-shirt over his fiddler's arms, driftwood hair drifting over his eyes, smile lighting his face. He more dances than lifts me off the stairs.

When the arms holding me are Jake's and the road travelled leads home, the bump and throw in the back of the truck matters none. Mary stops the truck before Skyfish. Jake jumps out then opens his arms. "Come on, love. Get yourself down here."

I tumble out. He seizes my hand, hurrying me across the grassy shore piece between Skyfish and the Butters'. If we kept going we'd fly off the edge into the ocean but we stop about middle of the field. "What are you doing?"

"Giving you your birthday present." He points to a large black rock with a fat vein of quartz running through it. "This is your rock. A piece of Cape Breton."

I test the movability of the Volkswagen-sized bit. "It's lovely, but how do you suppose I transport it?"

"You'll just have to leave it here. Build a house nearby."

"Won't Gus Mulligan have something to say about that?"

"Gus sold the place."

"Jake?"

"I picked it up for a song. Well, actually more like a thousand songs but still it was a deal." My legs snap around his waist nearly dashing him against my rock. He laughs, "So any chance I'm getting last dance, m'lady?"

"What if the cliff gives way and the whole lot falls into the ocean?"

"Then we'll live on our boat."

"What if I gain five hundred pounds and sink the boat?"

"Then I'll build us a tanker."

He gives me a foot up, then moves himself up like a mountain goat. We survey our kingdom. "It's the best present any girl ever got. I'll live on this rock forever."

"Aye, she's queen of the land."

We kiss, a wild missed-you-for-ten-long-months kiss then grudgingly, I let him go to haul in supplies for Nia before he and his fiddle have to head to St. John for a week. Mary scolds, "You best be taking your books with you, b'y."

"They're in the van." His head tilts asking for a walk out. I climb into the unloaded van, lying back with his sweater under my head. He crawls up, snuggling in close. "After this there's only local stuff, okay?"

"In a couple of weeks men are going to the moon. You could go that far and it wouldn't stretch thin my love for you." Hair, as soft and generous as Zodiac's fills my hand. "I'm sorry about Danny."

"He went so fast."

"Did his dad come?"

"Children's Aid couldn't locate him." He fidgets with a button on my sleeve. "He was one lost little kid. He saw a chorus of snowy owls on every crest of a wave. I don't know how many times he asked me to feed him to them."

"Did he ever tell you why he set the fires?"

"He said they ate up the disappointment, but it was always hungry for more." Jake's sigh falls like an iron band onto my neck. "He stopped when he saw the ocean swallowed it all and said enough."

"That's a poem."

"And here's the last line direct from him, 'My father's disappointment made me small and my death don't matter at all.'" Jake bites back tears. "How do people become such shit parents?"

"They feed the disappointment and they don't pay attention and . . . they stop being astonished by a snowy owl in the surf. I bet *you* told him he was magic, didn't you?"

"Maybe so, but all he really wanted was to hear it from his dad."

"Jake, listen for the voices that matter. Your dad was a liar, liar."

"We're talking Danny."

"We're talking all of us, the unthinkable ones, the invisible, the throwaways."

"I want so much to stay and talk away the hours, but I really do have to head out. I'll be back in a lamb's shake, then time will be ours."

Nia looks up from luring an ocean goddess out of burl maple when I return. "Jake okay?"

I sit on my stool, pick up my brush, and paint another friggin' lighthouse on a weathered piece of wood. "Danny's dying hit him like a thousand-pound tuna."

Mary says, "He's wearing himself ragged. If he's not playing, he's working at the docks or out on the boats, fishing or taking out tours. He's not giving himself a moment to think."

Nia hunches low as if telling the wood secrets. "He was eight when the Butters finally got him. There's a lot of hurt that went on before then that needs healing."

"Did you know his parents?"

"Betsy was a mute mouse. She took her two young girls back to her mum's in Newfoundland and left Jake here with his dad. A brute bastard. Wee Jake would exist for hours in that filthy hovel, scared, cold, and hungry while his dad was off. Kindest thing he ever did was drown."

"How could she leave Jake with him?"

"I don't know. Maybe two armfuls were all she could run with at three a.m."

Mary drops a pot, on purpose, skittering rusty bits of clay across the planked floor. "Bloody fucking fuckers. His dad and his mum." An intact chunk explodes under her foot.

Her anger is like a wave and it's maybe the safest I've felt in my sixteen years on this earth.

"Now, let's get *the talk* out of the way before Jake gets back."

"What talk?"

"Nia and I know there's about as much chance of keeping you out of each other's knickers as there is leashing a whale and taking it for a walk." Mary pulls up a stool. "We've had the talk with Jake and now, you listen up, missy. You will use protection. We'll joy in the day you give us a grandbaby, but that day is not today. Do I make myself clear?"

"Yes, ma'am. Does that mean we have your blessing?"

"I didn't say that."

Nia chimes in. "Well, you sure have mine. It'd do you both a world of good to discover the joy of it. Lord knows you've had an overdose of the evil."

FIFTY-SEVEN

I walk the shore then struggle up the craggy cliff to my rock.

Jake bought this for us, Ari. We'll live our days with him and my Jewel, between the Butters and Aunties M&N.

We will, Jasper.

Remnants of a split-rail fence zigzag around a small wood, maybe half an acre and two smaller stands. The foundation of the old Mulligan house possesses charred memories of an eight-kid family. Echoes of their dogs, Ginger and Tag, barking on my way past from school, linger in the long grass.

Jake has built a small screened summer house near the ridge. The air inside is spiced with sweet cedar and salt. Most nights we steal away from our beds and lie outside body to soul on the ancient quilt. I think about him inside me but fear is a sticky thing. Jake feels it and tells me he'll wait forever if that's what I need. My hand paints his canvas of skin and his fiddler fingers play out the music in me. Then comes the long afterholding where we dream talk about our ever after.

I saunter to my rock and stand atop. *I want a home, Jasper. One that's truly mine. Mine and Jake's. I don't care to count my life in miles travelled or money stored. I just want to love like those on my right and those at my left.*

I feel proud, noble even until Jasper whispers, *Then we have to go back at summer end, don't we?*

Shut it. I mean it. You say that once more during my worry-freed vacation and I'll pickle you and cork the lid. I swear.

I trudge back to Skyfish and take the wheel. Mary lifts my head. "Ari, you've been crying," I bend low. "Go on, salt the pots. It makes them more beautiful."

I look pretty, splayed on the summer grass. At least the look on Jake's face says I do.

"They're setting up a TV at the community centre to watch the moon landing tonight. You want to go?"

I sigh, the kind of sigh that takes a long while to work its way out. "Did you know they're landing on the Sea of Tranquility in a little ship called the Eagle? Let's take Huey's boat round to our little inlet and just watch the moon, imagine it all from there."

Jake elbows up; strokes my cheek. "You're too good for me, Ari."

I whap his head—firmly. "You say that again and I swear I'll murder you. You're the best man there is and that includes those two hurtling toward the moon." I brush myself off. "Stupid pigheaded boy'that has no clue how spectacular he is, tries my patience more than wet-afternoon mosquitoes. I'm gonna throttle him, I swear, Jasper." I yell at the indent in the grass as I head back to work. "Pick me up at seven and smell soap-nice."

Jasper prattles as I make preparations: featherbed and blankets.

In case a cold front moves in. Right?

Lacey bra and silk panties.

In case we crash against a rock and have to go to the hospital.

Fancy glasses for the ginger ale.

In case we need extra bailers.

Mason jars with candles.

Just in case Buzz and Neil short-circuit the light from the moon. Good planning, Ari.

Jake schleps the paraphernalia onto the *Tura Lura* and we sail into our own sea of tranquility.

"Not many people get to disappear into a sunset and rise with the moon." We make more of a nest than a bed. "You still mad?"

I hand him a glass. "One toast and I'll forgive you."

He clinks my glass. "To Ari, my earth, moon, and stars."

"Say, 'To Jake Tupper, the only man in this universe good enough for Ari Zajac.'" He wanders around my face. "Say it. There can't ever be an 'us' if you don't believe this one thing."

He says it slow and measured, filled with a small seed of belief.

I unbutton his shirt. Kiss his chest, down to an unzipping of his jeans, stripping away threads separating me from his skin. I sit back on my heels, pull off my sweater, my tank. Atlantic cool startles up my nipples as I unfasten my bra and let it fall. I stand, dropping my jeans. Pink panties float down my leg. I linger in

331

the moonmilk, letting him drink. He fills to the brim, pulling me down, shivering and heating me in the same breath.

The weight of him on me feels light. His lips, hungry but not greedy, taste my neck . . . my right breast, lingering on my left. His fingers play a slow song down my body. I open my legs, pulling him to me 'til he feels how much I want him inside. "Jesus, Ari, I . . . I didn't bring anything. Mary will take my pecker for a turn on her wheel if I don't keep you safe."

"Tonight you can be an astronaut without a suit. We won't make any little spacemen."

"How?"

"A pill that puts my eggs under lock and key until we're ready for them."

"You did that for me?"

"For me." My teeth capture his ear. "And you."

Feeling the sweet pain as he slides inside, our rocking with the rhythm of the water beneath us, opening my eyes to the graceful arc of his neck, the ecstasy on his face, and the seahorse spinning in the moonlight through his hair, colours over the darkness.

In the afterfall he catches me, reels me close. "You're shivering, love."

Our ocean is heavy with ghosts: my father, Jake's father, Danny . . . I force tears down into my belly. "Sing our world into place."

Unhurried and gentle, he fills the night around me with Gaelic jewels and soon the roiling inside me calms, grief transmutes into something nearing joy.

"Is it almost eleven?"

"Aye." He props our pillow against the coil of rope, tucks the blanket under my chin, then circles me with his arms. "They should be stepping out about now." He kisses my headtop. "For them it's a walk, but Jake Tupper just danced on the moon."

I tilt back to see his face. "Our first dance."

"Save me last?"

"What if that moon falls from the sky?"

He reaches down, cupping my bum. "No matter, I'll have this one."

Summer houses and boats, long grass and moonlit shores make love-making easy and each time I love it more than the last. Everything I create, think, touch, want, say . . . is connected to Jake, to us. I want, I need, to be with him forever.

I go looking for Mikey and find him tucked in a corner of the veranda. "You've been awfully quiet." I slide down beside him. "What's up?"

"Just thinking."

"About what?"

"I heard the Missus tell Huey it was a blessing you were finally free of having to go back." His voice sounds as small as one might expect of a dragonfly. "Kira wants me to tell you that it's okay. We'll be okay. I know how to do it now. You showed me."

"Chase said I'm not allowed to spend a minute thinking about this. So you tell Kira there's a lot more summer to enjoy before she can say another word about it. Now, don't waste a minute of happiness worrying about what's ahead or Nia will skin you. Go have fun. Go on." He buoys, floats, then takes off to the Butters', leaving me in a puddle of grief. I rake myself up and trudge over to Skyfish; get my hands good and mucky. My neck aches and my shoulders burn but I keep on working out the crack inside my chest.

"Excuse me."

I look up to an exquisitely aged woman. What I imagine Jennah will look like in thirty years—and my mother won't.

"The proprietor said I could get a picture of the potter at the wheel. I just bought *Dirt Music in the Key of Wonder*. You're the artist?"

I nod.

"Why are you crying?"

"Because I love this place," I catch a tear with the soft flesh of my arm, "and I love a boy who belongs to this ocean."

"Lovely. Just lovely."

My head bows over the wheel as she wanders around the studio focusing, studying the light, choosing angles and clicking thoughtfully.

"My name is Lorraine." She places a card on the workbench. "Lorraine Monk. Could I see the piece you're working on when it's finished? I'll be back this way two weeks from Saturday. Will you be here?"

"I hope to be. We'll hold it. If I'm not out front just ask to see, *Where Questions Sleep Answers Lie*."

No matter how late the hour when Jake returns from a gig, my body tingles at his touch. His whisper brushes my ear. "There's no music without you, Ari." His smile is felt more than seen when I turn to him. The goodness of his weight on me. The fit of us. The magic of our seahorse dance is more alluring than sky seen from the ocean's floor.

He sleeps.

Sunrise draws me to the shore. Nia and the dogs meet me between Skyfish and the piece Jake and I call Moondance. She says, "How's our girl?"

"How hard will you slug me if I tell you that the terror of leaving this happiness is deflating my cells?"

"You've done well, but summer is coming to an end."

"I want to stay here."

"I want that, too. You've given Mikey a solid footing and built up an army of support."

"But they'll be outside. It's not the same as being inside. Todd said the Dick got passed over for detective and he's pissing all over everyone."

"Maybe we should give keeping Mikey here a try. Really, what could Irwin do?"

"He'd go after Jory. I'm sure of it. She's an easy target and expendable. We take *his*, he'll destroy *mine*." The water tugs at my ankles while shore mush anchors me. "A couple of nights ago Jake said all I had to do was ask and he'd come to Toronto with me until we could see Mikey out of crapdom."

She whips a stick for the dogs. "And what do you think about that?"

"It felt like a rope thrown to save me. But then the Missus asked if Jake and I would move into the house after Mikey left. They've got a brood there now with night terrors."

"We'll hire someone to help out at the Butters'."

"Jake is still so tangled up in doing for the Butters what they did for him. Besides, for him, Toronto would be like a seahorse living in a toilet bowl."

"Don't forget, you're seahorse kin."

"I've adapted."

"You've evolved." Nia smiles as Jake crests the ridge, skitters down the cliff, whooping like a banshee as he runs toward the ocean. I'm stirred up as his lean frame streaks across the pebbly beach and plunges into the water. "Better go save him while I get some towels."

"Bring Mary, too. And coffee—and cinnamon buns."

"Light a fire."

I drop my jeans and ditch my sweater and do exactly that.

I feel Mikey's forehead for fever. "You feeling okay?"

"The cat just makes my eyes itchy."

I accept the excuse. It's easier than the reality that he's been off by himself crying—again.

"Ari, phone." Mary looks like a mirage behind the screen. "It's Chase."

"Yeah, I figured as much." I navigate the path like I'm walking the plank and take the receiver. "Chase Pace, it's August twenty-eighth. I thought you were going to give me a week."

"No need. It's an easy question."

"Okay. Let's hear it."

"You're ninety years old. What's the one regret you wish you could change?"

"That's it?"

"That's the question, but here are the rules. You have to look for the grace of it, not the judgment, yours or anyone else's. You have to look for the answer in your passions, your art, your writing, the ocean, the faces of those you love, the ethereal things that give you joy. It has to feel light and free. If it doesn't, you're convincing yourself of the wrong decision. Ari? How does that feel?"

"Kind of spectacular. Thank you."

"I love you. Bye."

"Bye."

I walk the shore, miles of it. *What would I regret when I'm ninety, Jasper?*

I'd regret not being with my Jewel.

Yeah, that's it, isn't. We belong with our matches. Seahorses don't belong in toilets, do they? Red rocks look like ancient creatures emerging from a long sleep. I climb over them and sit like I'm riding one home. My finger loops in the water, writing, freedom, passion, joy. *I'm allowed to stay, Jasper. I'm free to stay. We're free.*

Work pulls me back to Skyfish. Mary's fingers are pressed to her lips. Her eyes are ocean-full.

"What's wrong?"

She spins *Where Questions Sleep Answers Lie.* "Oh, m'girl, your salt pots are from a different dimension." In a fissure, a small child is folded tight, his back is the only thing seen. The sharp shoulder blades hint at wings. An iridescent dragonfly emerges, lightly, on the other side.

"It tells me Mikey is going to be okay."

I go over to the Butters to help Mikey pack. He wraps up treasures: a spiky shell, pretty stones, a lobster claw . . . and chatters about sand dollars and seaweed, crabs versus lobsters, and why great whites are rarely seen on these shores, what makes the sand red and the rocks black. *Listen to him. He's not scared, is he, Jasper?*

Jake gathers up fosters like he's an octopus, settling them with a story and dreamy fiddle tunes. He stretches out beside Mikey, drapes him with his arm, and sings a Gaelic lullaby.

What will I regret when I'm ninety? That every lost boy won't have Jake to sing him to sleep.

The Missus says, "I never met a child more like Jake in all my borned days."

"Mikey?"

"Them's like two peas."

"Thank you for raising him up."

"We dos what needs doing, eh, lamb?"

Jake stretches off the bed. "You want us to stay here?"

"Jesus no, yous two on that squeaky bed would be waking all the kids. Go visit with Mary and Nia. They've not had enoughs of you."

Middle of the night, water breaking against the rocks wakes me. The grass heaves with grace as wind rushes to greet the skin of me. It pushes me to Skyfish, invites me to lie on the scarred floor. The rafters above stretch like the ribcage of my goddess. Goddess of clay and colour, word pictures and piercing kindness. "I'm being reborn, Papa."

Into who, corka?

"Myself. The unthinkable one."

And what do you regret of your lives so far? The fire? The grit? The floods. The many hands that have shaped you?

"I don't regret any of it."

Look, you have arms and legs. Go feed the deer.

The un-weightedness is what I notice most. There is lightness in Jake's arms as he holds me. "I'll get a start on the house. Maybe by Christmas there will be a fireplace." I feel Jasper spine-up as his tail releases Jewel's.

Mary already has my small bag and a lunch packed. Nia tucks a new journal into my hand. "Do you know how proud we are of you marching back into that darkness?"

"You've known all along I was going back, haven't you?"

"Aye."

"I'm glad I didn't know."

"When did you?"

"Last night I saw my newest pot in a different light. It wasn't saying Mikey would be okay. That piece is the most unstable thing I've ever made. Those wings will break off if the dogs bark too loud. What regret would stay with me all my life? That all the broken kids coming up might not have Mikey because I didn't 'dos what needs doing.'"

"That's one side of it. Ask yourself where your salt-pots come from. What made you know that this time with Jake was so good?" Mary gentles my stress of hair. "There's still softness in your clay. I suspect there always will be."

"It's kinda hopeful not being fully baked." I pick up my bag.

"You think Mikey knows?"

Nia bolsters me out the door. "Could he ever imagine that you'd willingly go back into that hell?"

Jake takes the bag from me and plunks it in the truck. "I've been sick that he asked us not to come for the goodbye."

"I get why. Seeing your paradise disappear can make a kid really sulky." I hug Mary and Nia. "I don't know how I'm going to swing it, but I'm coming at Christmas."

"Hurry along now. That train's not going to wait."

Jake peels along the gravel and swings on to the road.

"Slow down. I can get the afternoon train."

"One, if I don't let you go while my head is winning over my busting heart, I never will." His down-home "heart" always sounds more like "art" and the ache of it creeps into my bones. "And two, I can't bear Mikey sitting alone on that train right now."

I wonder if Jake's terminal goodness will always make him soft or if he'll one day snap under the fierce weight of it. "I love you, Jake."

"Our ever after is down the road. I know that. Just tell me you'll save last dance."

What ifs crash through my head: *What if the Dick kills me? What if he cuts my face? What if O'Toole takes what he wants? What if more of Mum seeps into me?* "What if the pull of this leaving tears me in two?"

"Then I'll love you twice as much."

"I believe you would."

The train is kicking up noise. Jake takes the ticket that holds my fate from his pocket. "Run, love."

We sprint and I scramble up the steps of the caboose as the train lurches forward. Jake tosses my bag and I catch it. "Christmas."

"Just a few short months." His smile trembles. "Last dance?"

The clatter of the train swallows my, "First and last."

My stomach heaves at the interminable in-between.

He touches his eye, his heart, then points to me. Everything we shared gets bigger as he becomes a speck of light. *I'm scared, Jasper. What if there's no return trip for this train?*

Lioneagles can fly.

I open the door, shimmy between supply shelves, a couple of bunks, a desk, a stove, and through to the passenger cars. Three cars up, I see William crouched in the aisle. He looks up when I approach and shakes his head in a smile. He turns back to Mikey. "Dry your eyes, laddie, and listen to old William when he tells you there's good ahead. You can believe me when I say I see it." He ratchets up and takes my bag. "Let me help you with that, little miss."

Mikey is too broken to look up. I take William's spot. "I'm here, Mikey."

His sobs are gulpy and his little face, a mucousy mess. "No, Ari. I don't want to say goodbye."

I take a cold cloth from William's hand and sooth his swells and blotches. "I have no idea what waits ahead, but whatever it is we'll muddle through it together."

His inhale is a bumpy struggle. "What?"

"A seahorse never leaves a spirit brother behind." I feel the shiver in him as he takes hold. "Everything is okay. We'll be okay."

"No, you don't have to. I can do it."

"I know." I maneuver to a sit and he keeps hold. "But maybe I have to be with you to do what I need to do."

"You're really coming with me?"

"Really and truly."

His head lolls on my shoulder. "Jake will be so sad."

"And won't his music be more beautiful for it."

He clutches my hair like an otter staying afloat in a tangle of seaweed and rests in the hope of things. The closeness of Mary's voice startles-up my neck hairs. *Didn't I say you'd make a great potter?*

Mikey shifts and I feel the softness in him, the elasticity, the grit, the water. *You're right, Auntie. It's the best clay I'll ever place my hands on.*

Mikey sighs from a dreamy place, like the dragonfly in him has been flitting around my thoughts. "I have two spirit fathers like you have Mary and Nia."

"Huey and Jake?"

"Huey's my grandpa. I mean Jake and Aaron."

"I have lots of mums and dads. It's how I sort out my arms and legs. You gather as many as you need."

"He promised to meet my train." His breathing evens and calms. "He put a letter in my bag for you."

"Jake?"

"No." He yawns. "Aaron."

"Oh."

I attempt to navigate Mikey's bag with my foot as he sleeps heavy on me. A passenger on the way to the loo helps me out. I fish Aaron's note out of the zippered pocket.

June 22

Ari: When you walked away today that mysterious thing bumping around inside me said you'd be coming back in September. The possibility was like surfacing for air.

It's a dolphin, isn't it, Ari.

Yeah. How one landed in a boy from the prairies is a spectacular wonder, eh, Jasper.

I can scarcely believe anyone would have the courage to do it, yet, if you're reading this you are indeed on your way and I'll be waiting to give you and Mikey a lift. How do I explain this "spectacularly" weird friendship we have? I can't, but I have to say it means more to me than any connection I've ever had with another human being. That's over the top, I know, but it is what it is.

Travel the miles knowing you have a friend here who is so grateful for a little more time with you. A.

Hours pass in silence. The honey-coloured days behind me fade. Still, I feel their heat on my back. A few passing trees blush scarlet and I know autumn's flame is ahead. Jasper hums one of Iggy's quotes, *The sweetness we've left behind, the fire that is to come, is nothing compared to what lies inside us.*

Jasper, there's a war ahead. Isn't there?

He shelters in the curve of my ear. *Armageddon.*

A lie now and then wouldn't hurt you, you know.

Mikey is small for eight but still too big to fit on my lap. His legs spill onto the seat beside him while the rest of him puzzles tight into me. William comes, eases my arm with a plump pillow, and covers Mikey's boy-scraped legs with a blanket. His great black hand opens full on my head. "Old William loves to be surprised."

"You didn't see me coming?"

"Hope is a thing you let fly and land where it might."

"Is there good ahead?"

"Legions might set this old world on a wild spin. But one can turn it right side up." He tips his hat. "There's good right here, little miss."

ACKNOWLEDGEMENTS

This book is about family. Thank you to every perfectly imperfect family I have worked with over the years. Your resiliency inspires me. And to my own amazing children. Your compassion and creativity are woven throughout the pages. To my partner, Brian Tucker, I have written this through only your support, encouragement, and listening ear. Thank you for meeting my every "I can't," with "Yes, you can" and many cups of coffee.

To my sister, Sue Rayner, my cheerleader and best friend, I am so grateful to you, John Rayner, and Shauna Vaillancourt for being my first readers, and believers.

This book is also about the power of imagination. I am privileged to be part of the Writers' Community of Durham Region, a place where "hearing voices" and imaginary friends are celebrated. I am indebted to my WIP group, past and present, especially Kevin Craig, Heather O'Connor, Barb Hunt, Sherry Hinman, Myrna Marcelline, Anne MacLachlan, Sandra Clarke, Patrick Meade, Sylvia Chiang, and the wonderful Karen Cole, who has been with me start to finish. You have all enriched my writing.

I am grateful to the Ontario Arts Council for supporting my imagination. To the spectacular Hilary McMahon, at Westwood Creative Artists, thank you for loving this book and believing in me. To the incredible team at ECW Press, especially the insightful

Michael Holmes, my editor, thank you for bringing *The Clay Girl* to life.

Most of all, this book is about everyday heroes. My life is so rich with them that I can't name you all. Thank you, Cheryl Hermer, the most astonishing teacher any child could ever have. To Ally and Alycia Rayner/Fridkin for being the real-life aunties caring for a child. Thank you, Ruth Walker, a champion for writers. You encouraged me to jump and gave me the wings to make all this possible.

And, lastly, to my nieces, Frances McDowell, who faces mountains with wit, tenacity, brilliance and creativity, and Seana Rossi, the one who showed us all how to be heroes.

HEATHER TUCKER has won many prose and short-story writing competitions, and her stories have appeared in anthologies and literary journals. She lives in Ajax, Ontario.

Published by ECW Press
665 Gerrard Street East
Toronto, ON M4M 1Y2
416-694-3348 / info@ecwpress.com

Library and Archives Canada Cataloguing in Publication

Tucker, Heather, 1954–, author
The clay girl : a novel / Heather Tucker.

Issued in print and electronic formats.
ISBN 978-1-77041-303-0 (paperback); ISBN 978-1-77090-918-2 (pdf); ISBN 978-1-77090-917-5 (epub)

I. Title.

PS8639.U34C53 2016   C813'.6   C2016-902378-8
C2016-902379-6

Editor for the press: Michael Holmes
Cover design: Michel Vrana
Cover image: seahorse © nLd/Shutterstock
Interior images: "Hippocampus" from *Arcana, or, The museum of natural history* by James Stratford, c. 1811, courtesy of the Biodiversity Heritage Library
Author photo © Brian D. Tucker
Type: Rachel Ironstone

MISFIT

The publication of *The Clay Girl* has been generously supported by the Canada Council for the Arts, which last year invested $153 million to bring the arts to Canadians throughout the country, and by the Government of Canada through the Canada Book Fund. *Nous remercions le Conseil des arts du Canada de son soutien. L'an dernier, le Conseil a investi 153 millions de dollars pour mettre de l'art dans la vie des Canadiennes et des Canadiens de tout le pays. Ce livre est financé en partie par le gouvernement du Canada.* We also acknowledge the support of the Ontario Arts Council (OAC), an agency of the Government of Ontario, which last year funded 1,737 individual artists and 1,095 organizations in 223 communities across Ontario for a total of $52.1 million, and the contribution of the Government of Ontario through the Ontario Book Publishing Tax Credit and the Ontario Media Development Corporation.

Ontario
Ontario Media Development
Corporation

ONTARIO ARTS COUNCIL
CONSEIL DES ARTS DE L'ONTARIO
an Ontario government agency
un organisme du gouvernement de l'Ontario

**Canada Council
for the Arts**
**Conseil des Arts
du Canada**

Canadä

Printed and bound in Canada by Marquis   5   4   3   2

RECYCLED
Paper made from
recycled material
FSC
www.fsc.org   FSC® C103567